Ruggles of Red Gap

Harry Leon Wilson

Contents

RUGGLES OF RED GAP

by

Harry Leon Wilson

CHAPTER ONE

A T 6:30 in our Paris apartment I had finished the Honourable George, performing those final touches that make the difference between a man well turned out and a man merely dressed. In the main I was not dissatisfied. His dress waistcoats, it is true, no longer permit the inhalation of anything like a full breath, and his collars clasp too closely. (I have always held that a collar may provide quite ample room for the throat without sacrifice of smartness if the depth be at least two and one quarter inches.) And it is no secret to either the Honourable George or our intimates that I have never approved his fashion of beard, a reddish, enveloping, brushlike affair never nicely enough trimmed. I prefer, indeed, no beard at all, but he stubbornly refuses to shave, possessing a difficult chin. Still, I repeat, he was not nearly impossible as he now left my hands.

"Dining with the Americans," he remarked, as I conveyed the hat, gloves, and stick to him in their proper order.

"Yes, sir," I replied. "And might I suggest, sir, that your choice be a grilled undercut or something simple, bearing in mind the undoubted effects of shell-fish upon one's complexion?" The hard truth is that after even a very little lobster the Honourable George has a way of coming out in spots. A single oyster patty, too, will often spot him quite all over.

"What cheek! Decide that for myself," he retorted with a lame effort at dignity which he was unable to sustain. His eyes fell from mine. "Besides, I'm almost quite certain that the last time it was the melon. Wretched things, melons!"

Then, as if to divert me, he rather fussily refused the correct evening stick I had chosen for him and seized a knobby bit of thornwood suitable only for moor and upland work, and brazenly quite discarded the gloves.

"Feel a silly fool wearing gloves when there's no reason!" he exclaimed pettishly.

"Quite so, sir," I replied, freezing instantly.

"Now, don't play the juggins," he retorted. "Let me be comfortable. And I don't mind telling you I stand to win a hundred quid this very evening."

"I dare say," I replied. The sum was more than needed, but I had cause to be thus cynical.

"From the American Johnny with the eyebrows," he went on with a quite pathetic enthusiasm. "We're to play their American game of poker--drawing poker as they call it. I've watched them play for near a fortnight. It's beastly simple. One has only to know when to bluff."

"A hundred pounds, yes, sir. And if one loses----"

He flashed me a look so deucedly queer that it fair chilled me.

"I fancy you'll be even more interested than I if I lose," he remarked in tones of a curious evenness that were somehow rather deadly. The words seemed pregnant with meaning, but before I could weigh them I heard him noisily descending the stairs. It was only then I recalled having noticed that he had not changed to his varnished boots, having still on his feet the doggish and battered pair he most favoured. It was a trick of his to evade me with them. I did for them each day all that human boot-cream could do, but they were things no sensitive gentleman would endure with evening dress. I was glad to reflect that doubtless only Americans would observe them.

So began the final hours of a 14th of July in Paris that must ever be memorable. My own birthday, it is also chosen by the French as one on which to celebrate with carnival some one of those regrettable events in their own distressing past.

To begin with, the day was marked first of all by the breezing in of his lordship the Earl of Brinstead, brother of the Honourable George, on his way to England from the Engadine. More peppery than usual had his lordship been, his grayish side-whiskers in angry upheaval and his inflamed words exploding quite all over the place, so that the Honourable George and I had both perceived it to be no time for admitting our recent financial reverse at the gaming tables of Ostend. On the contrary, we had gamely affirmed the last quarter's allowance to be practically untouched--a desperate stand, indeed! But there was that in his lordship's manner to urge us to it, though even so he appeared to be not more than half deceived.

"No good greening me!" he exploded to both of us. "Tell in a flash--gambling, or a woman--typing-girl, milliner, dancing person, what, what! Guilty faces, both of you. Know you too well. My word, what, what!"

Again we stoutly protested while his lordship on the hearthrug rocked in his boots and glared. The Honourable George gamely rattled some loose coin of the baser sort in his pockets and tried in return for a glare of innocence foully aspersed. I dare say he fell short of it. His histrionic gifts are but meagre.

"Fools, quite fools, both of you!" exploded his lordship anew. "And, make it worse, no longer young fools. Young and a fool, people make excuses. Say, 'Fool? Yes, but so young!' But old and a fool--not a word to say, what, what! Silly rot at forty." He clutched his side-whiskers with frenzied hands. He seemed to comb them to a more bristling rage.

"Dare say you'll both come croppers. Not surprise me. Silly old George, course, course! Hoped better of Ruggles, though. Ruggles different from old George. Got a brain. But can't use it. Have old George wed to a charwoman presently. Hope she'll be a worker. Need to be--support you both, what, what!"

I mean to say, he was coming it pretty thick, since he could not have forgotten that each time I had warned him so he could hasten to save his brother from distressing mesalliances. I refer to the affair with the typing-girl and to the later entanglement with a Brixton milliner encountered informally under the portico of a theatre in Charing Cross Road. But he was in no mood to concede that I had thus far shown a scrupulous care in these emergencies. Peppery he was, indeed. He gathered hat and stick, glaring indignantly at each of them and then at us.

"Greened me fair, haven't you, about money? Quite so, quite so! Not hear from you then till next quarter. No telegraphing--no begging letters. Shouldn't a bit know what to make of them. Plenty you got to last. Say so yourselves." He laughed villainously here. "Morning," said he, and was out.

"Old Nevil been annoyed by something," said the Honourable George after a long silence. "Know the old boy too well. Always tell when he's been annoyed. Rather wish he hadn't been."

So we had come to the night of this memorable day, and to the Honourable George's departure on his mysterious words about the hundred pounds.

Left alone, I began to meditate profoundly. It was the closing of a day I had seen dawn with the keenest misgiving, having had reason to believe it might be fraught with significance if not disaster to myself. The year before a gypsy at Epsom had solemnly warned me that a great change would come into my life on or before my fortieth birthday. To this I might have paid less heed but for its disquieting confirmation on a later day at a psychic parlour in Edgware Road. Proceeding there in company with my eldest brother-in-law, a plate-layer and surfaceman on the Northern (he being uncertain about the Derby winner for that year), I was told by the person for a trifle of two shillings that I was soon to cross water and to meet many strange adventures. True, later events proved her to have been psychically unsound as to the Derby winner (so that my brother-in-law, who was out two pounds ten, thereby threatened to have an action against her); yet her reference to myself had confirmed the words of the gypsy; so it will be plain why I had been anxious the whole of this birthday.

For one thing, I had gone on the streets as little as possible, though I should naturally have done that, for the behaviour of the French on this bank holiday of theirs is repugnant in the extreme to the sane English point of view--I mean their frivolous public dancing and marked conversational levity. Indeed, in their soberest moments, they have too little of British weight. Their best-dressed men are apparently turned out not by menservants but by modistes. I will not say their women are without a gift for wearing gowns, and their chefs have unquestionably got at the inner meaning of food, but as a people at large they would never do with us. Even their language is not based on reason. I have had occasion, for example, to acquire their word for bread, which is "pain." As if that were not wild enough, they mispronounce it atrociously. Yet for years these people have been separated from us only by a narrow strip of water!

By keeping close to our rooms, then, I had thought to evade what of evil might have been in store for me on this day. Another evening I might have ventured abroad to a cinema palace, but this was no time for daring, and I took a further precaution of locking our doors. Then, indeed, I had no misgiving save that inspired by the last words of the Honourable George. In the event of his losing the game of poker I was to be even more concerned than he. Yet how could evil come to me, even should the American do him in the eye rather frightfully? In truth, I had not the faintest belief that the Honourable George would win the game. He fancies himself a card-player, though why he should, God knows. At bridge with him every hand is a no-trumper. I need not say more. Also it occurred to me that the American would be a person not accustomed to losing. There was that about him.

More than once I had deplored this rather Bohemian taste of the Honourable George which led him to associate with Americans as readily as with persons of his own class; and especially had I regretted his intimacy with the family in question. Several times I had observed them, on the occasion of bearing messages from the Honourable George--usually his acceptance of an invitation to dine. Too obviously they were rather a handful. I mean to say, they were people who could perhaps matter in their own wilds, but they would never do with us.

Their leader, with whom the Honourable George had consented to game this evening, was a tall, careless-spoken person, with a narrow, dark face marked with heavy black brows that were rather tremendous in their effect when he did not smile. Almost at my first meeting him I divined something of the public man in his bearing, a suggestion, perhaps, of the confirmed orator, a notion in which I was somehow further set by the gesture with which he swept back his carelessly falling forelock. I was not surprised, then, to hear him referred to as the "Senator." In some unexplained manner, the Honourable George, who is never as reserved in public as I could wish him to be, had chummed up with this person at one of the race-tracks, and had thereafter been almost quite too pally with him and with the very curious other members of his family--the name being Floud.

The wife might still be called youngish, a bit florid in type, plumpish, with yellow hair, though to this a stain had been applied, leaving it in deficient consonance with her eyebrows; these shading grayish eyes that crackled with determination. Rather on the large side she was, forcible of speech and manner, yet curiously eager, I had at once detected, for the exactly correct thing in dress and deportment.

The remaining member of the family was a male cousin of the so-called Senator, his senior evidently by half a score of years, since I took him to have reached the late fifties. "Cousin Egbert" he was called, and it was at once apparent to me that he had been most direly subjugated by the woman whom he addressed with great respect as "Mrs. Effie." Rather a seamed and drooping chap he was, with mild, whitish-blue eyes like a porcelain doll's, a mournfully drooped gray moustache, and a grayish jumble of hair. I early remarked his hunted look in the presence of the woman. Timid and soft-stepping he was beyond measure.

Such were the impressions I had been able to glean of these altogether queer people during the fortnight since the Honourable George had so lawlessly taken them up. Lodged they were in an hotel among the most expensive situated near what would have been our Trafalgar Square, and I later recalled that I had been most interestedly studied by the so-called "Mrs. Effie" on each of the few occasions I appeared there. I mean to say, she would not be above putting to me intimate questions concerning my term of service with the Honourable George Augustus Vane-Basingwell, the precise nature of the duties I performed for him, and even the exact sum of my honourarium. On the last occasion she had remarked--and too well I recall a strange glitter in her competent eyes--"You are just the man needed by poor Cousin Egbert there--you could make something of him. Look at the way he's tied that cravat after all I've said to him."

The person referred to here shivered noticeably, stroked his chin in a manner enabling him to conceal the cravat, and affected nervously to be taken with a sight in the street below. In some embarrassment I withdrew, conscious of a cold, speculative scrutiny bent upon me by the woman.

If I have seemed tedious in my recital of the known facts concerning these extraordinary North American natives, it will, I am sure, be forgiven me in the light of those tragic developments about to ensue.

Meantime, let me be pictured as reposing in fancied security from all evil predictions while I awaited the return of the Honourable George. I was only too certain he would come suffering from an acute acid dyspepsia, for I had seen lobster in his shifty eyes as he left me; but beyond this I apprehended nothing poignant, and I gave myself up to meditating profoundly upon our situation.

Frankly, it was not good. I had done my best to cheer the Honourable George, but since our brief sojourn at Ostend, and despite the almost continuous hospitality of the Americans, he had been having, to put it bluntly, an awful hump. At Ostend, despite my remonstrance, he had staked and lost the major portion of his quarter's allowance in testing a system at the wheel which had been warranted by the person who sold it to him in London to break any bank in a day's play. He had meant to pause but briefly at Ostend, for little more than a test of the system, then proceed to Monte Carlo, where his proposed terrific winnings would occasion less alarm to the managers. Yet at Ostend the system developed such grave faults in the first hour of play that we were forced to lay up in Paris to economize.

For myself I had entertained doubts of the system from the moment of its purchase, for it seemed awfully certain to me that the vendor would have used it himself instead of parting with it for a couple of quid, he being in plain need of fresh linen and smarter boots, to say nothing of the quite impossible lounge-suit he wore the night we met him in a cab shelter near Covent Garden. But the Honourable George had not listened to me. He insisted the chap had made it all enormously clear; that those mathematical Johnnies never valued money for its own sake, and that we should presently be as right as two sparrows in a crate.

Fearfully annoyed I was at the denouement. For now we were in Paris, rather meanly lodged in a dingy hotel on a narrow street leading from what with us might have been Piccadilly Circus. Our rooms were rather a good height with a carved cornice and plaster enrichments, but the furnishings were musty and the general air depressing, notwithstanding the effect of a few good mantel ornaments which I have long made it a rule to carry with me.

Then had come the meeting with the Americans. Glad I was to reflect that this had occurred in Paris instead of London. That sort of thing gets about so. Even from Paris I was not a little fearful that news of his mixing with this raffish set might get to the ears of his lordship either at the town house or at Chaynes-Wotten. True, his lordship is not over-liberal with his brother, but that is small reason for affronting the pride of a family that attained its earldom in the fourteenth century. Indeed the family had become important quite long before this time, the first Vane-Basingwell having been beheaded by no less a personage than William the Conqueror, as I learned in one of the many hours I have been privileged to browse in the Chaynes-Wotten library.

It need hardly be said that in my long term of service with the Honourable George, beginning almost from the time my mother nursed him, I have endeavoured to keep him up to his class, combating a certain laxness that has hampered him. And most stubborn he is, and wilful. At games he is almost quite a duffer. I once got him to play outside left on a hockey eleven and he excited much comment, some of which was of a favourable nature, but he cares little for hunting or shooting and, though it is scarce a matter to be gossiped of, he loathes cricket. Perhaps I have disclosed enough concerning him. Although the Vane-Basingwells have quite almost always married the right people, the Honourable George was beyond question born queer.

Again, in the matter of marriage, he was difficult. His lordship, having married early into a family of poor lifes, was now long a widower, and meaning to remain so he had been especially concerned that the Honourable George should contract a proper alliance. Hence our constant worry lest he prove too susceptible out of his class. More than once had he shamefully funked his fences. There was the distressing instance of the Honourable Agatha Cradleigh. Quite all that could be desired of family and dower she was, thirty-two years old, a bit faded though still eager, with the rather immensely high forehead and long, thin, slightly curved Cradleigh nose.

The Honourable George at his lordship's peppery urging had at last consented to a betrothal, and our troubles for a time promised to be over, but it came to precisely nothing. I gathered it might have been because she wore beads on her gown and was interested in uplift work, or that she bred canaries, these birds being loathed by the Honourable George with remarkable intensity, though it might equally have been that she still mourned a deceased fiance of her early girlhood, a curate, I believe, whose faded letters she had preserved and would read to the Honourable George at intimate moments, weeping bitterly the while. Whatever may have been his fancied objection--that is the time we disappeared and were not heard of for near a twelvemonth.

Wondering now I was how we should last until the next quarter's allowance. We always had lasted, but each time it was a different way. The Honourable George at a crisis of this sort invariably spoke of entering trade, and had actually talked of selling motor-cars, pointing out to me that even certain rulers of Europe had frankly entered this trade as agents. It might have proved remunerative had he known anything of motor-cars, but I was more than glad he did not, for I have always considered machinery to be unrefined. Much I preferred that he be a company promoter or something of that sort in the city, knowing about bonds and debentures, as many of the best of our families are not above doing. It seemed all he could do with propriety, having failed in examinations for the army and the church, and being incurably hostile to politics, which he declared silly rot.

Sharply at midnight I aroused myself from these gloomy thoughts and breathed a long sigh of relief. Both gipsy and psychic expert had failed in their prophecies. With a lightened heart I set about the preparations I knew would be needed against the Honourable George's return. Strong in my conviction that he would not have been able to resist lobster, I made ready his hot foot-bath with its solution of brine-crystals and put the absorbent fruit-lozenges close by, together with his sleeping-suit, his bed-cap, and his knitted night-socks. Scarcely was all ready when I heard his step.

He greeted me curtly on entering, swiftly averting his face as I took his stick, hat, and top-coat. But I had seen the worst at one glance. The Honourable George was more than spotted--he was splotchy. It was as bad as that.

"Lobster *and* oysters," I made bold to remark, but he affected not to have heard, and proceeded rapidly to disrobe. He accepted the foot-bath without demur, pulling a blanket well about his shoulders, complaining of the water's temperature, and demanding three of the fruit-lozenges.

"Not what you think at all," he then said. "It was that cursed bar-le-duc jelly. Always puts me this way, and you quite well know it."

"Yes, sir, to be sure," I answered gravely, and had the satisfaction of noting that he looked quite a little foolish. Too well he knew I could not be deceived, and even now I could surmise that the lobster had been supported by sherry. How many times have I not explained to him that sherry has double the tonic vinosity of any other wine and may not be tampered with by the sensitive. But he chose at present to make light of it, almost as if he were chaffing above his knowledge of some calamity.

"Some book Johnny says a chap is either a fool or a physician at forty," he remarked, drawing the blanket more closely about him.

"I should hardly rank you as a Harley Street consultant, sir," I swiftly retorted, which was slanging him enormously because he had turned forty. I mean to say, there was but one thing he could take me as meaning him to be, since at forty I considered him no physician. But at least I had not been too blunt, the touch about the Harley Street consultant being rather neat, I thought, yet not too subtle for him.

He now demanded a pipe of tobacco, and for a time smoked in silence. I could see that his mind worked painfully.

"Stiffish lot, those Americans," he said at last.

"They do so many things one doesn't do," I answered.

"And their brogue is not what one could call top-hole, is it now? How often they say 'I guess!' I fancy they must say it a score of times in a half-hour."

"I fancy they do, sir," I agreed.

"I fancy that Johnny with the eyebrows will say it even oftener."

"I fancy so, sir. I fancy I've counted it well up to that."

"I fancy you're quite right. And the chap 'guesses' when he awfully well knows, too. That's the essential rabbit. To-night he said 'I guess I've got you beaten to a pulp,' when I fancy he wasn't guessing at all. I mean to say, I swear he knew it perfectly."

"You lost the game of drawing poker?" I asked coldly, though I knew he had carried little to lose.

"I lost----" he began. I observed he was strangely embarrassed. He strangled over his pipe and began anew: "I said that to play the game soundly you've only to know when to bluff. Studied it out myself, and jolly well right I was, too, as far as I went. But there's further to go in the silly game. I hadn't observed that to play it greatly one must also know when one's opponent is bluffing."

"Really, sir?"

"Oh, really; quite important, I assure you. More important than one would have believed, watching their silly ways. You fancy a chap's bluffing when he's doing nothing of the sort. I'd enormously have liked to know it before we played. Things would have been so awfully different for us"--he broke off curiously, paused, then added--"for you."

"Different for me, sir?" His words seemed gruesome. They seemed open to some vaguely sinister interpretation. But I kept myself steady.

"We live and learn, sir," I said, lightly enough.

"Some of us learn too late," he replied, increasingly ominous.

"I take it you failed to win the hundred pounds, sir?"

"I have the hundred pounds; I won it--by losing."

Again he evaded my eye.

"Played, indeed, sir," said I.

"You jolly well won't believe that for long."

Now as he had the hundred pounds, I couldn't fancy what the deuce and all he meant by such prattle. I was half afraid he might be having me on, as I have known him do now and again when he fancied he could get me. I fearfully wanted to ask questions. Again I saw the dark, absorbed face of the gipsy as he studied my future.

"Rotten shift, life is," now murmured the Honourable George quite as if he had forgotten me. "If I'd have but put through that Monte Carlo affair I dare say I'd have chucked the whole business--gone to South Africa, perhaps, and set up a mine or a plantation. Shouldn't have come back. Just cut off, and good-bye to this mess. But no capital. Can't do things without capital. Where these American Johnnies have the pull of us. Do anything. Nearly do what they jolly well like to. No sense to money. Stuff that runs blind. Look at the silly beggars that have it----" On he went quite alarmingly with his tirade. Almost as violent he was as an ugly-headed chap I once heard ranting when I went with my brother-in-law to a meeting of the North Brixton Radical Club. Quite like an anarchist he was. Presently he quieted. After a long pull at his pipe he regarded me with an entire change of manner. Well I knew something was coming; coming swift as a rocketing woodcock. Word for word I put down our incredible speeches:

"You are going out to America, Ruggles."

"Yes, sir; North or South, sir?"

"North, I fancy; somewhere on the West coast--Ohio, Omaha, one of those Indian places."

"Perhaps Indiana or the Yellowstone Valley, sir."

"The chap's a sort of millionaire."

"The chap, sir?"

"Eyebrow chap. Money no end--mines, lumber, domestic animals, that sort of thing."

"Beg pardon, sir! I'm to go----"

"Chap's wife taken a great fancy to you. Would have you to do for the funny, sad beggar. So he's won you. Won you in a game of drawing poker. Another man would have done as well, but the creature was keen for you. Great strength of character. Determined sort. Hope you won't think I didn't play soundly, but it's not a forthright game. Think they're bluffing when they aren't. When they are you mayn't think it. So far as hiding one's intentions, it's a most rottenly immoral game. Low, animal cunning--that sort of thing."

"Do I understand I was the stake, sir?" I controlled myself to say. The heavens seemed bursting about my head.

"Ultimately lost you were by the very trifling margin of superiority that a hand known as a club flush bears over another hand consisting of three of the eights-- not quite all of them, you understand, only three, and two other quite meaningless cards."

I could but stammer piteously, I fear. I heard myself make a wretched failure of words that crowded to my lips.

"But it's quite simple, I tell you. I dare say I could show it you in a moment if you've cards in your box."

"Thank you, sir, I'll not trouble you. I'm certain it was simple. But would you mind telling me what exactly the game was played for?"

"Knew you'd not understand at once. My word, it was not too bally simple. If I won I'd a hundred pounds. If I lost I'd to give you up to them but still to receive a hundred pounds. I suspect the Johnny's conscience pricked him. Thought you were worth a hundred pounds, and guessed all the time he could do me awfully in the eye with his poker. Quite set they were on having you. Eyebrow chap seemed to think it a jolly good wheeze. She didn't, though. Quite off her head at having you for that glum one who does himself so badly."

Dazed I was, to be sure, scarce comprehending the calamity that had befallen us.

"Am I to understand, sir, that I am now in the service of the Americans?"

"Stupid! Of course, of course! Explained clearly, haven't I, about the club flush and the three eights. Only three of them, mind you. If the other one had been in my hand, I'd have done him. As narrow a squeak as that. But I lost. And you may be certain I lost gamely, as a gentleman should. No laughing matter, but I laughed with them--except the funny, sad one. He was worried and made no secret of it. They were good enough to say I took my loss like a dead sport."

More of it followed, but always the same. Ever he came back to the sickening, concise point that I was to go out to the American wilderness with these grotesque folk who had but the most elementary notions of what one does and what one does not do. Always he concluded with his boast that he had taken his loss like a dead sport. He became vexed at last by my painful efforts to understand how, precisely, the dreadful thing had come about. But neither could I endure more. I fled to my room. He had tried again to impress upon me that three eights are but slightly inferior to the flush of clubs.

I faced my glass. My ordinary smooth, full face seemed to have shrivelled. The marks of my anguish were upon me. Vainly had I locked myself in. The gipsy's warning had borne its evil fruit. Sold, I'd been; even as once the poor blackamoors were sold into American bondage. I recalled one of their pathetic folk-songs in which the wretches were wont to make light of their lamentable estate; a thing I had often heard sung by a black with a banjo on the pier at Brighton; not a genuine black, only dyed for the moment he was, but I had never lost the plaintive quality of the verses:

"Away down South in Michigan,   Where I was so happy and so gay,   'Twas there I mowed the cotton and the cane----"

How poignantly the simple words came back to me! A slave, day after day mowing his owner's cotton and cane, plucking the maize from the savannahs, yet happy and gay! Should I be equal to this spirit? The Honourable George had lost; so I, his pawn, must also submit like a dead sport.

How little I then dreamed what adventures, what adversities, what ignominies--yes, and what triumphs were to be mine in those back blocks of North America! I saw but a bleak wilderness, a distressing contact with people who never for a moment would do with us. I shuddered. I despaired.

And outside the windows gay Paris laughed and sang in the dance, ever unheeding my plight!

CHAPTER TWO

IN that first sleep how often do we dream that our calamity has been only a dream. It was so in my first moments of awakening. Vestiges of some grotesquely hideous nightmare remained with me. Wearing the shackles of the slave, I had been mowing the corn under the fierce sun that beats down upon the American savannahs. Sickeningly, then, a wind of memory blew upon me and I was alive to my situation.

Nor was I forgetful of the plight in which the Honourable George would now find himself. He is as good as lost when not properly looked after. In the ordinary affairs of life he is a simple, trusting, incompetent duffer, if ever there was one. Even in so rudimentary a matter as collar-studs he is like a storm-tossed mariner--I mean to say, like a chap in a boat on the ocean who doesn't know what sails to pull up nor how to steer the silly rudder.

One rather feels exactly that about him.

And now he was bound to go seedy beyond description--like the time at Mentone when he dreamed a system for playing the little horses, after which for a fortnight I was obliged to nurse a well-connected invalid in order that we might last over till next remittance day. The havoc he managed to wreak among his belongings in that time would scarce be believed should I set it down--not even a single boot properly treed--and his appearance when I was enabled to recover him (my client having behaved most handsomely on the eve of his departure for Spain) being such that I passed him in the hotel lounge without even a nod--climbing-boots, with trousers from his one suit of boating flannels, a blazered golfing waistcoat, his best morning-coat with the wide braid, a hunting-stock and a motoring-cap, with his beard more than discursive, as one might say, than I had ever seen it. If I disclose this thing it is only that my fears for him may be comprehended when I pictured him being permanently out of hand.

Meditating thus bitterly, I had but finished dressing when I was startled by a knock on my door and by the entrance, to my summons, of the elder and more subdued Floud, he of the drooping mustaches and the mournful eyes of pale blue. One glance at his attire brought freshly to my mind the atrocious difficulties of my new situation. I may be credited or not, but combined with tan boots and wretchedly fitting trousers of a purple hue he wore a black frock-coat, revealing far, far too much of a blue satin "made" cravat on which was painted a cluster of tiny white flowers--lilies of the valley, I should say. Unbelievably above this monstrous melange was a rather low-crowned bowler hat.

Hardly repressing a shudder, I bowed, whereupon he advanced solemnly to me and put out his hand. To cover the embarrassing situation tactfully I extended my own, and we actually shook hands, although the clasp was limply quite formal.

"How do you do, Mr. Ruggles?" he began.

I bowed again, but speech failed me.

"She sent me over to get you," he went on. He uttered the word "She" with such profound awe that I knew he could mean none other than Mrs. Effie. It was most extraordinary, but I dare say only what was to have been expected from persons of this sort. In any good-class club or among gentlemen at large it is customary to allow one at least twenty-four hours for the payment of one's gambling debts. Yet there I was being collected by the winner at so early an hour as half-after seven. If I had been a five-pound note instead of myself, I fancy it would have been quite the same. These Americans would most indecently have sent for their winnings before the Honourable George had awakened. One would have thought they had expected him to refuse payment of me after losing me the night before. How little they seemed to realize that we were both intending to be dead sportsmen.

"Very good, sir," I said, "but I trust I may be allowed to brew the Honourable George his tea before leaving? I'd hardly like to trust to him alone with it, sir."

"Yes, sir," he said, so respectfully that it gave me an odd feeling. "Take your time, Mr. Ruggles. I don't know as I am in any hurry on my own account. It's only account of Her."

I trust it will be remembered that in reporting this person's speeches I am making an earnest effort to set them down word for word in all their terrific peculiarities. I mean to say, I would not be held accountable for his phrasing, and if

I corrected his speech, as of course the tendency is, our identities might become confused. I hope this will be understood when I report him as saying things in ways one doesn't word them. I mean to say that it should not be thought that I would say them in this way if it chanced that I were saying the same things in my proper person. I fancy this should now be plain.

"Very well, sir," I said.

"If it was me," he went on, "I wouldn't want you a little bit. But it's Her. She's got her mind made up to do the right thing and have us all be somebody, and when she makes her mind up----" He hesitated and studied the ceiling for some seconds. "Believe me," he continued, "Mrs. Effie is some wildcat!"

"Yes, sir--some wildcat," I repeated.

"Believe *me*, Bill," he said again, quaintly addressing me by a name not my own--"believe me, she'd fight a rattlesnake and give it the first two bites."

Again let it be recalled that I put down this extraordinary speech exactly as I heard it. I thought to detect in it that grotesque exaggeration with which the Americans so distressingly embellish their humour. I mean to say, it could hardly have been meant in all seriousness. So far as my researches have extended, the rattlesnake is an invariably poisonous reptile. Fancy giving one so downright an advantage as the first two bites, or even one bite, although I believe the thing does not in fact bite at all, but does one down with its forked tongue, of which there is an excellent drawing in my little volume, "Inquire Within; 1,000 Useful Facts."

"Yes, sir," I replied, somewhat at a loss; "quite so, sir!"

"I just thought I'd wise you up beforehand."

"Thank you, sir," I said, for his intention beneath the weird jargon was somehow benevolent. "And if you'll be good enough to wait until I have taken tea to the Honourable George----"

"How is the Judge this morning?" he broke in.

"The Judge, sir?" I was at a loss, until he gestured toward the room of the Honourable George.

"The Judge, yes. Ain't he a justice of the peace or something?"

"But no, sir; not at all, sir."

"Then what do you call him 'Honourable' for, if he ain't a judge or something?"

"Well, sir, it's done, sir," I explained, but I fear he was unable to catch my meaning, for a moment later (the Honourable George, hearing our voices, had thrown a boot smartly against the door) he was addressing him as "Judge" and thereafter continued to do so, nor did the Honourable George seem to make any moment of being thus miscalled.

I served the Ceylon tea, together with biscuits and marmalade, the while our caller chatted nervously. He had, it appeared, procured his own breakfast while on his way to us.

"I got to have my ham and eggs of a morning," he confided. "But she won't let me have anything at that hotel but a continental breakfast, which is nothing but coffee and toast and some of that there sauce you're eating. She says when I'm on the continent I got to eat a continental breakfast, because that's the smart thing to do, and not stuff myself like I was on the ranch; but I got that game beat both ways from the jack. I duck out every morning before she's up. I found a place where you can get regular ham and eggs."

"Regular ham and eggs?" murmured the Honourable George.

"French ham and eggs is a joke. They put a slice of boiled ham in a little dish, slosh a couple of eggs on it, and tuck the dish into the oven a few minutes. Say, they won't ever believe that back in Red Gap when I tell it. But I found this here little place where they do it right, account of Americans having made trouble so much over the other way. But, mind you, don't let on to her," he warned me suddenly.

"Certainly not, sir," I said. "Trust me to be discreet, sir."

"All right, then. Maybe we'll get on better than what I thought we would. I was looking for trouble with you, the way she's been talking about what you'd do for me."

"I trust matters will be pleasant, sir," I replied.

"I can be pushed just so far," he curiously warned me, "and no farther--not by any man that wears hair."

"Yes, sir," I said again, wondering what the wearing of hair might mean to this process of pushing him, and feeling rather absurdly glad that my own face is smoothly shaven.

"You'll find Ruggles fairish enough after you've got used to his ways," put in the Honourable George.

"All right, Judge; and remember it wasn't my doings," said my new employer, rising and pulling down to his ears his fearful bowler hat. "And now we better report to her before she does a hot-foot over here. You can pack your grip later in the day," he added to me.

"Pack my grip--yes, sir," I said numbly, for I was on the tick of leaving the Honourable George helpless in bed. In a voice that I fear was broken I spoke of clothes for the day's wear which I had laid out for him the night before. He waved a hand bravely at us and sank back into his pillow as my new employer led me forth. There had been barely a glance between us to betoken the dreadfulness of the moment.

At our door I was pleased to note that a taximetre cab awaited us. I had acutely dreaded a walk through the streets, even of Paris, with my new employer garbed as he was. The blue satin cravat of itself would have been bound to insure us more attention than one would care for.

I fear we were both somewhat moody during the short ride. Each of us seemed to have matters of weight to reflect upon. Only upon reaching our destination did my companion brighten a bit. For a fare of five francs forty centimes he gave the driver a ten-franc piece and waited for no change.

"I always get around them that way," he said with an expression of the brightest cunning. "She used to have the laugh on me because I got so much counterfeit money handed to me. Now I don't take any change at all."

"Yes, sir," I said. "Quite right, sir."

"There's more than one way to skin a cat," he added as we ascended to the Floud's drawing-room, though why his mind should have flown to this brutal sport, if it be a sport, was quite beyond me. At the door he paused and hissed at me: "Remember, no matter what she says, if you treat me white I'll treat you white." And before I could frame any suitable response to this puzzling announcement he had opened the door and pushed me in, almost before I could remove my cap.

Seated at the table over coffee and rolls was Mrs. Effie. Her face brightened as she saw me, then froze to disapproval as her glance rested upon him I was to know as Cousin Egbert. I saw her capable mouth set in a straight line of determination.

"You did your very worst, didn't you?" she began. "But sit down and eat your breakfast. He'll soon change *that*." She turned to me. "Now, Ruggles, I hope you understand the situation, and I'm sure I can trust you to take no nonsense from him.

You see plainly what you've got to do. I let him dress to suit himself this morning, so that you could know the worst at once. Take a good look at him--shoes, coat, hat--that dreadful cravat!"

"I call this a right pretty necktie," mumbled her victim over a crust of toast. She had poured coffee for him.

"You hear that?" she asked me. I bowed sympathetically.

"What does he look like?" she insisted. "Just tell him for his own good, please."

But this I could not do. True enough, during our short ride he had been re-minding me of one of a pair of cross-talk comedians I had once seen in a music-hall. This, of course, was not a thing one could say.

"I dare say, Madam, he could be smartened up a bit. If I might take him to some good-class shop----"

"And burn the things he's got on----" she broke in.

"Not this here necktie," interrupted Cousin Egbert rather stubbornly. "It was give to me by Jeff Tuttle's littlest girl last Christmas; and this here Prince Albert coat--what's the matter of it, I'd like to know? It come right from the One Price Clothing Store at Red Gap, and it's plenty good to go to funerals in----"

"And then to a barber-shop with him," went on Mrs. Effie, who had paid no heed to his outburst. "Get him done right for once."

Her relative continued to nibble nervously at a bit of toast.

"I've done something with him myself," she said, watching him narrowly. "At first he insisted on having the whole bill-of-fare for breakfast, but I put my foot down, and now he's satisfied with the continental breakfast. That goes to show he has something in him, if we can only bring it out."

"Something in him, indeed, yes, Madam!" I assented, and Cousin Egbert, turn-ing to me, winked heavily.

"I want him to look like some one," she resumed, "and I think you're the man can make him if you're firm with him; but you'll have to be firm, because he's full of tricks. And if he starts any rough stuff, just come to me."

"Quite so, Madam," I said, but I felt I was blushing with shame at hearing one of my own sex so slanged by a woman. That sort of thing would never do with us. And yet there was something about this woman--something weirdly authoritative.

She showed rather well in the morning light, her gray eyes crackling as she talked. She was wearing a most elaborate peignoir, and of course she should not have worn the diamonds; it seemed almost too much like the morning hour of a stage favourite; but still one felt that when she talked one would do well to listen.

Hereupon Cousin Egbert startled me once more.

"Won't you set up and have something with us, Mr. Ruggles?" he asked me.

I looked away, affecting not to have heard, and could feel Mrs. Effie scowling at him. He coughed into his cup and sprayed coffee well over himself. His intention had been obvious in the main, though exactly what he had meant by "setting up" I couldn't fancy--as if I had been a performing poodle!

The moment's embarrassment was well covered by Mrs. Effie, who again renewed her instructions, and from an escritoire brought me a sheaf of the pretentiously printed sheets which the French use in place of our banknotes.

"You will spare no expense," she directed, "and don't let me see him again until he looks like some one. Try to have him back here by five. Some very smart friends of ours are coming for tea."

"I won't drink tea at that outlandish hour for any one," said Cousin Egbert rather snappishly.

"You will at least refuse it like a man of the world, I hope," she replied icily, and he drooped submissive once more. "You see?" she added to me.

"Quite so, Madam," I said, and resolved to be firm and thorough with Cousin Egbert. In a way I was put upon my mettle. I swore to make him look like some one. Moreover, I now saw that his half-veiled threats of rebellion to me had been pure swank. I had in turn but to threaten to report him to this woman and he would be as clay in my hands.

I presently had him tucked into a closed taxicab, half-heartedly muttering expostulations and protests to which I paid not the least heed. During my strolls I had observed in what would have been Regent Street at home a rather good-class shop with an English name, and to this I now proceeded with my charge. I am afraid I rather hustled him across the pavement and into the shop, not knowing what tricks he might be up to, and not until he was well to the back did I attempt to explain myself to the shop-walker who had followed us. To him I then gave details of my charge's escape from a burning hotel the previous night, which accounted for his extraordinary garb of the moment, he having been obliged to accept the loan of garments that neither fitted him nor harmonized with one another. I mean to say, I did not care to have the chap suspect we would don tan boots, a frock-coat, and bowler hat except under the most tremendous compulsion.

Cousin Egbert stared at me open mouthed during this recital, but the shop-walker was only too readily convinced, as indeed who would not have been, and called an intelligent assistant to relieve our distress. With his help I swiftly selected an outfit that was not half bad for ready-to-wear garments. There was a black morning-coat, snug at the waist, moderately broad at the shoulders, closing with two buttons, its skirt sharply cut away from the lower button and reaching to the bend of the knee. The lapels were, of course, soft-rolled and joined the collar with a triangular notch. It is a coat of immense character when properly worn, and I was delighted to observe in the trying on that Cousin Egbert filled it rather smartly. Moreover, he submitted more meekly than I had hoped. The trousers I selected were of gray cloth, faintly striped, the waistcoat being of the same material as the coat, relieved at the neck-opening by an edging of white.

With the boots I had rather more trouble, as he refused to wear the patent leathers that I selected, together with the pearl gray spats, until I grimly requested the telephone assistant to put me through to the hotel, desiring to speak to Mrs. Senator Floud. This brought him around, although muttering, and I had less trouble with shirts, collars, and cravats. I chose a shirt of white pique, a wing collar with small, square-cornered tabs, and a pearl ascot.

Then in a cabinet I superintended Cousin Egbert's change of raiment. We clashed again in the matter of sock-suspenders, which I was astounded to observe he did not possess. He insisted that he had never worn them--garters he called them--and never would if he were shot for it, so I decided to be content with what I had already gained.

By dint of urging and threatening I at length achieved my ground-work and was more than a little pleased with my effect, as was the shop-assistant, after I had tied the pearl ascot and adjusted a quiet tie-pin of my own choosing.

"Now I hope you're satisfied!" growled my charge, seizing his bowler hat and edging off.

"By no means," I said coldly. "The hat, if you please, sir."

He gave it up rebelliously, and I had again to threaten him with the telephone before he would submit to a top-hat with a moderate bell and broad brim. Surveying this in the glass, however, he became perceptibly reconciled. It was plain that he rather fancied it, though as yet he wore it consciously and would turn his head slowly and painfully, as if his neck were stiffened.

Having chosen the proper gloves, I was, I repeat, more than pleased with this severely simple scheme of black, white, and gray. I felt I had been wise to resist any tendency to colour, even to the most delicate of pastel tints. My last selection was a smartish Malacca stick, the ideal stick for town wear, which I thrust into the defenceless hands of my client.

"And now, sir," I said firmly, "it is but a step to a barber's stop where English is spoken." And ruefully he accompanied me. I dare say that by that time he had discovered that I was not to be trifled with, for during his hour in the barber's chair he did not once rebel openly. Only at times would he roll his eyes to mine in dumb appeal. There was in them something of the utter confiding helplessness I had noted in the eyes of an old setter at Chaynes-Wotten when I had been called upon to assist the undergardener in chloroforming him. I mean to say, the dog had jolly well known something terrible was being done to him, yet his eyes seemed to say he knew it must be all for the best and that he trusted us. It was this look I caught as I gave directions about the trimming of the hair, and especially when I directed that something radical should be done to the long, grayish moustache that fell to either side of his chin in the form of a horseshoe. I myself was puzzled by this difficulty, but the barber solved it rather neatly, I thought, after a whispered consultation with me. He snipped a bit off each end and then stoutly waxed the whole affair until the ends stood stiffly out with distinct military implications. I shall never forget, and indeed I was not a little touched by the look of quivering anguish in the eyes of my client when he first beheld this novel effect. And yet when we were once more in the street I could not but admit that the change was worth all that it had cost him in suffering. Strangely, he now looked like some one, especially after I had persuaded him to a carnation for his buttonhole. I cannot say that his carriage was all that it should have been, and he was still conscious of his smart attire, but I nevertheless felt a distinct thrill of pride in my own work, and was eager to reveal him to Mrs. Effie in his new guise.

But first he would have luncheon--dinner he called it--and I was not averse to this, for I had put in a long and trying morning. I went with him to the little restaurant where Americans had made so much trouble about ham and eggs, and there he insisted that I should join him in chops and potatoes and ale. I thought it only proper then to point out to him that there was certain differences in our walks of life which should be more or less denoted by his manner of addressing me. Among other things he should not address me as Mr. Ruggles, nor was it customary for a valet to eat at the same table with his master. He seemed much interested in these distinctions and thereupon addressed me as "Colonel," which was of course quite absurd, but this I could not make him see. Thereafter, I may say, that he called me impartially either "Colonel" or "Bill." It was a situation that I had never before been obliged to meet, and I found it trying in the extreme. He was a chap who seemed ready to pal up with any one, and I could not but recall the strange assertion I had so often heard that in America one never knows who is one's superior. Fancy that! It would never do with us. I could only determine to be on my guard.

Our luncheon done, he consented to accompany me to the hotel of the Honourable George, whence I wished to remove my belongings. I should have preferred to go alone, but I was too fearful of what he might do to himself or his clothes in my absence.

We found the Honourable George still in bed, as I had feared. He had, it seemed, been unable to discover his collar studs, which, though I had placed them in a fresh shirt for him, he had carelessly covered with a blanket. Begging Cousin Egbert to be seated in my room, I did a few of the more obvious things required by my late master.

"You'd leave me here like a rat in a trap," he said reproachfully, which I thought almost quite a little unjust. I mean to say, it had all been his own doing, he having lost me in the game of drawing poker, so why should he row me about it now? I silently laid out the shirt once more.

"You might have told me where I'm to find my brown tweeds and the body linen."

Again he was addressing me as if I had voluntarily left him without notice, but I observed that he was still mildly speckled from the night before, so I handed him the fruit-lozenges, and went to pack my own box. Cousin Egbert I found sitting as

I had left him, on the edge of a chair, carefully holding his hat, stick, and gloves, and staring into the wall. He had promised me faithfully not to fumble with his cravat, and evidently he had not once stirred. I packed my box swiftly--my "grip," as he called it--and we were presently off once more, without another sight of the Honourable George, who was to join us at tea. I could hear him moving about, using rather ultra-frightful language, but I lacked heart for further speech with him at the moment.

An hour later, in the Floud drawing-room, I had the supreme satisfaction of displaying to Mrs. Effie the happy changes I had been able to effect in my charge. Posing him, I knocked at the door of her chamber. She came at once and drew a long breath as she surveyed him, from varnished boots, spats, and coat to top-hat, which he still wore. He leaned rather well on his stick, the hand to his hip, the elbow out, while the other hand lightly held his gloves. A moment she looked, then gave a low cry of wonder and delight, so that I felt repaid for my trouble. Indeed, as she faced me to thank me I could see that her eyes were dimmed.

"Wonderful!" she exclaimed. "Now he looks like some one!" And I distinctly perceived that only just in time did she repress an impulse to grasp me by the hand. Under the circumstances I am not sure that I wouldn't have overlooked the lapse had she yielded to it. "Wonderful!" she said again.

Hereupon Cousin Egbert, much embarrassed, leaned his stick against the wall; the stick fell, and in reaching down for it his hat fell, and in reaching for that he dropped his gloves; but I soon restored him to order and he was safely seated where he might be studied in further detail, especially as to his moustaches, which I had considered rather the supreme touch.

"He looks exactly like some well-known clubman," exclaimed Mrs. Effie.

Her relative growled as if he were quite ready to savage her.

"Like a man about town," she murmured. "Who would have thought he had it in him until you brought it out?" I knew then that we two should understand each other.

The slight tension was here relieved by two of the hotel servants who brought tea things. At a nod from Mrs. Effie I directed the laying out of these.

At that moment came the other Floud, he of the eyebrows, and a cousin cub called Elmer, who, I understood, studied art. I became aware that they were both suddenly engaged and silenced by the sight of Cousin Egbert. I caught their amazed stares, and then terrifically they broke into gales of laughter. The cub threw himself on a couch, waving his feet in the air, and holding his middle as if he'd suffered a sudden acute dyspepsia, while the elder threw his head back and shrieked hysterically. Cousin Egbert merely glared at them and, endeavouring to stroke his moustache, succeeded in unwaxing one side of it so that it once more hung limply down his chin, whereat they renewed their boorishness. The elder Floud was now quite dangerously purple, and the cub on the couch was shrieking: "No matter how dark the clouds, remember she is still your stepmother," or words to some such silly effect as that. How it might have ended I hardly dare conjecture--perhaps Cousin Egbert would presently have roughed them--but a knock sounded, and it became my duty to open our door upon other guests, women mostly; Americans in Paris; that sort of thing.

I served the tea amid their babble. The Honourable George was shown up a bit later, having done to himself quite all I thought he might in the matter of dress. In spite of serious discrepancies in his attire, however, I saw that Mrs. Effie meant to lionize him tremendously. With vast ceremony he was presented to her guests--the Honourable George Augustus Vane-Basingwell, brother of his lordship the Earl of Brinstead. The women fluttered about him rather, though he behaved moodily, and at the first opportunity fell to the tea and cakes quite wholeheartedly.

In spite of my aversion to the American wilderness, I felt a bit of professional pride in reflecting that my first day in this new service was about to end so auspiciously. Yet even in that moment, being as yet unfamiliar with the room's lesser furniture, I stumbled slightly against a hassock hid from me by the tray I carried. A cup of tea was lost, though my recovery was quick. Too late I observed that the hitherto self-effacing Cousin Egbert was in range of my clumsiness.

"There goes tea all over my new pants!" he said in a high, pained voice.

"Sorry, indeed, sir," said I, a ready napkin in hand. "Let me dry it, sir!"

"Yes, sir, I fancy quite so, sir," said he.

I most truly would have liked to shake him smartly for this. I saw that my work was cut out for me among these Americans, from whom at their best one expects so little.

CHAPTER THREE

AS I brisked out of bed the following morning at half-after six, I could not but wonder rather nervously what the day might have in store for me. I was obliged to admit that what I was in for looked a bit thick. As I opened my door I heard stealthy footsteps down the hall and looked out in time to observe Cousin Egbert entering his own room. It was not this that startled me. He would have been abroad, I knew, for the ham and eggs that were forbidden him. Yet I stood aghast, for with the lounge-suit of tweeds I had selected the day before he had worn his top-hat! I am aware that these things I relate of him may not be credited. I can only put them down in all sincerity.

I hastened to him and removed the thing from his head. I fear it was not with the utmost deference, for I have my human moments.

"It's not done, sir," I protested. He saw that I was offended.

"All right, sir," he replied meekly. "But how was I to know? I thought it kind of set me off." He referred to it as a "stove-pipe" hat. I knew then that I should find myself overlooking many things in him. He was not a person one could be stern with, and I even promised that Mrs. Effie should not be told of his offence, he promising in turn never again to stir abroad without first submitting himself to me and agreeing also to wear sock-suspenders from that day forth. I saw, indeed, that diplomacy might work wonders with him.

At breakfast in the drawing-room, during which Cousin Egbert earned warm praise from Mrs. Effie for his lack of appetite (he winking violently at me during this), I learned that I should be expected to accompany him to a certain art gallery which corresponds to our British Museum. I was a bit surprised, indeed, to learn that he largely spent his days there, and was accustomed to make notes of the various objects of interest.

"I insisted," explained Mrs. Effie, "that he should absorb all the culture he could on his trip abroad, so I got him a notebook in which he puts down his impressions, and I must say he's done fine. Some of his remarks are so good that when he gets home I may have him read a paper before our Onwards and Upwards Club."

Cousin Egbert wriggled modestly at this and said: "Shucks!" which I took to be a term of deprecation.

"You needn't pretend," said Mrs. Effie. "Just let Ruggles here look over some of the notes you have made," and she handed me a notebook of ruled paper in which there was a deal of writing. I glanced, as bidden, at one or two of the paragraphs, and confess that I, too, was amazed at the fluency and insight displayed along lines in which I should have thought the man entirely uninformed. "This choice work represents the first or formative period of the Master," began one note, "but distinctly foreshadows that later method which made him at once the hope and despair of his contemporaries. In the 'Portrait of the Artist by Himself' we have a canvas that well repays patient study, since here is displayed in its full flower that ruthless realism, happily attenuated by a superbly subtle delicacy of brush work----" It was really quite amazing, and I perceived for the first time that Cousin Egbert must be "a diamond in the rough," as the well-known saying has it. I felt, indeed, that I would be very pleased to accompany him on one of his instructive strolls through this gallery, for I have always been of a studious habit and anxious to improve myself in the fine arts.

"You see?" asked Mrs. Effie, when I had perused this fragment. "And yet folks back home would tell you that he's just a----" Cousin Egbert here coughed alarmingly. "No matter," she continued. "He'll show them that he's got something in him, mark my words."

"Quite so, Madam," I said, "and I shall consider it a privilege to be present when he further prosecutes his art studies."

"You may keep him out till dinner-time," she continued. "I'm shopping this morning, and in the afternoon I shall motor to have tea in the Boy with the Senator and Mr. Nevil Vane-Basingwell."

Presently, then, my charge and I set out for what I hoped was to be a peaceful and instructive day among objects of art, though first I was obliged to escort him to a hatter's and glover's to remedy some minor discrepancies in his attire. He was very pleased when I permitted him to select his own hat. I was safe in this, as the shop was really artists in gentlemen's headwear, and carried only shapes, I observed, that were confined to exclusive firms so as to insure their being worn by the right set. As to gloves and a stick, he was again rather pettish and had to be set right with some firmness. He declared he had lost his stick and gloves of the previous day. I discovered later that he had presented them to the lift attendant. But I soon convinced him that he would not be let to appear without these adjuncts to a gentleman's toilet.

Then, having once more stood by at the barber's while he was shaved and his moustaches firmly waxed anew, I saw that he was fit at last for his art studies. The barber this day suggested curling the moustaches with a heated iron, but at this my charge fell into so unseemly a rage that I deemed it wise not to insist. He, indeed, bluntly threatened a nameless violence to the barber if he were so much as touched with the iron, and revealed an altogether shocking gift for profanity, saying loudly: "I'll be--dashed--if you will!" I mean to say, I have written "dashed" for what he actually said. But at length I had him once more quieted.

"Now, sir," I said, when I had got him from the barber's shop, to the barber's manifest relief: "I fancy we've time to do a few objects of art before luncheon. I've the book here for your comments," I added.

"Quite so," he replied, and led me at a rapid pace along the street in what I presumed was the direction of the art museum. At the end of a few blocks he paused at one of those open-air public houses that disgracefully line the streets of the French capital. I mean to say that chairs and tables are set out upon the pavement in the most brazen manner and occupied by the populace, who there drink their silly beverages and idle away their time. After scanning the score or so of persons present, even at so early an hour as ten of the morning, he fell into one of the iron chairs at one of the iron tables and motioned me to another at his side.

When I had seated myself he said "Beer" to the waiter who appeared, and held up two fingers.

"Now, look at here," he resumed to me, "this is a good place to do about four pages of art, and then we can go out and have some recreation somewhere." Seeing that I was puzzled, he added: "This way--you take that notebook and write in it out of this here other book till I think you've done enough, then I'll tell you to stop." And while I was still bewildered, he drew from an inner pocket a small, well-thumbed volume which I took from him and saw to be entitled "One Hundred Masterpieces of the Louvre."

"Open her about the middle," he directed, "and pick out something that begins good, like 'Here the true art-lover will stand entranced----' You got to write it, because I guess you can write faster than what I can. I'll tell her I dictated to you. Get a hustle on now, so's we can get through. Write down about four pages of that stuff."

Stunned I was for a moment at his audacity. Too plainly I saw through his deception. Each day, doubtless, he had come to a low place of this sort and copied into the notebook from the printed volume.

"But, sir," I protested, "why not at least go to the gallery where these art objects are stored? Copy the notes there if that must be done."

"I don't know where the darned place is," he confessed. "I did start for it the first day, but I run into a Punch and Judy show in a little park, and I just couldn't get away from it, it was so comical, with all the French kids hollering their heads off at it. Anyway, what's the use? I'd rather set here in front of this saloon, where everything is nice."

"It's very extraordinary, sir," I said, wondering if I oughtn't to cut off to the hotel and warn Mrs. Effie so that she might do a heated foot to him, as he had once expressed it.

"Well, I guess I've got my rights as well as anybody," he insisted. "I'll be pushed just so far and no farther, not if I never get any more cultured than a jack-rabbit. And now you better go on and write or I'll be--dashed--if I'll ever wear another thing you tell me to."

He had a most bitter and dangerous expression on his face, so I thought best to humour him once more. Accordingly I set about writing in his notebook from the volume of criticism he had supplied.

"Change a word now and then and skip around here and there," he suggested as I wrote, "so's it'll sound more like me."

"Quite so, sir," I said, and continued to transcribe from the printed page. I was beginning the fifth page in the notebook, being in the midst of an enthusiastic description of the bit of statuary entitled "The Winged Victory," when I was startled by a wild yell in my ear. Cousin Egbert had leaped to his feet and now danced in the middle of the pavement, waving his stick and hat high in the air and shouting in-coherently. At once we attracted the most undesirable attention from the loungers about us, the waiters and the passers-by in the street, many of whom stopped at once to survey my charge with the liveliest interest. It was then I saw that he had merely wished to attract the attention of some one passing in a cab. Half a block down the boulevard I saw a man likewise waving excitedly, standing erect in the cab to do so. The cab thereupon turned sharply, came back on the opposite side of the street, crossed over to us, and the occupant alighted.

He was an American, as one might have fancied from his behaviour, a tall, dark-skinned person, wearing a drooping moustache after the former style of Cousin Egbert, supplemented by an imperial. He wore a loose-fitting suit of black which had evidently received no proper attention from the day he purchased it. Under a folded collar he wore a narrow cravat tied in a bowknot, and in the bosom of his white shirt there sparkled a diamond such as might have come from a collection of crown-jewels. This much I had time to notice as he neared us. Cousin Egbert had not ceased to shout, nor had he paid the least attention to my tugs at his coat. When the cab's occupant descended to the pavement they fell upon each other and did for some moments a wild dance such as I imagine they might have seen the red Indians of western America perform. Most savagely they punched each other, calling out in the meantime: "Well, old horse!" and "Who'd ever expected to see you here, darn your old skin!" (Their actual phrases, be it remembered.)

The crowd, I was glad to note, fell rapidly away, many of them shrugging their shoulders in a way the French have, and even the waiters about us quickly lost interest in the pair, as if they were hardened to the sight of Americans greeting one another. The two were still saying: "Well! well!" rather breathlessly, but had become a bit more coherent.

"Jeff Tuttle, you--dashed--old long-horn!" exclaimed Cousin Egbert.

"Good old Sour-dough!" exploded the other. "Ain't this just like old home week!"

"I thought mebbe you wouldn't know me with all my beadwork and my new war-bonnet on," continued Cousin Egbert.

"Know you, why, you knock-kneed old Siwash, I could pick out your hide in a tanyard!"

"Well, well, well!" replied Cousin Egbert.

"Well, well, well!" said the other, and again they dealt each other smart blows.

"Where'd you turn up from?" demanded Cousin Egbert.

"Europe," said the other. "We been all over Europe and Italy--just come from some place up over the divide where they talk Dutch, the Madam and the two girls and me, with the Reverend Timmins and his wife riding line on us. Say, he's an out-and-out devil for cathedrals--it's just one church after another with him--Baptist, Methodist, Presbyterian, Lutheran, takes 'em all in--never overlooks a bet. He's got Addie and the girls out now. My gosh! it's solemn work! Me? I ducked out this morning."

"How'd you do it?"

"Told the little woman I had to have a tooth pulled--I was working it up on the train all day yesterday. Say, what you all rigged out like that for, Sour-dough, and what you done to your face?"

Cousin Egbert here turned to me in some embarrassment. "Colonel Ruggles, shake hands with my friend Jeff Tuttle from the State of Washington."

"Pleased to meet you, Colonel," said the other before I could explain that I had no military title whatever, never having, in fact, served our King, even in the ranks. He shook my hand warmly.

"Any friend of Sour-dough Floud's is all right with me," he assured me. "What's the matter with having a drink?"

"Say, listen here! I wouldn't have to be blinded and backed into it," said Cousin Egbert, enigmatically, I thought, but as they sat down I, too, seated myself. Something within me had sounded a warning. As well as I know it now I knew then in my inmost soul that I should summon Mrs. Effie before matters went farther.

"Beer is all I know how to say," suggested Cousin Egbert.

"Leave that to me," said his new friend masterfully. "Where's the boy? Here, boy! Veesky-soda! That's French for high-ball," he explained. "I've had to pick up a lot of their lingo."

Cousin Egbert looked at him admiringly. "Good old Jeff!" he said simply. He glanced aside to me for a second with downright hostility, then turned back to his friend. "Something tells me, Jeff, that this is going to be the first happy day I've had since I crossed the state line. I've been pestered to death, Jeff--what with Mrs. Effie after me to improve myself so's I can be a social credit to her back in Red Gap, and learn to wear clothes and go without my breakfast and attend art galleries. If you'd stand by me I'd throw her down good and hard right now, but you know what she is----"

"I sure do," put in Mr. Tuttle so fervently that I knew he spoke the truth. "That woman can bite through nails. But here's your drink, Sour-dough. Maybe it will cheer you up."

Extraordinary! I mean to say, biting through nails.

"Three rousing cheers!" exclaimed Cousin Egbert with more animation than I had ever known him display.

"Here's looking at you, Colonel," said his friend to me, whereupon I partook of the drink, not wishing to offend him. Decidedly he was not vogue. His hat was remarkable, being of a black felt with high crown and a wide and flopping brim. Across his waistcoat was a watch-chain of heavy links, with a weighty charm consisting of a sculptured gold horse in full gallop. That sort of thing would never do with us.

"Here, George," he immediately called to the waiter, for they had quickly drained their glasses, "tell the bartender three more. By gosh! but that's good, after the way I've been held down."

"Me, too," said Cousin Egbert. "I didn't know how to say it in French."

"The Reverend held me down," continued the Tuttle person. "'A glass of native wine,' he says, 'may perhaps be taken now and then without harm.' 'Well,' I says, 'leave us have ales, wines, liquors, and cigars,' I says, but not him. I'd get a thimble-ful of elderberry wine or something about every second Friday, except when I'd duck out the side door of a church and find some caffy. Here, George, foomer, foomer--bring us some seegars, and then stay on that spot--I may want you."

"Well, well!" said Cousin Egbert again, as if the meeting were still incredible.

"You old stinging-lizard!" responded the other affectionately. The cigars were brought and I felt constrained to light one.

"The State of Washington needn't ever get nervous over the prospect of losing me," said the Tuttle person, biting off the end of his cigar.

I gathered at once that the Americans have actually named one of our colonies

"Washington" after the rebel George Washington, though one would have thought that the indelicacy of this would have been only too apparent. But, then, I recalled, as well, the city where their so-called parliament assembles, Washington, D. C. Doubtless the initials indicate that it was named in "honour" of another member of this notorious family. I could not but reflect how shocked our King would be to learn of this effrontery.

Cousin Egbert, who had been for some moments moving his lips without sound, here spoke:

"I'm going to try it myself," he said. "Here, Charley, veesky-soda! He made me right off," he continued as the waiter disappeared. "Say, Jeff, I bet I could have learned a lot of this language if I'd had some one like you around."

"Well, it took me some time to get the accent," replied the other with a modesty which I could detect was assumed. More acutely than ever was I conscious of a psychic warning to separate these two, and I resolved to act upon it with the utmost diplomacy. The third whiskey and soda was served us.

"Three rousing cheers!" said Cousin Egbert.

"Here's looking at you!" said the other, and I drank. When my glass was drained I arose briskly and said:

"I think we should be getting along now, sir, if Mr. Tuttle will be good enough to excuse us." They both stared at me.

"Yes, sir--I fancy not, sir," said Cousin Egbert.

"Stop your kidding, you fat rascal!" said the other.

"Old Bill means all right," said Cousin Egbert, "so don't let him irritate you. Bill's our new hired man. He's all right--just let him talk along."

"Can't he talk setting down?" asked the other. "Does he have to stand up every time he talks? Ain't that a good chair?" he demanded of me. "Here, take mine," and to my great embarrassment he arose and offered me his chair in such a manner that I felt moved to accept it. Thereupon he took the chair I had vacated and beamed upon us, "Now that we're all home-folks, together once more, I would suggest a bit of refreshment. Boy, veesky-soda!"

"I fancy so, sir," said Cousin Egbert, dreamily contemplating me as the order was served. I was conscious even then that he seemed to be studying my attire with a critical eye, and indeed he remarked as if to himself: "What a coat!" I was rather shocked by this, for my suit was quite a decent lounge-suit that had become too snug for the Honourable George some two years before. Yet something warned me to ignore the comment.

"Three rousing cheers!" he said as the drink was served.

"Here's looking at you!" said the Tuttle person.

And again I drank with them, against my better judgment, wondering if I might escape long enough to be put through to Mrs. Floud on the telephone. Too plainly the situation was rapidly getting out of hand, and yet I hesitated. The Tuttle person under an exterior geniality was rather abrupt. And, moreover, I now recalled having observed a person much like him in manner and attire in a certain cinema drama of the far Wild West. He had been a constable or sheriff in the piece and had subdued a band of armed border ruffians with only a small pocket pistol. I thought it as well not to cross him.

When they had drunk, each one again said, "Well! well!"

"You old maverick!" said Cousin Egbert.

"You--dashed--old horned toad!" responded his friend.

"What's the matter with a little snack?"

"Not a thing on earth. My appetite ain't been so powerful craving since Heck was a pup."

These were their actual words, though it may not be believed. The Tuttle person now approached his cabman, who had waited beside the curb.

"Say, Frank," he began, "Ally restorong," and this he supplemented with a crude but informing pantomime of one eating. Cousin Egbert was already seated in the cab, and I could do nothing but follow. "Ally restorong!" commanded our new friend in a louder tone, and the cabman with an explosion of understanding drove rapidly off.

"It's a genuine wonder to me how you learned the language so quick," said Cousin Egbert.

"It's all in the accent," protested the other. I occupied a narrow seat in the front. Facing me in the back seat, they lolled easily and smoked their cigars. Down the thronged boulevard we proceeded at a rapid pace and were passing presently before an immense gray edifice which I recognized as the so-called Louvre from its illustration on the cover of Cousin Egbert's art book. He himself regarded it with interest, though I fancy he did not recognize it, for, waving his cigar toward it, he announced to his friend:

"The Public Library." His friend surveyed the building with every sign of approval.

"That Carnegie is a hot sport, all right," he declared warmly. "I'll bet that shack set him back some."

"Three rousing cheers!" said Cousin Egbert, without point that I could detect.

We now crossed their Thames over what would have been Westminster Bridge, I fancy, and were presently bowling through a sort of Battersea part of the city. The streets grew quite narrow and the shops smaller, and I found myself wondering not without alarm what sort of restaurant our abrupt friend had chosen.

"Three rousing cheers!" said Cousin Egbert from time to time, with almost childish delight.

Debouching from a narrow street again into what the French term a boulevard, we halted before what was indeed a restaurant, for several tables were laid on the pavement before the door, but I saw at once that it was anything but a nice place. "Au Rendezvous des Cochers Fideles," read the announcement on the flap of the awning, and truly enough it was a low resort frequented by cabbies--"The meeting-place of faithful coachmen." Along the curb half a score of horses were eating from their bags, while their drivers lounged before the place, eating, drinking, and conversing excitedly in their grotesque jargon.

We descended, in spite of the repellent aspect of the place, and our driver went to the foot of the line, where he fed his own horse. Cousin Egbert, already at one of the open-air tables, was rapping smartly for a waiter.

"What's the matter with having just one little one before grub?" asked the Tuttle person as we joined him. He had a most curious fashion of speech. I mean to say, when he suggested anything whatsoever he invariably wished to know what might be the matter with it.

"Veesky-soda!" demanded Cousin Egbert of the serving person who now appeared, "and ask your driver to have one," he then urged his friend.

The latter hereupon addressed the cabman who had now come up.

"Vooley-voos take something!" he demanded, and the cabman appeared to accept.

"Vooley-voos your friends take something, too?" he demanded further, with a gesture that embraced all the cabmen present, and these, too, appeared to accept with the utmost cordiality.

"You're a wonder, Jeff," said Cousin Egbert. "You talk it like a professor."

"It come natural to me," said the fellow, "and it's a good thing, too. If you know a little French you can go all over Europe without a bit of trouble."

Inside the place was all activity, for many cabmen were now accepting the proffered hospitality, and calling "votry santy!" to their host, who seemed much pleased. Then to my amazement Cousin Egbert insisted that our cabman should sit at table with us. I trust I have as little foolish pride as most people, but this did seem like crowding it on a bit thick. In fact, it looked rather dicky. I was glad to remember that we were in what seemed to be the foreign quarter of the town, where it was probable that no one would recognize us. The drink came, though our cabman refused the whiskey and secured a bottle of native wine.

"Three rousing cheers!" said Cousin Egbert as we drank once more, and added as an afterthought, "What a beautiful world we live in!"

"Vooley-voos make-um bring dinner!" said the Tuttle person to the cabman, who thereupon spoke at length in his native tongue to the waiter. By this means we secured a soup that was not half bad and presently a stew of mutton which Cousin Egbert declared was "some goo." To my astonishment I ate heartily, even in such raffish surroundings. In fact, I found myself pigging it with the rest of them. With coffee, cigars were brought from the tobacconist's next-door, each cabman present accepting one. Our own man was plainly feeling a vast pride in his party, and now circulated among his fellows with an account of our merits.

"This is what I call life," said the Tuttle person, leaning back in his chair.

"I'm coming right back here every day," declared Cousin Egbert happily.

"What's the matter with a little drive to see some well-known objects of interest?" inquired his friend.

"Not art galleries," insisted Cousin Egbert.

"And not churches," said his friend. "Every day's been Sunday with me long enough."

"And not clothing stores," said Cousin Egbert firmly. "The Colonel here is awful fussy about my clothes," he added.

"Is, heh?" inquired his friend. "How do you like this hat of mine?" he asked, turning to me. It was that sudden I nearly fluffed the catch, but recovered myself in time.

"I should consider it a hat of sound wearing properties, sir," I said.

He took it off, examined it carefully, and replaced it.

"So far, so good," he said gravely. "But why be fussy about clothes when God has given you only one life to live?"

"Don't argue about religion," warned Cousin Egbert.

"I always like to see people well dressed, sir," I said, "because it makes such a difference in their appearance."

He slapped his thigh fiercely. "My gosh! that's true. He's got you there, Sourdough. I never thought of that."

"He makes me wear these chest-protectors on my ankles," said Cousin Egbert bitterly, extending one foot.

"What's the matter of taking a little drive to see some well-known objects of interest?" said his friend.

"Not art galleries," said Cousin Egbert firmly.

"We said that before--and not churches."

"And not gents' furnishing goods."

"You said that before."

"Well, you said not churches before."

"Well, what's the matter with taking a little drive?"

"Not art galleries," insisted Cousin Egbert. The thing seemed interminable. I mean to say, they went about the circle as before. It looked to me as if they were having a bit of a spree.

"We'll have one last drink," said the Tuttle person.

"No," said Cousin Egbert firmly, "not another drop. Don't you see the condition poor Bill here is in?" To my amazement he was referring to me. Candidly, he was attempting to convey the impression that I had taken a drop too much. The other regarded me intently.

"Pickled," he said.

"Always affects him that way," said Cousin Egbert. "He's got no head for it."

"Beg pardon, sir," I said, wishing to explain, but this I was not let to do.

"Don't start anything like that here," broke in the Tuttle person, "the police wouldn't stand for it. Just keep quiet and remember you're among friends."

"Yes, sir; quite so, sir," said I, being somewhat puzzled by these strange words. "I was merely----"

"Look out, Jeff," warned Cousin Egbert, interrupting me; "he's a devil when he starts."

"Have you got a knife?" demanded the other suddenly.

"I fancy so, sir," I answered, and produced from my waistcoat pocket the small metal-handled affair I have long carried. This he quickly seized from me.

"You can keep your gun," he remarked, "but you can't be trusted with this in your condition. I ain't afraid of a gun, but I am afraid of a knife. You could have backed me off the board any time with this knife."

"Didn't I tell you?" asked Cousin Egbert.

"Beg pardon, sir," I began, for this was drawing it quite too thick, but again he interrupted me.

"We'd better get him away from this place right off," he said.

"A drive in the fresh air might fix him," suggested Cousin Egbert. "He's as good a scout as you want to know when he's himself." Hereupon, calling our waiting cab-man, they both, to my embarrassment, assisted me to the vehicle.

"Ally caffy!" directed the Tuttle person, and we were driven off, to the raised hats of the remaining cabmen, through many long, quiet streets.

"I wouldn't have had this happen for anything," said Cousin Egbert, indicating me.

"Lucky I got that knife away from him," said the other.

To this I thought it best to remain silent, it being plain that the men were both well along, so to say.

The cab now approached an open square from which issued discordant blasts of music. One glance showed it to be a street fair. I prayed that we might pass it, but my companions hailed it with delight and at once halted the cabby.

"Ally caffy on the corner," directed the Tuttle person, and once more we were seated at an iron table with whiskey and soda ordered. Before us was the street fair in all its silly activity. There were many tinselled booths at which games of chance or marksmanship were played, or at which articles of ornament or household decoration were displayed for sale, and about these were throngs of low-class French idling away their afternoon in that mad pursuit of pleasure which is so characteristic of this race. In the centre of the place was a carrousel from which came the blare of a steam orchestrion playing the "Marseillaise," one of their popular songs. From where I sat I could perceive the circle of gaudily painted beasts that revolved about this musical atrocity. A fashion of horses seemed to predominate, but there was also an ostrich (a bearded Frenchman being astride this bird for the moment), a zebra, a lion, and a gaudily emblazoned giraffe. I shuddered as I thought of the evil possibilities that might be suggested to my two companions by this affair. For the moment I was pleased to note that they had forgotten my supposed indisposition, yet another equally absurd complication ensued when the drink arrived.

"Say, don't your friend ever loosen up?" asked the Tuttle person of Cousin Egbert.

"Tighter than Dick's hatband," replied the latter.

"And then some! He ain't bought once. Say, Bo," he continued to me as I was striving to divine the drift of these comments, "have I got my fingers crossed or not?"

Seeing that he held one hand behind him I thought to humour him by saying, "I fancy so, sir."

"He means 'yes,'" said Cousin Egbert.

The other held his hand before me with the first two fingers spread wide apart. "You lost," he said. "How's that, Sour-dough? We stuck him the first rattle out of the box."

"Good work," said Cousin Egbert. "You're stuck for this round," he added to me. "Three rousing cheers!"

I readily perceived that they meant me to pay the score, which I accordingly did, though I at once suspected the fairness of the game. I mean to say, if my opponent had been a trickster he could easily have rearranged his fingers to defeat me before displaying them. I do not say it was done in this instance. I am merely pointing out that it left open a way to trickery. I mean to say, one would wish to be assured of his opponent's social standing before playing this game extensively.

No sooner had we finished the drink than the Tuttle person said to me:

"I'll give you one chance to get even. I'll guess your fingers this time." Accordingly I put one hand behind me and firmly crossed the fingers, fancying that he would guess them to be uncrossed. Instead of which he called out "Crossed," and I was obliged to show them in that wise, though, as before pointed out, I could easily have defeated him by uncrossing them before revealing my hand. I mean to say, it is not on the face of it a game one would care to play with casual acquaintances, and I questioned even then in my own mind its prevalence in the States. (As a matter of fact, I may say that in my later life in the States I could find no trace of it, and now believe it to have been a pure invention on the part of the Tuttle person. I mean to say, I later became convinced that it was, properly speaking, not a game at all.)

Again they were hugely delighted at my loss and rapped smartly on the table for more drink, and now to my embarrassment I discovered that I lacked the money to pay for this "round" as they would call it.

"Beg pardon, sir," said I discreetly to Cousin Egbert, "but if you could let me have a bit of change, a half-crown or so----" To my surprise he regarded me coldly and shook his head emphatically in the negative.

"Not me," he said; "I've been had too often. You're a good smooth talker and you may be all right, but I can't take a chance at my time of life."

"What's he want now?" asked the other.

"The old story," said Cousin Egbert: "come off and left his purse on the hatrack or out in the woodshed some place." This was the height of absurdity, for I had said nothing of the sort.

"I was looking for something like that," said the other "I never make a mistake in faces. You got a watch there haven't you?"

"Yes, sir," I said, and laid on the table my silver English half-hunter with Albert. They both fell to examining this with interest, and presently the Tuttle person spoke up excitedly:

"Well, darn my skin if he ain't got a genuine double Gazottz. How did you come by this, my man?" he demanded sharply.

"It came from my brother-in-law, sir," I explained, "six years ago as security for a trifling loan."

"He sounds honest enough," said the Tuttle person to Cousin Egbert.

"Yes, but maybe it ain't a regular double Gazottz," said the latter. "The market is flooded with imitations."

"No, sir, I can't be fooled on them boys," insisted the other. "Blindfold me and I could pick a double Gazottz out every time. I'm going to take a chance on it, anyway." Whereupon the fellow pocketed my watch and from his wallet passed me a note of the so-called French money which I was astounded to observe was for the equivalent of four pounds, or one hundred francs, as the French will have it. "I'll advance that much on it," he said, "but don't ask for another cent until I've had it thoroughly gone over by a plumber. It may have moths in it."

It seemed to me that the chap was quite off his head, for the watch was worth not more than ten shillings at the most, though what a double Gazottz might be I could not guess. However, I saw it would be wise to appear to accept the loan, and tendered the note in payment of the score.

When I had secured the change I sought to intimate that we should be leaving. I thought even the street fair would be better for us than this rapid consumption of stimulants.

"I bet he'd go without buying," said Cousin Egbert.

"No, he wouldn't," said the other. "He knows what's customary in a case like this. He's just a little embarrassed. Wait and see if I ain't right." At which they both sat and stared at me in silence for some moments until at last I ordered more drink, as I saw was expected of me.

"He wants the cabman to have one with him," said Cousin Egbert, whereat the other not only beckoned our cabby to join us, but called to two labourers who were passing, and also induced the waiter who served us to join in the "round."

"He seems to have a lot of tough friends," said Cousin Egbert as we all drank, though he well knew I had extended none of these invitations.

"Acts like a drunken sailor soon as he gets a little money," said the other.

"Three rousing cheers!" replied Cousin Egbert, and to my great chagrin he leaped to his feet, seized one of the navvies about the waist, and there on the public pavement did a crude dance with him to the strain of the "Marseillaise" from the steam orchestrion. Not only this, but when the music had ceased he traded hats with the navvy, securing a most shocking affair in place of the new one, and as they parted he presented the fellow with the gloves and stick I had purchased for him that very morning. As I stared aghast at this *faux pas* the navvy, with his new hat at an angle and twirling the stick, proceeded down the street with mincing steps and exaggerated airs of gentility, to the applause of the entire crowd, including Cousin Egbert.

"This ain't quite the hat I want," he said as he returned to us, "but the day is young. I'll have other chances," and with the help of the public-house window as a mirror he adjusted the unmentionable thing with affectations of great nicety.

"He always was a dressy old scoundrel," remarked the Tuttle person. And then, as the music came to us once more, he continued: "Say, Sour-dough, let's go over to the rodeo--they got some likely looking broncs over there."

Arm in arm, accordingly, they crossed the street and proceeded to the carrousel, first warning the cabby and myself to stay by them lest harm should come to us. What now ensued was perhaps their most remarkable behaviour at the day. At the time I could account for it only by the liquor they had consumed, but later experience in the States convinced me that they were at times consciously spoofing. I mean to say, it was quite too absurd--their seriously believing what they seemed to believe.

The carrousel being at rest when we approached, they gravely examined each one of the painted wooden effigies, looking into such of the mouths as were open, and cautiously feeling the forelegs of the different mounts, keeping up an elaborate pretence the while that the beasts were real and that they were in danger of being kicked. One absurdly painted horse they agreed would be the most difficult to ride. Examining his mouth, they disputed as to his age, and called the cabby to have his opinion of the thing's fetlocks, warning each other to beware of his rearing. The cabby, who was doubtless also intoxicated, made an equal pretence of the beast's realness, and indulged, I gathered, in various criticisms of its legs at great length.

"I think he's right," remarked the Tuttle person when the cabby had finished. "It's a bad case of splints. The leg would be blistered if I had him."

"I wouldn't give him corral room," said Cousin Egbert. "He's a bad actor. Look at his eye! Whoa! there--you would, would you!" Here he made a pretence that the beast had seized him by the shoulder. "He's a man-eater! What did I tell you? Keep him away!"

"I'll take that out of him," said the Tuttle person. "I'll show him who's his master."

"You ain't never going to try to ride him, Jeff? Think of the wife and little ones!"

"You know me, Sour-dough. No horse never stepped out from under me yet. I'll not only ride him, but I'll put a silver dollar in each stirrup and give you a thousand for each one I lose and a thousand for every time I touch leather."

Cousin Egbert here began to plead tearfully:

"Don't do it, Jeff--come on around here. There's a big five-year-old roan around here that will be safe as a church for you. Let that pinto alone. They ought to be arrested for having him here."

But the other seemed obdurate.

"Start her up, Professor, when I give the word!" he called to the proprietor, and handed him one of the French banknotes. "Play it all out!" he directed, as this person gasped with amazement.

Cousin Egbert then proceeded to the head of the beast.

"You'll have to blind him," he said.

"Sure!" replied the other, and with loud and profane cries to the animal they bound a handkerchief about his eyes.

"I can tell he's going to be a twister," warned Cousin Egbert. "I better ear him," and to my increased amazement he took one of the beast's leather ears between his teeth and held it tightly. Then with soothing words to the supposedly dangerous animal, the Tuttle person mounted him.

"Let him go!" he called to Cousin Egbert, who released the ear from between his teeth.

"Wait!" called the latter. "We're all going with you," whereupon he insisted that the cabby and I should enter a sort of swan-boat directly in the rear. I felt a silly fool, but I saw there was nothing else to be done. Cousin Egbert himself mounted a horse he had called a "blue roan," waved his hand to the proprietor, who switched a lever, the "Marseillaise" blared forth, and the platform began to revolve. As we moved, the Tuttle person whisked the handkerchief from off the eyes of his mount and with loud, shrill cries began to beat the sides of its head with his soft hat, bobbing about in his saddle, moreover, as if the beast were most unruly and like to dismount him. Cousin Egbert joined in the yelling, I am sorry to say, and lashed his beast as if he would overtake his companion. The cabman also became excited and shouted his utmost, apparently in the way of encouragement. Strange to say,

I presume on account of the motion, I felt the thing was becoming infectious and was absurdly moved to join in the shouts, restraining myself with difficulty. I could distinctly imagine we were in the hunting field and riding the tails off the hounds, as one might say.

In view of what was later most unjustly alleged of me, I think it as well to record now that, though I had partaken freely of the stimulants since our meeting with the Tuttle person, I was not intoxicated, nor until this moment had I felt even the slightest elation. Now, however, I did begin to feel conscious of a mild exhilaration, and to be aware that I was viewing the behaviour of my companions with a sort of superior but amused tolerance. I can account for this only by supposing that the swift revolutions of the carrousel had in some occult manner intensified or consummated, as one might say, the effect of my previous potations. I mean to say, the continued swirling about gave me a frothy feeling that was not unpleasant.

As the contrivance came to rest, Cousin Egbert ran to the Tuttle person, who had dismounted, and warmly shook his hand, as did the cabby.

"I certainly thought he had you there once, Jeff," said Cousin Egbert. "Of all the twisters I ever saw, that outlaw is the worst."

"Wanted to roll me," said the other, "but I learned him something."

It may not be credited, but at this moment I found myself examining the beast and saying: "He's crocked himself up, sir--he's gone tender at the heel." I knew perfectly, it must be understood, that this was silly, and yet I further added, "I fancy he's picked up a stone." I mean to say, it was the most utter rot, pretending seriously that way.

"You come away," said Cousin Egbert. "Next thing you'll be thinking you can ride him yourself." I did in truth experience an earnest craving for more of the revolutions and said as much, adding that I rode at twelve stone.

"Let him break his neck if he wants to," urged the Tuttle person.

"It wouldn't be right," replied Cousin Egbert, "not in his condition. Let's see if we can't find something gentle for him. Not the roan--I found she ain't bridle-wise. How about that pheasant?"

"It's an ostrich, sir," I corrected him, as indeed it most distinctly was, though at my words they both indulged in loud laughter, affecting to consider that I had misnamed the creature.

"Ostrich!" they shouted. "Poor old Bill--he thinks it's an ostrich!"

"Quite so, sir," I said, pleasantly but firmly, determining not to be hoaxed again.

"Don't drivel that way," said the Tuttle person.

"Leave it to the driver, Jeff--maybe he'll believe *him*," said Cousin Egbert almost sadly, whereupon the other addressed the cabby:

"Hey, Frank," he began, and continued with some French words, among which I caught "vooley-vous, ally caffy, foomer"; and something that sounded much like "kafoozleum," at which the cabby spoke at some length in his native language concerning the ostrich. When he had done, the Tuttle person turned to me with a superior frown.

"Now I guess you're satisfied," he remarked. "You heard what Frank said--it's an Arabian muffin bird." Of course I was perfectly certain that the chap had said nothing of the sort, but I resolved to enter into the spirit of the thing, so I merely said: "Yes, sir; my error; it was only at first glance that it seemed to be an ostrich."

"Come along," said Cousin Egbert. "I won't let him ride anything he can't guess the name of. It wouldn't be right to his folks."

"Well, what's that, then?" demanded the other, pointing full at the giraffe.

"It's a bally ant-eater, sir," I replied, divining that I should be wise not to seem too obvious in naming the beast.

"Well, well, so it is!" exclaimed the Tuttle person delightedly.

"He's got the eye with him this time," said Cousin Egbert admiringly.

"He's sure a wonder," said the other. "That thing had me fooled; I thought at first it was a Russian mouse hound."

"Well, let him ride it, then," said Cousin Egbert, and I was practically lifted into the saddle by the pair of them.

"One moment," said Cousin Egbert. "Can't you see the poor thing has a sore throat? Wait till I fix him." And forthwith he removed his spats and in another moment had buckled them securely high about the throat of the giraffe. It will be seen that I was not myself when I say that this performance did not shock me as it should have done, though I was, of course, less entertained by it than were the remainder of our party and a circle of the French lower classes that had formed about us.

"Give him his head! Let's see what time you can make!" shouted Cousin Egbert as the affair began once more to revolve. I saw that both my companions held opened watches in their hands.

It here becomes difficult for me to be lucid about the succeeding events of the day. I was conscious of a mounting exhilaration as my beast swept me around the circle, and of a marked impatience with many of the proprieties of behaviour that ordinarily with me matter enormously. I swung my cap and joyously urged my strange steed to a faster pace, being conscious of loud applause each time I passed my companions. For certain lapses of memory thereafter I must wholly blame this insidious motion.

For example, though I believed myself to be still mounted and whirling (indeed I was strongly aware of the motion), I found myself seated again at the corner public house and rapping smartly for drink, which I paid for. I was feeling remarkably fit, and suffered only a mild wonder that I should have left the carrousel without observing it. Having drained my glass, I then remember asking Cousin Egbert if he would consent to change hats with the cabby, which he willingly did. It was a top-hat of some strange, hard material brightly glazed. Although many unjust things were said of me later, this is the sole incident of the day which causes me to admit that I might have taken a glass too much, especially as I undoubtedly praised Cousin Egbert's appearance when the exchange had been made, and was heard to wish that we might all have hats so smart.

It was directly after this that young Mr. Elmer, the art student, invited us to his studio, though I had not before remarked his presence, and cannot recall now where we met him. The occurrence in the studio, however, was entirely natural. I wished to please my friends and made no demur whatever when asked to don the things--a trouserish affair, of sheep's wool, which they called "chapps," a flannel shirt of blue (they knotted a scarlet handkerchief around my neck), and a wide-brimmed white hat with four indentations in the crown, such as one may see worn in the cinema dramas by cow-persons and other western-coast desperadoes. When they had strapped around my waist a large pistol in a leather jacket, I considered the effect picturesque in the extreme, and my friends were loud in their approval of it.

I repeat, it was an occasion when it would have been boorish in me to refuse to meet them halfway. I even told them an excellent wheeze I had long known, which I thought they might not, have heard. It runs: "Why is Charing Cross? Because the

Strand runs into it." I mean to say, this is comic providing one enters wholly into the spirit of it, as there is required a certain nimbleness of mind to get the point, as one might say. In the present instance some needed element was lacking, for they actually drew aloof from me and conversed in low tones among themselves, pointedly ignoring me. I repeated the thing to make sure they should see it, whereat I heard Cousin Egbert say. "Better not irritate him--he'll get mad if we don't laugh," after which they burst into laughter so extravagant that I knew it to be feigned. Hereupon, feeling quite drowsy, I resolved to have forty winks, and with due apologies reclined upon the couch, where I drifted into a refreshing slumber.

Later I inferred that I must have slept for some hours. I was awakened by a light flashed in my eyes, and beheld Cousin Egbert and the Tuttle person, the latter wishing to know how late I expected to keep them up. I was on my feet at once with apologies, but they instantly hustled me to the door, down a flight of steps, through a court-yard, and into the waiting cab. It was then I noticed that I was wearing the curious hat of the American Far-West, but when I would have gone back to leave it, and secure my own, they protested vehemently, wishing to know if I had not given them trouble enough that day.

In the cab I was still somewhat drowsy, but gathered that my companions had left me, to dine and attend a public dance-hall with the cubbish art student. They had not seemed to need sleep and were still wakeful, for they sang from time to time, and Cousin Egbert lifted the cabby's hat, which he still wore, bowing to imaginary throngs along the street who were supposed to be applauding him. I at once became conscience-stricken at the thought of Mrs. Effie's feelings when she should discover him to be in this state, and was on the point of suggesting that he seek another apartment for the night, when the cab pulled up in front of our own hotel.

Though I protest that I was now entirely recovered from any effect that the alcohol might have had upon me, it was not until this moment that I most horribly discovered myself to be in the full cow-person's regalia I had donned in the studio in a spirit of pure frolic. I mean to say, I had never intended to wear the things beyond the door and could not have been hired to do so. What was my amazement then to find my companions laboriously lifting me from the cab in this impossible tenue. I objected vehemently, but little good it did me.

"Get a policeman if he starts any of that rough stuff," said the Tuttle person, and in sheer horror of a scandal I subsided, while one on either side they hustled me through the hotel lounge--happily vacant of every one but a tariff manager--and into the lift. And now I perceived that they were once more pretending to themselves that I was in a bad way from drink, though I could not at once suspect the full iniquity of their design.

As we reached our own floor, one of them still seeming to support me on either side, they began loud and excited admonitions to me to be still, to come along as quickly as possible, to stop singing, and not to shoot. I mean to say, I was entirely quiet, I was coming along as quickly as they would let me, I had not sung, and did not wish to shoot, yet they persisted in making this loud ado over my supposed intoxication, aimlessly as I thought, until the door of the Floud drawing-room opened and Mrs. Effie appeared in the hallway. At this they redoubled their absurd violence with me, and by dint of tripping me they actually made it appear that I was scarce able to walk, nor do I imagine that the costume I wore was any testimonial to my sobriety.

"Now we got him safe," panted Cousin Egbert, pushing open the door of my room.

"Get his gun, first!" warned the Tuttle person, and this being taken from me, I was unceremoniously shoved inside.

"What does all this mean?" demanded Mrs. Effie, coming rapidly down the hall. "Where have you been till this time of night? I bet it's your fault, Jeff Tuttle--you've been getting him going."

They were both voluble with denials of this, and though I could scarce believe my ears, they proceeded to tell a story that laid the blame entirely on me.

"No, ma'am, Mis' Effie," began the Tuttle person. "It ain't that way at all. You wrong me if ever a man was wronged."

"You just seen what state he was in, didn't you?" asked Cousin Egbert in tones of deep injury. "Do you want to take another look at him?" and he made as if to push the door farther open upon me.

"Don't do it--don't get him started again!" warned the Tuttle person. "I've had trouble enough with that man to-day."

"I seen it coming this morning," said Cousin Egbert, "when we was at the art gallery. He had a kind of wild look in his eyes, and I says right then: 'There's a man ought to be watched,' and, well, one thing led to another--look at this hat he made me wear--nothing would satisfy him but I should trade hats with some cab-driver----"

"I was coming along from looking at two or three good churches," broke in the Tuttle person, "when I seen Sour-dough here having a kind of a mix-up with this man because of him insisting he must ride a kangaroo or something on a merry-go-round, and wanting Sour-dough to ride an ostrich with him, and then when we got him quieted down a little, nothing would do him but he's got to be a cowboy--you seen his clothes, didn't you? And of course I wanted to get back to Addie and the girls, but I seen Sour-dough here was in trouble, so I stayed right by him, and between us we got the maniac here."

"He's one of them should never touch liquor," said Cousin Egbert; "it makes a demon of him."

"I got his knife away from him early in the game," said the other.

"I don't suppose I got to wear this cabman's hat just because he told me to, have I?" demanded Cousin Egbert.

"And here I'd been looking forward to a quiet day seeing some well-known objects of interest," came from the other, "after I got my tooth pulled, that is."

"And me with a tooth, too, that nearly drove me out of my mind," said Cousin Egbert suddenly.

I could not see Mrs. Effie, but she had evidently listened to this outrageous tale with more or less belief, though not wholly credulous.

"You men have both been drinking yourselves," she said shrewdly.

"We had to take a little; he made us," declared the Tuttle person brazenly.

"He got so he insisted on our taking something every time he did," added Cousin Egbert. "And, anyway, I didn't care so much, with this tooth of mine aching like it does."

"You come right out with me and around to that dentist I went to this morning," said the Tuttle person. "You'll suffer all night if you don't."

"Maybe I'd better," said Cousin Egbert, "though I hate to leave this comfortable hotel and go out into the night air again."

"I'll have the right of this in the morning," said Mrs. Effie. "Don't think it's going to stop here!" At this my door was pulled to and the key turned in the lock.

Frankly I am aware that what I have put down above is incredible, yet not a single detail have I distorted. With a quite devilish ingenuity they had fastened upon some true bits: I had suggested the change of hats with the cabby, I had wished to ride the giraffe, and the Tuttle person had secured my knife, but how monstrously untrue of me was the impression conveyed by these isolated facts. I could believe now quite all the tales I had ever heard of the queerness of Americans. Queerness, indeed! I went to bed resolving to let the morrow take care of itself.

Again I was awakened by a light flashing in my eyes, and became aware that Cousin Egbert stood in the middle of the room. He was reading from his notebook of art criticisms, with something of an oratorical effect. Through the half-drawn curtains I could see that dawn was breaking. Cousin Egbert was no longer wearing the cabby's hat. It was now the flat cap of the Paris constable or policeman.

CHAPTER FOUR

THE sight was a fair crumpler after the outrageous slander that had been put upon me by this elderly inebriate and his accomplice. I sat up at once, prepared to bully him down a bit. Although I was not sure that I engaged his attention, I told him that his reading could be very well done without and that he might take himself off. At this he became silent and regarded me solemnly.

"Why did Charing Cross the Strand? Because three rousing cheers," said he.

Of course he had the wheeze all wrong and I saw that he should be in bed. So with gentle words I lured him to his own chamber. Here, with a quite unexpected perversity, he accused me of having kept him up the night long and begged now to be allowed to retire. This he did with muttered complaints of my behaviour, and was almost instantly asleep. I concealed the constable's cap in one of his boxes, for I feared that he had not come by this honestly. I then returned to my own room, where for a long time I meditated profoundly upon the situation that now confronted me.

It seemed probable that I should be shopped by Mrs. Effie for what she had been led to believe was my rowdyish behaviour. However dastardly the injustice to me, it was a solution of the problem that I saw I could bring myself to meet with considerable philosophy. It meant a return to the quiet service of the Honourable George and that I need no longer face the distressing vicissitudes of life in the back blocks of unexplored America. I would not be obliged to muddle along in the blind fashion of the last two days, feeling a frightful fool. Mrs. Effie would surely not keep me on, and that was all about it. I had merely to make no defence of myself. And even if I chose to make one I was not certain that she would believe me, so cunning had been the accusations against me, with that tiny thread of fact which I make no doubt has so often enabled historians to give a false colouring to their recitals without stating downright untruths. Indeed, my shameless appearance in the garb of a cow person would alone have cast doubt upon the truth as I knew it to be.

Then suddenly I suffered an illumination. I perceived all at once that to make any sort of defence of myself would not be cricket. I mean to say, I saw the proceedings of the previous day in a new light. It is well known that I do not hold with the abuse of alcoholic stimulants, and yet on the day before, in moments that I now confess to have been slightly elevated, I had been conscious of a certain feeling of fellowship with my two companions that was rather wonderful. Though obviously they were not university men, they seemed to belong to what in America would be called the landed gentry, and yet I had felt myself on terms of undoubted equality with them. It may be believed or not, but there had been brief spaces when I forgot that I was a gentleman's man. Astoundingly I had experienced the confident ease of a gentleman among his equals. I was obliged to admit now that this might have been a mere delusion of the cup, and yet I wondered, too, if perchance I might not have caught something of that American spirit of equality which is said to be peculiar to republics. Needless to say I had never believed in the existence of this spirit, but had considered it rather a ghastly jest, having been a reader of our own periodical press since earliest youth. I mean to say, there could hardly be a stable society in which one had no superiors, because in that case one would not know who were one's inferiors. Nevertheless, I repeat that I had felt a most novel enlargement of myself; had, in fact, felt that I was a gentleman among gentlemen, using the word in its strictly technical sense. And so vividly did this conviction remain with me that I now saw any defence of my course to be out of the question.

I perceived that my companions had meant to have me on toast from the first. I mean to say, they had started a rag with me--a bit of chaff--and I now found myself rather preposterously enjoying the manner in which they had chivied me. I mean to say, I felt myself taking it as one gentleman would take a rag from other gentlemen--not as a bit of a sneak who would tell the truth to save his face. A couple of chaffing old beggars they were, but they had found me a topping dead sportsman of their own sort. Be it remembered I was still uncertain whether I had caught something of that alleged American spirit, or whether the drink had made me feel equal at least to Americans. Whatever it might be, it was rather great, and I was prepared to face Mrs. Effie without a tremor--to face her, of course, as one overtaken by a weakness for spirits.

When the bell at last rang I donned my service coat and, assuming a look of profound remorse, I went to the drawing-room to serve the morning coffee. As I suspected, only Mrs. Effie was present. I believe it has been before remarked that she is a person of commanding presence, with a manner of marked determination. She favoured me with a brief but chilling glance, and for some moments thereafter affected quite to ignore me. Obviously she had been completely greened the night before and was treating me with a proper contempt. I saw that it was no use grousing at fate and that it was better for me not to go into the American wilderness, since a rolling stone gathers no moss. I was prepared to accept instant dismissal without a character.

She began upon me, however, after her first cup of coffee, more mildly than I had expected.

"Ruggles, I'm horribly disappointed in you."

"Not more so than I myself, Madam," I replied.

"I am more disappointed," she continued, "because I felt that Cousin Egbert had something in him----"

"Something in him, yes, Madam," I murmured sympathetically.

"And that you were the man to bring it out. I was quite hopeful after you got him into those new clothes. I don't believe any one else could have done it. And now it turns out that you have this weakness for drink. Not only that, but you have a mania for insisting that other men drink with you. Think of those two poor fellows trailing you over Paris yesterday trying to save you from yourself."

"I shall never forget it, Madam," I said.

"Of course I don't believe that Jeff Tuttle always has to have it forced on him. Jeff Tuttle is an Indian. But Cousin Egbert is different. You tore him away from that art gallery where he was improving his mind, and led him into places that must have been disgusting to him. All he wanted was to study the world's masterpieces in canvas and marble, yet you put a cabman's hat on him and made him ride an antelope, or whatever the thing was. I can't think where you got such ideas."

"I was not myself. I can only say that I seemed to be subject to an attack." And the Tuttle person was one of their Indians! This explained so much about him.

"You don't look like a periodical souse," she remarked.

"Quite so, Madam."

"But you must be a wonder when you do start. The point is: am I doing right to intrust Cousin Egbert to you again?"

"Quite so, Madam."

"It seems doubtful if you are the person to develop his higher nature."

Against my better judgment I here felt obliged to protest that I had always been given the highest character for quietness and general behaviour and that I could safely promise that I should be guilty of no further lapses of this kind. Frankly, I was wishing to be shopped, and yet I could not resist making this mild defence of myself. Such I have found to be the way of human nature. To my surprise I found that Mrs. Effie was more than half persuaded by these words and was on the point of giving me another trial. I cannot say that I was delighted at this. I was ready to give up all Americans as problems one too many for me, and yet I was strangely a little warmed at thinking I might not have seen the last of Cousin Egbert, whom I had just given a tuckup.

"You shall have your chance," she said at last, "and just to show you that I'm not narrow, you can go over to the sideboard there and pour yourself out a little one. It ought to be a lifesaver to you, feeling the way you must this morning."

"Thank you, Madam," and I did as she suggested. I was feeling especially fit, but I knew that I ought to play in character, as one might say.

"Three rousing cheers!" I said, having gathered the previous day that this was a popular American toast. She stared at me rather oddly, but made no comment other than to announce her departure on a shopping tour. Her bonnet, I noted, was quite wrong. Too extremely modish it was, accenting its own lines at the expense of a face to which less attention should have been called. This is a mistake common to the sex, however. They little dream how sadly they mock and betray their own faces. Nothing I think is more pathetic than their trustful unconsciousness of the tragedy--the rather plainish face under the contemptuous structure that points to it and shrieks derision. The rather plain woman who knows what to put upon her head is a woman of genius. I have seen three, perhaps.

I now went to the room of Cousin Egbert. I found him awake and cheerful, but disinclined to arise. It was hard for me to realize that his simple, kindly face could mask the guile he had displayed the night before. He showed no sign of regret for the false light in which he had placed me. Indeed he was sitting up in bed as cheerful and independent as if he had paid two-pence for a park chair.

"I fancy," he began, "that we ought to spend a peaceful day indoors. The trouble with these foreign parts is that they don't have enough home life. If it isn't one thing it's another."

"Sometimes it's both, sir," I said, and he saw at once that I was not to be wheedled. Thereupon he grinned brazenly at me, and demanded:

"What did she say?"

"Well, sir," I said, "she was highly indignant at me for taking you and Mr. Tuttle into public houses and forcing you to drink liquor, but she was good enough, after I had expressed my great regret and promised to do better in the future, to promise that I should have another chance. It was more than I could have hoped, sir, after the outrageous manner in which I behaved."

He grinned again at this, and in spite of my resentment I found myself grinning with him. I am aware that this was a most undignified submission to the injustice he had put upon me, and it was far from the line of stern rebuke that I had fully meant to adopt with him, but there seemed no other way. I mean to say, I couldn't help it.

"I'm glad to hear you talk that way," he said. "It shows you may have something in you after all. What you want to do is to learn to say no. Then you won't be so much trouble to those who have to look after you."

"Yes, sir," I said, "I shall try, sir."

"Then I'll give you another chance," he said sternly.

I mean to say, it was all spoofing, the way we talked. I am certain he knew it as well as I did, and I am sure we both enjoyed it. I am not one of those who think it shows a lack of dignity to unbend in this manner on occasion. True, it is not with every one I could afford to do so, but Cousin Egbert seemed to be an exception to almost every rule of conduct.

At his earnest request I now procured for him another carafe of iced water (he seemed already to have consumed two of these), after which he suggested that I read to him. The book he had was the well-known story, "Robinson Crusoe," and I began a chapter which describes some of the hero's adventures on his lonely island.

Cousin Egbert, I was glad to note, was soon sleeping soundly, so I left him and retired to my own room for a bit of needed rest. The story of "Robinson Crusoe" is one in which many interesting facts are conveyed regarding life upon remote islands where there are practically no modern conveniences and one is put to all sorts of crude makeshifts, but for me the narrative contains too little dialogue.

For the remainder of the day I was left to myself, a period of peace that I found most welcome. Not until evening did I meet any of the family except Cousin Egbert, who partook of some light nourishment late in the afternoon. Then it was that Mrs. Effie summoned me when she had dressed for dinner, to say:

"We are sailing for home the day after to-morrow. See that Cousin Egbert has everything he needs."

The following day was a busy one, for there were many boxes to be packed against the morrow's sailing, and much shopping to do for Cousin Egbert, although he was much against this.

"It's all nonsense," he insisted, "her saying all that truck helps to 'finish' me. Look at me! I've been in Europe darned near four months and I can't see that I'm a lick more finished than when I left Red Gap. Of course it may show on me so other people can see it, but I don't believe it does, at that." Nevertheless, I bought him no end of suits and smart haberdashery.

When the last box had been strapped I hastened to our old lodgings on the chance of seeing the Honourable George once more. I found him dejectedly studying an ancient copy of the "Referee." Too evidently he had dined that night in a costume which would, I am sure, have offended even Cousin Egbert. Above his dress trousers he wore a golfing waistcoat and a shooting jacket. However, I could not allow myself to be distressed by this. Indeed, I knew that worse would come. I forebore to comment upon the extraordinary choice of garments he had made. I knew it was quite useless. From any word that he let fall during our chat, he might have supposed himself to be dressed as an English gentleman should be.

He bade me seat myself, and for some time we smoked our pipes in a friendly silence. I had feared that, as on the last occasion, he would row me for having deserted him, but he no longer seemed to harbour this unjust thought. We spoke of America, and I suggested that he might some time come out to shoot big game along the Ohio or the Mississippi. He replied moodily, after a long interval, that if he ever did come out it would be to set up a cattle plantation. It was rather agreed that he would come should I send for him. "Can't sit around forever waiting for old Nevil's toast crumbs," said he.

We chatted for a time of home politics, which was, of course, in a wretched state. There was a time when we might both have been won to a sane and reasoned liberalism, but the present so-called government was coming it a bit too thick for us. We said some sharp things about the little Welsh attorney who was beginning to be England's humiliation. Then it was time for me to go.

The moment was rather awkward, for the Honourable George, to my great embarrassment, pressed upon me his dispatch-case, one that we had carried during all our travels and into which tidily fitted a quart flask. Brandy we usually carried in it. I managed to accept it with a word of thanks, and then amazingly he shook hands twice with me as we said good-night. I had never dreamed he could be so greatly affected. Indeed, I had always supposed that there was nothing of the sentimentalist about him.

So the Honourable George and I were definitely apart for the first time in our lives.

It was with mingled emotions that I set sail next day for the foreign land to which I had been exiled by a turn of the cards. Not only was I off to a wilderness where a life of daily adventure was the normal life, but I was to mingle with foreigners who promised to be quite almost impossibly queer, if the family of Flouds could be taken as a sample of the native American--knowing Indians like the Tuttle person; that sort of thing. If some would be less queer, others would be even more queer, with queerness of a sort to tax even my *savoir faire*, something which had been sorely taxed, I need hardly say, since that fatal evening when the Honourable George's intuitions had played him false in the game of drawing poker. I was not the first of my countrymen, however, to find himself in desperate straits, and I resolved to behave as England expects us to.

I have said that I was viewing the prospect with mingled emotions. Before we had been out many hours they became so mingled that, having crossed the Channel many times, I could no longer pretend to ignore their true nature. For three days I was at the mercy of the elements, and it was then I discovered a certain hardness in the nature of Cousin Egbert which I had not before suspected. It was only by speaking in the sharpest manner to him that I was able to secure the nursing my condition demanded. I made no doubt he would actually have left me to the care of a steward had I not been firm with him. I have known him leave my bedside for an hour at a time when it seemed probable that I would pass away at any moment. And more than once, when I summoned him in the night to administer one of the remedies with which I had provided myself, or perhaps to question him if the ship were out of danger, he exhibited something very like irritation. Indeed he was never properly impressed by my suffering, and at times when he would answer my call it was plain to be seen that he had been passing idle moments in the smoke-room or elsewhere, quite as if the situation were an ordinary one.

It is only fair to say, however, that toward the end of my long and interesting illness I had quite broken his spirit and brought him to be as attentive as even I could wish. By the time I was able with his assistance to go upon deck again he was bringing me nutritive wines and jellies without being told, and so attentive did he remain that I overheard a fellow-passenger address him as Florence Nightingale. I also overheard the Senator tell him that I had got his sheep, whatever that may have meant--a sheep or a goat--some domestic animal. Yet with all his willingness he was clumsy in his handling of me; he seemed to take nothing with any proper seriousness, and in spite of my sharpest warning he would never wear the proper clothes, so that I always felt he was attracting undue attention to us. Indeed, I should hardly care to cross with him again, and this I told him straight.

Of the so-called joys of ship-life, concerning which the boat companies speak so enthusiastically in their folders, the less said the better. It is a childish mind, I think, that can be impressed by the mere wabbly bulk of water. It is undoubtedly tremendous, but nothing to kick up such a row about. The truth is that the prospect from a ship's deck lacks that variety which one may enjoy from almost any English hillside. One sees merely water, and that's all about it.

It will be understood, therefore, that I hailed our approach to the shores of foreign America with relief if not with enthusiasm. Even this was better than an ocean which has only size in its favour and has been quite too foolishly overrated.

We were soon steaming into the harbour of one of their large cities. Chicago, I had fancied it to be, until the chance remark of an American who looked to be a well-informed fellow identified it as New York. I was much annoyed now at the behaviour of Cousin Egbert, who burst into silly cheers at the slightest excuse, a passing steamer, a green hill, or a rusty statue of quite ungainly height which seemed to be made of crude iron. Do as I would, I could not restrain him from these unseemly shouts. I could not help contrasting his boisterousness with the fine reserve which, for example, the Honourable George would have maintained under these circumstances.

A further relief it was, therefore, when we were on the dock and his mind was diverted to other matters. A long time we were detained by customs officials who seemed rather overwhelmed by the gowns and millinery of Mrs. Effie, but we were at last free and taken through the streets of the crude new American city of New York to a hotel overlooking what I dare say in their simplicity they call their Hyde Park.

CHAPTER FIVE

I must admit that at this inn they did things quite nicely, doubtless because it seemed to be almost entirely staffed by foreigners. One would scarce have known within its walls that one had come out to North America, nor that savage wilderness surrounded one on every hand. Indeed I was surprised to learn that we were quite at the edge of the rough Western frontier, for in but one night's journey we were to reach the American mountains to visit some people who inhabited a camp in their dense wilds.

A bit of romantic thrill I felt in this adventure, for we should encounter, I inferred, people of the hardy pioneer stock that has pushed the American civilization, such as it is, ever westward. I pictured the stalwart woodsman, axe in hand, braving the forest to fell trees for his rustic home, while at night the red savages prowled about to scalp any who might stray from the blazing campfire. On the day of our landing I had read something of this--of depredations committed by their Indians at Arizona.

From what would, I take it, be their Victoria station, we three began our journey in one of the Pullman night coaches, the Senator of this family having proceeded to their home settlement of Red Gap with word that he must "look after his fences," referring, doubtless, to those about his cattle plantation.

As our train moved out Mrs. Effie summoned me for a serious talk concerning the significance of our present visit; not of the wilderness dangers to which we might be exposed, but of its social aspects, which seemed to be of prime importance. We were to visit, I learned, one Charles Belknap-Jackson of Boston and Red Gap, he being a person who mattered enormously, coming from one of the very oldest families of Boston, a port on their east coast, and a place, I gathered, in which some decent attention is given to the matter of who has been one's family. A bit of a shock it was to learn that in this rough land they had their castes and precedences.

I saw I had been right to suspect that even a crude society could not exist without its rules for separating one's superiors from the lower sorts. I began to feel at once more at home and I attended the discourse of Mrs. Effie with close attention.

The Boston person, in one of those irresponsibly romantic moments that sometimes trap the best of us, had married far beneath him, espousing the simple daughter of one of the crude, old-settling families of Red Gap. Further, so inattentive to details had he been, he had neglected to secure an ante-nuptial settlement as our own men so wisely make it their rule to do, and was now suffering a painful embarrassment from this folly; for the mother-in-law, controlling the rather sizable family fortune, had harshly insisted that the pair reside in Red Gap, permitting no more than an occasional summer visit to his native Boston, whose inhabitants she affected not to admire.

"Of course the poor fellow suffers frightfully," explained Mrs. Effie, "shut off there away from all he'd been brought up to, but good has come of it, for his presence has simply done wonders for us. Before he came our social life was too awful for words--oh, a *mixture*! Practically every one in town attended our dances; no one had ever told us any better. The Bohemian set mingled freely with the very oldest families--oh, in a way that would never be tolerated in London society, I'm sure. And everything so crude! Why, I can remember when no one thought of putting doilies under the finger-bowls. No tone to it at all. For years we had no country club, if you can believe that. And even now, in spite of the efforts of Charles and a few of us, there are still some of the older families that are simply sloppy in their entertaining. And promiscuous. The trouble I've had with the Senator and Cousin Egbert!"

"The Flouds are an old family?" I suggested, wishing to understand these matters deeply.

"The Flouds," she answered impressively, "were living in Red Gap before the spur track was ever run out to the canning factory--and I guess you know what that means!"

"Quite so, Madam," I suggested; and, indeed, though it puzzled me a bit, it sounded rather tremendous, as meaning with us something like since the battle of Hastings.

"But, as I say, Charles at once gave us a glimpse of the better things. Thanks to him, the Bohemian set and the North Side set are now fairly distinct. The scraps we've had with that Bohemian set! He has a real genius for leadership, Charles has, but I know he often finds it so discouraging, getting people to know their places. Even his own mother-in-law, Mrs. Lysander John Pettengill--but you'll see to-morrow how impossible she is, poor old soul! I shouldn't talk about her, I really shouldn't. Awfully good heart the poor old dear has, but--well, I don't see why I shouldn't tell you the exact truth in plain words--you'd find it out soon enough. She is simply a confirmed *mixer*. The trial she's been and is to poor Charles! Almost no respect for any of the higher things he stands for--and temper? Well, I've heard her swear at him till you'd have thought it was Jeff Tuttle packing a green cayuse for the first time. Words? Talk about words! And Cousin Egbert always standing in with her. He's been another awful trial, refusing to play tennis at the country club, or to take up golf, or do any of those smart things, though I got him a beautiful lot of sticks. But no: when he isn't out in the hills, he'd rather sit down in that back room at the Silver Dollar saloon, playing cribbage all day with a lot of drunken loafers. But I'm so hoping that will be changed, now that I've made him see there are better things in life. Don't you really think he's another man?"

"To an extent, Madam, I dare say," I replied cautiously.

"It's chiefly what I got you for," she went on. "And then, in a general way you will give tone to our establishment. The moment I saw you I knew you could be an influence for good among us. No one there has ever had anything like you. Not even Charles. He's tried to have American valets, but you never can get them to understand their place. Charles finds them so offensively familiar. They don't seem to realize. But of course you realize."

I inclined my head in sympathetic understanding.

"I'm looking forward to Charles meeting you. I guess he'll be a little put out at our having you, but there's no harm letting him see I'm to be reckoned with. Naturally his wife, Millie, is more or less mentioned as a social leader, but I never could see that she is really any more prominent than I am. In fact, last year after our Bazaar of All Nations our pictures in costume were in the Spokane paper as 'Red Gap's Rival Society Queens,' and I suppose that's what we are, though we work together pretty well as a rule. Still, I must say, having you puts me a couple of notches ahead of her. Only, for heaven's sake, keep your eye on Cousin Egbert!"

"I shall do my duty, Madam," I returned, thinking it all rather morbidly interesting, these weird details about their county families.

"I'm sure you will," she said at parting. "I feel that we shall do things right this year. Last year the Sunday Spokane paper used to have nearly a column under the heading 'Social Doings of Red Gap's Smart Set.' This year we'll have a good two columns, if I don't miss my guess."

In the smoking-compartment I found Cousin Egbert staring gloomily into vacancy, as one might say, the reason I knew being that he had vainly pleaded with Mrs. Effie to be allowed to spend this time at their Coney Island, which is a sort of Brighton. He transferred his stare to me, but it lost none of its gloom.

"Hell begins to pop!" said he.

"Referring to what, sir?" I rejoined with some severity, for I have never held with profanity.

"Referring to Charles Belknap Hyphen Jackson of Boston, Mass.," said he, "the greatest little trouble-maker that ever crossed the hills--with a bracelet on one wrist and a watch on the other and a one-shot eyeglass and a gold cigareet case and key chains, rings, bangles, and jewellery till he'd sink like lead if he ever fell into the crick with all that metal on."

"You are speaking, sir, about a person who matters enormously," I rebuked him.

"If I hadn't been afraid of getting arrested I'd have shot him long ago."

"It's not done, sir," I said, quite horrified by his rash words.

"It's liable to be," he insisted. "I bet Ma Pettengill will go in with me on it any time I give her the word. Say, listen! there's one good mixer."

"The confirmed Mixer, sir?" For I remembered the term.

"The best ever. Any one can set into her game that's got a stack of chips." He uttered this with deep feeling, whatever it might exactly mean.

"I can be pushed just so far," he insisted sullenly. It struck me then that he should perhaps have been kept longer in one of the European capitals. I feared his brief contact with those refining influences had left him less polished than Mrs. Effie seemed to hope. I wondered uneasily if he might not cause her to miss her guess. Yet I saw he was in no mood to be reasoned with, and I retired to my bed which the blackamoor guard had done out. Here I meditated profoundly for some time before

I slept.

Morning found our coach shunted to a siding at a backwoods settlement on the borders of an inland sea. The scene was wild beyond description, where quite almost anything might be expected to happen, though I was a bit reassured by the presence of a number of persons of both sexes who appeared to make little of the dangers by which we were surrounded. I mean to say since they thus took their women into the wilds so freely, I would still be a dead sportsman.

After a brief wait at a rude quay we embarked on a launch and steamed out over the water. Mile after mile we passed wooded shores that sloped up to mountains of prodigious height. Indeed the description of the Rocky Mountains, of which I take these to be a part, have not been overdrawn. From time to time, at the edge of the primeval forest, I could make out the rude shelters of hunter and trapper who braved these perils for the sake of a scanty livelihood for their hardy wives and little ones.

Cousin Egbert, beside me, seemed unimpressed, making no outcry at the fearsome wildness of the scene, and when I spoke of the terrific height of the mountains he merely admonished me to "quit my kidding." The sole interest he had thus far displayed was in the title of our craft-- *Storm King*.

"Think of the guy's imagination, naming this here chafing dish the *Storm King*!" said he; but I was impatient of levity at so solemn a moment, and promptly rebuked him for having donned a cravat that I had warned him was for town wear alone; whereat he subsided and did not again intrude upon me.

Far ahead, at length, I could descry an open glade at the forest edge, and above this I soon spied floating the North American flag, or national emblem. It is, of course, known to us that the natives are given to making rather a silly noise over this flag of theirs, but in this instance--the pioneer fighting his way into the wilderness and hoisting it above his frontier home--I felt strangely indisposed to criticise. I understood that he could be greatly cheered by the flag of the country he had left behind.

We now neared a small dock from which two ladies brandished handkerchiefs at us, and were presently welcomed by them. I had no difficulty in identifying the Mrs. Charles Belknap-Jackson, a lively featured brunette of neutral tints, rather stubby as to figure, but modishly done out in white flannels. She surveyed us interestedly through a lorgnon, observing which Mrs. Effie was quick with her own. I surmised that neither of them was skilled with this form of glass (which must really be raised with an air or it's no good); also that each was not a little chagrined to note that the other possessed one.

Nor was it less evident that the other lady was the mother of Mrs. Belknap-Jackson; I mean to say, the confirmed Mixer--an elderly person of immense bulk in gray walking-skirt, heavy boots, and a flowered blouse that was overwhelming. Her face, under her grayish thatch of hair, was broad and smiling, the eyes keen, the mouth wide, and the nose rather a bit blobby. Although at every point she was far from vogue, she impressed me not unpleasantly. Even her voice, a magnificently hoarse rumble, was primed with a sort of uncouth good-will which one might accept in the States. Of course it would never do with us.

I fancied I could at once detect why they had called her the "Mixer." She embraced Mrs. Effie with an air of being about to strangle the woman; she affectionately wrung the hands of Cousin Egbert, and had grasped my own tightly before I could evade her, not having looked for that sort of thing.

"That's Cousin Egbert's man!" called Mrs. Effie. But even then the powerful creature would not release me until her daughter had called sharply, "Maw! Don't you hear? He's a *man*!" Nevertheless she gave my hand a parting shake before turning to the others.

"Glad to see a human face at last!" she boomed. "Here I've been a month in this dinky hole," which I thought strange, since we were surrounded by league upon league of the primal wilderness. "Cooped up like a hen in a barrel," she added in tones that must have carried well out over the lake.

"Cousin Egbert's man," repeated Mrs. Effie, a little ostentatiously, I thought. "Poor Egbert's so dependent on him--quite helpless without him."

Cousin Egbert muttered sullenly to himself as he assisted me with the bags. Then he straightened himself to address them.

"Won him in a game of freeze-out," he remarked quite viciously.

"Does he doll Sour-dough up like that all the time?" demanded the Mixer, "or has he just come from a masquerade? What's he represent, anyway?" And these words when I had taken especial pains and resorted to all manner of threats to turn him smartly out in the walking-suit of a pioneer!

"Maw!" cried our hostess, "do try to forget that dreadful nickname of Egbert's."

"I sure will if he keeps his disguise on," she rumbled back. "The old horned toad is most as funny as Jackson."

Really, I mean to say, they talked most amazingly. I was but too glad when they moved on and we could follow with the bags.

"Calls her 'Maw' all right now," hissed Cousin Egbert in my ear, "but when that begoshed husband of hers is around the house she calls her 'Mater.'"

His tone was vastly bitter. He continued to mutter sullenly to himself--a way he had--until we had disposed of the luggage and I was laying out his afternoon and evening wear in one of the small detached houses to which we had been assigned. Nor did he sink his grievance on the arrival of the Mixer a few moments later. He now addressed her as "Ma" and asked if she had "the makings," which puzzled me until she drew from the pocket of her skirt a small cloth sack of tobacco and some bits of brown paper, from which they both fashioned cigarettes.

"The smart set of Red Gap is holding its first annual meeting for the election of officers back there," she began after she had emitted twin jets of smoke from the widely separated corners of her set mouth.

"I say, you know, where's Hyphen old top?" demanded Cousin Egbert in a quite vile imitation of one speaking in the correct manner.

"Fishing," answered the Mixer with a grin. "In a thousand dollars' worth of clothes. These here Eastern trout won't notice you unless you dress right." I thought this strange indeed, but Cousin Egbert merely grinned in his turn.

"How'd he get you into this awfully horrid rough place?" he next demanded.

"Made him. 'This or Red Gap for yours,' I says. The two weeks in New York wasn't so bad, what with Millie and me getting new clothes, though him and her both jumped on me that I'm getting too gay about clothes for a party of my age. 'What's age to me,' I says, 'when I like bright colours?' Then we tried his home-folks in Boston, but I played that string out in a week.

"Two old-maid sisters, thin noses and knitted shawls! Stick around in the back parlour talking about families--whether it was Aunt Lucy's Abigail or the Concord cousin's Hester that married an Adams in '78 and moved out west to Buffalo. I thought first I could liven them up some, *you* know. Looked like it would help a lot for them to get out in a hack and get a few shots of hooch under their belts, stop at a few roadhouses, take in a good variety show; get 'em to feeling good, understand? No use. Wouldn't start. Darn it! they held off from me. Don't know why. I sure wore clothes for them. Yes, sir. I'd get dressed up like a broken arm every afternoon; and, say, I got one sheath skirt, black and white striped, that just has to be looked at. Never phased them, though.

"I got to thinking mebbe it was because I made my own smokes instead of using those vegetable cigarettes of Jackson's, or maybe because I'd get parched and demand a slug of booze before supper. Like a Sunday afternoon all the time, when you eat a big dinner and everybody's sleepy and mad because they can't take a nap, and have to set around and play a few church tunes on the organ or look through the album again."

"Ain't that right? Don't it fade you?" murmured Cousin Egbert with deep feeling.

"And little Lysander, my only grandson, poor kid, getting the fidgets because they try to make him talk different, and raise hell every time he knocks over a vase or busts a window. Say, would you believe it? they wanted to keep him there--yes, sir--make him refined. Not for me! 'His father's about all he can survive in those respects,' I says. What do you think? Wanted to let his hair grow so he'd have curls. Some dames, yes? I bet they'd have give the kid lovely days. 'Boston may be all O.K. for grandfathers,' I says; 'not for grandsons, though.'

"Then Jackson was set on Bar Harbor, and I had to be firm again. Darn it! that man is always making me be firm. So here we are. He said it was a camp, and that sounded good. But my lands! he wears his full evening dress suit for supper every night, and you had ought to heard him go on one day when the patent ice-machine went bad."

"My good gosh!" said Cousin Egbert quite simply.

I had now finished laying out his things and was about to withdraw.

"Is he always like that?" suddenly demanded the Mixer, pointing at me.

"Oh, Bill's all right when you get him out with a crowd," explained the other. "Bill's really got the makings of one fine little mixer."

They both regarded me genially. It was vastly puzzling. I mean to say, I was at a loss how to take it, for, of course, that sort of thing would never do with us.

And yet I felt a queer, confused sort of pleasure in the talk. Absurd though it may seem, I felt there might come moments in which America would appear almost not impossible.

As I went out Cousin Egbert was telling her of Paris. I lingered to hear him disclose that all Frenchmen have "M" for their first initial, and that the Louer family must be one of their wealthiest, the name "A. Louer" being conspicuous on millions of dollars' worth of their real estate. This family, he said, must be like the Rothschilds. Of course the poor soul was absurdly wrong. I mean to say, the letter "M" merely indicates "Monsieur," which is their foreign way of spelling Mister, while "A Louer" signifies "to let." I resolved to explain this to him at the first opportunity, not thinking it right that he should spread such gross error among a race still but half-enlightened.

Having now a bit of time to myself, I observed the construction of this rude homestead, a dozen or more detached or semi-detached structures of the native log, yet with the interiors more smartly done out than I had supposed was common even with the most prosperous of their scouts and trappers. I suspected a false idea of this rude life had been given by the cinema dramas. I mean to say, with pianos, ice-machines, telephones, objects of art, and servants, one saw that these woodsmen were not primitive in any true sense of the word.

The butler proved to be a genuine blackamoor, a Mr. Waterman, he informed me, his wife, also a black, being the cook. An elderly creature of the utmost gravity of bearing, he brought to his professional duties a finish, a dignity, a manner in short that I have scarce known excelled among our own serving people. And a creature he was of the most eventful past, as he informed me at our first encounter. As a slave he had commanded an immensely high price, some twenty thousand dollars, as the American money is called, and two prominent slaveholders had once fought a duel to the death over his possession. Not many, he assured me, had been so eagerly sought after, they being for the most part held cheaper--"common black trash," he put it.

Early tiring of the life of slavery, he had fled to the wilds and for some years led a desperate band of outlaws whose crimes soon put a price upon his head. He spoke frankly and with considerable regret of these lawless years. At the outbreak of the American war, however, with a reward of fifty thousand dollars offered for his body, he had boldly surrendered to their Secretary of State for War, receiving a full pardon for his crimes on condition that he assist in directing the military operations against the slaveholding aristocracy. Invaluable he had been in this service, I gathered, two generals, named respectively Grant and Sherman, having repeatedly assured him that but for his aid they would more than once in sheer despair have laid down their swords.

I could readily imagine that after these years of strife he had been glad to embrace the peaceful calling in which I found him engaged. He was, as I have intimated, a person of lofty demeanour, with a vein of high seriousness. Yet he would unbend at moments as frankly as a child and play at a simple game of chance with a pair of dice. This he was good enough to teach to myself and gained from me quite a number of shillings that I chanced to have. For his consort, a person of tremendous bulk named Clarice, he showed a most chivalric consideration, and even what I might have mistaken for timidity in one not a confessed desperado. In truth, he rather flinched when she interrupted our chat from the kitchen doorway by roundly calling him "an old black liar." I saw that his must indeed be a complex nature.

From this encounter I chanced upon two lads who seemed to present the marks of the backwoods life as I had conceived it. Strolling up a woodland path, I discovered a tent pitched among the trees, before it a smouldering campfire, over which a cooking-pot hung. The two lads, of ten years or so, rushed from the tent to regard me, both attired in shirts and leggings of deerskin profusely fringed after the manner in which the red Indians decorate their outing or lounge-suits. They were armed with sheath knives and revolvers, and the taller bore a rifle.

"Howdy, stranger?" exclaimed this one, and the other repeated the simple American phrase of greeting. Responding in kind, I was bade to seat myself on a fallen log, which I did. For some moments they appeared to ignore me, excitedly discussing an adventure of the night before, and addressing each other as Dead Shot and Hawk Eye. From their quaint backwoods speech I gathered that Dead Shot, the taller lad, had the day before been captured by a band of hostile redskins who would have burned him at the stake but for the happy chance that the chieftain's daughter had become enamoured of him and cut his bonds.

They now planned to return to the encampment at nightfall to fetch away the daughter, whose name was White Fawn, and cleaned and oiled their weapons for the enterprise. Dead Shot was vindictive in the extreme, swearing to engage the chieftain in mortal combat and to cut his heart out, the same chieftain in former years having led his savage band against the forest home of Dead Shot while he was yet too young to defend it, and scalped both of his parents. "I was a mere stripling then, but now the coward will feel my steel!" he coldly declared.

It had become absurdly evident as I listened that the whole thing was but spoofing of a silly sort that lads of this age will indulge in, for I had seen the younger one take his seat at the luncheon table. But now they spoke of a raid on the settlement to procure "grub," as the American slang for food has it. Bidding me stop on there and to utter the cry of the great horned owl if danger threatened, they stealthily crept toward the buildings of the camp. Presently came a scream, followed by a hoarse shout of rage. A second later the two dashed by me into the dense woods, Hawk Eye bearing a plucked fowl. Soon Mr. Waterman panted up the path brandishing a barge pole and demanding to know the whereabouts of the marauders. As he had apparently for the moment reverted to his primal African savagery, I deliberately misled him by indicating a false direction, upon which he went off, muttering the most frightful threats.

The two culprits returned, put their fowl in the pot to boil, and swore me eternal fidelity for having saved them. They declared I should thereafter be known as Keen Knife, and that, needing a service, I might call upon them freely.

"Dead Shot never forgets a friend," affirmed the taller lad, whereupon I formally shook hands with the pair and left them to their childish devices. They were plotting as I left to capture "that nigger," as they called him, and put him to death by slow torture.

But I was now shrewd enough to suspect that I might still be far from the western frontier of America. The evidence had been cumulative but was no longer questionable. I mean to say, one might do here somewhat after the way of our own people at a country house in the shires. I resolved at the first opportunity to have a look at a good map of our late colonies.

Late in the afternoon our party gathered upon the small dock and I understood that our host now returned from his trouting. Along the shore of the lake he came, propelled in a native canoe by a hairy backwoods person quite wretchedly gotten up, even for a wilderness. Our host himself, I was quick to observe, was vogue to the last detail, with a sense of dress and equipment that can never be acquired, having to be born in one. As he stepped from his frail craft I saw that he was rather slight of stature, dark, with slender moustaches, a finely sensitive nose, and eyes of an almost austere repose. That he had much of the real manner was at once apparent. He greeted the Flouds and his own family with just that faint touch of easy superiority which would stamp him to the trained eye as one that really mattered. Mrs. Effie beckoned me to the group.

"Let Ruggles take your things--Cousin Egbert's man," she was saying. After a startled glance at Cousin Egbert, our host turned to regard me with flattering interest for a moment, then transferred to me his oddments of fishing machinery: his rod, his creel, his luncheon hamper, landing net, small scales, ointment for warding off midges, a jar of cold cream, a case containing smoked glasses, a rolled map, a camera, a book of flies. As I was stowing these he explained that his sport had been wretched; no fish had been hooked because his guide had not known where to find them. I here glanced at the backwoods person referred to and at once did not like the look in his eyes. He winked swiftly at Cousin Egbert, who coughed rather formally.

"Let Ruggles help you to change," continued Mrs. Effie. "He's awfully handy. Poor Cousin Egbert is perfectly helpless now without him."

So I followed our host to his own detached hut, though feeling a bit queer at being passed about in this manner, I mean to say, as if I were a basket of fruit. Yet I found it a grateful change to be serving one who knew our respective places and what I should do for him. His manner of speech, also, was less barbarous than that of the others, suggesting that he might have lived among our own people a fortnight or so and have tried earnestly to correct his deficiencies. In fact he remarked to me after a bit: "I fancy I talk rather like one of yourselves, what?" and was pleased as Punch when I assured him that I had observed this. He questioned me at length regarding my association with the Honourable George, and the houses at which we would have stayed, being immensely particular about names and titles.

"You'll find us vastly different here," he said with a sigh, as I held his coat for him. "Crude, I may say. In truth, Red Gap, where my interests largely confine me, is a town of impossible persons. You'll see in no time what I mean."

"I can already imagine it, sir," I said sympathetically.

"It's not for want of example," he added. "Scores of times I show them better ways, but they're eaten up with commercialism--money-grubbing."

I perceived him to be a person of profound and interesting views, and it was with regret I left him to bully Cousin Egbert into evening dress. It is undoubtedly true that he will never wear this except it have the look of having been forced upon him by several persons of superior physical strength.

The evening passed in a refined manner with cards and music, the latter being emitted from a phonograph which I was asked to attend to and upon which I reproduced many of their quaint North American folksongs, such as "Everybody Is Doing It," which has a rare native rhythm. At ten o'clock, it being noticed by the three playing dummy bridge that Cousin Egbert and the Mixer were absent, I accompanied our host in search of them. In Cousin Egbert's hut we found them, seated at a bare table, playing at cards--a game called seven-upwards, I learned. Cousin Egbert had removed his coat, collar, and cravat, and his sleeves were rolled to his elbows like a navvy's. Both smoked the brown paper cigarettes.

"You see?" murmured Mr. Belknap-Jackson as we looked in upon them.

"Quite so, sir," I said discreetly.

The Mixer regarded her son-in-law with some annoyance, I thought.

"Run off to bed, Jackson!" she directed. "We're busy. I'm putting a nick in Sour-dough's bank roll."

Our host turned away with a contemptuous shrug that I dare say might have offended her had she observed it, but she was now speaking to Cousin Egbert, who had stared at us brazenly.

"Ring that bell for the coon, Sour-dough. I'll split a bottle of Scotch with you."

It queerly occurred to me that she made this monstrous suggestion in a spirit of bravado to annoy Mr. Belknap-Jackson.

CHAPTER SIX

THERE are times when all Nature seems to smile, yet when to the sensitive mind it will be faintly brought that the possibilities are quite tremendously otherwise if one will consider them pro and con. I mean to say, one often suspects things may happen when it doesn't look so.

The succeeding three days passed with so ordered a calm that little would any but a profound thinker have fancied tragedy to lurk so near their placid surface. Mrs. Effie and Mrs. Belknap-Jackson continued to plan the approaching social campaign at Red Gap. Cousin Egbert and the Mixer continued their card game for the trifling stake of a shilling a game, or "two bits," as it is known in the American monetary system. And our host continued his recreation.

Each morning I turned him out in the smartest of fishing costumes and each evening I assisted him to change. It is true I was now compelled to observe at these times a certain lofty irritability in his character, yet I more than half fancied this to be queerly assumed in order to inform me that he was not unaccustomed to services such as I rendered him. There was that about him. I mean to say, when he sharply rebuked me for clumsiness or cried out "Stupid!" it had a perfunctory languor, as if meant to show me he could address a servant in what he believed to be the grand manner. In this, to be sure, he was so oddly wrong that the pathos of it quite drowned what I might otherwise have felt of resentment.

But I next observed that he was sharp in the same manner with the hairy backwoods person who took him to fish each day, using words to him which I, for one, would have employed, had I thought them merited, only after the gravest hesitation. I have before remarked that I did not like the gleam in this person's eyes: he was very apparently a not quite nice person. Also I more than once observed him to wink at Cousin Egbert in an evil manner.

As I have so truly said, how close may tragedy be to us when life seems most correct! It was Belknap-Jackson's custom to raise a view halloo each evening when he returned down the lake, so that we might gather at the dock to oversee his landing. I must admit that he disembarked with somewhat the manner of a visiting royalty, demanding much attention and assistance with his impedimenta. Undoubtedly he liked to be looked at. This was what one rather felt. And I can fancy that this very human trait of his had in a manner worn upon the probably undisciplined nerves of the backwoods josser--had, in fact, deprived him of his "goat," as the native people have it.

Be this as it may, we gathered at the dock on the afternoon of the third day of our stay to assist at the return. As the native log craft neared the dock our host daringly arose to a graceful kneeling posture in the bow and saluted us charmingly, the woods person in the stern wielding his single oar in gloomy silence. At the moment a most poetic image occurred to me--that he was like a dull grim figure of Fate that fetches us low at the moment of our highest seeming. I mean to say, it was a silly thought, perhaps, yet I afterward recalled it most vividly.

Holding his creel aloft our host hailed us:

"Full to-day, thanks to going where I wished and paying no attention to silly guides' talk." He beamed upon us in an unquestionably superior manner, and again from the moody figure at the stern I intercepted the flash of a wink to Cousin Egbert. Then as the frail craft had all but touched the dock and our host had half risen, there was a sharp dipping of the thing and he was ejected into the chilling waters, where he almost instantly sank. There were loud cries of alarm from all, including the woodsman himself, who had kept the craft upright, and in these Mr. Belknap-Jackson heartily joined the moment his head appeared above the surface, calling "Help!" in the quite loudest of tones, which was thoughtless enough, as we were close at hand and could easily have heard his ordinary speaking voice.

The woods person now stepped to the dock, and firmly grasping the collar of the drowning man hauled him out with but little effort, at the same time becoming voluble with apologies and sympathy. The rescued man, however, was quite off his head with rage and bluntly berated the fellow for having tried to assassinate him. Indeed he put forth rather a torrent of execration, but to all of this the fellow merely repeated his crude protestations of regret and astonishment, seeming to be sincerely grieved that his intentions should have been doubted.

From his friends about him the unfortunate man was receiving the most urgent advice to seek dry garments lest he perish of chill, whereupon he turned abruptly to me and cried: "Well, Stupid, don't you see the state that fellow has put me in? What are you doing? Have you lost your wits?"

Now I had suffered a very proper alarm and solicitude for him, but the injustice of this got a bit on me. I mean to say, I suddenly felt a bit of temper myself, though to be sure retaining my control.

"Yes, sir; quite so, sir," I replied smoothly. "I'll have you right as rain in no time at all, sir," and started to conduct him off the dock. But now, having gone a little distance, he began to utter the most violent threats against the woods person, declaring, in fact, he would pull the fellow's nose. However, I restrained him from rushing back, as I subtly felt I was wished to do, and he at length consented again to be led toward his hut.

But now the woods person called out: "You're forgetting all your pretties!" By which I saw him to mean the fishing impedimenta he had placed on the dock. And most unreasonably at this Mr. Belknap-Jackson again turned upon me, wishing anew to be told if I had lost my wits and directing me to fetch the stuff. Again I was conscious of that within me which no gentleman's man should confess to. I mean to say, I felt like shaking him. But I hastened back to fetch the rod, the creel, the luncheon hamper, the midge ointment, the camera, and other articles which the woods fellow handed me.

With these somewhat awkwardly carried, I returned to our still turbulent host. More like a volcano he was than a man who has had a narrow squeak from drowning, and before we had gone a dozen feet more he again turned and declared he would "go back and thrash the unspeakable cad within an inch of his life." Their relative sizes rendering an attempt of this sort quite too unwise, I was conscious of renewed irritation toward him; indeed, the vulgar words, "Oh, stow that piffle!" swiftly formed in the back of my mind, but again I controlled myself, as the chap was now sneezing violently.

"Best hurry on, sir," I said with exemplary tact. "One might contract a severe head-cold from such a wetting," and further endeavoured to sooth him while I started ahead to lead him away from the fellow. Then there happened that which fulfilled my direst premonitions. Looking back from a moment of calm, the psychology of the crisis is of a rudimentary simplicity.

Enraged beyond measure at the woods person, Mr. Belknap-Jackson yet retained a fine native caution which counselled him to attempt no violence upon that offender; but his mental tension was such that it could be relieved only by his attacking some one; preferably some one forbidden to retaliate. I walked there temptingly but a pace ahead of him, after my well-meant word of advice.

I make no defence of my own course. I am aware there can be none. I can only plead that I had already been vexed not a little by his unjust accusations of stupidity, and dismiss with as few words as possible an incident that will ever seem to me quite too indecently criminal. Briefly, then, with my well-intended "Best not lower yourself, sir," Mr. Belknap-Jackson forgot himself and I forgot myself. It will be recalled that I was in front of him, but I turned rather quickly. (His belongings I had carried were widely disseminated.)

Instantly there were wild outcries from the others, who had started toward the main, or living house.

"He's killed Charles!" I heard Mrs. Belknap-Jackson scream; then came the deep-chested rumble of the Mixer, "Jackson kicked him first!" They ran for us. They had reached us while our host was down, even while my fist was still clenched. Now again the unfortunate man cried "Help!" as his wife assisted him to his feet.

"Send for an officer!" cried she.

"The man's an anarchist!" shouted her husband.

"Nonsense!" boomed the Mixer. "Jackson got what he was looking for. Do it myself if he kicked me!"

"Oh, Maw! Oh, Mater!" cried her daughter tearfully.

"Gee! He done it in one punch!" I heard Cousin Egbert say with what I was aghast to suspect was admiration.

Mrs. Effie, trembling, could but glare at me and gasp. Mercifully she was beyond speech for the moment.

Mr. Belknap-Jackson was now painfully rubbing his right eye, which was not what he should have done, and I said as much.

"Beg pardon, sir, but one does better with a bit of raw beef."

"How dare you, you great hulking brute!" cried his wife, and made as if to shield her husband from another attack from me, which I submit was unjust.

"Bill's right," said Cousin Egbert casually. "Put a piece of raw steak on it. Gee! with one wallop!" And then, quite strangely, for a moment we all amiably discussed whether cold compresses might not be better. Presently our host was led off by his wife. Mrs. Effie followed them, moaning: "Oh, oh, oh!" in the keenest distress.

At this I took to my own room in dire confusion, making no doubt I would presently be given in charge and left to languish in gaol, perhaps given six months' hard.

Cousin Egbert came to me in a little while and laughed heartily at my fear that anything legal would be done. He also made some ill-timed compliments on the neatness of the blow I had dealt Mr. Belknap-Jackson, but these I found in wretched taste and was begging him to desist, when the Mixer entered and began to speak much in the same strain.

"Don't you ever dare do a thing like that again," she warned me, "unless I got a ringside seat," to which I remained severely silent, for I felt my offence should not be made light of.

"Three rousing cheers!" exclaimed Cousin Egbert, whereat the two most unfeelingly went through a vivid pantomime of cheering.

Our host, I understood, had his dinner in bed that night, and throughout the evening, as I sat solitary in remorse, came the mocking strains of another of their American folksongs with the refrain:

"You made me what I am to-day,
I hope you're satisfied!"

I conceived it to be the Mixer and Cousin Egbert who did this and, considering the plight of our host, I thought it in the worst possible taste. I had raised my hand against the one American I had met who was at all times vogue. And not only this: For I now recalled a certain phrase I had flung out as I stood over him, ranting indeed no better than an anarchist, a phrase which showed my poor culture to be the flimsiest veneer.

Late in the night, as I lay looking back on the frightful scene, I recalled with wonder a swift picture of Cousin Egbert caught as I once looked back to the dock. He had most amazingly shaken the woods person by the hand, quickly but with marked cordiality. And yet I am quite certain he had never been presented to the fellow.

Promptly the next morning came the dreaded summons to meet Mrs. Effie. I was of course prepared to accept instant dismissal without a character, if indeed I were not to be given in charge. I found her wearing an expression of the utmost sternness, erect and formidable by the now silent phonograph. Cousin Egbert, who was present, also wore an expression of sternness, though I perceived him to wink at me.

"I really don't know what we're to do with you, Ruggles," began the stricken woman, and so done out she plainly was that I at once felt the warmest sympathy for her as she continued: "First you lead poor Cousin Egbert into a drunken debauch----"

Cousin Egbert here coughed nervously and eyed me with strong condemnation.

"--then you behave like a murderer. What have you to say for yourself?"

At this I saw there was little I could say, except that I had coarsely given way to the brute in me, and yet I knew I should try to explain.

"I dare say, Madam, it may have been because Mr. Belknap-Jackson was quite sober at the unfortunate moment."

"Of course Charles was sober. The idea! What of it?"

"I was remembering an occasion at Chaynes-Wotten when Lord Ivor Cradleigh behaved toward me somewhat as Mr. Belknap-Jackson did last night and when my own deportment was quite all that could be wished. It occurs to me now that it was because his lordship was, how shall I say?--quite far gone in liquor at the time, so that I could without loss of dignity pass it off as a mere prank. Indeed, he regarded it as such himself, performing the act with a good nature that I found quite irresistible, and I am certain that neither his lordship nor I have ever thought the less of each other because of it. I revert to this merely to show that I have not always acted in a ruffianly manner under these circumstances. It seems rather to depend upon how the thing is done--the mood of the performer--his mental state. Had Mr. Belknap-Jackson been--pardon me--quite drunk, I feel that the outcome would have been happier for us all. So far as I have thought along these lines, it seems to me that if one is to be kicked at all, one must be kicked good-naturedly. I mean to say, with a certain camaraderie, a lightness, a gayety, a genuine good-will that for the moment expresses itself uncouthly--an element, I regret to say, that was conspicuously lacking from the brief activities of Mr. Belknap-Jackson."

"I never heard such crazy talk," responded Mrs. Effie, "and really I never saw such a man as you are for wanting people to become disgustingly drunk. You made poor Cousin Egbert and Jeff Tuttle act like beasts, and now nothing will satisfy you but that Charles should roll in the gutter. Such dissipated talk I never did hear, and poor Charles rarely taking anything but a single glass of wine, it upsets him so; even our reception punch he finds too stimulating!"

I mean to say, the woman had cleanly missed my point, for never have I advocated the use of fermented liquors to excess; but I saw it was no good trying to tell her this.

"And the worst of it," she went rapidly on, "Cousin Egbert here is acting stranger than I ever knew him to act. He swears if he can't keep you he'll never have another man, and you know yourself what that means in his case--and Mrs. Pettengill saying she means to employ you herself if we let you go. Heaven knows what the poor woman can be thinking of! Oh, it's awful--and everything was going so beautifully. Of course Charles would simply never be brought to accept an apology----"

"I am only too anxious to make one," I submitted.

"Here's the poor fellow now," said Cousin Egbert almost gleefully, and our host entered. He carried a patch over his right eye and was not attired for sport on the lake, but in a dark morning suit of quietly beautiful lines that I thought showed a fine sense of the situation. He shot me one superior glance from his left eye and turned to Mrs. Effie.

"I see you still harbour the ruffian?"

"I've just given him a call-down," said Mrs. Effie, plainly ill at ease, "and he says it was all because you were sober; that if you'd been in the state Lord Ivor Cradleigh was the time it happened at Chaynes-Wotten he wouldn't have done anything to you, probably."

"What's this, what's this? Lord Ivor Cradleigh--Chaynes-Wotten?" The man seemed to be curiously interested by the mere names, in spite of himself. "His lordship was at Chaynes-Wotten for the shooting, I suppose?" This, most amazingly, to me.

"A house party at Whitsuntide, sir," I explained.

"Ah! And you say his lordship was----"

"Oh, quite, quite in his cups, sir. If I might explain, it was that, sir--its being done under circumstances and in a certain entirely genial spirit of irritation to which I could take no offence, sir. His lordship is a very decent sort, sir. I've known him intimately for years."

"Dear, dear!" he replied. "Too bad, too bad! And I dare say you thought me out of temper last night? Nothing of the sort. You should have taken it in quite the same spirit as you did from Lord Ivor Cradleigh."

"It seemed different, sir," I said firmly. "If I may take the liberty of putting it so, I felt quite offended by your manner. I missed from it at the most critical moment, as one might say, a certain urbanity that I found in his lordship, sir."

"Well, well, well! It's too bad, really. I'm quite aware that I show a sort of brusqueness at times, but mind you, it's all on the surface. Had you known me as long as you've known his lordship, I dare say you'd have noticed the same rough urbanity in me as well. I rather fancy some of us over here don't do those things so very differently. A few of us, at least."

"I'm glad, indeed, to hear it, sir. It's only necessary to understand that there is a certain mood in which one really cannot permit one's self to be--you perceive, I trust."

"Perfectly, perfectly," said he, "and I can only express my regret that you should have mistaken my own mood, which, I am confident, was exactly the thing his lordship might have felt."

"I gladly accept your apology, sir," I returned quickly, "as I should have accepted his lordship's had his manner permitted any misapprehension on my part. And in return I wish to apologize most contritely for the phrase I applied to you just after it happened, sir. I rarely use strong language, but----"

"I remember hearing none," said he.

"I regret to say, sir, that I called you a blighted little mug----"

"You needn't have mentioned it," he replied with just a trace of sharpness, "and I trust that in future----"

"I am sure, sir, that in future you will give me no occasion to misunderstand your intentions--no more than would his lordship," I added as he raised his brows.

Thus in a manner wholly unexpected was a frightful situation eased off.

"I'm so glad it's settled!" cried Mrs. Effie, who had listened almost breathlessly to our exchange.

"I fancy I settled it as Cradleigh would have--eh, Ruggles?" And the man actually smiled at me.

"Entirely so, sir," said I.

"If only it doesn't get out," said Mrs. Effie now. "We shouldn't want it known in Red Gap. Think of the talk!"

"Certainly," rejoined Mr. Belknap-Jackson jauntily, "we are all here above gossip about an affair of that sort. I am sure--" He broke off and looked uneasily at Cousin Egbert, who coughed into his hand and looked out over the lake before he spoke.

"What would I want to tell a thing like that for?" he demanded indignantly, as if an accusation had been made against him. But I saw his eyes glitter with an evil light.

An hour later I chanced to be with him in our detached hut, when the Mixer entered.

"What happened?" she demanded.

"What do you reckon happened?" returned Cousin Egbert. "They get to talking about Lord Ivy Craddles, or some guy, and before we know it Mr. Belknap Hyphen Jackson is apologizing to Bill here."

"No?" bellowed the Mixer.

"Sure did he!" affirmed Cousin Egbert.

Here they grasped each other's arms and did a rude native dance about the room, nor did they desist when I sought to explain that the name was not at all Ivy Craddles.

CHAPTER SEVEN

NOW once more it seemed that for a time I might lead a sanely ordered existence. Not for long did I hope it. I think I had become resigned to the unending series of shocks that seemed to compose the daily life in North America. Few had been my peaceful hours since that fatal evening in Paris. And the shocks had become increasingly violent. When I tried to picture what the next might be I found myself shuddering. For the present, like a stag that has eluded the hounds but hears their distant baying, I lay panting in momentary security, gathering breath for some new course. I mean to say, one couldn't tell what might happen next. Again and again I found myself coming all over frightened.

Wholly restored I was now in the esteem of Mr. Belknap-Jackson, who never tired of discussing with me our own life and people. Indeed he was quite the most intelligent foreigner I had encountered. I may seem to exaggerate in the American fashion, but I doubt if a single one of the others could have named the counties of England or the present Lord Mayor of London. Our host was not like that. Also he early gave me to know that he felt quite as we do concerning the rebellion of our American colonies, holding it a matter for the deepest regret; and justly proud he was of the circumstance that at the time of that rebellion his own family had put all possible obstacles in the way of the traitorous Washington. To be sure, I dare say he may have boasted a bit in this.

It was during the long journey across America which we now set out upon that I came to this sympathetic understanding of his character and of the chagrin he constantly felt at being compelled to live among people with whom he could have as little sympathy as I myself had.

This journey began pleasantly enough, and through the farming counties of Philadelphia, Ohio, and Chicago was not without interest. Beyond came an incredibly large region, much like the steppes of Siberia, I fancy: vast uninhabited stretches of heath and down, with but here and there some rude settlement about which the poor peasants would eagerly assemble as our train passed through. I could not wonder that our own travellers have always spoken so disparagingly of the American civilization. It is a country that would never do with us.

Although we lived in this train a matter of nearly four days, I fancy not a single person dressed for dinner as one would on shipboard. Even Belknap-Jackson dined in a lounge-suit, though he wore gloves constantly by day, which was more than I could get Cousin Egbert to do.

As we went ever farther over these leagues of fen and fell and rolling veldt, I could but speculate unquietly as to what sort of place the Red Gap must be. A residential town for gentlemen and families, I had understood, with a little colony of people that really mattered, as I had gathered from Mrs. Effie. And yet I was unable to divine their object in going so far away to live. One goes to distant places for the winter sports or for big game shooting, but this seemed rather grotesquely perverse.

Little did I then dream of the spiritual agencies that were to insure my gradual understanding of the town and its people. Unsuspectingly I fronted a future so wildly improbable that no power could have made me credit it had it then been foretold by the most rarely endowed gypsy. It is always now with a sort of terror that I look back to those last moments before my destiny had unfolded far enough to be actually alarming. I was as one floating in fancied security down the calm river above their famous Niagara Falls--to be presently dashed without warning over the horrible verge. I mean to say, I never suspected.

Our last day of travel arrived. We were now in a roughened and most untidy welter of mountain and jungle and glen, with violent tarns and bleak bits of moorland that had all too evidently never known the calming touch of the landscape gardener; a region, moreover, peopled by a much more lawless appearing peasantry than I had observed back in the Chicago counties, people for the most part quite wretchedly gotten up and distinctly of the lower or working classes.

Late in the afternoon our train wound out of a narrow cutting and into a valley that broadened away on every hand to distant mountains. Beyond doubt this prospect could, in a loose way of speaking, be called scenery, but of too violent a character it was for cultivated tastes. Then, as my eye caught the vague outlines of a settlement or village in the midst of this valley, Cousin Egbert, who also looked from, the coach window, amazed me by crying out:

"There she is--little old Red Gap! The fastest growing town in the State, if any one should ask you."

"Yes, sir; I'll try to remember, sir," I said, wondering why I should be asked this.

"Garden spot of the world," he added in a kind of ecstasy, to which I made no response, for this was too preposterous. Nearing the place our train passed an immense hoarding erected by the roadway, a score of feet high, I should say, and at least a dozen times as long, upon which was emblazoned in mammoth red letters on a black ground, "Keep Your Eye on Red Gap!" At either end of this lettering was painted a gigantic staring human eye. Regarding this monstrosity with startled interest, I heard myself addressed by Belknap-Jackson:

"The sort of vulgarity I'm obliged to contend with," said he, with a contemptuous gesture toward the hoarding. Indeed the thing lacked refinement in its diction, while the painted eyes were not Art in any true sense of the word. "The work of our precious Chamber of Commerce," he added, "though I pleaded with them for days and days."

"It's a sort of thing would never do with us, sir," I said.

"It's what one has to expect from a commercialized bourgeoise," he returned bitterly. "And even our association, 'The City Beautiful,' of which I was president, helped to erect the thing. Of course I resigned at once."

"Naturally, sir; the colours are atrocious."

"And the words a mere blatant boast!" He groaned and left me, for we were now well into a suburb of detached villas, many of them of a squalid character, and presently we had halted at the station. About this bleak affair was the usual gathering of peasantry and the common people, villagers, agricultural labourers, and the like, and these at once showed a tremendous interest in our party, many of them hailing various members of us with a quite offensive familiarity.

Belknap-Jackson, of course, bore himself through this with a proper aloofness, as did his wife and Mrs. Effie, but I heard the Mixer booming salutations right and left. It was Cousin Egbert, however, who most embarrassed me by the freedom of his manner with these persons. He shook hands warmly with at least a dozen of them and these hailed him with rude shouts, dealt him smart blows on the back and, forming a circle about him, escorted him to a carriage where Mrs. Effie and I awaited him. Here the driver, a loutish and familiar youth, also seized his hand and, with some crude effect of oratory, shouted to the crowd.

"What's the matter with Sour-dough?" To this, with a flourish of their impossible hats, they quickly responded in unison,

"He's all right!" accenting the first word terrifically.

Then, to the immense relief of Mrs. Effie and myself, he was released and we were driven quickly off from the raffish set. Through their Regent and Bond streets we went, though I mean to say they were on an unbelievably small or village scale, to an outlying region of detached villas that doubtless would be their St. John's Wood, but my efforts to observe closely were distracted by the extraordinary freedom with which our driver essayed to chat with us, saying he "guessed" we were glad to get back to God's country, and things of a similar intimate nature. This was even more embarrassing to Mrs. Effie than it was to me, since she more than once felt obliged to answer the fellow with a feigned cordiality.

Relieved I was when we drew up before the town house of the Flouds. Set well back from the driveway in a faded stretch of common, it was of rather a garbled architecture, with the Tudor, late Gothic, and French Renaissance so intermixed that one was puzzled to separate the periods. Nor was the result so vast as this might sound. Hardly would the thing have made a wing of the manor house at Chaynes-Wotten. The common or small park before it was shielded from the main thoroughfare by a fence of iron palings, and back of this on either side of a gravelled walk that led to the main entrance were two life-sized stags not badly sculptured from metal.

Once inside I began to suspect that my position was going to be more than a bit dicky. I mean to say, it was not an establishment in our sense of the word, being staffed, apparently, by two China persons who performed the functions of cook, housemaids, footmen, butler, and housekeeper. There was not even a billiard room.

During the ensuing hour, marked by the arrival of our luggage and the unpacking of boxes, I meditated profoundly over the difficulties of my situation. In a wilderness, beyond the confines of civilization, I would undoubtedly be compelled to endure the hardships of the pioneer; yet for the present I resolved to let no inkling of my dismay escape.

The evening meal over--dinner in but the barest technical sense--I sat alone in my own room, meditating thus darkly. Nor was I at all cheered by the voice of Cousin Egbert, who sang in his own room adjoining. I had found this to be a habit of his, and his songs are always dolorous to the last degree. Now, for example, while life seemed all too black to me, he sang a favourite of his, the pathetic ballad of two small children evidently begging in a business thoroughfare:

"Lone and weary through the streets we wander,
For we have no place to lay our head;
Not a friend is left on earth to shelter us,
For both our parents now are dead."

It was a fair crumpler in my then mood. It made me wish to be out of North America--made me long for London; London with a yellow fog and its greasy pavements, where one knew what to apprehend. I wanted him to stop, but still he atrociously sang in his high, cracked voice:

"Dear mother died when we were both young,
And father built for us a home,
But now he's killed by falling timbers,
And we are left here all alone."

I dare say I should have rushed madly into the night had there been another verse, but now he was still. A moment later, however, he entered nay room with the suggestion that I stroll about the village streets with him, he having a mission to perform for Mrs. Effie. I had already heard her confide this to him. He was to proceed to the office of their newspaper and there leave with the press chap a notice of our arrival which from day to day she had been composing on the train.

"I just got to leave this here piece for the *Recorder*," he said; "then we can sasshay up and down for a while and meet some of the boys."

How profoundly may our whole destiny be affected by the mood of an idle moment; by some superficial indecision, mere fruit of a transient unrest. We lightly debate, we hesitate, we yawn, unconscious of the brink. We half-heartedly decline a suggested course, then lightly accept from sheer ennui, and "life," as I have read in a quite meritorious poem, "is never the same again." It was thus I now toyed there with my fate in my hands, as might a child have toyed with a bauble. I mean to say, I was looking for nothing thick.

"She's wrote a very fancy piece for that newspaper," Cousin Egbert went on, handing me the sheets of manuscript. Idly I glanced down the pages.

"Yesterday saw the return to Red Gap of Mrs. Senator James Knox Floud and Egbert G. Floud from their extensive European tour," it began. Farther I caught vagrant lines, salient phrases: "--the well-known social leader of our North Side set ... planning a series of entertainments for the approaching social season that promise to eclipse all previous gayeties of Red Gap's smart set ... holding the reins of social leadership with a firm grasp ... distinguished for her social graces and tact as a hostess ... their palatial home on Ophir Avenue, the scene of so much of the smart social life that has distinguished our beautiful city."

It left me rather unmoved from my depression, even the concluding note: "The Flouds are accompanied by their English manservant, secured through the kind offices of the brother of his lordship Earl of Brinstead, the well-known English peer, who will no doubt do much to impart to the coming functions that air of smartness which distinguishes the highest social circles of London, Paris, and other capitals of the great world of fashion."

"Some mess of words, that," observed Cousin Egbert, and it did indeed seem to be rather intimately phrased.

"Better come along with me," he again urged. There was a moment's fateful silence, then, quite mechanically, I arose and prepared to accompany him. In the hall below I handed him his evening stick and gloves, which he absently took from me, and we presently traversed that street of houses much in the fashion of the Floud house and nearly all boasting some sculptured bit of wild life on their terraces.

It was a calm night of late summer; all Nature seemed at peace. I looked aloft and reflected that the same stars were shining upon the civilization I had left so far behind. As we walked I lost myself in musing pensively upon this curious astronomical fact and upon the further vicissitudes to which I would surely be exposed.

I compared myself whimsically to an explorer chap who has ventured among a tribe of natives and who must seem to adopt their weird manners and customs to save himself from their fanatic violence.

From this I was aroused by Cousin Egbert, who, with sudden dismay regarding his stick and gloves, uttered a low cry of anguish and thrust them into my hands before I had divined his purpose.

"You'll have to tote them there things," he swiftly explained. "I forgot where I was." I demurred sharply, but he would not listen.

"I didn't mind it so much in Paris and Europe, where I ain't so very well known, but my good gosh! man, this is my home town. You'll have to take them. People won't notice it in you so much, you being a foreigner, anyway."

Without further objection I wearily took them, finding a desperate drollery in being regarded as a foreigner, whereas I was simply alone among foreigners; but I knew that Cousin Egbert lacked the subtlety to grasp this point of view and made no effort to lay it before him. It was clear to me then, I think, that he would forever remain socially impossible, though perhaps no bad sort from a mere human point of view.

We continued our stroll, turning presently from this residential avenue to a street of small unlighted shops, and from this into a wider and brilliantly lighted thoroughfare of larger shops, where my companion presently began to greet native acquaintances. And now once more he affected that fashion of presenting me to his friends that I had so deplored in Paris. His own greeting made, he would call out heartily: "Shake hands with my friend Colonel Ruggles!" Nor would he heed my protests at this, so that in sheer desperation I presently ceased making them, reflecting that after all we were encountering the street classes of the town.

At a score of such casual meetings I was thus presented, for he seemed to know quite almost every one and at times there would be a group of natives about us on the pavement. Twice we went into "saloons," as they rather pretentiously style their public houses, where Cousin Egbert would stand the drinks for all present, not omitting each time to present me formally to the bar-man. In all these instances I was at once asked what I thought of their town, which was at first rather embarrassing, as I was confident that any frank disclosure of my opinion, being necessarily hurried, might easily be misunderstood. I at length devised a conventional formula of praise which, although feeling a frightful fool, I delivered each time thereafter.

Thus we progressed the length of their commercial centre, the incidents varying but little.

"Hello, Sour-dough, you old shellback! When did you come off the trail?"

"Just got in. My lands! but it's good to be back. Billy, shake hands with my friend Colonel Ruggles."

I mean to say, the persons were not all named "Billy," that being used only by way of illustration. Sometimes they would be called "Doc" or "Hank" or "Al" or "Chris." Nor was my companion invariably called "shellback." "Horned-toad" and "Stinging-lizard" were also epithets much in favour with his friends.

At the end of this street we at length paused before the office, as I saw, of "The Red Gap *Recorder*; Daily and Weekly." Cousin Egbert entered here, but came out almost at once.

"Henshaw ain't there, and she said I got to be sure and give him this here piece personally; so come on. He's up to a lawn-feet."

"A social function, sir?" I asked.

"No; just a lawn-feet up in Judge Ballard's front yard to raise money for new uniforms for the band--that's what the boy said in there."

"But would it not be highly improper for me to appear there, sir?" I at once objected. "I fear it's not done, sir."

"Shucks!" he insisted, "don't talk foolish that way. You're a peach of a little mixer all right. Come on! Everybody goes. They'll even let me in. I can give this here piece to Henshaw and then we'll spend a little money to help the band-boys along."

My misgivings were by no means dispelled, yet as the affair seemed to be public rather than smart, I allowed myself to be led on.

Into another street of residences we turned, and after a brisk walk I was able to identify the "front yard" of which my companion had spoken. The strains of an orchestra came to us and from the trees and shrubbery gleamed the lights of paper lanterns. I could discern tents and marquees, a throng of people moving among them. Nearer, I observed a refreshment pavilion and a dancing platform.

Reaching the gate, Cousin Egbert paid for us an entrance fee of two shillings to a young lady in gypsy costume whom he greeted cordially as Beryl Mae, not omitting to present me to her as Colonel Ruggles.

We moved into the thick of the crowd. There was much laughter and hearty speech, and it at once occurred to me that Cousin Egbert had been right: it would not be an assemblage of people that mattered, but rather of small tradesmen, artisans, tenant-farmers and the like with whom I could properly mingle.

My companion was greeted by several of the throng, to whom he in turn presented me, among them after a bit to a slight, reddish-bearded person wearing thick nose-glasses whom I understood to be the pressman we were in search of. Nervous of manner he was and preoccupied with a notebook in which he frantically scribbled items from time to time. Yet no sooner was I presented to him than he began a quizzing sort of conversation with me that lasted near a half-hour, I should say. Very interested he seemed to hear of my previous life, having in full measure that naive curiosity about one which Americans take so little pains to hide. Like the other natives I had met that evening, he was especially concerned to know what I thought of Red Gap. The chat was not at all unpleasant, as he seemed to be a well-informed person, and it was not without regret that I noted the approach of Cousin Egbert in company with a pleasant-faced, middle-aged lady in Oriental garb, carrying a tambourine.

"Mrs. Ballard, allow me to make you acquainted with my friend Colonel Ruggles!" Thus Cousin Egbert performed his ceremony. The lady grasped my hand with great cordiality.

"You men have monopolized the Colonel long enough," she began with a large coquetry that I found not unpleasing, and firmly grasping my arm she led me off in the direction of the refreshment pavilion, where I was playfully let to know that I should purchase her bits of refreshment, coffee, plum-cake, an ice, things of that sort. Through it all she kept up a running fire of banter, from time to time presenting me to other women young and old who happened about us, all of whom betrayed an interest in my personality that was not unflattering, even from this commoner sort of the town's people.

Nor would my new friend release me when she had refreshed herself, but had it that I must dance with her. I had now to confess that I was unskilled in the native American folk dances which I had observed being performed, whereupon she briskly chided me for my backwardness, but commanded a valse from the musicians, and this we danced together.

I may here say that I am not without a certain finesse on the dancing-floor and I rather enjoyed the momentary abandon with this village worthy. Indeed I had rather enjoyed the whole affair, though I felt that my manner was gradually marking me as one apart from the natives; made conscious I was of a more finished, a suaver formality in myself--the Mrs. Ballard I had met came at length to be by way of tapping me coquettishly with her tambourine in our lighter moments. Also my presence increasingly drew attention, more and more of the village belles and matrons demanding in their hearty way to be presented to me. Indeed the society was vastly more enlivening, I reflected, than I had found it in a similar walk of life at home.

Rather regretfully I left with Cousin Egbert, who found me at last in one of the tents having my palm read by the gypsy young person who had taken our fees at the gate. Of course I am aware that she was probably without any real gifts for this science, as so few are who undertake it at charity bazaars, yet she told me not a few things that were significant: that my somewhat cold exterior and air of sternness were but a mask to shield a too-impulsive nature; that I possessed great firmness of character and was fond of Nature. She added peculiarly at the last "I see trouble ahead, but you are not to be downcast--the skies will brighten."

It was at this point that Cousin Egbert found me, and after he had warned the young woman that I was "some mixer" we departed. Not until we had reached the Floud home did he discover that he had quite forgotten to hand the press-chap Mrs. Effie's manuscript.

"Dog on the luck!" said he in his quaint tone of exasperation, "here I've went and forgot to give Mrs. Effie's piece to the editor." He sighed ruefully. "Well, to-morrow's another day."

And so the die was cast. To-morrow was indeed another day!

Yet I fell asleep on a memory of the evening that brought me a sort of shamed pleasure--that I had falsely borne the stick and gloves of Cousin Egbert. I knew they had given me rather an air.

CHAPTER EIGHT

I have never been able to recall the precise moment the next morning when I began to feel a strange disquietude but the opening hours of the day were marked by a series of occurrences slight in themselves yet so cumulatively ominous that they seemed to lower above me like a cloud of menace.

Looking from my window, shortly after the rising hour, I observed a paper boy pass through the street, whistling a popular melody as he ran up to toss folded journals into doorways. Something I cannot explain went through me even then; some premonition of disaster slinking furtively under my casual reflection that even in this remote wild the public press was not unknown.

Half an hour later the telephone rang in a lower room and I heard Mrs. Effie speak in answer. An unusual note in her voice caused me to listen more attentively. I stepped outside my door. To some one she was expressing amazement, doubt, and quick impatience which seemed to culminate, after she had again, listened, in a piercing cry of consternation. The term is not too strong. Evidently by the unknown speaker she had been first puzzled, then startled, then horrified; and now, as her anguished cry still rang in my ears, that snaky premonition of evil again writhed across my consciousness.

Presently I heard the front door open and close. Peering into the hallway below I saw that she had secured the newspaper I had seen dropped. Her own door now closed upon her. I waited, listening intently. Something told me that the incident was not closed. A brief interval elapsed and she was again at the telephone, excitedly demanding to be put through to a number.

"Come at once!" I heard her cry. "It's unspeakable! There isn't a moment to lose! Come as you are!" Hereupon, banging the receiver into its place with frenzied roughness, she ran halfway up the stairs to shout:

"Egbert Floud! Egbert Floud! You march right down here this minute, sir!"

From his room I heard an alarmed response, and a moment later knew that he had joined her. The door closed upon them, but high words reached me. Mostly the words of Mrs. Effie they were, though I could detect muffled retorts from the other. Wondering what this could portend, I noted from my window some ten minutes later the hurried arrival of the C. Belknap-Jacksons. The husband clenched a crumpled newspaper in one hand and both he and his wife betrayed signs to the trained eye of having performed hasty toilets for this early call.

As the door of the drawing-room closed upon them there ensued a terrific out-burst carrying a rich general effect of astounded rage. Some moments the sinister chorus continued, then a door sharply opened and I heard my own name cried out by Mrs. Effie in a tone that caused me to shudder. Rapidly descending the stairs, I entered the room to face the excited group. Cousin Egbert crouched on a sofa in a far corner like a hunted beast, but the others were standing, and all glared at me furiously.

The ladies addressed me simultaneously, one of them, I believe, asking me what I meant by it and the other demanding how dared I, which had the sole effect of adding to my bewilderment, nor did the words of Cousin Egbert diminish this.

"Hello, Bill!" he called, adding with a sort of timid bravado: "Don't you let 'em bluff you, not for a minute!"

"Yes, and it was probably all that wretched Cousin Egbert's fault in the first place," snapped Mrs. Belknap-Jackson almost tearfully.

"Say, listen here, now; I don't see as how I've done anything wrong," he feebly protested. "Bill's human, ain't he? Answer me that!"

"One sees it all!" This from Belknap-Jackson in bitter and judicial tones. He flung out his hands at Cousin Egbert in a gesture of pitiless scorn. "I dare say," he continued, "that poor Ruggles was merely a tool in his hands--weak, possibly, but not vicious."

"May I inquire----" I made bold to begin, but Mrs. Effie shut me off, brandish-ing the newspaper before me.

"Read it!" she commanded in hoarse, tragic tones. "There!" she added, pointing at monstrous black headlines on the page as I weakly took it from her. And then I saw. There before them, divining now the enormity of what had come to pass, I controlled myself to master the following screed:

RED GAP'S DISTINGUISHED VISITOR

Colonel Marmaduke Ruggles of London and Paris, late of the British army, bon-vivant and man of the world, is in our midst for an indefinite stay, being at present the honoured house guest of Senator and Mrs. James Knox Floud, who returned from foreign parts on the 5:16 flyer yesterday afternoon. Colonel Ruggles has long been intimately associated with the family of his lordship the Earl of Brinstead, and especially with his lordship's brother, the Honourable George Augustus Vane-Basingwell, with whom he has recently been sojourning in la belle France. In a brief interview which the Colonel genially accorded ye scribe, he expressed himself as delighted with our thriving little city.

"It's somewhat a town--if I've caught your American slang," he said with a merry twinkle in his eyes. "You have the garden spot of the West, if not of the civilized world, and your people display a charm that must be, I dare say, typically American. Altogether, I am enchanted with the wonders I have beheld since landing at your New York, particularly with the habit your best people have of roughing it in camps like that of Mr. C. Belknap-Jackson among the mountains of New York, where I was most pleasantly entertained by himself and his delightful wife. The length of my stay among you is uncertain, though I have been pressed by the Flouds, with whom I am stopping, and by the C. Belknap-Jacksons to prolong it indefinitely, and in fact to identify myself to an extent with your social life."

The Colonel is a man of distinguished appearance, with the seasoned bearing of an old campaigner, and though at moments he displays that cool reserve so typical of the English gentleman, evidence was not lacking last evening that he can unbend on occasion. At the lawn fete held in the spacious grounds of Judge Ballard, where a myriad Japanese lanterns made the scene a veritable fairyland, he was quite the most sought-after notable present, and gayly tripped the light fantastic toe with the elite of Red Gap's smart set there assembled.

From his cordial manner of entering into the spirit of the affair we predict that Colonel Ruggles will be a decided acquisition to our social life, and we understand that a series of recherche entertainments in his honour has already been planned by Mrs. County Judge Ballard, who took the distinguished guest under her wing the moment he appeared last evening. Welcome to our city, Colonel! And may the warm hearts of Red Gap cause you to forget that European world of fashion of which you have long been so distinguished an ornament!

In a sickening silence I finished the thing. As the absurd sheet fell from my nerveless fingers Mrs. Effie cried in a voice hoarse with emotion:

"Do you realize the dreadful thing you've done to us?"

Speechless I was with humiliation, unequal even to protesting that I had said nothing of the sort to the press-chap. I mean to say, he had wretchedly twisted my harmless words.

"Have you nothing to say for yourself?" demanded Mrs. Belknap-Jackson, also in a voice hoarse with emotion. I glanced at her husband. He, too, was pale with anger and trembling, so that I fancied he dared not trust himself to speak.

"The wretched man," declared Mrs. Effie, addressing them all, "simply can't realize--how disgraceful it is. Oh, we shall never be able to live it down!"

"Imagine those flippant Spokane sheets dressing up the thing," hissed Belknap-Jackson, speaking for the first time. "Imagine their blackguardly humour!"

"And that awful Cousin Egbert," broke in Mrs. Effie, pointing a desperate finger toward him. "Think of the laughing-stock he'll become! Why, he'll simply never be able to hold up his head again."

"Say, you listen here," exclaimed Cousin Egbert with sudden heat; "never you mind about my head. I always been able to hold up my head any time I felt like it." And again to me he threw out, "Don't you let 'em bluff you, Bill!"

"I gave him a notice for the paper," explained Mrs. Effie plaintively; "I'd written it all nicely out to save them time in the office, and that would have prevented this disgrace, but he never gave it in."

"I clean forgot it," declared the offender. "What with one thing and another, and gassing back and forth with some o' the boys, it kind of went out o' my head."

"Meeting our best people--actually dancing with them!" murmured Mrs. Belknap-Jackson in a voice vibrant with horror. "My dear, I truly am so sorry for you."

"You people entertained him delightfully at your camp," murmured Mrs. Effie quickly in her turn, with a gesture toward the journal.

"Oh, we're both in it, I know. I know. It's appalling!"

"We'll never be able to live it down!" said Mrs. Effie. "We shall have to go away somewhere."

"Can't you imagine what Jen' Ballard will say when she learns the truth?" asked the other bitterly. "Say we did it on purpose to humiliate her, and just as all our little scraps were being smoothed out, so we could get together and put that Bohemian set in its place. Oh, it's so dreadful!" On the verge of tears she seemed.

"And scarcely a word mentioned of our own return--when I'd taken such pains with the notice!"

"Listen here!" said Cousin Egbert brightly. "I'll take the piece down now and he can print it in his paper for you to-morrow."

"You can't understand," she replied impatiently. "I casually mentioned our having brought an English manservant. Print that now and insult all our best people who received him!"

"Pathetic how little the poor chap understands," sighed Belknap-Jackson. "No sense at all of our plight--naturally, naturally!"

"'A series of entertainments being planned in his honour!'" quavered Mrs.

Belknap-Jackson.

"'The most sought-after notable present!'" echoed Mrs. Effie viciously.

Again and again I had essayed to protest my innocence, only to provoke renewed outbursts. I could but stand there with what dignity I retained and let them savage me. Cousin Egbert now spoke again:

"Shucks! What's all the fuss? Just because I took Bill out and give him a good time! Didn't you say yourself in that there very piece that he'd impart to coming functions an air of smartiness like they have all over Europe? Didn't you write them very words? And ain't he already done it the very first night he gets here, right at that there lawn-feet where I took him? What for do you jump on me then? I took him and he done it; he done it good. Bill's a born mixer. Why, he had all them North Side society dames stung the minute I flashed him; after him quicker than hell could scorch a feather; run out from under their hats to get introduced to him-- and now you all turn on me like a passel of starved wolves." He finished with a note of genuine irritation I had never heard in his voice.

"The poor creature's demented," remarked Mrs. Belknap-Jackson pityingly.

"Always been that way," said Mrs. Effie hopelessly.

Belknap-Jackson contented himself with a mere clicking sound of commiseration.

"All right, then, if you're so smart," continued Cousin Egbert. "Just the same Bill, here, is the most popular thing in the whole Kulanche Valley this minute, so all I got to say is if you want to play this here society game you better stick close by him. First thing you know, some o' them other dames'll have him won from you. That Mis' Ballard's going to invite him to supper or dinner or some other doings right away. I heard her say so."

To my amazement a curious and prolonged silence greeted this amazing tirade. The three at length were regarding each other almost furtively. Belknap-Jackson began to pace the floor in deep thought.

"After all, no one knows except ourselves," he said in curiously hushed tones at last.

"Of course it's one way out of a dreadful mess," observed his wife.

"Colonel Marmaduke Ruggles of the British army," said Mrs. Effie in a peculiar tone, as if she were trying over a song.

"It may indeed be the best way out of an impossible situation," continued Belknap-Jackson musingly. "Otherwise we face a social upheaval that might leave us demoralized for years--say nothing of making us a laughingstock with the rabble. In fact, I see nothing else to be done."

"Cousin Egbert would be sure to spoil it all again," objected Mrs. Effie, glaring at him.

"No danger," returned the other with his superior smile. "Being quite unable to realize what has happened, he will be equally unable to realize what is going to happen. We may speak before him as before a babe in arms; the amenities of the situation are forever beyond him."

"I guess I always been able to hold up my head when I felt like it," put in Cousin Egbert, now again both sullen and puzzled. Once more he threw out his encouragement to me: "Don't let 'em run any bluffs, Bill! They can't touch you, and they know it."

"'Touch him,'" murmured Mrs. Belknap-Jackson with an able sneer. "My dear, what a trial he must have been to you. I never knew. He's as bad as the mater, actually."

"And such hopes I had of him in Paris," replied Mrs. Effie, "when he was taking up Art and dressing for dinner and everything!"

"I can be pushed just so far!" muttered the offender darkly.

There was now a ring at the door which I took the liberty of answering, and received two notes from a messenger. One bore the address of Mrs. Floud and the other was quite astonishingly to myself, the name preceded by "Colonel."

"That's Jen' Ballard's stationery!" cried Mrs. Belknap-Jackson. "Trust her not to lose one second in getting busy!"

"But he mustn't answer the door that way," exclaimed her husband as I handed Mrs. Effie her note.

They were indeed both from my acquaintance of the night before. Receiving permission to read my own, I found it to be a dinner invitation for the following Friday. Mrs. Effie looked up from hers.

"It's all too true," she announced grimly. "We're asked to dinner and she earnestly hopes dear Colonel Ruggles will have made no other engagement. She also says hasn't he the darlingest English accent. Oh, isn't it a mess!"

"You see how right I am," said Belknap-Jackson.

"I guess we've got to go through with it," conceded Mrs. Effie.

"The pushing thing that Ballard woman is!" observed her friend.

"Ruggles!" exclaimed Belknap-Jackson, addressing me with sudden decision.

"Yes, sir."

"Listen carefully--I'm quite serious. In future you will try to address me as if I were your equal. Ah! rather you will try to address me as if you were *my* equal. I dare say it will come to you easily after a bit of practice. Your employers will wish you to address them in the same manner. You will cultivate toward us a manner of easy friendliness--remember I'm entirely serious--quite as if you were one of us. You must try to be, in short, the Colonel Marmaduke Ruggles that wretched penny-a-liner has foisted upon these innocent people. We shall thus avert a most humiliating contretemps."

The thing fair staggered me. I fell weakly into the chair by which I had stood, for the first time in a not uneventful career feeling that my *savoir faire* had been over-taxed.

"Quite right," he went on. "Be seated as one of us," and he amazingly proffered me his cigarette case. "Do take one, old chap," he insisted as I weakly waved it away, and against my will I did so. "Dare say you'll fancy them--a non-throat cigarette especially prescribed for me." He now held a match so that I was obliged to smoke. Never have I been in less humour for it.

"There, not so hard, is it? You see, we're getting on famously."

"Ain't I always said Bill was a good mixer?" called Cousin Egbert, but his gaucherie was pointedly ignored.

"Now," continued Belknap-Jackson, "suppose you tell us in a chatty, friendly way just what you think about this regrettable affair." All sat forward interestedly.

"But I met what I supposed were your villagers," I said; "your small tradesmen, your artisans, clerks, shop-assistants, tenant-farmers, and the like, I'd no idea in the world they were your county families. Seemed quite a bit too jolly for that. And your press-chap--preposterous, quite! He quizzed me rather, I admit, but he made it vastly different. Your pressmen are remarkable. That thing is a fair crumpler."

"But surely," put in Mrs. Effie, "you could see that Mrs. Judge Ballard must be one of our best people."

"I saw she was a goodish sort," I explained, "but it never occurred to me one would meet her in your best houses. And when she spoke of entertaining me I fancied I might stroll by her cottage some fair day and be asked in to a slice from one of her own loaves and a dish of tea. There was that about her."

"Mercy!" exclaimed both ladies, Mrs. Belknap-Jackson adding a bit maliciously I thought, "Oh, don't you awfully wish she could hear him say it just that way?"

"As to the title," I continued, "Mr. Egbert has from the first had a curious American tendency to present me to his many friends as 'Colonel.' I am sure he means as little by it as when he calls me 'Bill,' which I have often reminded him is not a name of mine."

"Oh, we understand the poor chap is a social incompetent," said Belknap-Jackson with a despairing shrug.

"Say, look here," suddenly exclaimed Cousin Egbert, a new heat in his tone, "what I call Bill ain't a marker to what I call you when I really get going. You ought to hear me some day when I'm feeling right!"

"Really!" exclaimed the other with elaborate sarcasm.

"Yes, sir. Surest thing you know. I could call you a lot of good things right now if so many ladies wasn't around. You don't think I'd be afraid, do you? Why, Bill there had you licked with one wallop."

"But really, really!" protested the other with a helpless shrug to the ladies, who were gasping with dismay.

"You ruffian!" cried his wife.

"Egbert Floud," said Mrs. Effie fiercely, "you will apologize to Charles before you leave this room. The idea of forgetting yourself that way. Apologize at once!"

"Oh, very well," he grumbled, "I apologize like I'm made to." But he added quickly with even more irritation, "only don't you get the idea it's because I'm afraid of you."

"Tush, tush!" said Belknap-Jackson.

"No, sir; I apologize, but it ain't for one minute because I'm afraid of you."

"Your bare apology is ample; I'm bound to accept it," replied the other, a bit uneasily I thought.

"Come right down to it," continued Cousin Egbert, "I ain't afraid of hardly any person. I can be pushed just so far." Here he looked significantly at Mrs. Effie.

"After all I've tried to do for him!" she moaned. "I thought he had something in him."

"Darn it all, I like to be friendly with my friends," he bluntly persisted. "I call a man anything that suits me. And I ain't ever apologized yet because I was afraid. I want all parties here to get that."

"Say no more, please. It's quite understood," said Belknap-Jackson hastily. The other subsided into low mutterings.

"I trust you fully understand the situation, Ruggles--Colonel Ruggles," he continued to me.

"It's preposterous, but plain as a pillar-box," I answered. "I can only regret it as keenly as any right-minded person should. It's not at all what I've been accustomed to."

"Very well. Then I suggest that you accompany me for a drive this afternoon. I'll call for you with the trap, say at three."

"Perhaps," suggested his wife, "it might be as well if Colonel Ruggles were to come to us as a guest." She was regarding me with a gaze that was frankly speculative.

"Oh, not at all, not at all!" retorted Mrs. Effie crisply. "Having been announced as our house guest--never do in the world for him to go to you so soon. We must be careful in this. Later, perhaps, my dear."

Briefly the ladies measured each other with a glance. Could it be, I asked myself, that they were sparring for the possession of me?

"Naturally he will be asked about everywhere, and there'll be loads of entertaining to do in return."

"Of course," returned Mrs. Effie, "and I'd never think of putting it off on to you, dear, when we're wholly to blame for the awful thing."

"That's so thoughtful of you, dear," replied her friend coldly.

"At three, then," said Belknap-Jackson as we arose.

"I shall be delighted," I murmured.

"I bet you won't," said Cousin Egbert sourly. "He wants to show you off." This, I could see, was ignored as a sheer indecency.

"We shall have to get a reception in quick," said Mrs. Effie, her eyes narrowed in calculation.

"I don't see what all the fuss was about," remarked Cousin Egbert again, as if to himself; "tearing me to pieces like a passel of wolves!"

The Belknap-Jacksons left hastily, not deigning him a glance. And to do the poor soul justice, I believe he did not at all know what the "fuss" had been about. The niceties of the situation were beyond him, dear old sort though he had shown himself to be. I knew then I was never again to be harsh with him, let him dress as he would.

"Say," he asked, the moment we were alone, "you remember that thing you called him back there that night--'blighted little mug,' was it?"

"It's best forgotten, sir," I said.

"Well, sir, some way it sounded just the thing to call him. It sounded bully. What does it mean?"

So far was his darkened mind from comprehending that I, in a foreign land, among a weird people, must now have a go at being a gentleman; and that if I fluffed my catch we should all be gossipped to rags!

Alone in my room I made a hasty inventory of my wardrobe. Thanks to the circumstance that the Honourable George, despite my warning, had for several years refused to bant, it was rather well stocked. The evening clothes were irreproachable; so were the frock coat and a morning suit. Of waistcoats there were a number showing but slight wear. The three lounge-suits of tweed, though slightly demoded, would still be vogue in this remote spot. For sticks, gloves, cravats, and body-linen I saw that I should be compelled to levy on the store I had laid in for Cousin Egbert, and I happily discovered that his top-hat set me quite effectively.

Also in a casket of trifles that had knocked about in my box I had the good fortune to find the monocle that the Honourable George had discarded some years before on the ground that it was "bally nonsense." I screwed the glass into my eye. The effect was tremendous.

Rather a lark I might have thought it but for the false military title. That was rank deception, and I have always regarded any sort of wrongdoing as detestable. Perhaps if he had introduced me as a mere subaltern in a line regiment--but I was powerless.

For the afternoon's drive I chose the smartest of the lounge-suits, a Carlsbad hat which Cousin Egbert had bitterly resented for himself, and for top-coat a light weight, straight-hanging Chesterfield with velvet collar which, although the cut studiously avoids a fitted effect, is yet a garment that intrigues the eye when carried with any distinction. So many top-coats are but mere wrappings! I had, too, gloves of a delicately contrasting tint.

Altogether I felt I had turned myself out well, and this I found to be the verdict of Mrs. Effie, who engaged me in the hall to say that I was to have anything in the way of equipment I liked to ask for. Belknap-Jackson also, arriving now in a smart trap to which he drove two cobs tandem, was at once impressed and made me compliments upon my tenue. I was aware that I appeared not badly beside him. I mean to say, I felt that I was vogue in the finest sense of the word.

Mrs. Effie waved us a farewell from the doorway, and I was conscious that from several houses on either side of the avenue we attracted more than a bit of attention. There were doors opened, blinds pushed aside, faces--that sort of thing.

At a leisurely pace we progressed through the main thoroughfares. That we created a sensation, especially along the commercial streets, where my host halted at shops to order goods, cannot be denied. Furore is perhaps the word. I mean to say, almost quite every one stared. Rather more like a parade it was than I could have wished, but I was again resolved to be a dead sportsman.

Among those who saluted us from time to time were several of the lesser townsmen to whom Cousin Egbert had presented me the evening before, and I now perceived that most of these were truly persons I must not know in my present station--hodmen, road-menders, grooms, delivery-chaps, that sort. In responding to the often florid salutations of such, I instilled into my barely perceptible nod a certain frigidity that I trusted might be informing. I mean to say, having now a position to keep up, it would never do at all to chatter and pal about loosely as Cousin Egbert did.

When we had done a fairish number of streets, both of shops and villas, we drove out a winding roadway along a tarn to the country club. The house was an unpretentious structure of native wood, fronting a couple of tennis courts and a golf links, but although it was tea-time, not a soul was present. Having unlocked the door, my host suggested refreshment and I consented to partake of a glass of sherry and a biscuit. But these, it seemed, were not to be had; so over pegs of ginger ale, found in an ice-chest, we sat for a time and chatted.

"You will find us crude, Ruggles, as I warned you," my host observed. "Take this deserted clubhouse at this hour. It tells the story. Take again the matter of sherry and a biscuit--so simple! Yet no one ever thinks of them, and what you mean by a biscuit is in this wretched hole spoken of as a cracker."

I thanked him for the item, resolving to add it to my list of curious American-isms. Already I had begun a narrative of my adventures in this wild land, a thing I had tentatively entitled, "Alone in North America."

"Though we have people in abundance of ample means," he went on, "you will regret to know that we have not achieved a leisured class. Barely once in a fortnight will you see this club patronized, after all the pains I took in its organization. They simply haven't evolved to the idea yet; sometimes I have moments in which I de-spair of their ever doing so."

As usual he grew depressed when speaking of social Red Gap, so that we did not tarry long in the silent place that should have been quite alive with people smartly having their tea. As we drove back he touched briefly and with all delicacy on our changed relations.

"What made me only too glad to consent to it," he said, "is the sodden depravity of that Floud chap. Really he's a menace to the community. I saw from the degener-ate leer on his face this morning that he will not be able to keep silent about that little affair of ours back there. Mark my words, he'll talk. And fancy how embar-rassing had you continued in the office for which you were engaged. Fancy it being known I had been assaulted by a--you see what I mean. But now, let him talk his vilest. What is it? A mere disagreement between two gentlemen, generous, hot-tempered chaps, followed by mutual apologies. A mere nothing!"

I was conscious of more than a little irritation at his manner of speaking of Cousin Egbert, but this in my new character I could hardly betray.

When he set me down at the Floud house, "Thanks for the breeze-out," I said; then, with an easy wave of the hand and in firm tones, "Good day, Jackson! See you again, old chap!"

I had nerved myself to it as to an icy tub and was rewarded by a glow such as had suffused me that morning in Paris after the shameful proceedings with Cousin Egbert and the Indian Tuttle. I mean to say, I felt again that wonderful thrill of equality--quite as if my superiors were not all about me.

Inside the house Mrs. Effie addressed the last of a heap of invitations for an early reception--"To meet Colonel Marmaduke Ruggles," they read.

CHAPTER NINE

OF the following fortnight I find it difficult to write coherently. I found myself in a steady whirl of receptions, luncheons, dinners, teas, and assemblies of rather a pretentious character, at the greater number of which I was obliged to appear as the guest of honour. It began with the reception of Mrs. Floud, at which I may be said to have made my first formal bow to the smarter element of Red Gap, followed by the dinner of the Mrs. Ballard, with whom I had formed acquaintance on that first memorable evening.

I was during this time like a babe at blind play with a set of chess men, not knowing king from pawn nor one rule of the game. Senator Floud--who was but a member of their provincial assembly, I discovered--sought an early opportunity to felicitate me on my changed estate, though he seemed not a little amused by it.

"Good work!" he said. "You know I was afraid our having an English valet would put me in bad with the voters this fall. They're already saying I wear silk stockings since I've been abroad. My wife did buy me six pair, but I've never worn any. Shows how people talk, though. And even now they'll probably say I'm making up to the British army. But it's better than having a valet in the house. The plain people would never stand my having a valet and I know it."

I thought this most remarkable, that his constituency should resent his having proper house service. American politics were, then, more debased than even we of England had dreamed.

"Good work!" he said again. "And say, take out your papers--become one of us. Be a citizen. Nothing better than an American citizen on God's green earth. Read the Declaration of Independence. Here----" From a bookcase at his hand he reached me a volume. "Read and reflect, my man! Become a citizen of a country where true worth has always its chance and one may hope to climb to any heights whatsoever." Quite like an advertisement he talked, but I read their so-called Declaration, finding it snarky in the extreme and with no end of silly rot about equality. In no way at all did it solve the problems by which I had been so suddenly confronted.

Social lines in the town seemed to have been drawn by no rule whatever. There were actually tradesmen who seemed to matter enormously; on the other hand, there were those of undoubted qualifications, like Mrs. Pettengill, for example, and Cousin Egbert, who deliberately chose not to matter, and mingled as freely with the Bohemian set as they did with the county families. Thus one could never be quite certain whom one was meeting. There was the Tuttle person. I had learned from Mrs. Effie in Paris that he was an Indian (accounting for much that was startling in his behaviour there) yet despite his being an aborigine I now learned that his was one of the county families and he and his white American wife were guests at that first dinner. Throughout the meal both Cousin Egbert and he winked atrociously at me whenever they could catch my eye.

There was, again, an English person calling himself Hobbs, a baker, to whom Cousin Egbert presented me, full of delight at the idea that as compatriots we were bound to be congenial. Yet it needed only a glance and a moment's listening to the fellow's execrable cockney dialect to perceive that he was distinctly low-class, and I was immensely relieved, upon inquiry, to learn that he affiliated only with the Bohemian set. I felt a marked antagonism between us at that first meeting; the fellow eyed me with frank suspicion and displayed a taste for low chaffing which I felt bound to rebuke. He it was, I may now disclose, who later began a fashion of referring to me as "Lord Algy," which I found in the worst possible taste. "Sets himself up for a gentleman, does he? He ain't no more a gentleman than wot I be!" This speech of his reported to me will show how impossible the creature was. He was simply a person one does not know, and I was not long in letting him see it.

And there was the woman who was to play so active a part in my later history, of whom it will be well to speak at once. I had remarked her on the main street before I knew her identity. I am bound to say she stood out from the other women of Red Gap by reason of a certain dash, not to say beauty. Rather above medium height and of pleasingly full figure, her face was piquantly alert, with long-lashed eyes of a peculiar green, a small nose, the least bit raised, a lifted chin, and an abundance of yellowish hair. But it was the expertness of her gowning that really held my attention at that first view, and the fact that she knew what to put on her head. For the most part, the ladies I had met were well enough gotten up yet looked curiously all wrong, lacking a genius for harmony of detail.

This person, I repeat, displayed a taste that was faultless, a knowledge of the peculiar needs of her face and figure that was unimpeachable. Rather with regret it was I found her to be a Mrs. Kenner, the leader of the Bohemian set. And then came the further items that marked her as one that could not be taken up. Perhaps a summary of these may be conveyed when I say that she had long been known as Klondike Kate. She had some years before, it seemed, been a dancing person in the far Alaska north and had there married the proprietor of one of the resorts in which she disported herself--a man who had accumulated a very sizable fortune in his public house and who was shot to death by one of his patrons who had alleged unfairness in a game of chance. The widow had then purchased a townhouse in Red Gap and had quickly gathered about her what was known as the Bohemian set, the county families, of course, refusing to know her.

After that first brief study of her I could more easily account for the undercurrents of bitterness I had felt in Red Gap society. She would be, I saw, a dangerous woman in any situation where she was opposed; there was that about her--a sort of daring disregard of the established social order. I was not surprised to learn that the men of the community strongly favoured her, especially the younger dancing set who were not restrained by domestic considerations. Small wonder then that the women of the "old noblesse," as I may call them, were outspokenly bitter in their comments upon her. This I discovered when I attended an afternoon meeting of the ladies' "Onwards and Upwards Club," which, I had been told, would be devoted to a study of the English Lake poets, and where, it having been discovered that I read rather well, I had consented to favour the assembly with some of the more significant bits from these bards. The meeting, I regret to say, after a formal enough opening was diverted from its original purpose, the time being occupied in a quite heated discussion of a so-called "Dutch Supper" the Klondike person had given the evening before, the same having been attended, it seemed, by the husbands of at least three of those present, who had gone incognito, as it were. At no time during the ensuing two hours was there a moment that seemed opportune for the introduction of some of our noblest verse.

And so, by often painful stages, did my education progress. At the country club I played golf with Mr. Jackson. At social affairs I appeared with the Flouds. I played bridge. I danced the more dignified dances. And, though there was no proper church in the town--only dissenting chapels, Methodist, Presbyterian, and such outlandish persuasions--I attended services each Sabbath, and more than once had tea with what at home would have been the vicar of the parish.

It was now, when I had begun to feel a bit at ease in my queer foreign environment, that Mr. Belknap-Jackson broached his ill-starred plan for amateur theatricals. At the first suggestion of this I was immensely taken with the idea, suspecting that he would perhaps present "Hamlet," a part to which I have devoted long and intelligent study and to which I feel that I could bring something which has not yet been imparted to it by even the most skilled of our professional actors. But at my suggestion of this Mr. Belknap-Jackson informed me that he had already played Hamlet himself the year before, leaving nothing further to be done in that direction, and he wished now to attempt something more difficult; something, moreover, that would appeal to the little group of thinking people about us--he would have "a little theatre of ideas," as he phrased it--and he had chosen for his first offering a play entitled "Ghosts" by the foreign dramatist Ibsen.

I suspected at first that this might be a farce where a supposititious ghost brings about absurd predicaments in a country house, having seen something along these lines, but a reading of the thing enlightened me as to its character, which, to put it bluntly, is rather thick. There is a strain of immorality running through it which I believe cannot be too strongly condemned if the world is to be made better, and this is rendered the more repugnant to right-thinking people by the fact that the participants are middle-class persons who converse in quite commonplace language such as one may hear any day in the home.

Wrongdoing is surely never so objectionable as when it is indulged in by common people and talked about in ordinary language, and the language of this play is not stage language at all. Immorality such as one gets in Shakespeare is of so elevated a character that one accepts it, the language having a grandeur incomparably above what any person was ever capable of in private life, being always elegant and unnatural.

Though I felt this strongly, I was in no position to urge my objections, and at length consented to take a part in the production, reflecting that the people depicted were really foreigners and the part I would play was that of a clergyman whose behaviour throughout is above reproach. For himself Mr. Jackson had chosen the part of Oswald, a youth who goes quite dotty at the last for reasons which are better not talked about. His wife was to play the part of a serving-maid, who was rather a baggage, while Mrs. Judge Ballard was to enact his mother. (I may say in passing I have learned that the plays of this foreigner are largely concerned with people who have been queer at one time or another, so that one's parentage is often uncertain, though they always pay for it by going off in the head before the final curtain. I mean to say, there is too much neighbourhood scandal in them.)

There remained but one part to fill, that of the father of the serving-maid, an uncouth sort of drinking-man, quite low-class, who, in my opinion, should never have been allowed on the stage at all, since no moral lesson is taught by him. It was in the casting of this part that Mr. Jackson showed himself of a forgiving nature. He offered it to Cousin Egbert, saying he was the true "type"--"with his weak, dissolute face"--and that "types" were all the rage in theatricals.

At first the latter heatedly declined the honour, but after being urged and browbeaten for three days by Mrs. Effie he somewhat sullenly consented, being shown that there were not many lines for him to learn. From the first, I think, he was rendered quite miserable by the ordeal before him, yet he submitted to the rehearsals with a rather pathetic desire to please, and for a time all seemed well. Many an hour found him mugging away at the book, earnestly striving to memorize the part, or, as he quaintly expressed it, "that there piece they want me to speak." But as the day of our performance drew near it became evident to me, at least, that he was in a desperately black state of mind. As best I could I cheered him with words of praise, but his eye met mine blankly at such times and I could see him shudder poignantly while waiting the moment of his entrance.

And still all might have been well, I fancy, but for the extremely conscientious views of Mr. Jackson in the matter of our costuming and make-up. With his lines fairly learned, Cousin Egbert on the night of our dress rehearsal was called upon first to don the garb of the foreign carpenter he was to enact, the same involving shorts and gray woollen hose to his knees, at which he protested violently. So far as I could gather, his modesty was affronted by this revelation of his lower legs. Being at length persuaded to this sacrifice, he next submitted his face to Mr. Jackson, who adjusted it to a labouring person's beard and eyebrows, crimsoning the cheeks and nose heavily with grease-paint and crowning all with an unkempt wig.

The result, I am bound to say, was artistic in the extreme. No one would have suspected the identity of Cousin Egbert, and I had hopes that he would feel a new courage for his part when he beheld himself. Instead, however, after one quick glance into the glass he emitted a gasp of horror that was most eloquent, and thereafter refused to be comforted, holding himself aloof and glaring hideously at all who approached him. Rather like a mad dog he was.

Half an hour later, when all was ready for our first act, Cousin Egbert was not to be found. I need not dwell upon the annoyance this occasioned, nor upon how a substitute in the person of our hall's custodian, or janitor, was impressed to read the part. Suffice it to tell briefly that Cousin Egbert, costumed and bedizened as he was, had fled not only the theatre but the town as well. Search for him on the morrow was unavailing. Not until the second day did it become known that he had been seen at daybreak forty miles from Red Gap, goading a spent horse into the wilds of the adjacent mountains. Our informant disclosed that one side of his face was still bearded and that he had kept glancing back over his shoulder at frequent intervals, as if fearful of pursuit. Something of his frantic state may also be gleaned from the circumstance that the horse he rode was one he had found hitched in a side street near the hall, its ownership being unknown to him.

For the rest it may be said that our performance was given as scheduled, announcement being made of the sudden illness of Mr. Egbert Floud, and his part being read from the book in a rich and cultivated voice by the superintendent of the high school. Our efforts were received with respectful attention by a large audience, among whom I noted many of the Bohemian set, and this I took as an especial tribute to our merits. Mr. Belknap-Jackson, however, to whom I mentioned the circumstance, was pessimistic.

"I fear," said he, "we have not heard the last of it. I am sure they came for no good purpose."

"They were quite orderly in their behaviour," I suggested

"Which is why I suspect them. That Kenner woman, Hobbs, the baker, the others of their set--they're not thinking people; I dare say they never consider social problems seriously. And you may have noticed that they announce an amateur minstrel performance for a week hence. I'm quite convinced that they mean to be vulgar to the last extreme--there has been so much talk of the behaviour of the wretched Floud, a fellow who really has no place in our modern civilization. He should be compelled to remain on his ranche."

And indeed these suspicions proved to be only too well founded. That which followed was so atrociously personal that in any country but America we could have had an action against them. As Mr. Belknap-Jackson so bitterly said when all was over, "Our boasted liberty has degenerated into license."

It is best told in a few words, this affair of the minstrel performance, which I understood was to be an entertainment wherein the participants darkened themselves to resemble blackamoors. Naturally, I did not attend, it being agreed that the best people should signify their disapproval by staying away, but the disgraceful affair was recounted to me in all its details by more than one of the large audience that assembled. In the so-called "grand first part" there seemed to have been little that was flagrantly insulting to us, although in their exchange of conundrums, which is a peculiar feature of this form of entertainment, certain names were bandied about with a freedom that boded no good.

It was in the after-piece that the poltroons gave free play to their vilest fancies. Our piece having been announced as "Ghosts; a Drama for Thinking People," this part was entitled on their programme, "Gloats; a Dram for Drinking People," a transposition that should perhaps suffice to show the dreadful lengths to which they went; yet I feel that the thing should be set down in full.

The stage was set as our own had been, but it would scarce be credited that the Kenner woman in male attire had made herself up in a curiously accurate resemblance to Belknap-Jackson as he had rendered the part of Oswald, copying not alone his wig, moustache, and fashion of speech, but appearing in a golfing suit which was recognized by those present as actually belonging to him.

Nor was this the worst, for the fellow Hobbs had copied my own dress and make-up and persisted in speaking in an exaggerated manner alleged to resemble mine. This, of course, was the most shocking bad taste, and while it was quite to have been expected of Hobbs, I was indeed rather surprised that the entire assembly did not leave the auditorium in disgust the moment they perceived his base intention. But it was Cousin Egbert whom they had chosen to rag most unmercifully, and they were not long in displaying their clumsy attempts at humour.

As the curtain went up they were searching for him, affecting to be uncon-scious of the presence of their audience, and declaring that the play couldn't go on without him. "Have you tried all the saloons?" asked one, to which another re-sponded, "Yes, and he's been in all of them, but now he has fled. The sheriff has put bloodhounds on his trail and promises to have him here, dead or alive."

"Then while we are waiting," declared the character supposed to represent my-self, "I will tell you a wheeze," whereupon both the female characters fell to their knees shrieking, "Not that! My God, not that!" while Oswald sneered viciously and muttered, "Serves me right for leaving Boston."

To show the infamy of the thing, I must here explain that at several social gath-erings, in an effort which I still believe was praiseworthy, I had told an excellent wheeze which runs: "Have you heard the story of the three holes in the ground?" I mean to say, I would ask this in an interested manner, as if I were about to relate the anecdote, and upon being answered "No!" I would exclaim with mock seriousness, "Well! Well! Well!" This had gone rippingly almost quite every time I had favoured a company with it, hardly any one of my hearers failing to get the joke at a second telling. I mean to say, the three holes in the ground being three "Wells!" uttered in rapid succession.

Of course if one doesn't see it at once, or finds it a bit subtle, it's quite silly to attempt to explain it, because logically there is no adequate explanation. It is merely a bit of nonsense, and that's quite all to it. But these boors now fell upon it with their coarse humour, the fellow Hobbs pretending to get it all wrong by asking if they had heard the story about the three wells and the others replying: "No, tell us the hole thing," which made utter nonsense of it, whereupon they all began to cry, "Well! well! well!" at each other until interrupted by a terrific noise in the wings, which was followed by the entrance of the supposed Cousin Egbert, a part enacted by the cab-driver who had conveyed us from the station the day of our arrival. Dragged on he was by the sheriff and two of the town constables, the latter being armed with fowling-pieces and the sheriff holding two large dogs in leash. The character himself was heavily manacled and madly rattled his chains, his face being disguised to resemble Cousin Egbert's after the beard had been adjusted.

"Here he is!" exclaimed the supposed sheriff; "the dogs ran him into the third hole left by the well-diggers, and we lured him out by making a noise like sour dough." During this speech, I am told, the character snarled continuously and tried to bite his captors. At this the woman, who had so deplorably unsexed herself for the character of Mr. Belknap-Jackson as he had played Oswald, approached the prisoner and smartly drew forth a handful of his beard which she stuffed into a pipe and proceeded to smoke, after which they pretended that the play went on. But no more than a few speeches had been uttered when the supposed Cousin Egbert eluded his captors and, emitting a loud shriek of horror, leaped headlong through the window at the back of the stage, his disappearance being followed by the sounds of breaking glass as he was supposed to fall to the street below.

"How lovely!" exclaimed the mimic Oswald. "Perhaps he has broken both his legs so he can't run off any more," at which the fellow Hobbs remarked in his affected tones: "That sort of thing would never do with us."

This I learned aroused much laughter, the idea being that the remark had been one which I am supposed to make in private life, though I dare say I have never uttered anything remotely like it.

"The fellow is quite impossible," continued the spurious Oswald, with a doubtless rather clever imitation of Mr. Belknap-Jackson's manner. "If he is killed, feed him to the goldfish and let one of the dogs read his part. We must get along with this play. Now, then. 'Ah! why did I ever leave Boston where every one is nice and proper?'" To which his supposed mother replied with feigned emotion: "It was because of your father, my poor boy. Ah, what I had to endure through those years when he cursed and spoke disrespectfully of our city. 'Scissors and white aprons,' he would cry out, 'Why is Boston?' But I bore it all for your sake, and now you, too, are smoking--you will go the same way."

"But promise me, mother," returns Oswald, "promise me if I ever get dusty in the garret, that Lord Algy here will tell me one of his funny wheezes and put me out of pain. You could not bear to hear me knocking Boston as poor father did. And I feel it coming--already my mother-in-law has bluffed me into admitting that Red Gap has a right to be on the same map with Boston if it's a big map."

And this was the coarsely wretched buffoonery that refined people were expected to sit through! Yet worse followed, for at their climax, the mimic Oswald having gone quite off his head, the Hobbs person, still with the preposterous affectation of taking me off in speech and manner, was persuaded by the stricken mother to sing. "Sing that dear old plantation melody from London," she cried, "so that my poor boy may know there are worse things than death." And all this witless piffle because of a quite natural misunderstanding of mine.

I have before referred to what I supposed was an American plantation melody which I had heard a black sing at Brighton, meaning one of the English blacks who colour themselves for the purpose, but on reciting the lines at an evening affair, when the American folksongs were under discussion, I was told that it could hardly have been written by an American at all, but doubtless by one of our own composers who had taken too little trouble with his facts. I mean to say, the song as I had it, betrayed misapprehensions both of a geographical and faunal nature, but I am certain that no one thought the worse of me for having been deceived, and I had supposed the thing forgotten. Yet now what did I hear but that a garbled version of this song had been supposedly sung by myself, the Hobbs person meantime mincing across the stage and gesturing with a monocle which he had somehow procured, the words being quite simply:

"Away down south in Michigan,
   Where I was a slave, so happy and so gay,
'Twas there I mowed the cotton and the cane.
I used to hunt the elephants, the tigers, and giraffes,
   And the alligators at the break of day.
But the blooming Injuns prowled about my cabin every night,
   So I'd take me down my banjo and I'd play,
And I'd sing a little song and I'd make them dance with glee,
   On the banks of the Ohio far away."

I mean to say, there was nothing to make a dust about even if the song were not of a true American origin, yet I was told that the creature who sang it received hearty applause and even responded to an encore.

CHAPTER TEN

I need hardly say that this public ridicule left me dazed. Desperately I recalled our calm and orderly England where such things would not be permitted. There we are born to our stations and are not allowed to forget them. We matter from birth, or we do not matter, and that's all to it. Here there seemed to be no stations to which one was born; the effect was sheer anarchy, and one might ridicule any one whomsoever. As was actually said in that snarky manifesto drawn up by the rebel leaders at the time our colonies revolted, "All men are created free and equal"--than which absurdity could go no farther--yet the lower middle classes seemed to behave quite as if it were true.

And now through no fault of my own another awkward circumstance was threatening to call further attention to me, which was highly undesirable at this moment when the cheap one-and-six Hobbs fellow had so pointedly singled me out for his loathsome buffoonery.

Some ten days before, walking alone at the edge of town one calm afternoon, where I might commune with Nature, of which I have always been fond, I noted an humble vine-clad cot, in the kitchen garden of which there toiled a youngish, neat-figured woman whom I at once recognized as a person who did occasional charring for the Flouds on the occasion of their dinners or receptions. As she had appeared to be cheerful and competent, of respectful manners and a quite marked intelligence, I made nothing of stopping at her gate for a moment's chat, feeling a quite decided relief in the thought that here was one with whom I need make no pretence, her social position being sharply defined.

We spoke of the day's heat, which was bland, of the vegetables which she watered with a lawn hose, particularly of the tomatoes of which she was pardonably proud, and of the flowering vine which shielded her piazza from the sun. And when she presently and with due courtesy invited me to enter, I very affably did so, finding the atmosphere of the place reposeful and her conversation of a character that I could approve. She was dressed in a blue print gown that suited her no end, the sleeves turned back over her capable arms; her brown hair was arranged with scrupulous neatness, her face was pleasantly flushed from her agricultural labours, and her blue eyes flashed a friendly welcome and a pleased acknowledgment of the compliments I made her on the garden. Altogether, she was a person with whom I at once felt myself at ease, and a relief, I confess it was, after the strain of my high social endeavours.

After a tour of the garden I found myself in the cool twilight of her little parlour, where she begged me to be seated while she prepared me a dish of tea, which she did in the adjoining kitchen, to a cheerful accompaniment of song, quite with an honest, unpretentious good-heartedness. Glad I was for the moment to forget the social rancors of the town, the affronted dignities of the North Side set, and the pernicious activities of the Bohemians, for here all was of a simple humanity such as I would have found in a farmer's cottage at home.

As I rested in the parlour I could not but approve its general air of comfort and good taste--its clean flowered wall-paper, the pair of stuffed birds on the mantel, the comfortable chairs, the neat carpet, the pictures, and, on a slender-legged stand, the globe of goldfish. These I noted with an especial pleasure, for I have always found an intense satisfaction in their silent companionship. Of the pictures I noted particularly a life-sized drawing in black-and-white in a large gold frame, of a man whom I divined was the deceased husband of my hostess. There was also a spirited reproduction of "The Stag at Bay" and some charming coloured prints of villagers, children, and domestic animals in their lighter moments.

Tea being presently ready, I genially insisted that it should be served in the kitchen where it had been prepared, though to this my hostess at first stoutly objected, declaring that the room was in no suitable state. But this was a mere womanish hypocrisy, as the place was spotless, orderly, and in fact quite meticulous in its neatness. The tea was astonishingly excellent, so few Americans I had observed having the faintest notion of the real meaning of tea, and I was offered with it bread and butter and a genuinely satisfying compote of plums of which my hostess confessed herself the fabricator, having, as she quaintly phrased the thing, "put it up."

And so, over this collation, we chatted for quite all of an hour. The lady did, as

I have intimated, a bit of charring, a bit of plain sewing, and also derived no small revenue from her vegetables and fruit, thus managing, as she owned the free-hold of the premises, to make a decent living for herself and child. I have said that she was cheerful and competent, and these epithets kept returning to me as we talked. Her husband--she spoke of him as "poor Judson"--had been a carter and odd-job fellow, decent enough, I dare say, but hardly the man for her, I thought, after studying his portrait. There was a sort of foppish weakness in his face. And indeed his going seemed to have worked her no hardship, nor to have left any incurable sting of loss.

Three cups of the almost perfect tea I drank, as we talked of her own simple affairs and of the town at large, and at length of her child who awakened noisily from slumber in an adjacent room and came voraciously to partake of food. It was a male child of some two and a half years, rather suggesting the generous good-nature of the mother, but in the most shocking condition, a thing I should have spoken strongly to her about at once had I known her better. Queer it seemed to me that a woman of her apparently sound judgment should let her offspring reach this terrible state without some effort to alleviate it. The poor thing, to be blunt, was grossly corpulent, legs, arms, body, and face being wretchedly fat, and yet she now fed it a large slice of bread thickly spread with butter and loaded to overflowing with the fattening sweet. Banting of the strictest sort was of course what it needed. I have had but the slightest experience with children, but there could be no doubt of this if its figure was to be maintained. Its waistline was quite impossible, and its eyes, as it owlishly scrutinized me over its superfluous food, showed from a face already quite as puffy as the Honourable George's. I did, indeed, venture so far as suggesting that food at untimely hours made for a too-rounded outline, but to my surprise the mother took this as a tribute to the creature's grace, crying, "Yes, he wuzzum wuzzums a fatty ole sing," with an air of most fatuous pride, and followed this by announcing my name to it with concerned precision.

"Ruggums," it exclaimed promptly, getting the name all wrong and staring at me with cold detachment; then "Ruggums-Ruggums-Ruggums!" as if it were a game, but still stuffing itself meanwhile. There was a sort of horrid fascination in the sight, but I strove as well as I could to keep my gaze from it, and the mother and I again talked of matters at large.

I come now to speak of an incident which made this quite harmless visit memorable and entailed unforeseen consequences of an almost quite serious character.

As we sat at tea there stalked into the kitchen a nondescript sort of dog, a creature of fairish size, of a rambling structure, so to speak, coloured a puzzling grayish brown with underlying hints of yellow, with vast drooping ears, and a long and most saturnine countenance.

Quite a shock it gave me when I looked up to find the beast staring at me with what I took to be the most hearty disapproval. My hostess paused in silence as she noted my glance. The beast then approached me, sniffed at my boots inquiringly, then at my hands with increasing animation, and at last leaped into my lap and had licked my face before I could prevent it.

I need hardly say that this attention was embarrassing and most distasteful, since I have never held with dogs. They are doubtless well enough in their place, but there is a vast deal of sentiment about them that is silly, and outside the hunting field the most finely bred of them are too apt to be noisy nuisances. When I say that the beast in question was quite an American dog, obviously of no breeding whatever, my dismay will be readily imagined. Rather impulsively, I confess, I threw him to the floor with a stern, "Begone, sir!" whereat he merely crawled to my feet and whimpered, looking up into my eyes with a most horrid and sickening air of devotion. Hereupon, to my surprise, my hostess gayly called out:

"Why, look at Mr. Barker--he's actually taken up with you right away, and him usually so suspicious of strangers. Only yesterday he bit an agent that was calling with silver polish to sell--bit him in the leg so I had to buy some from the poor fellow--and now see! He's as friendly with you as you could wish. They do say that dogs know when people are all right. Look at him trying to get into your lap again." And indeed the beast was again fawning upon me in the most abject manner, licking my hands and seeming to express for me some hideous admiration. Seeing that I repulsed his advances none too gently, his owner called to him:

"Down, Mr. Barker, down, sir! Get out!" she continued, seeing that he paid her no attention, and then she thoughtfully seized him by the collar and dragged him to a safe distance where she held him, he nevertheless continuing to regard me with the most servile affection.

"Ruggums, Ruggums, Ruggums!" exploded the child at this, excitedly waving the crust of its bread.

"Behave, Mr. Barker!" called his owner again. "The gentleman probably doesn't want you climbing all over him."

The remainder of my visit was somewhat marred by the determination of Mr. Barker, as he was indeed quite seriously called, to force his monstrous affections upon me, and by the well-meant but often careless efforts of his mistress to restrain him. She, indeed, appeared to believe that I would feel immensely pleased at these tokens of his liking.

As I took my leave after sincere expressions of my pleasure in the call, the child with its face one fearful smear of jam again waved its crust and shouted, "Ruggums!" while the dog was plainly bent on departing with me. Not until he had been secured by a rope to one of the porch stanchions could I safely leave, and as I went he howled dismally after violent efforts to chew the detaining rope apart.

I finished my stroll with the greatest satisfaction, for during the entire hour I had been enabled to forget the manifold cares of my position. Again it seemed to me that the portrait in the little parlour was not that of a man who had been entirely suited to this worthy and energetic young woman. Highly deserving she seemed, and when I knew her better, as I made no doubt I should, I resolved to instruct her in the matter of a more suitable diet for her offspring, the present one, as I have said, carrying quite too large a preponderance of animal fats. Also, I mused upon the extraordinary tolerance she accorded to the sad-faced but too demonstrative Mr. Barker. He had been named, I fancied, by some one with a primitive sense of humour, I mean to say, he might have been facetiously called "Barker" because he actually barked a bit, though adding the "Mister" to it seemed to be rather forcing the poor drollery. At any rate, I was glad to believe I should see little of him in his free state.

And yet it was precisely the curious fondness of this brute for myself that now added to my embarrassments. On two succeeding days I paused briefly at Mrs. Judson's in my afternoon strolls, finding the lady as wholesomely reposeful as ever in her effect upon my nature, but finding the unspeakable dog each time more lavish of his disgusting affection for me.

Then, one day, when I had made back to the town and was in fact traversing the main commercial thoroughfare in a dignified manner, I was made aware that the brute had broken away to follow me. Close at my heels he skulked. Strong words hissed under my breath would not repulse him, and to blows I durst not proceed, for I suddenly divined that his juxtaposition to me was exciting amused comment among certain of the natives who observed us. The fellow Hobbs, in the doorway of his bake-shop, was especially offensive, bursting into a shout of boorish laughter and directing to me the attention of a nearby group of loungers, who likewise professed to become entertained. So situated, I was of course obliged to affect unconsciousness of the awful beast, and he was presently running joyously at my side as if secure in my approval, or perhaps his brute intelligence divined that for the moment I durst not turn upon him with blows.

Nor did the true perversity of the situation at once occur to me. Not until we had gained one of the residence avenues did I realize the significance of the ill-concealed merriment we had aroused. It was not that I had been followed by a random cur, but by one known to be the dog of the lady I had called upon. I mean to say, the creature had advertised my acquaintance with his owner in a way that would lead base minds to misconstrue its extent.

Thoroughly maddened by this thought, and being now safely beyond close observers, I turned upon the animal to give it a hearty drubbing with my stick, but it drew quickly off, as if divining my intention, and when I hurled the stick at it, retrieved it, and brought it to me quite as if it forgave my hostility. Discovering at length that this method not only availed nothing but was bringing faces to neighbouring windows, and that it did not the slightest good to speak strongly to the beast, I had perforce to accompany it to its home, where I had the satisfaction of seeing its owner once more secure it firmly with the rope.

Thus far a trivial annoyance one might say, but when the next day the creature bounded up to me as I escorted homeward two ladies from the Onwards and Upwards Club, leaping upon me with extravagant manifestations of delight and trailing a length of gnawed rope, it will be seen that the thing was little short of serious.

"It's Mr. Barker," exclaimed one of the ladies, regarding me brightly.

At a cutlery shop I then bought a stout chain, escorted the brute to his home, and saw him tethered. The thing was rather getting on me. The following morning he waited for me at the Floud door and was beside himself with rapture when I appeared. He had slipped his collar. And once more I saw him moored. Each time I had apologized to Mrs. Judson for seeming to attract her pet from home, for I could not bring myself to say that the beast was highly repugnant to me, and least of all could I intimate that his public devotion to me would be seized upon by the coarser village wits to her disadvantage.

"I never saw him so fascinated with any one before," explained the lady as she once more adjusted his leash. But that afternoon, as I waited in the trap for Mr. Jackson before the post-office, the beast seemed to appear from out the earth to leap into the trap beside me. After a rather undignified struggle I ejected him, whereupon he followed the trap madly to the country club and made a farce of my golf game by retrieving the ball after every drive. This time, I learned, the child had released him.

It is enough to add that for those remaining days until the present the unspeakable creature's mad infatuation for me had made my life well-nigh a torment, to say nothing of its being a matter of low public jesting. Hardly did I dare show myself in the business centres, for as surely as I did the animal found me and crawled to fawn upon me, affecting his release each day in some novel manner. Each morning I looked abroad from my window on arising, more than likely detecting his outstretched form on the walk below, patiently awaiting my appearance, and each night I was liable to dreams of his coming upon me, a monstrous creature, sad-faced but eager, tireless, resolute, determined to have me for his own.

Musing desperately over this impossible state of affairs, I was now surprised to receive a letter from the wretched Cousin Egbert, sent by the hand of the Tuttle person. It was written in pencil on ruled sheets apparently torn from a cheap notebook, quite as if proper pens and decent stationery were not to be had, and ran as follows:

DEAR FRIEND BILL:

Well, Bill, I know God hates a quitter, but I guess I got
a streak of yellow in me wider than the Comstock lode. I was
kicking at my stirrups even before I seen that bunch of whiskers,
and when I took a flash of them and seen he was intending I

should go out before folks without any regular pants on, I says I can be pushed just so far. Well, Bill, I beat it like a bat out of hell, as I guess you know by this time, and I would like to seen them catch me as I had a good bronc. If you know whose bronc it was tell him I will make it all O.K. The bronc will be all right when he rests up some. Well, Bill, I am here on the ranche, where everything is nice, and I would never come back unless certain parties agree to do what is right. I would not speak pieces that way for the President of the U.S. if he ask me to on his bended knees. Well, Bill, I wish you would come out here yourself, where everything is nice. You can't tell what that bunch of crazies would be wanting you to do next thing with false whiskers and no right pants. I would tell them "I can be pushed just so far, and now I will go out to the ranche with Sour-dough for some time, where things are nice." Well, Bill, if you will come out Jeff Tuttle will bring you Wednesday when he comes with more grub, and you will find everything nice. I have told Jeff to bring you, so no more at present, with kind regards and hoping to see you here soon.

Your true friend,

E.G. FLOUD.

P.S. Mrs. Effie said she would broaden me out. Maybe she did, because I felt pretty flat. Ha! ha!

Truth to tell, this wild suggestion at once appealed to me. I had an impulse to withdraw for a season from the social whirl, to seek repose among the glens and gorges of this cattle plantation, and there try to adjust myself more intelligently to my strange new environment. In the meantime, I hoped, something might happen to the dog of Mrs. Judson; or he might, perhaps, in my absence outlive his curious mania for me.

Mrs. Effie, whom I now consulted, after reading the letter of Cousin Egbert, proved to be in favour of my going to him to make one last appeal to his higher nature.

"If only he'd stick out there in the brush where he belongs, I'd let him stay," she explained. "But he won't stick; he gets tired after awhile and drops in perhaps on the very night when we're entertaining some of the best people at dinner--and of course we're obliged to have him, though he's dropped whatever manners I've taught him and picked up his old rough talk, and he eats until you wonder how he can. It's awful! Sometimes I've wondered if it couldn't be adenoids--there's a lot of talk about those just now--some very select people have them, and perhaps they're what kept him back and made him so hopelessly low in his tastes, but I just know he'd never go to a doctor about them. For heaven's sake, use what influence you have to get him back here and to take his rightful place in society."

I had a profound conviction that he would never take his rightful place in society, be it the fault of adenoids or whatever; that low passion of his for being pally with all sorts made it seem that his sense of values must have been at fault from birth, and yet I could not bring myself to abandon him utterly, for, as I have intimated, something in the fellow's nature appealed to me. I accordingly murmured my sympathy discreetly and set about preparations for my journey.

Feeling instinctively that Cousin Egbert would not now be dressing for dinner, I omitted evening clothes from my box, including only a morning-suit and one of form-fitting tweeds which I fancied would do me well enough. But no sooner was my box packed than the Tuttle person informed me that I could take no box whatever. It appeared that all luggage would be strapped to the backs of animals and thus transported. Even so, when I had reduced myself to one park riding-suit and a small bundle of necessary adjuncts, I was told that the golf-sticks must be left behind. It appeared there would be no golf.

And so quite early one morning I started on this curious pilgrimage from what was called a "feed corral" in a low part of the town. Here the Tuttle person had assembled a goods-train of a half-dozen animals, the luggage being adjusted to their backs by himself and two assistants, all using language of the most disgraceful character throughout the process. The Tuttle person I had half expected to appear garbed in his native dress--Mrs. Effie had once more referred to "that Indian Jeff

Tuttle"--but he wore instead, as did his two assistants, the outing or lounge suit of the Western desperado, nor, though I listened closely, could I hear him exclaim, "Ugh! Ugh!" in moments of emotional stress as my reading had informed me that the Indian frequently does.

The two assistants, solemn-faced, ill-groomed fellows, bore the curious American names of Hank and Buck, and furiously chewed the tobacco plant at all times. After betraying a momentary interest in my smart riding-suit, they paid me little attention, at which I was well pleased, for their manners were often repellent and their abrupt, direct fashion of speech quite disconcerting.

The Tuttle person welcomed me heartily and himself adjusted the saddle to my mount, expressing the hope that I would "get my fill of scenery," and volunteering the information that my destination was "one sleep" away.

CHAPTER ELEVEN

ALTHOUGH fond of rural surroundings and always interested in nature, the adventure in which I had become involved is not one I can recommend to a person of refined tastes. I found it little enough to my own taste even during the first two hours of travel when we kept to the beaten thoroughfare, for the sun was hot, the dust stifling, and the language with which the goods-animals were berated coarse in the extreme.

Yet from this plain roadway and a country of rolling down and heather which was at least not terrifying, our leader, the Tuttle person, swerved all at once into an untried jungle, in what at the moment I supposed to be a fit of absent-mindedness, following a narrow path that led up a fearsomely slanted incline among trees and boulders of granite thrown about in the greatest disorder. He was followed, however, by the goods-animals and by the two cow-persons, so that I soon saw the new course must be intended.

The mountains were now literally quite everywhere, some higher than others, but all of a rough appearance, and uninviting in the extreme. The narrow path, moreover, became more and more difficult, and seemed altogether quite insane with its twistings and fearsome declivities. One's first thought was that at least a bit of road-metal might have been put upon it. But there was no sign of this throughout our toilsome day, nor did I once observe a rustic seat along the way, although I saw an abundance of suitable nooks for these. Needless to say, in all England there is not an estate so poorly kept up.

There being no halt made for luncheon, I began to look forward to tea-time, but what was my dismay to observe that this hour also passed unnoted. Not until night was drawing upon us did our caravan halt beside a tarn, and here I learned that we would sup and sleep, although it was distressing to observe how remote we were from proper surroundings. There was no shelter and no modern conveniences; not even a wash-hand-stand or water-jug. There was, of course, no central heating, and no electricity for one's smoothing-iron, so that one's clothing must become quite disreputable for want of pressing. Also the informal manner of cooking and eating was not what I had been accustomed to, and the idea of sleeping publicly on the bare ground was repugnant in the extreme. I mean to say, there was no *vie intime*. Truly it was a coarser type of wilderness than that which I had encountered near New York City.

The animals, being unladen, were fitted with a species of leather bracelet about their forefeet and allowed to stray at their will. A fire was built and coarse food made ready. It is hardly a thing to speak of, but their manner of preparing tea was utterly depraved, the leaves being flung into a tin of boiling water and allowed to *stew*. The result was something that I imagine etchers might use in making lines upon their metal plates. But for my day's fast I should have been unequal to this, or to the crude output of their frying-pans.

Yet I was indeed glad that no sign of my dismay had escaped me, for the cow-persons, Hank and Buck, as I discovered, had given unusual care to the repast on my account, and I should not have liked to seem unappreciative. Quite by accident I overheard the honest fellows quarrelling about an oversight: they had, it seemed, left the finger-bowls behind; each was bitterly blaming the other for this, seeming to feel that the meal could not go forward. I had not to be told that they would not ordinarily carry finger-bowls for their own use, and that the forgotten utensils must have been meant solely for my comfort. Accordingly, when the quarrel was at its highest I broke in upon it, protesting that the oversight was of no consequence, and that I was quite prepared to roughen it with them in the best of good fellowship. They were unable to conceal their chagrin at my having overheard them, and slunk off abashed to the cooking-fire. It was plain that under their repellent exteriors they concealed veins of the finest chivalry, and I took pains during the remainder of the evening to put them at their ease, asking them many questions about their wild life.

Of the dangers of the jungle by which we were surrounded the most formidable, it seemed, was not the grizzly bear, of which I had read, but an animal quaintly called the "high-behind," which lurks about camping-places such as ours and is often known to attack man in its search for tinned milk of which it is inordinately fond. The spoor of one of these beasts had been detected near our campfire by the cow-person called Buck, and he now told us of it, though having at first resolved to be silent rather than alarm us.

As we carried a supply of the animal's favourite food, I was given two of the tins with instructions to hurl them quickly at any high-behind that might approach during the night, my companions arming themselves in a similar manner. It appears that the beast has tushes similar in shape to tin openers with which it deftly bites into any tins of milk that may be thrown at it. The person called Hank had once escaped with his life only by means of a tin of milk which had caught on the sabrelike tushes of the animal pursuing him, thus rendering him harmless and easy of capture.

Needless to say, I was greatly interested in this animal of the quaint name, and resolved to remain on watch during the night in the hope of seeing one, but at this juncture we were rejoined by the Tuttle person, who proceeded to recount to Hank and Buck a highly coloured version of my regrettable encounter with Mr. C. Belknap-Jackson back in the New York wilderness, whereat they both lost interest in the high-behind and greatly embarrassed me with their congratulations upon this lesser matter. Cousin Egbert, it seemed, had most indiscreetly talked of the thing, which was now a matter of common gossip in Red Gap. Thereafter I could get from them no further information about the habits of the high-behind, nor did I remain awake to watch for one as I had resolved to, the fatigues of the day proving too much for me. But doubtless none approached during the night, as the two tins of milk with which I was armed were untouched when I awoke at dawn.

Again we set off after a barbarous breakfast, driving our laden animals ever deeper into the mountain fastness, until it seemed that none of us could ever emerge, for I had ascertained that there was not a compass in the party. There was now a certain new friendliness in the manner of the two cow-persons toward me, born, it would seem, of their knowledge of my assault upon Belknap-Jackson, and I was somewhat at a loss to know how to receive this, well intentioned though it was. I mean to say, they were undoubtedly of the servant-class, and of course one must remember one's own position, but I at length decided to be quite friendly and American with them.

The truth must be told that I was now feeling in quite a bit of a funk and should have welcomed any friendship offered me; I even found myself remembering with rather a pensive tolerance the attentions of Mr. Barker, though doubtless back in Red Gap I should have found them as loathsome as ever. My hump was due, I made no doubt, first, to my precarious position in the wilderness, but more than that to my anomalous social position, for it seemed to me now that I was neither fish nor fowl. I was no longer a gentleman's man--the familiar boundaries of that office had been swept away; on the other hand, I was most emphatically not the gentleman I had set myself up to be, and I was weary of the pretence. The friendliness of these uncouth companions, then, proved doubly welcome, for with them I could conduct myself in a natural manner, happily forgetting my former limitations and my present quite fictitious dignities.

I even found myself talking to them of cricket as we rode, telling them I had once hit an eight--fully run out it was and not an overthrow--though I dare say it meant little to them. I also took pains to describe to them the correct method of brewing tea, which they promised thereafter to observe, though this I fear they did from mere politeness.

Our way continued adventurously upward until mid-afternoon, when we began an equally adventurous descent through a jungle of pine trees, not a few of which would have done credit to one of our own parks, though there were, of course, too many of them here to be at all effective. Indeed, it may be said that from a scenic standpoint everything through which we had passed was overdone: mountains, rocks, streams, trees, all sounding a characteristic American note of exaggeration.

Then at last we came to the wilderness abode of Cousin Egbert. A rude hut of native logs it was, set in this highland glen beside a tarn. From afar we descried its smoke, and presently in the doorway observed Cousin Egbert himself, who waved cheerfully at us. His appearance gave me a shock. Quite aware of his inclination to laxness, I was yet unprepared for his present state. Never, indeed, have I seen a man so badly turned out. Too evidently unshaven since his disappearance, he was gotten up in a faded flannel shirt, open at the neck and without the sign of cravat, a pair of overalls, also faded and quite wretchedly spotty, and boots of the most shocking description. Yet in spite of this dreadful tenue he greeted me without embarrassment and indeed with a kind of artless pleasure. Truly the man was impossible, and when I observed the placard he had allowed to remain on the waistband of his overalls, boastfully alleging their indestructibility, my sympathies flew back to Mrs. Effie. There was a cartoon emblazoned on this placard, depicting the futile efforts of two teams of stout horses, each attached to a leg of the garment, to wrench it in twain. I mean to say, one might be reduced to overalls, but this blatant emblem was not a thing any gentleman need have retained. And again, observing his footgear, I was glad to recall that I had included a plentiful supply of boot-cream in my scanty luggage.

Three of the goods-animals were now unladen, their burden of provisions being piled beside the door while Cousin Egbert chatted gayly with the cow-persons and the Indian Tuttle, after which these three took their leave, being madly bent, it appeared, upon penetrating still farther into the wilderness to another cattle farm. Then, left alone with Cousin Egbert, I was not long in discovering that, strictly speaking, he had no establishment. Not only were there no servants, but there were no drains, no water-taps, no ice-machine, no scullery, no central heating, no electric wiring. His hut consisted of but a single room, and this without a floor other than the packed earth, while the appointments were such as in any civilized country would have indicated the direst poverty. Two beds of the rudest description stood in opposite corners, and one end of the room was almost wholly occupied by a stone fireplace of primitive construction, over which the owner now hovered in certain feats of cookery.

Thanks to my famished state I was in no mood to criticise his efforts, which he presently set forth upon the rough deal table in a hearty but quite inelegant manner. The meal, I am bound to say, was more than welcome to my now indiscriminating palate, though at a less urgent moment I should doubtless have found the bread soggy and the beans a pernicious mass. There was a stew of venison, however, which only the most skilful hands could have bettered, though how the man had obtained a deer was beyond me, since it was evident he possessed no shooting or deer-stalking costume. As to the tea, I made bold to speak my mind and succeeded in brewing some for myself.

Throughout the repast Cousin Egbert was constantly attentive to my needs and was more cheerful of demeanour than I had ever seen him. The hunted look about his eyes, which had heretofore always distinguished him, was now gone, and he bore himself like a free man.

"Yes, sir," he said, as we smoked over the remains of the meal, "you stay with me and I'll give you one swell little time. I'll do the cooking, and between whiles we can sit right here and play cribbage day in and day out. You can get a taste of real life without moving."

I saw then, if never before, that his deeper nature would not be aroused. Doubtless my passing success with him in Paris had marked the very highest stage of his spiritual development. I did not need to be told now that he had left off sock-suspenders forever, nor did I waste words in trying to recall him to his better self. Indeed for the moment I was too overwhelmed by fatigue even to remonstrate about his wretched lounge-suit, and I early fell asleep on one of the beds while he was still engaged in washing the metal dishes upon which we had eaten, singing the while the doleful ballad of "Rosalie, the Prairie Flower."

It seemed but a moment later that I awoke, for Cousin Egbert was again busy among the dishes, but I saw that another day had come and his song had changed to one equally sad but quite different. "In the hazel dell my Nellie's sleeping," he sang, though in a low voice and quite cheerfully. Indeed his entire repertoire of ballads was confined to the saddest themes, chiefly of desirable maidens taken off untimely either by disease or accident. Besides "Rosalie, the Prairie Flower," there was "Lovely Annie Lisle," over whom the willows waved and earthly music could not waken; another named "Sweet Alice Ben Bolt" lying in the churchyard, and still another, "Lily Dale," who was pictured "'neath the trees in the flowery vale," with the wild rose blossoming o'er the little green grave.

His face was indeed sad as he rendered these woful ballads and yet his voice and manner were of the cheeriest, and I dare say he sang without reference to their real tragedy. It was a school of American balladry quite at variance with the cheerful optimism of those I had heard from the Belknap-Jackson phonograph, where the persons are not dead at all but are gayly calling upon one another to come on and do a folkdance, or hear a band or crawl under--things of that sort. As Cousin Egbert bent over a frying pan in which ham was cooking he crooned softly:

"In the hazel dell my Nellie's sleeping,
Nellie loved so long,

While my lonely, lonely watch I'm keeping,
Nellie lost and gone."

I could attribute his choice only to that natural perversity which prompted him always to do the wrong thing, for surely this affecting verse was not meant to be sung at such a moment.

Attempting to arise, I became aware that the two days' journey had left me sadly lame and wayworn, also that my face was burned from the sun and that I had been awakened too soon. Fortunately I had with me a shilling jar of Ridley's Society Complexion Food, "the all-weather wonder," which I applied to my face with cooling results, and I then felt able to partake of a bit of the breakfast which Cousin Egbert now brought to my bedside. The ham was of course not cooked correctly and the tea was again a mere corrosive, but so anxious was my host to please me that I refrained from any criticism, though at another time I should have told him straight what I thought of such cookery.

When we had both eaten I slept again to the accompaniment of another sad song and the muted rattle of the pans as Cousin Egbert did the scullery work, and it was long past the luncheon hour when I awoke, still lame from the saddle, but greatly refreshed.

It was now that another blow befell me, for upon arising and searching through my kit I discovered that my razors had been left behind. By any thinking man the effect of this oversight will be instantly perceived. Already low in spirits, the prospect of going unshaven could but aggravate my funk. I surrendered to the wave of homesickness that swept over me. I wanted London again, London with its yellow fog and greasy pavements, I wished to buy cockles off a barrow, I longed for toasted crumpets, and most of all I longed for my old rightful station; longed to turn out a gentleman, longed for the Honourable George and our peaceful if sometimes precarious existence among people of the right sort. The continued shocks since that fateful night of the cards had told upon me. I knew now that I had not been meant for adventure. Yet here I had turned up in the most savage of lands after leading a life of dishonest pretence in a station to which I had not been born--and, for I knew not how many days, I should not be able to shave my face.

But here again a ferment stirred in my blood, some electric thrill of anarchy which had come from association with these Americans, a strange, lawless impulse toward their quite absurd ideals of equality, a monstrous ambition to be in myself some one that mattered, instead of that pretended Colonel Ruggles who, I now recalled, was to-day promised to bridge at the home of Mrs. Judge Ballard, where he would talk of hunting in the shires, of the royal enclosure at Ascot, of Hurlingham and Ranleigh, of Cowes in June, of the excellence of the converts at Chaynes-Wotten. No doubt it was a sort of madness now seized me, consequent upon the lack of shaving utensils.

I wondered desperately if there was a true place for me in this life. I had tasted their equality that day of debauch in Paris, but obviously the sensation could not permanently be maintained upon spirits. Perhaps I might obtain a post in a bank; I might become a shop-assistant, bag-man, even a pressman. These moody and unwholesome thoughts were clouding my mind as I surveyed myself in the wrinkled mirror which had seemed to suffice the uncritical Cousin Egbert for his toilet. It hung between the portrait of a champion middle-weight crouching in position and the calendar advertisement of a brewery which, as I could not fancy Cousin Egbert being in the least concerned about the day of the month, had too evidently been hung on his wall because of the coloured lithograph of a blond creature in theatrical undress who smirked most immorally.

Studying the curiously wavy effect this glass produced upon my face, I chanced to observe in a corner of the frame a printed card with the heading "Take Courage!" To my surprise the thing, when I had read it, capped my black musings upon my position in a rather uncanny way. Briefly it recited the humble beginnings of a score or more of the world's notable figures.

"Demosthenes was the son of a cutler," it began. "Horace was the son of a shopkeeper. Virgil's father was a porter. Cardinal Wolsey was the son of a butcher. Shakespeare the son of a wool-stapler." Followed the obscure parentage of such well-known persons as Milton, Napoleon, Columbus, Cromwell. Even Mohammed was noted as a shepherd and camel-driver, though it seemed rather questionable taste to include in the list one whose religion, as to family life, was rather scandalous. More to the point was the citation of various Americans who had sprung from humble beginnings: Lincoln, Johnson, Grant, Garfield, Edison. It is true that there was not, apparently, a gentleman's servant among them; they were rail-splitters, boatmen, tailors, artisans of sorts, but the combined effect was rather overwhelming.

From the first moment of my encountering the American social system, it seemed, I had been by way of becoming a rabid anarchist--that is, one feeling that he might become a gentleman regardless of his birth--and here were the disconcerting facts concerning a score of notables to confirm me in my heresy. It was not a thing to be spoken lightly of in loose discussion, but there can be no doubt that at this moment I coldly questioned the soundness of our British system, the vital marrow of which is to teach that there is a difference between men and men. To be sure, it will have been seen that I was not myself, having for a quarter year been subjected to a series of nervous shocks, and having had my mind contaminated, moreover, by being brought into daily contact with this unthinking American equality in the person of Cousin Egbert, who, I make bold to assert, had never for one instant since his doubtless obscure birth considered himself the superior of any human being whatsoever.

This much I advance for myself in extenuation of my lawless imaginings, but of them I can abate no jot; it was all at once clear to me, monstrous as it may seem, that Nature and the British Empire were at variance in their decrees, and that somehow a system was base which taught that one man is necessarily inferior to another. I dare say it was a sort of poisonous intoxication--that I should all at once declare:

"His lordship tenth Earl of Brinstead and Marmaduke Ruggles are two men; one has made an acceptable peer and one an acceptable valet, yet the twain are equal, and the system which has made one inferior socially to the other is false and bad and cannot endure." For a moment, I repeat, I saw myself a gentleman in the making--a clear fairway without bunkers from tee to green--meeting my equals with a friendly eye; and then the illumining shock, for I unconsciously added to myself, "Regarding my inferiors with a kindly tolerance." It was there I caught myself. So much a part of the system was I that, although I could readily conceive a society in which I had no superiors, I could not picture one in which I had not inferiors. The same poison that ran in the veins of their lordships ran also in the veins of their servants. I was indeed, it appeared, hopelessly inoculated. Again I read the card. Horace was the son of a shopkeeper, but I made no doubt that, after he became a popular and successful writer of Latin verse, he looked down upon his own father.

Only could it have been otherwise, I thought, had he been born in this fermenting America to no station whatever and left to achieve his rightful one.

So I mused thus licentiously until one clear conviction possessed me: that I would no longer pretend to the social superiority of one Colonel Marmaduke Ruggles. I would concede no inferiority in myself, but I would not again, before Red Gap's county families vaunt myself as other than I was. That this was more than a vagrant fancy on my part will be seen when I aver that suddenly, strangely, alarmingly, I no longer cared that I was unshaven and must remain so for an untold number of days. I welcomed the unhandsome stubble that now projected itself upon my face; I curiously wished all at once to be as badly gotten up as Cousin Egbert, with as little thought for my station in life. I would no longer refrain from doing things because they were "not done." My own taste would be the law.

It was at this moment that Cousin Egbert appeared in the doorway with four trout from the stream nearby, though how he had managed to snare them I could not think, since he possessed no correct equipment for angling. I fancy I rather overwhelmed him by exclaiming, "Hello, Sour-dough!" since never before had I addressed him in any save a formal fashion, and it is certain I embarrassed him by my next proceeding, which was to grasp his hand and shake it heartily, an action that I could explain no more than he, except that the violence of my self-communion was still upon me and required an outlet. He grinned amiably, then regarded me with a shrewd eye and demanded if I had been drinking.

"This," I said; "I am drunk with this," and held the card up to him. But when he took it interestedly he merely read the obverse side which I had not observed until now. "Go to Epstein's for Everything You Wear," it said in large type, and added, "The Square Deal Mammoth Store."

"They carry a nice stock," he said, still a bit puzzled by my tone, "though I generally trade at the Red Front." I turned the card over for him and he studied the list of humble-born notables, though from a point of view peculiarly his own. "I don't see," he began, "what right they got to rake up all that stuff about people that's dead and gone. Who cares what their folks was!" And he added, "'Horace was the son of a shopkeeper'--Horace who?" Plainly the matter did not excite him, and I saw it would be useless to try to convey to him what the items had meant to me.

"I mean to say, I'm glad to be here with you," I said.

"I knew you'd like it," he answered. "Everything is nice here."

"America is some country," I said.

"She is, she is," he answered. "And now you can bile up a pot of tea in your own way while I clean these here fish for sapper."

I made the tea. I regret to say there was not a tea cozy in the place; indeed the linen, silver, and general table equipment were sadly deficient, but in my reckless mood I made no comment.

"Your tea smells good, but it ain't got no kick to it," he observed over his first cup. "When I drench my insides with tea I sort of want it to take a hold." And still I made no effort to set him right. I now saw that in all true essentials he did not need me to set him right. For so uncouth a person he was strangely commendable and worthy.

As we sipped our tea in companionable silence, I busy with my new and disturbing thoughts, a long shout came to us from the outer distance. Cousin Egbert brightened.

"I'm darned if that ain't Ma Pettengill!" he exclaimed. "She's rid over from the Arrowhead."

We rushed to the door, and in the distance, riding down upon us at terrific speed, I indeed beheld the Mixer. A moment later she reigned in her horse before us and hoarsely rumbled her greetings. I had last seen her at a formal dinner where she was rather formidably done out in black velvet and diamonds. Now she appeared in a startling tenue of khaki riding-breeches and flannel shirt, with one of the wide-brimmed cow-person hats. Even at the moment of greeting her I could not but reflect how shocked our dear Queen would be at the sight of this riding habit.

She dismounted with hearty explanations of how she had left her "round-up" and ridden over to visit, having heard from the Tuttle person that we were here. Cousin Egbert took her horse and she entered the hut, where to my utter amazement she at once did a feminine thing. Though from her garb one at a little distance might have thought her a man, a portly, florid, carelessly attired man, she made at once for the wrinkled mirror where, after anxiously scanning her burned face for an instant, she produced powder and puff from a pocket of her shirt and daintily powdered her generous blob of a nose. Having achieved this to her apparent satisfaction, she unrolled a bundle she had carried at her saddle and donned a riding skirt, buttoning it about the waist and smoothing down its folds--before I could retire.

"There, now," she boomed, as if some satisfying finality had been brought about. Such was the Mixer. That sort of thing would never do with us, and yet I suddenly saw that she, like Cousin Egbert, was strangely commendable and worthy. I mean to say, I no longer felt it was my part to set her right in any of the social niceties. Some curious change had come upon me. I knew then that I should no longer resist America.

CHAPTER TWELVE

WITH a curious friendly glow upon me I set about helping Cousin Egbert in the preparation of our evening meal, a work from which, owing to the number and apparent difficulty of my suggestions, he presently withdrew, leaving me in entire charge. It is quite true that I have pronounced views as to the preparation and serving of food, and I dare say I embarrassed the worthy fellow without at all meaning to do so, for too many of his culinary efforts betray the fumbling touch of the amateur. And as I worked over the open fire, doing the trout to a turn, stirring the beans, and perfecting the stew with deft touches of seasoning, I worded to myself for the first time a most severe indictment against the North American cookery, based upon my observations across the continent and my experience as a diner-out in Red Gap.

I saw that it would never do with us, and that it ought, as a matter of fact, to be uplifted. Even then, while our guest chattered gossip of the town over her brown paper cigarettes, I felt the stirring of an impulse to teach Americans how to do themselves better at table. For the moment, of course, I was hampered by lack of equipment (there was not even a fish slice in the establishment), but even so I brewed proper tea and was able to impart to the simple viands a touch of distinction which they had lacked under Cousin Egbert's all-too-careless manipulation.

As I served the repast Cousin Egbert produced a bottle of the brown American whiskey at which we pegged a bit before sitting to table.

"Three rousing cheers!" said he, and the Mixer responded with "Happy days!"

As on that former occasion, the draught of spirits flooded my being with a vast consciousness of personal worth and of good feeling toward my companions. With a true insight I suddenly perceived that one might belong to the great lower middle-class in America and still matter in the truest, correctest sense of the term.

As we fell hungrily to the food, the Mixer did not fail to praise my cooking of the trout, and she and Cousin Egbert were presently lamenting the difficulty of obtaining a well-cooked meal in Red Gap. At this I boldly spoke up, declaring that American cookery lacked constructive imagination, making only the barest use of its magnificent opportunities, following certain beaten and all-too-familiar roads with a slavish stupidity.

"We nearly had a good restaurant," said the Mixer. "A Frenchman came and showed us a little flash of form, but he only lasted a month because he got home-sick. He had half the people in town going there for dinner, too, to get away from their Chinamen--and after I spent a lot of money fixing the place up for him, too."

I recalled the establishment, on the main street, though I had not known that our guest was its owner. Vacant it was now, and looking quite as if the bailiffs had been in.

"He couldn't cook ham and eggs proper," suggested Cousin Egbert. "I tried him three times, and every time he done something French to 'em that nobody had ought to do to ham and eggs."

Hereupon I ventured to assert that a too-intense nationalism would prove the ruin of any chef outside his own country; there must be a certain breadth of treatment, a blending of the best features of different schools. One must know English and French methods and yet be a slave to neither; one must even know American cookery and be prepared to adapt its half-dozen or so undoubted excellencies. From this I ventured further into a general criticism of the dinners I had eaten at Red Gap's smartest houses. Too profuse they were, I said, and too little satisfying in any one feature; too many courses, constructed, as I had observed, after photographs printed in the back pages of women's magazines; doubtless they possessed a certain artistic value as sights for the eye, but considered as food they were devoid of any inner meaning.

"Bill's right," said Cousin Egbert warmly. "Mrs. Effie, she gets up about nine of them pictures, with nuts and grated eggs and scrambled tomatoes all over 'em, and nobody knowing what's what, and even when you strike one that tastes good they's only a dab of it and you mustn't ask for any more. When I go out to dinner, what I want is to have 'em say, 'Pass up your plate, Mr. Floud, for another piece of the steak and some potatoes, and have some more squash and help yourself to the quince jelly.' That's how it had ought to be, but I keep eatin' these here little plates of cut-up things and waiting for the real stuff, and first thing I know I get a spoon-ful of coffee in something like you put eye medicine into, and I know it's all over. Last time I was out I hid up a dish of these here salted almuns under a fern and et the whole lot from time to time, kind of absent like. It helped some, but it wasn't dinner."

"Same here," put in the Mixer, saturating half a slice of bread in the sauce of the stew. "I can't afford to act otherwise than like I am a lady at one of them din-ners, but the minute I'm home I beat it for the icebox. I suppose it's all right to be socially elegant, but we hadn't ought to let it contaminate our food none. And even at that New York hotel this summer you had to make trouble to get fed proper. I wanted strawberry shortcake, and what do you reckon they dealt me? A thing look-ing like a marble palace--sponge cake and whipped cream with a few red spots in between. Well, long as we're friends here together, I may say that I raised hell until I had the chef himself up and told him exactly what to do; biscuit dough baked and prized apart and buttered, strawberries with sugar on 'em in between and on top, and plenty of regular cream. Well, after three days' trying he finally managed to get simple--he just couldn't believe I meant it at first, and kept building on the whipped cream--and the thing cost eight dollars, but you can bet he had me, even then; the bonehead smarty had sweetened the cream and grated nutmeg into it. I give up.

"And if you can't get right food in New York, how can you expect to here? And Jackson, the idiot, has just fired the only real cook in Red Gap. Yes, sir; he's let the coons go. It come out that Waterman had sneaked out that suit of his golf clothes that Kate Kenner wore in the minstrel show, so he fired them both, and now I got to support 'em, because, as long as we're friends here, I don't mind telling you I egged the coon on to do it."

I saw that she was referring to the black and his wife whom I had met at the New York camp, though it seemed quaint to me that they should be called "coons," which is, I take it, a diminutive for "raccoon," a species of ground game to be found in America.

Truth to tell, I enjoyed myself immensely at this simple but satisfying meal, feeling myself one with these homely people, and I was sorry when we had fin-ished.

"That was some little dinner itself," said the Mixer as she rolled a cigarette; "and now you boys set still while I do up the dishes." Nor would she allow either of us to assist her in this work. When she had done, Cousin Egbert proceeded to mix hot toddies from the whiskey, and we gathered about the table before the open fire.

"Now we'll have a nice home evening," said the Mixer, and to my great embarrassment she began at once to speak to myself.

"A strong man like him has got no business becoming a social butterfly," she remarked to Cousin Egbert.

"Oh, Bill's all right," insisted the latter, as he had done so many times before.

"He's all right so far, but let him go on for a year or so and he won't be a darned bit better than what Jackson is, mark my words. Just a social butterfly, wearing funny clothes and attending afternoon affairs."

"Well, I don't say you ain't right," said Cousin Egbert thoughtfully; "that's one reason I got him out here where everything is nice. What with speaking pieces like an actor, I was afraid they'd have him making more kinds of a fool of himself than what Jackson does, him being a foreigner, and his mind kind o' running on what clothes a man had ought to wear."

Hereupon, so flushed was I with the good feeling of the occasion, I told them straight that I had resolved to quit being Colonel Ruggles of the British army and associate of the nobility; that I had determined to forget all class distinctions and to become one of themselves, plain, simple, and unpretentious. It is true that I had consumed two of the hot grogs, but my mind was clear enough, and both my companions applauded this resolution.

"If he can just get his mind off clothes for a bit he might amount to something," said Cousin Egbert, and it will scarcely be credited, but at the moment I felt actually grateful to him for this admission.

"We'll think about his case," said the Mixer, taking her own second toddy, whereupon the two fell to talking of other things, chiefly of their cattle plantations and the price of beef-stock, which then seemed to be six and one half, though what this meant I had no notion. Also I gathered that the Mixer at her own cattle-farm had been watching her calves marked with her monogram, though I would never have credited her with so much sentiment.

When the retiring hour came, Cousin Egbert and I prepared to take our blankets outside to sleep, but the Mixer would have none of this.

"The last time I slept in here," she remarked, "mice was crawling over me all night, so you keep your shack and I'll bed down outside. I ain't afraid of mice, understand, but I don't like to feel their feet on my face."

And to my great dismay, though Cousin Egbert took it calmly enough, she took a roll of blankets and made a crude pallet on the ground outside, under a spreading pine tree. I take it she was that sort. The least I could do was to secure two tins of milk from our larder and place them near her cot, in case of some lurking highbehind, though I said nothing of this, not wishing to alarm her needlessly.

Inside the hut Cousin Egbert and I partook of a final toddy before retiring. He was unusually thoughtful and I had difficulty in persuading him to any conversation. Thus having noted a bearskin before my bed, I asked him if he had killed the animal.

"No," said he shortly, "I wouldn't lie for a bear as small as that." As he was again silent, I made no further approaches to him.

From my first sleep I was awakened by a long, booming yell from our guest outside. Cousin Egbert and I reached the door at the same time.

"I've got it!" bellowed the Mixer, and we went out to her in the chill night. She sat up with the blankets muffled about her.

"We start Bill in that restaurant," she began. "It come to me in a flash. I judge he's got the right ideas, and Waterman and his wife can cook for him."

"Bully!" exclaimed Cousin Egbert. "I was thinking he ought to have a gents' furnishing store, on account of his mind running to dress, but you got the best idea."

"I'll stake him to the rent," she put in.

"And I'll stake him to the rest," exclaimed Cousin Egbert delightedly, and, strange as it may seem, I suddenly saw myself a licensed victualler.

"I'll call it the 'United States Grill,'" I said suddenly, as if by inspiration.

"Three rousing cheers for the U.S. Grill!" shouted Cousin Egbert to the surrounding hills, and repairing to the hut he brought out hot toddies with which we drank success to the new enterprise. For a half-hour, I dare say, we discussed details there in the cold night, not seeing that it was quite preposterously bizarre. Returning to the hut at last, Cousin Egbert declared himself so chilled that he must have another toddy before retiring, and, although I was already feeling myself the equal of any American, I consented to join him.

Just before retiring again my attention centred a second time upon the bearskin before my bed and, forgetting that I had already inquired about it, I demanded of him if he had killed the animal. "Sure," said he; "killed it with one shot just as it was going to claw me. It was an awful big one."

Morning found the three of us engrossed with the new plan, and by the time our guest rode away after luncheon the thing was well forward and I had the Mixer's order upon her estate agent at Red Gap for admission to the vacant premises. During the remainder of the day, between games of cribbage, Cousin Egbert and I discussed the venture. And it was now that I began to foresee a certain difficulty.

How, I asked myself, would the going into trade of Colonel Marmaduke Ruggles be regarded by those who had been his social sponsors in Red Gap? I mean to say, would not Mrs. Effie and the Belknap-Jacksons feel that I had played them false? Had I not given them the right to believe that I should continue, during my stay in their town, to be one whom their county families would consider rather a personage? It was idle, indeed, for me to deny that my personality as well as my assumed origin and social position abroad had conferred a sort of prestige upon my sponsors; that on my account, in short, the North Side set had been newly armed in its battle with the Bohemian set. And they relied upon my continued influence. How, then, could I face them with the declaration that I meant to become a tradesman? Should I be doing a caddish thing, I wondered?

Putting the difficulty to Cousin Egbert, he dismissed it impatiently by saying: "Oh, shucks!" In truth I do not believe he comprehended it in the least. But then it was that I fell upon my inspiration. I might take Colonel Marmaduke Ruggles from the North Side set, but I would give them another and bigger notable in his place. This should be none other than the Honourable George, whom I would now summon. A fortnight before I had received a rather snarky letter from him demanding to know how long I meant to remain in North America and disclosing that he was in a wretched state for want of some one to look after him. And he had even hinted that in the event of my continued absence he might himself come out to America and fetch me back. His quarter's allowance, would, I knew, be due in a fortnight, and my letter would reach him, therefore, before some adventurer had sold him a system for beating the French games of chance. And my letter would be compelling.

I would make it a summons he could not resist. Thus, when I met the reproachful gaze of the C. Belknap-Jacksons and of Mrs. Effie, I should be able to tell them: "I go from you, but I leave you a better man in my place." With the Honourable George Augustus Vane-Basingwell, next Earl of Brinstead, as their house guest, I made no doubt that the North Side set would at once prevail as it never had before, the Bohemian set losing at once such of its members as really mattered, who would of course be sensible of the tremendous social importance of the Honourable George.

Yet there came moments in which I would again find myself in no end of a funk, foreseeing difficulties of an insurmountable character. At such times Cousin Egbert strove to cheer me with all sorts of assurances, and to divert my mind he took me upon excursions of the roughest sort into the surrounding jungle, in search either of fish or ground game. After three days of this my park-suit became almost a total ruin, particularly as to the trousers, so that I was glad to borrow a pair of overalls such as Cousin Egbert wore. They were a tidy fit, but, having resolved not to resist America any longer, I donned them without even removing the advertising placard.

With my ever-lengthening stubble of beard it will be understood that I now appeared as one of their hearty Western Americans of the roughest type, which was almost quite a little odd, considering my former principles. Cousin Egbert, I need hardly say, was immensely pleased with my changed appearance, and remarked that I was "sure a live wire." He also heartened me in the matter of the possible disapproval of C. Belknap-Jackson, which he had divined was the essential rabbit in my moodiness.

"I admit the guy uses beautiful language," he conceded, "and probably he's top-notched in education, but jest the same he ain't the whole seven pillars of the house of wisdom, not by a long shot. If he gets fancy with you, soak him again. You done it once." So far was the worthy fellow from divining the intimate niceties involved in my giving up a social career for trade. Nor could he properly estimate the importance of my plan to summon the Honourable George to Red Gap, merely remarking that the "Judge" was all right and a good mixer and that the boys would give him a swell time.

Our return journey to Red Gap was made in company with the Indian Tuttle, and the two cow-persons, Hank and Buck, all of whom professed themselves glad to meet me again, and they, too, were wildly enthusiastic at hearing from Cousin Egbert of my proposed business venture. Needless to say they were of a class that would bother itself little with any question of social propriety involved in my entering trade, and they were loud in their promises of future patronage. At this I again felt some misgiving, for I meant the United States Grill to possess an atmosphere of quiet refinement calculated to appeal to particular people that really mattered; and yet it was plain that, keeping a public house, I must be prepared to entertain agricultural labourers and members of the lower or working classes. For a time I debated having an ordinary for such as these, where they could be shut away from my selecter patrons, but eventually decided upon a tariff that would be prohibitive to all but desirable people. The rougher or Bohemian element, being required to spring an extra shilling, would doubtless seek other places.

For two days we again filed through mountain gorges of a most awkward character, reaching Red Gap at dusk. For this I was rather grateful, not only because of my beard and the overalls, but on account of a hat of the most shocking description which Cousin Egbert had pressed upon me when my own deer-stalker was lost in a glen. I was willing to roughen it in all good-fellowship with these worthy Americans, but I knew that to those who had remarked my careful taste in dress my present appearance would seem almost a little singular. I would rather I did not shock them to this extent.

Yet when our animals had been left in their corral, or rude enclosure, I found it would be ungracious to decline the hospitality of my new friends who wished to drink to the success of the U.S. Grill, and so I accompanied them to several public houses, though with the shocking hat pulled well down over my face. Also, as the dinner hour passed, I consented to dine with them at the establishment of a Chinese, where we sat on high stools at a counter and were served ham and eggs and some of the simpler American foods.

The meal being over, I knew that we ought to cut off home directly, but Cousin Egbert again insisted upon visiting drinking-places, and I had no mind to leave him, particularly as he was growing more and more bitter in my behalf against Mr. Belknap-Jackson. I had a doubtless absurd fear that he would seek the gentleman out and do him a mischief, though for the moment he was merely urging me to do this. It would, he asserted, vastly entertain the Indian Tuttle and the cow-persons if I were to come upon Mr. Belknap-Jackson and savage him without warning, or at least with only a paltry excuse, which he seemed proud of having devised.

"You go up to the guy," he insisted, "very polite, you understand, and ask him what day this is. If he says it's Tuesday, soak him."

"But it is Tuesday," I said.

"Sure," he replied, "that's where the joke comes in."

Of course this was the crudest sort of American humour and not to be given a moment's serious thought, so I redoubled my efforts to detach him from our honest but noisy friends, and presently had the satisfaction of doing so by pleading that I must be up early on the morrow and would also require his assistance. At parting, to my embarrassment, he insisted on leading the group in a cheer. "What's the matter with Ruggles?" they loudly demanded in unison, following the query swiftly with: "He's all right!" the "he" being eloquently emphasized.

But at last we were away from them and off into the darker avenue, to my great relief, remembering my garb. I might be a living wire, as Cousin Egbert had said, but I was keenly aware that his overalls and hat would rather convey the impression that I was what they call in the States a bad person from a bitter creek.

To my further relief, the Floud house was quite dark as we approached and let ourselves in. Cousin Egbert, however, would enter the drawing-room, flood it with light, and seat himself in an easy-chair with his feet lifted to a sofa. He then raised his voice in a ballad of an infant that had perished, rendering it most tearfully, the refrain being, "Empty is the cradle, baby's gone!" Apprehensive at this, I stole softly up the stairs and had but reached the door of my own room when I heard Mrs. Effie below. I could fancy the chilling gaze which she fastened upon the singer, and I heard her coldly demand, "Where are your feet?" Whereupon the plaintive voice of Cousin Egbert arose to me, "Just below my legs." I mean to say, he had taken the thing as a quiz in anatomy rather than as the rebuke it was meant to be. As I closed my door, I heard him add that he could be pushed just so far.

CHAPTER THIRTEEN

HAVING written and posted my letter to the Honourable George the following morning, I summoned Mr. Belknap-Jackson, conceiving it my first duty to notify him and Mrs. Effie of my trade intentions. I also requested Cousin Egbert to be present, since he was my business sponsor.

All being gathered at the Floud house, including Mrs. Belknap-Jackson, I told them straight that I had resolved to abandon my social career, brilliant though it had been, and to enter trade quite as one of their middle-class Americans. They all gasped a bit at my first words, as I had quite expected them to do, but what was my surprise, when I went on to announce the nature of my enterprise, to find them not a little intrigued by it, and to discover that in their view I should not in the least be lowering myself.

"Capital, capital!" exclaimed Belknap-Jackson, and the ladies emitted little exclamations of similar import.

"At last," said Mrs. Belknap-Jackson, "we shall have a place with tone to it. The hall above will be splendid for our dinner dances, and now we can have smart luncheons and afternoon teas."

"And a red-coated orchestra and after-theatre suppers," said Mrs. Effie.

"Only," put in Belknap-Jackson thoughtfully, "he will of course be compelled to use discretion about his patrons. The rabble, of course----" He broke off with a wave of his hand which, although not pointedly, seemed to indicate Cousin Egbert, who once more wore the hunted look about his eyes and who sat by uneasily. I saw him wince.

"Some people's money is just as good as other people's if you come right down to it," he muttered, "and Bill is out for the coin. Besides, we all got to eat, ain't we?"

Belknap-Jackson smiled deprecatingly and again waved his hand as if there were no need for words.

"That rowdy Bohemian set----" began Mrs. Effie, but I made bold to interrupt. There might, I said, be awkward moments, but I had no doubt that I should be able to meet them with a flawless tact. Meantime, for the ultimate confusion of the Bohemian set of Red Gap, I had to announce that the Honourable George Augustus Vane-Basingwell would presently be with us. With him as a member of the North Side set, I pointed out, it was not possible to believe that any desirable members of the Bohemian set would longer refuse to affiliate with the smartest people.

My announcement made quite all the sensation I had anticipated. Belknap-Jackson, indeed, arose quickly and grasped me by the hand, echoing, "The Honourable George Augustus Vane-Basingwell, brother of the Earl of Brinstead," with little shivers of ecstasy in his voice, while the ladies pealed their excitement incoherently, with "Really! really!" and "Actually coming to Red Gap--the brother of a lord!"

Then almost at once I detected curiously cold glances being darted at each other by the ladies.

"Of course we will be only too glad to put him up," said Mrs. Belknap-Jackson quickly.

"But, my dear, he will of course come to us first," put in Mrs. Effie. "Afterward, to be sure----"

"It's so important that he should receive a favourable impression," responded Mrs. Belknap-Jackson.

"That's exactly why----" Mrs. Effie came back with not a little obvious warmth. Belknap-Jackson here caught my eye.

"I dare say Ruggles and I can be depended upon to decide a minor matter like that," he said.

The ladies both broke in at this, rather sputteringly, but Cousin Egbert silenced them.

"Shake dice for him," he said--"poker dice, three throws, aces low."

"How shockingly vulgar!" hissed Mrs. Belknap-Jackson.

"Even if there were no other reason for his coming to us," remarked her husband coldly, "there are certain unfortunate associations which ought to make his entertainment here quite impossible."

"If you're calling me 'unfortunate associations,'" remarked Cousin Egbert, "you want to get it out of your head right off. I don't mind telling you, the Judge and I get along fine together. I told him when I was in Paris and Europe to look me up the first thing if ever he come here, and he said he sure would. The Judge is some mixer, believe me!"

"The 'Judge'!" echoed the Belknap-Jacksons in deep disgust.

"You come right down to it--I bet a cookie he stays just where I tell him to stay," insisted Cousin Egbert. The evident conviction of his tone alarmed his hearers, who regarded each other with pained speculation.

"Right where I tell him to stay and no place else," insisted Cousin Egbert, sensing the impression he had made.

"But this is too monstrous!" said Mr. Jackson, regarding me imploringly.

"The Honourable George," I admitted, "has been known to do unexpected things, and there have been times when he was not as sensitive as I could wish to the demands of his caste----"

"Bill is stalling--he knows darned well the Judge is a mixer," broke in Cousin Egbert, somewhat to my embarrassment, nor did any reply occur to me. There was a moment's awkward silence during which I became sensitive to a radical change in the attitude which these people bore to Cousin Egbert. They shot him looks of furtive but unmistakable respect, and Mrs. Effie remarked almost with tenderness: "We must admit that Cousin Egbert has a certain way with him."

"I dare say Floud and I can adjust the matter satisfactorily to all," remarked Belknap-Jackson, and with a jaunty affection of good-fellowship, he opened his cigarette case to Cousin Egbert.

"I ain't made up my mind yet where I'll have him stay," announced the latter, too evidently feeling his newly acquired importance. "I may have him stay one place, then again I may have him stay another. I can't decide things like that off-hand."

And here the matter was preposterously left, the aspirants for this social honour patiently bending their knees to the erstwhile despised Cousin Egbert, and the latter being visibly puffed up. By rather awkward stages they came again to a discussion of the United States Grill.

"The name, of course, might be thought flamboyant," suggested Belknap-Jackson delicately.

"But I have determined," I said, "no longer to resist America, and so I can think of no name more fitting."

"Your determination," he answered, "bears rather sinister implications. One may be vanquished by America as I have been. One may even submit; but surely one may always resist a little, may not one? One need not abjectly surrender one's finest convictions, need one?"

"Oh, shucks," put in Cousin Egbert petulantly, "what's the use of all that 'one' stuff? Bill wants a good American name for his place. Me? I first thought the 'Bon Ton Eating House' would be kind of a nice name for it, but as soon as he said the 'United States Grill' I knew it was a better one. It sounds kind of grand and important."

Belknap-Jackson here made deprecating clucks, but not too directly toward Cousin Egbert, and my choice of a name was not further criticised. I went on to assure them that I should have an establishment quietly smart rather than noisily elegant, and that I made no doubt the place would give a new tone to Red Gap, whereat they all expressed themselves as immensely pleased, and our little conference came to an end.

In company with Cousin Egbert I now went to examine the premises I was to take over. There was a spacious corner room, lighted from the front and side, which would adapt itself well to the decorative scheme I had in mind. The kitchen with its ranges I found would be almost quite suitable for my purpose, requiring but little alteration, but the large room was of course atrociously impossible in the American fashion, with unsightly walls, the floors covered with American cloth of a garish pattern, and the small, oblong tables and flimsy chairs vastly uninviting.

As to the gross ideals of the former tenant, I need only say that he had made, as I now learned, a window display of foods, quite after the manner of a draper's window: moulds of custard set in a row, flanked on either side by "pies," as the natives call their tarts, with perhaps a roast fowl or ham in the centre. Artistic vulgarity could of course go little beyond this, but almost as offensive were the abundant wall-placards pathetically remaining in place.

"Coffee like mother used to make," read one. Impertinently intimate this, professing a familiarity with one's people that would never do with us. "Try our Boston

Baked Beans," pleaded another, quite abjectly. And several others quite indelicately stated the prices at which different dishes might be had: "Irish Stew, 25 cents"; "Philadelphia Capon, 35 cents"; "Fried Chicken, Maryland, 50 cents"; "New York Fancy Broil, 40 cents." Indeed the poor chap seemed to have been possessed by a geographical mania, finding it difficult to submit the simplest viands without crediting them to distant towns or provinces.

Upon Cousin Egbert's remarking that these bedizened placards would "come in handy," I took pains to explain to him just how different the United States Grill would be. The walls would be done in deep red; the floor would be covered with a heavy Turkey carpet of the same tone; the present crude electric lighting fixtures must be replaced with indirect lighting from the ceiling and electric candlesticks for the tables. The latter would be massive and of stained oak, my general colour-scheme being red and brown. The chairs would be of the same style, comfortable chairs in which patrons would be tempted to linger. The windows would be heavily draped. In a word, the place would have atmosphere; not the loud and blaring, elegance which I had observed in the smartest of New York establishments, with shrieking decorations and tables jammed together, but an atmosphere of distinction which, though subtle, would yet impress shop-assistants, plate-layers and road-menders, hodmen, carters, cattle-persons--in short the middle-class native.

Cousin Egbert, I fear, was not properly impressed with my plan, for he looked longingly at the wall-placards, yet he made the most loyal pretence to this effect, even when I explained further that I should probably have no printed menu, which I have always regarded as the ultimate vulgarity in a place where there are any proper relations between patrons and steward. He made one wistful, timid reference to the "Try Our Merchant's Lunch for 35 cents," after which he gave in entirely, particularly when I explained that ham and eggs in the best manner would be forthcoming at his order, even though no placard vaunted them or named their price. Advertising one's ability to serve ham and eggs, I pointed out to him, would be quite like advertising that one was a member of the Church of England.

After this he meekly enough accompanied me to his bank, where he placed a thousand pounds to my credit, adding that I could go as much farther as I liked, whereupon I set in motion the machinery for decorating and furnishing the place, with particular attention to silver, linen, china, and glassware, all of which, I was resolved, should have an air of its own.

Nor did I neglect to seek out the pair of blacks and enter into an agreement with them to assist in staffing my place. I had feared that the male black might have resolved to return to his adventurous life of outlawry after leaving the employment of Belknap-Jackson, but I found him peacefully inclined and entirely willing to accept service with me, while his wife, upon whom I would depend for much of the actual cooking, was wholly enthusiastic, admiring especially my colour-scheme of reds. I observed at once that her almost exclusive notion of preparing food was to fry it, but I made no doubt that I would be able to broaden her scope, since there are of course things that one simply does not fry.

The male black, or raccoon, at first alarmed me not a little by reason of threats he made against Belknap-Jackson on account of having been shopped. He nursed an intention, so he informed me, of putting snake-dust in the boots of his late employer and so bringing evil upon him, either by disease or violence, but in this I discouraged him smartly, apprising him that the Belknap-Jacksons would doubtless be among our most desirable patrons, whereupon his wife promised for him that he would do nothing of the sort. She was a native of formidable bulk, and her menacing glare at her consort as she made this promise gave me instant confidence in her power to control him, desperate fellow though he was.

Later in the day, at the door of the silversmith's, Cousin Egbert hailed the pressman I had met on the evening of my arrival, and insisted that I impart to him the details of my venture. The chap seemed vastly interested, and his sheet the following morning published the following:

THE DELMONICO OF THE WEST

Colonel Marmaduke Ruggles of London and Paris, for the past two months a social favourite in Red Gap's select North Side set, has decided to cast his lot among us and will henceforth be reckoned as one of our leading business men. The plan of the Colonel is nothing less than to give Red Gap a truly elite and recherche restaurant after the best models of London and Paris, to which purpose he will devote a considerable portion

of his ample means. The establishment will occupy the roomy
corner store of the Pettengill block, and orders have already
been placed for its decoration and furnishing, which will be
sumptuous beyond anything yet seen in our thriving metropolis.

In speaking of his enterprise yesterday, the Colonel remarked,
with a sly twinkle in his eye, "Demosthenes was the son of a
cutler, Cromwell's father was a brewer, your General Grant was
a tanner, and a Mr. Garfield, who held, I gather, an important
post in your government, was once employed on a canal-ship, so
I trust that in this land of equality it will not be presumptuous
on my part to seek to become the managing owner of a restaurant
that will be a credit to the fastest growing town in the state.

"You Americans have," continued the Colonel in his dry, inimitable
manner, "a bewildering variety of foodstuffs, but I trust I may
be forgiven for saying that you have used too little constructive
imagination in the cooking of it. In the one matter of tea,
for example, I have been obliged to figure in some episodes
that were profoundly regrettable. Again, amid the profusion of
fresh vegetables and meats, you are becoming a nation of tinned
food eaters, or canned food as you prefer to call it. This,
I need hardly say, adds to your cost of living and also makes
you liable to one of the most dreaded of modern diseases, a
disease whose rise can be traced to the rise of the tinned-food
industry. Your tin openers rasp into the tin with the result
that a fine sawdust of metal must drop into the contents and
so enter the human system. The result is perhaps negligible in
a large majority of cases, but that it is not universally so
is proved by the prevalence of appendicitis. Not orange or
grape pips, as was so long believed, but the deadly fine rain
of metal shavings must be held responsible for this scourge.
I need hardly say that at the United States Grill no tinned

food will be used."

This latest discovery of the Colonel's is important if true.
Be that as it may, his restaurant will fill a long-felt want,
and will doubtless prove to be an important factor in the social
gayeties of our smart set. Due notice of its opening will be
given in the news and doubtless in the advertising columns of
this journal.

Again I was brought to marvel at a peculiarity of the American press, a certain childish eagerness for marvels and grotesque wonders. I had given but passing thought to my remarks about appendicitis and its relation to the American tinned-food habit, nor, on reading the chap's screed, did they impress me as being fraught with vital interest to thinking people; in truth, I was more concerned with the comparison of myself to a restaurateur of the crude new city of New York, which might belittle rather than distinguish me, I suspected. But what was my astonishment to perceive in the course of a few days that I had created rather a sensation, with attending newspaper publicity which, although bizarre enough, I am bound to say contributed not a little to the consideration in which I afterward came to be held by the more serious-minded persons of Red Gap.

Busied with the multitude of details attending my installation, I was called upon by another press chap, representing a Spokane sheet, who wished me to elaborate my views concerning the most probable cause of appendicitis, which I found myself able to do with some eloquence, reciting among other details that even though the metal dust might be of an almost microscopic fineness, it could still do a mischief to one's appendix. The press chap appeared wholly receptive to my views, and, after securing details of my plan to smarten Red Gap with a restaurant of real distinction, he asked so civilly for a photographic portrait of myself that I was unable to refuse him. The thing was a snap taken of me one morning at Chaynes-Wotten by Higgins, the butler, as I stood by his lordship's saddle mare. It was not by any means the best likeness I have had, but there was a rather effective bit of background disclosing the driveway and the facade of the East Wing.

This episode I had well-nigh forgotten when on the following Sunday I found the thing emblazoned across a page of the Spokane sheet under a shrieking head-line: "Can Opener Blamed for Appendicitis." A secondary heading ran, "Famous British Sportsman and Bon Vivant Advances Novel Theory." Accompanying this was a print of the photograph entitled, "Colonel Marmaduke Ruggles with His Favourite Hunter, at His English Country Seat."

Although the article made suitable reference to myself and my enterprise, it was devoted chiefly to a discussion of my tin-opening theory and was supplemented by a rather snarky statement signed by a physician declaring it to be nonsense. I thought the fellow might have chosen his words with more care, but again dismissed the matter from my mind. Yet this was not to be the last of it. In due time came a New York sheet with a most extraordinary page. "Titled Englishman Learns Cause of Appendicitis," read the heading in large, muddy type. Below was the photograph of myself, now entitled, "Sir Marmaduke Ruggles and His Favourite Hunter." But this was only one of the illustrations. From the upper right-hand corner a gigantic hand wielding a tin-opener rained a voluminous spray of metal, presumably, upon a cowering wretch in the lower left-hand corner, who was quite plainly all in. There were tables of statistics showing the increase, side by side of appendicitis and the tinned-food industry, a matter to which I had devoted, said the print, years of research before announcing my discovery. Followed statements from half a dozen distinguished surgeons, each signed autographically, all but one rather bluntly dis-agreeing with me, insisting that the tin-opener cuts cleanly and, if not man's best friend, should at least be considered one of the triumphs of civilization. The only exception announced that he was at present conducting laboratory experiments with a view to testing my theory and would disclose his results in due time. Mean-time, he counselled the public to be not unduly alarmed.

Of the further flood of these screeds, which continued for the better part of a year, I need not speak. They ran the gamut from serious leaders in medical journals to paid ridicule of my theory in advertisements printed by the food-tinning per-sons, and I have to admit that in the end the public returned to a full confidence in its tinned foods. But that is beside the point, which was that Red Gap had become intensely interested in the United States Grill, and to this I was not averse, though I would rather I had been regarded as one of their plain, common sort, instead of the fictitious Colonel which Cousin Egbert's well-meaning stupidity had foisted upon the town. The "Sir Marmaduke Ruggles and His Favourite Hunter" had been especially repugnant to my finer taste, particularly as it was seized upon by the cheap one-and-six fellow Hobbs for some of his coarsest humour, he more than once referring to that detestable cur of Mrs. Judson's, who had quickly resumed his allegiance to me, as my "hunting pack."

The other tradesmen of the town, I am bound to say, exhibited a friendly interest in my venture which was always welcome and often helpful. Even one of my competitors showed himself to be a dead sport by coming to me from time to time with hints and advice. He was an entirely worthy person who advertised his restaurant as "Bert's Place." "Go to Bert's Place for a Square Meal," was his favoured line in the public prints. He, also, I regret to say, made a practice of displaying cooked foods in his show-window, the window carrying the line in enamelled letters, "Tables Reserved for Ladies."

Of course between such an establishment and my own there could be little in common, and I was obliged to reject a placard which he offered me, reading, "No Checks Cashed. This Means You!" although he and Cousin Egbert warmly advised that I display it in a conspicuous place. "Some of them dead beats in the North Side set will put you sideways if you don't," warned the latter, but I held firmly to the line of quiet refinement which I had laid down, and explained that I could allow no such inconsiderate mention of money to be obtruded upon the notice of my guests. I would devise some subtler protection against the dead beet-roots.

In the matter of music, however, I was pleased to accept the advice of Cousin Egbert. "Get one of them musical pianos that you put a nickel in," he counselled me, and this I did, together with an assorted repertoire of selections both classical and popular, the latter consisting chiefly of the ragging time songs to which the native Americans perform their folkdances.

And now, as the date of my opening drew near, I began to suspect that its social values might become a bit complicated. Mrs. Belknap-Jackson, for example, approached me in confidence to know if she might reserve all the tables in my establishment for the opening evening, remarking that it would be as well to put the correct social cachet upon the place at once, which would be achieved by her inviting only the desirable people. Though she was all for settling the matter at once, something prompted me to take it under consideration.

The same evening Mrs. Effie approached me with a similar suggestion, remarking that she would gladly take it upon herself to see that the occasion was unmarred by the presence of those one would not care to meet in one's own home. Again I was non-committal, somewhat to her annoyance.

The following morning I was sought by Mrs. Judge Ballard with the information that much would depend upon my opening, and if the matter were left entirely in her hands she would be more than glad to insure its success. Of her, also, I begged a day's consideration, suspecting then that I might be compelled to ask these three social leaders to unite amicably as patronesses of an affair that was bound to have a supreme social significance. But as I still meditated profoundly over the complication late that afternoon, overlooking in the meanwhile an electrician who was busy with my shaded candlesticks, I was surprised by the self-possessed entrance of the leader of the Bohemian set, the Klondike person of whom I have spoken. Again I was compelled to observe that she was quite the most smartly gowned woman in Red Gap, and that she marvellously knew what to put on her head.

She coolly surveyed my decorations and such of the furnishings as were in place before addressing me.

"I wish to engage one of your best tables," she began, "for your opening night--the tenth, isn't it?--this large one in the corner will do nicely. There will be eight of us. Your place really won't be half bad, if your food is at all possible."

The creature spoke with a sublime effrontery, quite as if she had not helped a few weeks before to ridicule all that was best in Red Gap society, yet there was that about her which prevented me from rebuking her even by the faintest shade in my manner. More than this, I suddenly saw that the Bohemian set would be a factor in my trade which I could not afford to ignore. While I affected to consider her request she tapped the toe of a small boot with a correctly rolled umbrella, lifting her chin rather attractively meanwhile to survey my freshly done ceiling. I may say here that the effect of her was most compelling, and I could well understand the bitterness with which the ladies of the Onwards and Upwards Society had gossiped her to rags. Incidently, this was the first correctly rolled umbrella, saving my own, that I had seen in North America.

"I shall be pleased," I said, "to reserve this table for you--eight places, I believe you said?"

She left me as a duchess might have. She was that sort. I felt almost quite un-equal to her. And the die was cast. I faced each of the three ladies who had previously approached me with the declaration that I was a licensed victualler, bound to serve all who might apply. That while I was keenly sensitive to the social aspects of my business, it was yet a business, and I must, therefore, be in supreme control. In justice to myself I could not exclusively entertain any faction of the North Side set, nor even the set in its entirety. In each instance, I added that I could not debar from my tables even such members of the Bohemian set as conducted themselves in a seemly manner. It was a difficult situation, calling out all my tact, yet I faced it with a firmness which was later to react to my advantage in ways I did not yet dream of.

So engrossed for a month had I been with furnishers, decorators, char persons, and others that the time of the Honourable George's arrival drew on quite before I realized it. A brief and still snarky note had apprised me of his intention to come out to North America, whereupon I had all but forgotten him, until a telegram from Chicago or one of those places had warned me of his imminence. This I displayed to Cousin Egbert, who, much pleased with himself, declared that the Honourable George should be taken to the Floud home directly upon his arrival.

"I meant to rope him in there on the start," he confided to me, "but I let on I wasn't decided yet, just to keep 'em stirred up. Mrs. Effie she butters me up with soft words every day of my life, and that Jackson lad has offered me about ten thousand of them vegetable cigarettes, but I'll have to throw him down. He's the human fliv-ver. Put him in a car of dressed beef and he'd freeze it between here and Spokane. Yes, sir; you could cut his ear off and it wouldn't bleed. I ain't going to run the Judge against no such proposition like that." Of course the poor chap was speaking his own backwoods metaphor, as I am quite sure he would have been incapable of mu-tilating Belknap-Jackson, or even of imprisoning him in a goods van of beef. I mean to say, it was merely his way of speaking and was not to be taken at all literally.

As a result of his ensuing call upon the pressman, the sheet of the following morning contained word of the Honourable George's coming, the facts being not garbled more than was usual with this chap.

RED GAP'S NOTABLE GUEST

En route for our thriving metropolis is a personage no
less distinguished than the Honourable George Augustus
Vane-Basingwell, only brother and next in line of
succession to his lordship the Earl of Brinstead, the
well-known British peer of London, England. Our noble
visitor will be the house guest of Senator and Mrs.
J. K. Floud, at their palatial residence on Ophir Avenue,
where he will be extensively entertained, particularly by
our esteemed fellow-townsman, Egbert G. Floud, with whom
he recently hobnobbed during the latter's stay in Paris,
France. His advent will doubtless prelude a season of
unparalleled gayety, particularly as Mr. Egbert Floud
assures us that the "Judge," as he affectionately calls
him, is "sure some mixer." If this be true, the gentleman
has selected a community where his talent will find ample
scope, and we bespeak for his lordship a hearty welcome.

CHAPTER FOURTEEN

I must do Cousin Egbert the justice to say that he showed a due sense of his responsibility in meeting the Honourable George. By general consent the honour had seemed to fall to him, both the Belknap-Jacksons and Mrs. Effie rather timidly conceding his claim that the distinguished guest would prefer it so. Indeed, Cousin Egbert had been loudly arrogant in the matter, speaking largely of his European intimacy with the "Judge" until, as he confided to me, he "had them all bisoned," or, I believe, "buffaloed" is the term he used, referring to the big-game animal that has been swept from the American savannahs.

At all events no one further questioned his right to be at the station when the Honourable George arrived, and for the first time almost since his own homecoming he got himself up with some attention to detail. If left to himself I dare say he would have donned frock-coat and top-hat, but at my suggestion he chose his smartest lounge-suit, and I took pains to see that the minor details of hat, boots, hose, gloves, etc., were studiously correct without being at all assertive.

For my own part, I was also at some pains with my attire going consciously a bit further with details than Cousin Egbert, thinking it best the Honourable George should at once observe a change in my bearing and social consequence so that nothing in his manner toward me might embarrassingly publish our former relations. The stick, gloves, and monocle would achieve this for the moment, and once alone I meant to tell him straight that all was over between us as master and man, we having passed out of each other's lives in that respect. If necessary, I meant to read to him certain passages from the so-called "Declaration of Independence," and to show him the fateful little card I had found, which would acquaint him, I made no doubt, with the great change that had come upon me, after which our intimacy would rest solely upon the mutual esteem which I knew to exist between us. I mean to say, it would never have done for one moment at home, but finding ourselves together in this wild and lawless country we would neither of us try to resist America, but face each other as one equal native to another.

Waiting on the station platform with Cousin Egbert, he confided to the loungers there that he was come to meet his friend Judge Basingwell, whereat all betrayed a friendly interest, though they were not at all persons that mattered, being of the semi-leisured class who each day went down, as they put it, "to see Number Six go through." There was thus a rather tense air of expectancy when the train pulled in. From one of the Pullman night coaches emerged the Honourable George, preceded by a blackamoor or raccoon bearing bags and bundles, and followed by another uniformed raccoon and a white guard, also bearing bags and bundles, and all betraying a marked anxiety.

One glance at the Honourable George served to confirm certain fears I had suffered regarding his appearance. Topped by a deer-stalking fore-and-aft cap in an inferior state of preservation, he wore the jacket of a lounge-suit, once possible, doubtless, but now demoded, and a blazered golfing waistcoat, striking for its poisonous greens, trousers from an outing suit that I myself had discarded after it came to me, and boots of an entirely shocking character. Of his cravat I have not the heart to speak, but I may mention that all his garments were quite horrid with wrinkles and seemed to have been slept in repeatedly.

Cousin Egbert at once rushed forward to greet his guest, while I busied myself in receiving the hand-luggage, wishing to have our guest effaced from the scene and secluded, with all possible speed. There were three battered handbags, two rolls of travelling rugs, a stick-case, a dispatch-case, a pair of binoculars, a hat-box, a topcoat, a storm-coat, a portfolio of correspondence materials, a camera, a medicine-case, some of these lacking either strap or handle. The attendants all emitted hearty sighs of relief when these articles had been deposited upon the platform. Without being told, I divined that the Honourable George had greatly worried them during the long journey with his fretful demands for service, and I tipped them handsomely while he was still engaged with Cousin Egbert and the latter's station-lounging friends to whom he was being presented. At last, observing me, he came forward, but halted on surveying the luggage, and screamed hoarsely to the last attendant who was now boarding the train. The latter vanished, but reappeared, as the train moved off, with two more articles, a vacuum night-flask and a tin of charcoal biscuits, the absence of which had been swiftly detected by their owner.

It was at that moment that one of the loungers nearby made a peculiar observation. "Gee!" said he to a native beside him, "it must take an awful lot of trouble to be an Englishman." At the moment this seemed to me to be pregnant with meaning, though doubtless it was because I had so long been a resident of the North American wilds.

Again the Honourable George approached me and grasped my hand before certain details of my attire and, I fancy, a certain change in my bearing, attracted his notice. Perhaps it was the single glass. His grasp of my hand relaxed and he rubbed his eyes as if dazed from a blow, but I was able to carry the situation off quite nicely under cover of the confusion attending his many bags and bundles, being helped also at the moment by the deeply humiliating discovery of a certain omission from his attire. I could not at first believe my eyes and was obliged to look again and again, but there could be no doubt about it: the Honourable George was wearing a single spat!

I cried out at this, pointing, I fancy, in a most undignified manner, so terrific had been the shock of it, and what was my amazement to hear him say: "But I *had* only one, you silly! How could I wear 'em both when the other was lost in that bally rabbit-hutch they put me in on shipboard? No bigger than a parcels-lift!" And he had too plainly crossed North America in this shocking state! Glad I was then that Belknap-Jackson was not present. The others, I dare say, considered it a mere freak of fashion. As quickly as I could, I hustled him into the waiting carriage, piling his luggage about him to the best advantage and hurrying Cousin Egbert after him as rapidly as I could, though the latter, as on the occasion of my own arrival, halted our departure long enough to present the Honourable George to the driver.

"Judge, shake hands with my friend Eddie Pierce." adding as the ceremony was performed, "Eddie keeps a good team, any time you want a hack-ride."

"Sure, Judge," remarked the driver cordially. "Just call up Main 224, any time. Any friend of Sour-dough's can have anything they want night or day." Whereupon he climbed to his box and we at last drove away.

The Honourable George had continued from the moment of our meeting to glance at me in a peculiar, side-long fashion. He seemed fascinated and yet unequal to a straight look at me. He was undoubtedly dazed, as I could discern from his absent manner of opening the tin of charcoal biscuits and munching one. I mean to say, it was too obviously a mere mechanical impulse.

"I say," he remarked to Cousin Egbert, who was beaming fondly at him, "how strange it all is! It's quite foreign."

"The fastest-growing little town in the State," said Cousin Egbert.

"But what makes it grow so silly fast?" demanded the other.

"Enterprise and industries," answered Cousin Egbert loftily.

"Nothing to make a dust about," remarked the Honourable George, staring glassily at the main business thoroughfare. "I've seen larger towns--scores of them."

"You ain't begun to see this town yet," responded Cousin Egbert loyally, and he called to the driver, "Has he, Eddie?"

"Sure, he ain't!" said the driver person genially. "Wait till he sees the new waterworks and the sash-and-blind factory!"

"Is he one of your gentleman drivers?" demanded the Honourable George. "And why a blind factory?"

"Oh, Eddie's good people all right," answered the other, "and the factory turns out blinds and things."

"Why turn them out?" he left this and continued: "He's like that American Johnny in London that drives his own coach to Brighton, yes? Ripping idea! Gentleman driver. But I say, you know, I'll sit on the box with him. Pull up a bit, old son!"

To my consternation the driver chap halted, and before I could remonstrate the Honourable George had mounted to the box beside him. Thankful I was we had left the main street, though in the residence avenue where the change was made we attracted far more attention than was desirable. "Didn't I tell you he was some mixer?" demanded Cousin Egbert of me, but I was too sickened to make any suitable response. The Honourable George's possession of a single spat was now flaunted, as it were, in the face of Red Gap's best families.

"How foreign it all is!" he repeated, turning back to us, yet with only his sideglance for me. "But the American Johnny in London had a much smarter coach than this, and better animals, too. You're not up to his class yet, old thing!"

"That dish-faced pinto on the off side," remarked the driver, "can outrun anything in this town for fun, money, or marbles."

"Marbles!" called the Honourable George to us; "why marbles? Silly things! It's all bally strange! And why do your villagers stare so?"

"Some little mixer, all right, all right," murmured Cousin Egbert in a sort of ecstasy, as we drew up at the Floud home. "And yet one of them guys back there called him a typical Britisher. You bet I shut him up quick--saying a thing like that about a plumb stranger. I'd 'a' mixed it with him right there except I thought it was better to have things nice and not start something the minute the Judge got here."

With all possible speed I hurried the party indoors, for already faces were appearing at the windows of neighbouring houses. Mrs. Effie, who met us, allowed her glare at Cousin Egbert, I fancy, to affect the cordiality of her greeting to the Honourable George; at least she seemed to be quite as dazed as he, and there was a moment of constraint before he went on up to the room that had been prepared for him. Once safely within the room I contrived a moment alone with him and removed his single spat, not too gently, I fear, for the nervous strain since his arrival had told upon me.

"You have reason to be thankful," I said, "that Belknap-Jackson was not present to witness this."

"They cost seven and six," he muttered, regarding the one spat wistfully. "But why Belknap-Jackson?"

"Mr. C. Belknap-Jackson of Boston and Red Gap," I returned sternly. "He does himself perfectly. To think he might have seen you in this rowdyish state!" And I hastened to seek a presentable lounge-suit from his bags.

"Everything is so strange," he muttered again, quite helplessly. "And why the mural decoration at the edge of the settlement? Why keep one's eye upon it? Why should they do such things? I say, it's all quite monstrous, you know."

I saw that indeed he was quite done for with amazement, so I ran him a bath and procured him a dish of tea. He rambled oddly at moments of things the guard on the night-coach had told him of North America, of Niagara Falls, and Missouri and other objects of interest. He was still almost quite a bit dotty when I was obliged to leave him for an appointment with the raccoon and his wife to discuss the menu of my opening dinner, but Cousin Egbert, who had rejoined us, was listening sympathetically. As I left, the two were pegging it from a bottle of hunting sherry which the Honourable George had carried in his dispatch-case. I was about to warn him that he would come out spotted, but instantly I saw that there must be an end to such surveillance. I could not manage an enterprise of the magnitude of the United States Grill and yet have an eye to his meat and drink. I resolved to let spots come as they would.

On all hands I was now congratulated by members of the North Side set upon the master-stroke I had played in adding the Honourable George to their number. Not only did it promise to reunite certain warring factions in the North Side set itself, but it truly bade fair to disintegrate the Bohemian set. Belknap-Jackson wrung my hand that afternoon, begging me to inform the Honourable George that he would call on the morrow to pay his respects. Mrs. Judge Ballard besought me to engage him for an early dinner, and Mrs. Effie, it is needless to say, after recovering from the shock of his arrival, which she attributed to Cousin Egbert's want of taste, thanked me with a wealth of genuine emotion.

Only by slight degrees, then, did it fall to be noticed that the Honourable George did not hold himself to be too strictly bound by our social conventions as to whom one should be pally with. Thus, on the morrow, at the hour when the Belknap-Jacksons called, he was regrettably absent on what Cousin Egbert called "a hack-ride" with the driver person he had met the day before, nor did they return until after the callers had waited the better part of two hours. Cousin Egbert, as usual, received the blame for this, yet neither of the Belknap-Jacksons nor Mrs. Effie dared to upbraid him.

Being presented to the callers, I am bound to say that the Honourable George showed himself to be immensely impressed by Belknap-Jackson, whom I had never beheld more perfectly vogue in all his appointments. He became, in fact, rather moody in the presence of this subtle niceness of detail, being made conscious, I dare say, of his own sloppy lounge-suit, rumpled cravat, and shocking boots, and despite Belknap-Jackson's amiable efforts to draw him into talk about hunting in the shires and our county society at home, I began to fear that they would not hit it off together. The Honourable George did, however, consent to drive with his caller the following day, and I relied upon the tandem to recall him to his better self. But when the callers had departed he became quite almost plaintive to me.

"I say, you know, I shan't be wanted to pal up much with that chap, shall I? I mean to say, he wears so many clothes. They make me writhe as if I wore them myself. It won't do, you know."

I told him very firmly that this was piffle of the most wretched sort. That his caller wore but the prescribed number of garments, each vogue to the last note, and that he was a person whom one must know. He responded pettishly that he vastly preferred the gentleman driver with whom he had spent the afternoon, and "Sourdough," as he was now calling Cousin Egbert.

"Jolly chaps, with no swank," he insisted. "We drove quite almost everywhere--waterworks, cemetery, sash-and-blind factory. You know I thought 'blind factory' was some of their bally American slang for the shop of a chap who made eyeglasses and that sort of thing, but nothing of the kind. They saw up timbers there quite all over the place and nail them up again into articles. It's all quite foreign."

Nor was his account of his drive with Belknap-Jackson the following day a bit more reassuring.

"He wouldn't stop again at the sash-and-blind factory, where I wished to see the timbers being sawed and nailed, but drove me to a country club which was not in the country and wasn't a club; not a human there, not even a barman. Fancy a club of that sort! But he took me to his own house for a glass of sherry and a biscuit, and there it wasn't so rotten. Rather a mother-in-law I think, she is--bally old booming grenadier--topping sort--no end of fun. We palled up immensely and I quite forgot the Jackson chap till it was time for him to drive me back to these diggings. Rather sulky he was, I fancy; uppish sort. Told him the old one was quite like old Caroline, dowager duchess of Clewe, but couldn't tell if it pleased him. Seemed to like it and seemed not to: rather uncertain.

"Asked him why the people of the settlement pronounced his name 'Belknap Hyphen Jackson,' and that seemed to make him snarky again. I mean to say names with hyphen marks in 'em--I'd never heard the hyphen pronounced before, but everything is so strange. He said only the lowest classes did it as a form of coarse wit, and that he was wasting himself here. Wouldn't stay another day if it were not for family reasons. Queer sort of wheeze to say 'hyphen' in a chap's name as if it were a word, when it wasn't at all. The old girl, though--bellower she is--perfectly top-hole; familiar with cattle--all that sort of thing. Sent away the chap's sherry and had 'em bring whiskey and soda. The hyphen chap fidgeted a good bit--nervous sort, I take it. Looked through a score of magazines, I dare say, when he found we didn't notice him much; turned the leaves too fast to see anything, though; made noises and coughed--that sort of thing. Fine old girl. Daughter, hyphen chap's wife, tried to talk, too, some rot about the season being well on here, and was there a good deal of society in London, and would I be free for dinner on the ninth?

"Silly chatter! old girl talked sense: cattle, mines, timber, blind factory, two-year olds, that kind of thing. Shall see her often. Not the hyphen chap, though; too much like one of those Bond Street milliner-chap managers."

Vague misgivings here beset me as to the value of the Honourable George to the North Side set. Nor could I feel at all reassured on the following day when Mrs. Effie held an afternoon reception in his honour. That he should be unaware of the event's importance was to be expected, for as yet I had been unable to get him to take the Red Gap social crisis seriously. At the hour when he should have been dressed and ready I found him playing at cribbage with Cousin Egbert in the latter's apartment, and to my dismay he insisted upon finishing the rubber although guests were already arriving.

Even when the game was done he flatly refused to dress suitably, declaring that his lounge-suit should be entirely acceptable to these rough frontier people, and he consented to go down at all only on condition that Cousin Egbert would accompany him. Thereafter for an hour the two of them drank tea uncomfortably as often as it was given them, and while the Honourable George undoubtedly made his impression, I could not but regret that he had so few conversational graces.

How different, I reflected, had been my own entree into this county society! As well as I might I again carried off the day for the Honourable George, endeavouring from time to time to put him at his ease, yet he breathed an unfeigned sigh of relief when the last guest had left and he could resume his cribbage with Cousin Egbert. But he had received one impression of which I was glad: an impression of my own altered social quality, for I had graced the occasion with an urbanity which was as far beyond him as it must have been astonishing. It was now that he began to take seriously what I had told him of my business enterprise, so many of the guests having mentioned it to him in terms of the utmost enthusiasm. After my first accounts to him he had persisted in referring to it as a tuck-shop, a sort of place where schoolboys would exchange their halfpence for toffy, sweet-cakes, and marbles.

Now he demanded to be shown the premises and was at once duly impressed both with their quiet elegance and my own business acumen. How it had all come about, and why I should be addressed as "Colonel Ruggles" and treated as a person of some importance in the community, I dare say he has never comprehended to this day. As I had planned to do, I later endeavoured to explain to him that in North America persons were almost quite equal to one another--being born so--but at this he told me not to be silly and continued to regard my rise as an insoluble part of the strangeness he everywhere encountered, even after I added that Demosthenes was the son of a cutler, that Cardinal Wolsey's father had been a pork butcher, and that Garfield had worked on a canal-boat. I found him quite hopeless. "Chaps go dotty talkin' that piffle," was his comment.

At another time, I dare say, I should have been rather distressed over this inability of the Honourable George to comprehend and adapt himself to the peculiarities of American life as readily as I had done, but just now I was quite too taken up with the details of my opening to give it the deeper consideration it deserved. In fact, there were moments when I confessed to myself that I did not care tuppence about it, such was the strain upon my executive faculties. When decorators and furnishers had done their work, when the choice carpet was laid, when the kitchen and table equipments were completed to the last detail, and when the lighting was artistically correct, there was still the matter of service.

As to this, I conceived and carried out what I fancy was rather a brilliant stroke, which was nothing less than to eliminate the fellow Hobbs as a social factor of even the Bohemian set. In contracting with him for my bread and rolls, I took an early opportunity of setting the chap in his place, as indeed it was not difficult to do when he had observed the splendid scale on which I was operating. At our second interview he was removing his hat and addressing me as "sir."

While I have found that I can quite gracefully place myself on a level with the middle-class American, there is a serving type of our own people to which I shall eternally feel superior; the Hobbs fellow was of this sort, having undeniably the soul of a lackey. In addition to jobbing his bread and rolls, I engaged him as pantry man, and took on such members of his numerous family as were competent. His wife was to assist my raccoon cook in the kitchen, three of his sons were to serve as waiters, and his youngest, a lad in his teens, I installed as vestiare, garbing him in a smart uniform and posting him to relieve my gentleman patrons of their hats and top-coats. A daughter was similarly installed as maid, and the two achieved an effect of smartness unprecedented in Red Gap, an effect to which I am glad to say that the community responded instantly.

In other establishments it was the custom for patrons to hang their garments on hat-pegs, often under a printed warning that the proprietor would disclaim responsibility in case of loss. In the one known as "Bert's Place" indeed the warning was positively vulgar: "Watch Your Overcoat." Of course that sort of coarseness would have been impossible in my own place.

As another important detail I had taken over from Mrs. Judson her stock of jellies and compotes which I had found to be of a most excellent character, and had ordered as much more as she could manage to produce, together with cut flowers from her garden for my tables. She, herself, being a young woman of the most pleasing capabilities, had done a bit of charring for me and was now to be in charge of the glassware, linen, and silver. I had found her, indeed, highly sympathetic with my highest aims, and not a few of her suggestions as to management proved to be entirely sound. Her unspeakable dog continued his quite objectionable advances to me at every opportunity, in spite of my hitting him about, rather, when I could do so unobserved, but the sinister interpretation that might be placed upon this by the baser-minded was now happily answered by the circumstance of her being in my employment. Her child, I regret to say, was still grossly overfed, seldom having its face free from jam or other smears. It persisted, moreover, in twisting my name into "Ruggums," which I found not a little embarrassing.

The night of my opening found me calmly awaiting the triumph that was due me. As some one has said of Napoleon, I had won my battle in my tent before the firing of a single shot. I mean to say, I had looked so conscientiously after details, even to assuring myself that Cousin Egbert and the Honourable George would appear in evening dress, my last act having been to coerce each of them into purchasing varnished boots, the former submitting meekly enough, though the Honourable George insisted it was a silly fuss.

At seven o'clock, having devoted a final inspection to the kitchen where the female raccoon was well on with the dinner, and having noted that the members of my staff were in their places, I gave a last pleased survey of my dining-room, with its smartly equipped tables, flower-bedecked, gleaming in the softened light from my shaded candlesticks. Truly it was a scene of refined elegance such as Red Gap had never before witnessed within its own confines, and I had seen to it that the dinner as well would mark an epoch in the lives of these simple but worthy people.

Not a heavy nor a cloying repast would they find. Indeed, the bare simplicity of my menu, had it been previously disclosed, would doubtless have disappointed more than one of my dinner-giving patronesses; but each item had been perfected to an extent never achieved by them. Their weakness had ever been to serve a profusion of neutral dishes, pleasing enough to the eye, but unedifying except as a spectacle. I mean to say, as food it was noncommittal; it failed to intrigue.

I should serve only a thin soup, a fish, small birds, two vegetables, a salad, a sweet and a savoury, but each item would prove worthy of the profoundest consideration. In the matter of thin soup, for example, the local practice was to serve a fluid of which, beyond the circumstance that it was warmish and slightly tinted, nothing of interest could ever be ascertained. My own thin soup would be a revelation to them. Again, in the matter of fish. This course with the hostesses of Red Gap had seemed to be merely an excuse for a pause. I had truly sympathized with Cousin Egbert's bitter complaint: "They hand you a dab of something about the size of a watch-charm with two strings of potato."

For the first time, then, the fish course in Red Gap was to be an event, an abundant portion of native fish with a lobster sauce which I had carried out to its highest power. My birds, hot from the oven, would be food in the strictest sense of the word, my vegetables cooked with a zealous attention, and my sweet immensely appealing without being pretentiously spectacular. And for what I believed to be quite the first time in the town, good coffee would be served. Disheartening, indeed, had been the various attenuations of coffee which had been imposed upon me in my brief career as a diner-out among these people. Not one among them had possessed the genius to master an acceptable decoction of the berry, the bald simplicity of the correct formula being doubtless incredible to them.

The blare of a motor horn aroused me from this musing, and from that moment I had little time for meditation until the evening, as the *Journal* recorded the next morning, "had gone down into history." My patrons arrived in groups, couples, or singly, almost faster than I could seat them. The Hobbs lad, as vestiare, would halt them for hats and wraps, during which pause they would emit subdued cries of surprise and delight at my beautifully toned ensemble, after which, as they walked to their tables, it was not difficult to see that they were properly impressed.

Mrs. Effie, escorted by the Honourable George and cousin Egbert, was among the early arrivals; the Senator being absent from town at a sitting of the House. These were quickly followed by the Belknap-Jacksons and the Mixer, resplendent in purple satin and diamonds, all being at one of my large tables, so that the Honourable George sat between Mrs. Belknap-Jackson and Mrs. Effie, though he at first made a somewhat undignified essay to seat himself next the Mixer. Needless to say, all were in evening dress, though the Honourable George had fumbled grossly with his cravat and rumpled his shirt, nor had he submitted to having his beard trimmed, as I had warned him to do. As for Belknap-Jackson, I had never beheld him more truly vogue in every detail, and his slightly austere manner in any Red Gap gathering had never set him better. Both Mrs. Belknap-Jackson and Mrs. Effie wielded their lorgnons upon the later comers, thus giving their table quite an air.

Mrs. Judge Ballard, who had come to be one of my staunchest adherents, occupied an adjacent table with her family party and two or three of the younger dancing set. The Indian Tuttle with his wife and two daughters were also among the early comers, and I could not but marvel anew at the red man's histrionic powers. In almost quite correct evening attire, and entirely decorous in speech and gesture, he might readily have been thought some one that mattered, had he not at an early opportunity caught my eye and winked with a sly significance.

Quite almost every one of the North Side set was present, imparting to my room a general air of distinguished smartness, and in addition there were not a few of what Belknap-Jackson had called the "rabble," persons of no social value, to be sure, but honest, well-mannered folk, small tradesmen, shop-assistants, and the like. These plain people, I may say, I took especial pains to welcome and put at their ease, for I had resolved, in effect, to be one of them, after the manner prescribed by their Declaration thing.

With quite all of them I chatted easily a moment or two, expressing the hope that they would be well pleased with their entertainment. I noted while thus engaged that Belknap-Jackson eyed me with frank and superior cynicism, but this affected me quite not at all and I took pains to point my indifference, chatting with increased urbanity with the two cow-persons, Hank and Buck, who had entered rather uncertainly, not in evening dress, to be sure, but in decent black as befitted their stations. When I had prevailed upon them to surrender their hats to the vestiare and had seated them at a table for two, they informed me in hoarse undertones that they were prepared to "put a bet down on every card from soda to hock," so that I at first suspected they had thought me conducting a gaming establishment, but ultimately gathered that they were merely expressing a cordial determination to enter into the spirit of the occasion.

There then entered, somewhat to my uneasiness, the Klondike woman and her party. Being almost the last, it will be understood that they created no little sensation as she led them down the thronged room to her table. She was wearing an evening gown of lustrous black with the apparently simple lines that are so baffling to any but the expert maker, with a black picture hat that suited her no end. I saw more than one matron of the North Side set stiffen in her seat, while Mrs. Belknap-Jackson and Mrs. Effie turned upon her the chilling broadside of their lorgnons. Belknap-Jackson merely drew himself up austerely. The three other women of her party, flutterers rather, did little but set off their hostess. The four men were of a youngish sort, chaps in banks, chemists' assistants, that sort of thing, who were constantly to be seen in her train. They were especially reprobated by the matrons of the correct set by reason of their deliberately choosing to ally themselves with the Bohemian set.

Acutely feeling the antagonism aroused by this group, I was momentarily discouraged in a design I had half formed of using my undoubted influence to unite the warring social factions of Red Gap, even as Bismarck had once brought the warring Prussian states together in a federated Germany. I began to see that the Klondike woman would forever prove unacceptable to the North Side set. The cliques would unite against her, even if one should find in her a spirit of reconciliation, which I supremely doubted.

The bustle having in a measure subsided, I gave orders for the soup to be served, at the same time turning the current into the electric pianoforte. I had wished for this opening number something attractive yet dignified, which would in a manner of speaking symbolize an occasion to me at least highly momentous. To this end I had chosen Handel's celebrated Largo, and at the first strains of this highly meritorious composition I knew that I had chosen surely. I am sure the piece was indelibly engraved upon the minds of those many dinner-givers who were for the first time in their lives realizing that a thin soup may be made a thing to take seriously.

Nominally, I occupied a seat at the table with the Belknap-Jacksons and Mrs. Effie, though I apprehended having to be more or less up and down in the direction of my staff. Having now seated myself to soup, I was for the first time made aware of the curious behaviour of the Honourable George. Disregarding his own soup, which was of itself unusual with him, he was staring straight ahead with a curious intensity. A half turn of my head was enough. He sat facing the Klondike woman. As I again turned a bit I saw that under cover of her animated converse with her table companions she was at intervals allowing her very effective eyes to rest, as if absently, upon him. I may say now that a curious chill seized me, bringing with it a sudden psychic warning that all was not going to be as it should be. Some calamity impended. The man was quite apparently fascinated, staring with a fixed, hypnotic intensity that had already been noted by his companions on either side.

With a word about the soup, shot quickly and directly at him, I managed to divert his gaze, but his eyes had returned even before the spoon had gone once to his lips. The second time there was a soup stain upon his already rumpled shirt front. Presently it became only too horribly certain that the man was out of himself, for when the fish course was served he remained serenely unconscious that none of the lobster sauce accompanied his own portion. It was a rich sauce, and the almost immediate effect of shell-fish upon his complexion being only too well known to me, I had directed that his fish should be served without it, though I had fully expected him to row me for it and perhaps create a scene. The circumstance of his blindly attacking the unsauced fish was eloquent indeed.

The Belknap-Jacksons and Mrs. Effie were now plainly alarmed, and somewhat feverishly sought to engage his attention, with the result only that he snapped monosyllables at them without removing his gaze from its mark. And the woman was now too obviously pluming herself upon the effect she had achieved; upon us all she flashed an amused consciousness of her power, yet with a fine affectation of quite ignoring us. I was here obliged to leave the table to oversee the serving of the wine, returning after an interval to find the situation unchanged, save that the woman no longer glanced at the Honourable George. Such were her tactics. Having enmeshed him, she confidently left him to complete his own undoing. I had returned with the serving of the small birds. Observing his own before him, the Honourable George wished to be told why he had not been served with fish, and only with difficulty could be convinced that he had partaken of this. "Of course in public places one must expect to come into contact with persons of that sort," remarked Mrs. Effie.

"Something should be done about it," observed Mrs. Belknap-Jackson, and they both murmured "Creature!" though it was plain that the Honourable George had little notion to whom they referred. Observing, however, that the woman no longer glanced at him, he fell to his bird somewhat whole-heartedly, as indeed did all my guests.

From every side I could hear eager approval of the repast which was now being supplemented at most of the tables by a sound wine of the Burgundy type which I had recommended or by a dry champagne. Meantime, the electric pianoforte played steadily through a repertoire that had progressed from the Largo to more vivacious pieces of the American folkdance school. As was said in the press the following day, "Gayety and good-feeling reigned supreme, and one and all felt that it was indeed good to be there."

Through the sweet and the savoury the dinner progressed, the latter proving to be a novelty that the hostesses of Red Gap thereafter slavishly copied, and with the advent of the coffee ensued a noticeable relaxation. People began to visit one another's tables and there was a blithe undercurrent of praise for my efforts to smarten the town's public dining.

The Klondike woman, I fancy, was the first to light a cigarette, though quickly followed by the ladies of her party. Mrs. Belknap-Jackson and Mrs. Effie, after a period of futile glaring at her through the lorgnons, seemed to make their resolves simultaneously, and forthwith themselves lighted cigarettes.

"Of course it's done in the smart English restaurants," murmured Belknap-Jackson as he assisted the ladies to their lights. Thereupon Mrs. Judge Ballard, farther down the room, began to smoke what I believe was her first cigarette, which proved to be a signal for other ladies of the Onwards and Upwards Society to do the same, Mrs. Ballard being their president. It occurred to me that these ladies were grimly bent on showing the Klondike woman that they could trifle quite as gracefully as she with the lesser vices of Bohemia; or perhaps they wished to demonstrate to the younger dancing men in her train that the North Side set was not desolately austere in its recreation. The Honourable George, I regret to say, produced a smelly pipe which he would have lighted; but at a shocked and cold glance from me he put it by and allowed the Mixer to roll him one of the yellow paper cigarettes from a sack of tobacco which she had produced from some secret recess of her costume.

Cousin Egbert had been excitedly happy throughout the meal and now paid me a quaint compliment upon the food. "Some eats, Bill!" he called to me. "I got to hand it to you," though what precisely it was he wished to hand me I never ascertained, for the Mixer at that moment claimed my attention with a compliment of her own. "That," said she, "is the only dinner I've eaten for a long time that was composed entirely of food."

This hour succeeding the repast I found quite entirely agreeable, more than one person that mattered assuring me that I had assisted Red Gap to a notable advance in the finest and correctest sense of the word, and it was with a very definite regret that I beheld my guests departing. Returning to our table from a group of these who had called me to make their adieus, I saw that a most regrettable incident had occurred--nothing less than the formal presentation of the Honourable George to the Klondike woman. And the Mixer had appallingly done it!

"Everything is so strange here," I heard him saying as I passed their table, and the woman echoed, "Everything!" while her glance enveloped him with a curious effect of appraisal. The others of her party were making much of him, I could see, quite as if they had preposterous designs of wresting him from the North Side set to be one of themselves. Mrs. Belknap-Jackson and Mrs. Effie affected to ignore the meeting. Belknap-Jackson stared into vacancy with a quite shocked expression as if vandals had desecrated an altar in his presence. Cousin Egbert having drawn off one of his newly purchased boots during the dinner was now replacing it with audible groans, but I caught his joyous comment a moment later: "Didn't I tell you the Judge was some mixer?"

"Mixing, indeed," snapped the ladies.

A half-hour later the historic evening had come to an end. The last guest had departed, and all of my staff, save Mrs. Judson and her male child. These I begged to escort to their home, since the way was rather far and dark. The child, incautiously left in the kitchen at the mercy of the female black, had with criminal stupidity been stuffed with food, traces of almost every course of the dinner being apparent upon its puffy countenance. Being now in a stupor from overfeeding, I was obliged to lug the thing over my shoulder. I resolved to warn the mother at an early opportunity of the perils of an unrestricted diet, although the deluded creature seemed actually to glory in its corpulence. I discovered when halfway to her residence that the thing was still tightly clutching the gnawed thigh-bone of a fowl which was spotting the shoulder of my smartest top-coat. The mother, however, was so ingenuously delighted with my success and so full of prattle concerning my future triumphs that I forbore to instruct her at this time. I may say that of all my staff she had betrayed the most intelligent understanding of my ideals, and I bade her good-night with a strong conviction that she would greatly assist me in the future. She also promised that Mr. Barker should thereafter be locked in a cellar at such times as she was serving me.

Returning through the town, I heard strains of music from the establishment known as "Bert's Place," and was shocked on staring through his show window to observe the Honourable George and Cousin Egbert waltzing madly with the cow-persons, Hank and Buck, to the strains of a mechanical piano. The Honourable George had exchanged his top-hat for his partner's cow-person hat, which came down over his ears in a most regrettable manner.

I thought it best not to intrude upon their coarse amusement and went on to the grill to see that all was safe for the night. Returning from my inspection some half-hour later, I came upon the two, Cousin Egbert in the lead, the Honourable George behind him. They greeted me somewhat boisterously, but I saw that they were now content to return home and to bed. As they walked somewhat mincingly, I noticed that they were in their hose, carrying their varnished boots in either hand.

Of the Honourable George, who still wore the cow-person's hat, I began now to have the gravest doubts. There had been an evil light in the eyes of the Klondike woman and her Bohemian cohorts as they surveyed him. As he preceded me I heard him murmur ecstatically: "Sush is life."

CHAPTER FIFTEEN

L AUNCHED now upon a business venture that would require my unremitting attention if it were to prosper, it may be imagined that I had little leisure for the social vagaries of the Honourable George, shocking as these might be to one's finer tastes. And yet on the following morning I found time to tell him what. To put it quite bluntly, I gave him beans for his loose behaviour the previous evening, in publicly ogling and meeting as an equal one whom one didn't know.

To my amazement, instead of being heartily ashamed of his licentiousness, I found him recalcitrant. Stubborn as a mule he was and with a low animal cunning that I had never given him credit for. "Demosthenes was the son of a cutler," said he, "and Napoleon worked on a canal-boat, what? Didn't you say so yourself, you juggins, what? Fancy there being upper and lower classes among natives! What rot! And I like North America. I don't mind telling you straight I'm going to take it up."

Horrified by these reckless words, I could only say "Noblesse oblige," meaning to convey that whatever the North Americans did, the next Earl of Brinstead must not meet persons one doesn't know, whereat he rejoined tartly that I was "to stow that piffle!"

Being now quite alarmed, I took the further time to call upon Belknap-Jackson, believing that he, if any one, could recall the Honourable George to his better nature. He, too, was shocked, as I had been, and at first would have put the blame entirely upon the shoulders of Cousin Egbert, but at this I was obliged to admit that the Honourable George had too often shown a regrettable fondness for the society of persons that did not matter, especially females, and I cited the case of the typing-girl and the Brixton millinery person, with either of whom he would have allied himself in marriage had not his lordship intervened. Belknap-Jackson was quite properly horrified at these revelations.

"Has he no sense of 'Noblesse oblige'?" he demanded, at which I quoted the result of my own use of this phrase to the unfortunate man. Quite too plain it was that "Noblesse oblige!" would never stop him from yielding to his baser impulses.

"We must be tactful, then," remarked Belknap-Jackson. "Without appearing to oppose him we must yet show him who is really who in Red Gap. We shall let him see that we have standards which must be as rigidly adhered to as those of an older civilization. I fancy it can be done."

Privately I fancied not, yet I forbore to say this or to prolong the painful interview, particularly as I was due at the United States Grill.

The *Recorder* of that morning had done me handsomely, declaring my opening to have been a social event long to be remembered, and describing the costumes of a dozen or more of the smartly gowned matrons, quite as if it had been an assembly ball. My task now was to see that the Grill was kept to the high level of its opening, both as a social ganglion, if one may use the term, and as a place to which the public would ever turn for food that mattered. For my first luncheon the raccoons had prepared, under my direction, a steak-and-kidney pie, in addition to which I offered a thick soup and a pudding of high nutritive value.

To my pleased astonishment the crowd at midday was quite all that my staff could serve, several of the Hobbs brood being at school, and the luncheon was received with every sign of approval by the business persons who sat to it. Not only were there drapers, chemists, and shop-assistants, but solicitors and barristers, bankers and estate agents, and all quite eager with their praise of my fare. To each of these I explained that I should give them but few things, but that these would be food in the finest sense of the word, adding that the fault of the American school lay in attempting a too-great profusion of dishes, none of which in consequence could be raised to its highest power.

So sound was my theory and so nicely did my simple-dished luncheon demonstrate it that I was engaged on the spot to provide the bi-monthly banquet of the Chamber of Commerce, the president of which rather seriously proposed that it now be made a monthly affair, since they would no longer be at the mercy of a hotel caterer whose ambition ran inversely to his skill. Indeed, after the pudding, I was this day asked to become a member of the body, and I now felt that I was indubitably one of them--America and I had taken each other as seriously as could be desired.

More than once during the afternoon I wondered rather painfully what the Honourable George might be doing. I knew that he had been promised to a meeting of the Onwards and Upwards Club through the influence of Mrs. Effie, where it had been hoped that he would give a talk on Country Life in England. At least she had hinted to them that he might do this, though I had known from the beginning that he would do nothing of the sort, and had merely hoped that he would appear for a dish of tea and stay quiet, which was as much as the North Side set could expect of him. Induced to speak, I was quite certain he would tell them straight that Country Life in England was silly rot, and that was all to it. Now, not having seen him during the day, I could but hope that he had attended the gathering in suitable afternoon attire, and that he would have divined that the cattle-person's hat did not coordinate with this.

At four-thirty, while I was still concerned over the possible misadventures of the Honourable George, my first patrons for tea began to arrive, for I had let it be known that I should specialize in this. Toasted crumpets there were, and muffins, and a tea cake rich with plums, and tea, I need not say, which was all that tea could be. Several tables were filled with prominent ladies of the North Side set, who were loud in their exclamations of delight, especially at the finished smartness of my service, for it was perhaps now that the profoundly serious thought I had given to my silver, linen, and glassware showed to best advantage. I suspect that this was the first time many of my guests had encountered a tea cozy, since from that day they began to be prevalent in Red Gap homes. Also my wagon containing the crumpets, muffins, tea cake, jam and bread-and-butter, which I now used for the first time created a veritable sensation.

There was an agreeable hum of chatter from these early comers when I found myself welcoming Mrs. Judge Ballard and half a dozen members of the Onwards and Upwards Club, all of them wearing what I made out to be a baffled look. From these I presently managed to gather that their guest of honour for the afternoon had simply not appeared, and that the meeting, after awaiting him for two hours, had dissolved in some resentment, the time having been spent chiefly in an unflattering dissection of the Klondike woman's behaviour the evening before.

"He is a naughty man to disappoint us so cruelly!" declared Mrs. Judge Ballard of the Honourable George, but the coquetry of it was feigned to cover a very real irritation. I made haste with possible excuses. I said that he might be ill, or that important letters in that day's post might have detained him. I knew he had been astonishingly well that morning, also that he loathed letters and almost practically never received any; but something had to be said.

"A naughty, naughty fellow!" repeated Mrs. Ballard, and the members of her party echoed it. They had looked forward rather pathetically, I saw, to hearing about Country Life in England from one who had lived it.

I was now drawn to greet the Belknap-Jacksons, who entered, and to the pleasure of winning their hearty approval for the perfection of my arrangements. As the wife presently joined Mrs. Ballard's group, the husband called me to his table and disclosed that almost the worst might be feared of the Honourable George. He was at that moment, it appeared, with a rabble of cow-persons and members of the lower class gathered at a stockade at the edge of town, where various native horses fresh from the wilderness were being taught to be ridden.

"The wretched Floud is with him," continued my informant, "also the Tuttle chap, who continues to be received by our best people in spite of my remonstrances, and he yells quite like a demon when one of the riders is thrown. I passed as quickly as I could. The spectacle was--of course I make allowances for Vane-Basingwell's ignorance of our standards--it was nothing short of disgusting; a man of his position consorting with the herd!"

"He told me no longer ago than this morning," I said, "that he was going to take up America."

"He *has*!" said Belknap-Jackson with bitter emphasis. "You should see what he has on--a cowboy hat and chapps! And the very lowest of them are calling him 'Judge'!"

"He flunked a meeting of the Onwards and Upwards Society," I added.

"I know! I know! And who could have expected it in one of his lineage? At this very moment he should be conducting himself as one of his class. Can you wonder at my impatience with the West? Here at an hour when our social life should be in evidence, when all trade should be forgotten, I am the only man in the town who shows himself in a tea-room; and Vane-Basingwell over there debasing himself with our commonest sort!"

All at once I saw that I myself must bear the brunt of this scandal. I had brought hither the Honourable George, promising a personage who would for once and all unify the North Side set and perhaps disintegrate its rival. I had been felicitated upon my master-stroke. And now it seemed I had come a cropper. But I resolved not to give up, and said as much now to Belknap-Jackson.

"I may be blamed for bringing him among you, but trust me if things are really as bad as they seem. I'll get him off again. I'll not let myself be bowled by such a silly lob as that. Trust me to devote profound thought to this problem."

"We all have every confidence in you," he assured me, "but don't be too severe all at once with the chap. He might recover a sane balance even yet."

"I shall use discretion," I assured him, "but if it proves that I have fluffed my catch, rely upon me to use extreme measures."

"Red Gap needs your best effort," he replied in a voice that brimmed with feeling.

At five-thirty, my rush being over, I repaired to the neighbourhood where the Honourable George had been reported. The stockade now contained only a half-score of the untaught horses, but across the road from it was a public house, or saloon, from which came unmistakable sounds of carousing. It was an unsavoury place, frequented only by cattle and horse persons, the proprietor being an abandoned character named Spilmer, who had once done a patron to death in a drunken quarrel. Only slight legal difficulties had been made for him, however, it having been pleaded that he acted in self-defence, and the creature had at once resumed his trade as publican. There was even public sympathy for him at the time on the ground that he possessed a blind mother, though I have never been able to see that this should have been a factor in adjudging him.

I paused now before the low place, imagining I could detect the tones of the Honourable George high above the chorus that came out to me. Deciding that in any event it would not become me to enter a resort of this stamp, I walked slowly back toward the more reputable part of town, and was presently rewarded by seeing the crowd emerge. It was led, I saw, by the Honourable George. The cattle-hat was still down upon his ears, and to my horror he had come upon the public thoroughfare with his legs encased in the chapps--a species of leathern pantalettes covered with goat's wool--a garment which I need not say no gentleman should be seen abroad in. As worn by the cow-persons in their daily toil they are only just possible, being as far from true vogue as anything well could be.

Accompanying him were Cousin Egbert, the Indian Tuttle, the cow-persons, Hank and Buck, and three or four others of the same rough stamp. Unobtrusively I followed them to our main thoroughfare, deeply humiliated by the atrocious spectacle the Honourable George was making of himself, only to observe them turn into another public house entitled "The Family Liquor Store," where if seemed only too certain, since the bearing of all was highly animated, that they would again carouse.

At once seeing my duty, I boldly entered, finding them aligned against the American bar and clamouring for drink. My welcome was heartfelt, even enthusiastic, almost every one of them beginning to regale me with incidents of the afternoon's horse-breaking. The Honourable George, it seemed, had himself briefly mounted one of the animals, having fallen into the belief that the cow-persons did not try earnestly enough to stay on their mounts. I gathered that one experience had dissuaded him from this opinion.

"That there little paint horse," observed Cousin Egbert genially, "stepped out from under the Judge the prettiest you ever saw."

"He sure did," remarked the Honourable George, with a palpable effort to speak the American brogue. "A most flighty beast he was--nerves all gone--I dare say a hopeless neurasthenic."

And then when I would have rebuked him for so shamefully disappointing the ladies of the Onwards and Upwards Society, he began to tell me of the public house he had just left.

"I say, you know that Spilmer chap, he's a genuine murderer--he let me hold the weapon with which he did it--and he has blind relatives dependent upon him, or something of that sort, otherwise I fancy they'd have sent him to the gallows. And, by Gad! he's a witty scoundrel, what! Looking at his sign--leaving the settlement it reads, 'Last Chance,' but entering the settlement it reads, 'First Chance.' Last chance and first chance for a peg, do you see what I mean? I tried it out; walked both ways under the sign and looked up; it worked perfectly. Enter the settlement, 'First Chance'; leave the settlement, 'Last Chance.' Do you see what I mean? Suggestive, what! Witty! You'd never have expected that murderer-Johnny to be so subtle. Our own murderers aren't that way. I say, it's a tremendous wheeze. I wonder the press-chaps don't take it up. It's better than the blind factory, though the chap's mother or something is blind. What ho! But that's silly! To be sure one has nothing to do with the other. I say, have another, you chaps! I've not felt so fit in ages. I'm going to take up America!"

Plainly it was no occasion to use serious words to the man. He slapped his companions smartly on their backs and was slapped in turn by all of them. One or two of them called him an old horse! Not only was I doing no good for the North Side set, but I had felt obliged to consume two glasses of spirits that I did not wish. So I discreetly withdrew. As I went, the Honourable George was again telling them that he was "going in" for North America, and Cousin Egbert was calling "Three rousing cheers!"

Thus luridly began, I may say, a scandal that was to be far-reaching in its dreadful effects. Far from feeling a proper shame on the following day, the Honourable George was as pleased as Punch with himself, declaring his intention of again consorting with the cattle and horse persons and very definitely declining an invitation to play at golf with Belknap-Jackson.

"Golf!" he spluttered. "You do it, and then you've directly to do it all over again. I mean to say, one gets nowhere. A silly game--what!"

Wishing to be in no manner held responsible for his vicious pursuits, I that day removed my diggings from the Floud home to chambers in the Pettengill block above the Grill, where I did myself quite nicely with decent mantel ornaments, some vivacious prints of old-world cathedrals, and a few good books, having for body-servant one of the Hobbs lads who seemed rather teachable. I must admit, however, that I was frequently obliged to address him more sharply than one should ever address one's servant, my theory having always been that a serving person should be treated quite as if he were a gentleman temporarily performing menial duties, but there was that strain of lowness in all the Hobbses which often forbade this, a blending of servility with more or less skilfully dissembled impertinence, which I dare say is the distinguishing mark of our lower-class serving people.

Removed now from the immediate and more intimate effects of the Honourable George's digressions, I was privileged for days at a time to devote my attention exclusively to my enterprise. It had thriven from the beginning, and after a month I had so perfected the minor details of management that everything was right as rain. In my catering I continued to steer a middle course between the British school of plain roast and boiled and a too often piffling French complexity, seeking to retain the desirable features of each. My luncheons for the tradesmen rather held to a cut from the joint with vegetables and a suitable sweet, while in my dinners I relaxed a bit into somewhat imaginative salads and entrees. For the tea-hour I constantly strove to provide some appetizing novelty, often, I confess, sacrificing nutrition to mere sightliness in view of my almost exclusive feminine patronage, yet never carrying this to an undignified extreme.

As a result of my sound judgment, dinner-giving in Red Gap began that winter to be done almost entirely in my place. There might be small informal affairs at home, but for dinners of any pretension the hostesses of the North Side set came to me, relying almost quite entirely upon my taste in the selection of the menu. Although at first I was required to employ unlimited tact in dissuading them from strange and laboured concoctions, whose photographs they fetched me from their women's magazines, I at length converted them from this unwholesome striving for novelty and laid the foundations for that sound scheme of gastronomy which to-day distinguishes this fastest-growing town in the state, if not in the West of America.

It was during these early months, I ought perhaps to say, that I rather distinguished myself in the matter of a relish which I compounded one day when there was a cold round of beef for luncheon. Little dreaming of the magnitude of the moment, I brought together English mustard and the American tomato catsup, in proportions which for reasons that will be made obvious I do not here disclose, together with three other and lesser condiments whose identity also must remain a secret. Serving this with my cold joint, I was rather amazed at the sensation it created. My patrons clamoured for it repeatedly and a barrister wished me to prepare a flask of it for use in his home. The following day it was again demanded and other requests were made for private supplies, while by the end of the week my relish had become rather famous. Followed a suggestion from Mrs. Judson as she overlooked my preparation of it one day from her own task of polishing the glassware.

"Put it on the market," said she, and at once I felt the inspiration of her idea.

To her I entrusted the formula. I procured a quantity of suitable flasks, while in her own home she compounded the stuff and filled them. Having no mind to claim credit not my own, I may now say that this rather remarkable woman also evolved the idea of the label, including the name, which was pasted upon the bottles when our product was launched.

"Ruggles' International Relish" she had named it after a moment's thought. Below was a print of my face taken from an excellent photographic portrait, followed by a brief summary of the article's unsurpassed excellence, together with a list of the viands for which it was commended. As the International Relish is now a matter of history, the demand for it having spread as far east as Chicago and those places, I may add that it was this capable woman again who devised the large placard for hoardings in which a middle-aged but glowing bon-vivant in evening dress rebukes the blackamoor who has served his dinner for not having at once placed Ruggles' International Relish upon the table. The genial annoyance of the diner and the apologetic concern of the black are excellently depicted by the artist, for the original drawing of which I paid a stiffish price to the leading artist fellow of Spokane. This now adorns the wall of my sitting-room.

It must not be supposed that I had been free during these months from annoyance and chagrin at the manner in which the Honourable George was conducting himself. In the beginning it was hoped both by Belknap-Jackson and myself that he might do no worse than merely consort with the rougher element of the town. I mean to say, we suspected that the apparent charm of the raffish cattle-persons might suffice to keep him from any notorious alliance with the dreaded Bohemian set. So long as he abstained from this he might still be received at our best homes, despite his regrettable fondness for low company. Even when he brought the murderer Spilmer to dine with him at my place, the thing was condoned as a freakish grotesquerie in one who, of unassailable social position, might well afford to stoop momentarily.

I must say that the murderer--a heavy-jowled brute of husky voice, and quite lacking a forehead--conducted himself on this occasion with an entirely decent restraint of manner, quite in contrast to the Honourable George, who betrayed an expansively naive pride in his guest, seeming to wish the world to know of the event. Between them they consumed a fair bottle of the relish. Indeed, the Honourable George was inordinately fond of this, as a result of which he would often come out quite spotty again. Cousin Egbert was another who became so addicted to it that his fondness might well have been called a vice. Both he and the Honourable George would drench quite every course with the sauce, and Cousin Egbert, with that explicit directness which distinguished his character, would frankly sop his bread-crusts in it, or even sip it with a coffee-spoon.

As I have intimated, in spite of the Honourable George's affiliations with the slum-characters of what I may call Red Gap's East End, he had not yet publicly identified himself with the Klondike woman and her Bohemian set, in consequence of which--let him dine and wine a Spilmer as he would--there was yet hope that he would not alienate himself from the North Side set.

At intervals during the early months of his sojourn among us he accepted dinner invitations at the Grill from our social leaders; in fact, after the launching of the International Relish, I know of none that he declined, but it was evident to me that he moved but half-heartedly in this higher circle. On one occasion, too, he appeared in the trousers of a lounge-suit of tweeds instead of his dress trousers, and with tan boots. The trousers, to be sure, were of a sombre hue, but the brown boots were quite too dreadfully unmistakable. After this I may say that I looked for anything, and my worst fears were soon confirmed.

It began as the vaguest sort of gossip. The Honourable George, it was said, had been a guest at one of the Klondike woman's evening affairs. The rumour crystallized. He had been asked to meet the Bohemian set at a Dutch supper and had gone. He had lingered until a late hour, dancing the American folkdances (for which he had shown a surprising adaptability) and conducting himself generally as the next Earl of Brinstead should not have done. He had repeated his visit, repairing to the woman's house both afternoon and evening. He had become a constant visitor. He had spoken regrettably of the dulness of a meeting of the Onwards and Upwards Society which he had attended. He was in the woman's toils.

With gossip of this sort there was naturally much indignation, and yet the leaders of the North Side set were so delicately placed that there was every reason for concealing it. They redoubled their attentions to the unfortunate man, seeking to leave him not an unoccupied evening or afternoon. Such was the gravity of the crisis. Belknap-Jackson alone remained finely judicial.

"The situation is of the gravest character," he confided to me, "but we must be wary. The day isn't lost so long as he doesn't appear publicly in the creature's train. For the present we have only unverified rumour. As a man about town Vane-Basingwell may feel free to consort with vicious companions and still maintain his proper standing. Deplore it as all right-thinking people must, under present social conditions he is undoubtedly free to lead what is called a double life. We can only wait."

Such was the state of the public mind, be it understood, up to the time of the notorious and scandalous defection of this obsessed creature, an occasion which I cannot recall without shuddering, and which inspired me to a course that was later to have the most inexplicable and far-reaching consequences.

Theatrical plays had been numerous with us during the season, with the natural result of many after-theatre suppers being given by those who attended, among them the North Side leaders, and frequently the Klondike woman with her following. On several of these occasions, moreover, the latter brought as supper guests certain representatives of the theatrical profession, both male and female, she apparently having a wide acquaintance with such persons. That this sort of thing increased her unpopularity with the North Side set will be understood when I add that now and then her guests would be of undoubted respectability in their private lives, as theatrical persons often are, and such as our smartest hostesses would have been only too glad to entertain.

To counteract this effect Belknap-Jackson now broached to me a plan of undoubted merit, which was nothing less than to hold an afternoon reception at his home in honour of the world's greatest pianoforte artist, who was presently to give a recital in Red Gap.

"I've not met the chap myself," he began, "but I knew his secretary and travelling companion quite well in a happier day in Boston. The recital here will be Saturday evening, which means that they will remain here on Sunday until the evening train East. I shall suggest to my friend that his employer, to while away the tedium of the Sunday, might care to look in upon me in the afternoon and meet a few of our best people. Nothing boring, of course. I've no doubt he will arrange it. I've written him to Portland, where they now are."

"Rather a card that will be," I instantly cried. "Rather better class than entertaining strolling players." Indeed the merit of the proposal rather overwhelmed me. It would be dignified and yet spectacular. It would show the Klondike woman that we chose to have contact only with artists of acknowledged preeminence and that such were quite willing to accept our courtesies. I had hopes, too, that the Honourable George might be aroused to advantages which he seemed bent upon casting to the American winds.

A week later Belknap-Jackson joyously informed me that the great artist had consented to accept his hospitality. There would be light refreshments, with which I was charged. I suggested tea in the Russian manner, which he applauded.

"And everything dainty in the way of food," he warned me. "Nothing common, nothing heavy. Some of those tiny lettuce sandwiches, a bit of caviare, macaroons-- nothing gross--a decanter of dry sherry, perhaps, a few of the lightest wafers; things that cultivated persons may trifle with--things not repugnant to the artist soul."

I promised my profoundest consideration to these matters.

"And it occurs to me," he thoughtfully added, "that this may be a time for Vane-Basingwell to silence the slurs upon himself that are becoming so common. I shall beg him to meet our guest at his hotel and escort him to my place. A note to my friend, 'the bearer, the Honourable George Augustus Vane-Basingwell, brother of his lordship the Earl of Brinstead, will take great pleasure in escorting to my home----' You get the idea? Not bad!"

Again I applauded, resolving that for once the Honourable George would be suitably attired even if I had to bully him. And so was launched what promised to be Red Gap's most notable social event of the season. The Honourable George, being consulted, promised after a rather sulky hesitation to act as the great artist's escort, though he persisted in referring to him as "that piano Johnny," and betrayed a suspicion that Belknap-Jackson was merely bent upon getting him to perform without price.

"But no," cried Belknap-Jackson, "I should never think of anything so indelicate as asking him to play. My own piano will be tightly closed and I dare say removed to another room."

At this the Honourable George professed to wonder why the chap was desired if he wasn't to perform. "All hair and bad English--silly brutes when they don't play," he declared. In the end, however, as I have said, he consented to act as he was wished to. Cousin Egbert, who was present at this interview, took somewhat the same view as the Honourable George, even asserting that he should not attend the recital.

"He don't sing, he don't dance, he don't recite; just plays the piano. That ain't any kind of a show for folks to set up a whole evening for," he protested bitterly, and he went on to mention various theatrical pieces which he had considered worthy, among them I recall being one entitled "The Two Johns," which he regretted not having witnessed for several years, and another called "Ben Hur," which was better than all the piano players alive, he declared. But with the Honourable George enlisted, both Belknap-Jackson and I considered the opinions of Cousin Egbert to be quite wholly negligible.

Saturday's *Recorder*, in its advance notice of the recital, announced that the Belknap-Jacksons of Boston and Red Gap would entertain the artist on the following afternoon at their palatial home in the Pettengill addition, where a select few of the North Side set had been invited to meet him. Belknap-Jackson himself was as a man uplifted. He constantly revised and re-revised his invitation list; he sought me out each day to suggest subtle changes in the very artistic menu I had prepared for the affair. His last touch was to supplement the decanter of sherry with a bottle of vodka. About the caviare he worried quite fearfully until it proved upon arrival to be fresh and of prime quality. My man, the Hobbs boy, had under my instructions pressed and smarted the Honourable George's suit for afternoon wear. The carriage was engaged. Saturday night it was tremendously certain that no hitch could occur to mar the affair. We had left no detail to chance.

The recital itself was quite all that could have been expected, but underneath the enthusiastic applause there ran even a more intense fervour among those fortunate ones who were to meet the artist on the morrow.

Belknap-Jackson knew himself to be a hero. He was elaborately cool. He smiled tolerantly at intervals and undoubtedly applauded with the least hint of languid proprietorship in his manner. He was heard to speak of the artist by his first name. The Klondike woman and many of her Bohemian set were prominently among those present and sustained glances of pitying triumph from those members of the North Side set so soon to be distinguished above her.

The morrow dawned auspiciously, very cloudy with smartish drives of wind and rain. Confined to the dingy squalor of his hotel, how gladly would the artist, it was felt, seek the refined cheer of one of our best homes where he would be enlivened by an hour or so of contact with our most cultivated people. Belknap-Jackson telephoned me with increasing frequency as the hour drew near, nervously seeming to dread that I would have overlooked some detail of his refined refreshments, or that I would not have them at his house on time. He telephoned often to the Honourable George to be assured that the carriage with its escort would be prompt. He telephoned repeatedly to the driver chap, to impress upon him the importance of his mission.

His guests began to arrive even before I had decked his sideboard with what was, I have no hesitation in declaring, the most superbly dainty buffet collation that Red Gap had ever beheld. The atmosphere at once became tense with expectation.

At three o'clock the host announced from the telephone: "Vane-Basingwell has started from the Floud house." The guests thrilled and hushed the careless chatter of new arrivals. Belknap-Jackson remained heroically at the telephone, having demanded to be put through to the hotel. He was flushed with excitement. A score of minutes later he announced with an effort to control his voice: "They have left the hotel--they are on the way."

The guests stiffened in their seats. Some of them nervously and for no apparent reason exchanged chairs with others. Some late arrivals bustled in and were immediately awed to the same electric silence of waiting. Belknap-Jackson placed the sherry decanter where the vodka bottle had been and the vodka bottle where the sherry decanter had been. "The effect is better," he remarked, and went to stand where he could view the driveway. The moments passed.

At such crises, which I need not say have been plentiful in my life, I have always known that I possessed an immense reserve of coolness. Seldom have I ever been so much as slightly flustered. Now I was calmness itself, and the knowledge brought me no little satisfaction as I noted the rather painful distraction of our host. The moments passed--long, heavy, silent moments. Our host ascended trippingly to an upper floor whence he could see farther down the drive. The guests held themselves in smiling readiness. Our host descended and again took up his post at a lower window.

The moments passed--stilled, leaden moments. The silence had become intolerable. Our host jiggled on his feet. Some of the quicker-minded guests made a pretence of little conversational flurries: "That second movement--oh, exquisitely rendered!... No one has ever read Chopin so divinely.... How his family must idolize him!... They say.... That exquisite concerto!... Hasn't he the most stunning hair.... Those staccato passages left me actually limp--I'm starting Myrtle in Tuesday to take of Professor Gluckstein. She wants to take stenography, but I tell her.... Did you think the preludes were just the tiniest bit idealized.... I always say if one has one's music, and one's books, of course--He must be very, *very* fond of music!"

Such were the hushed, tentative fragments I caught.

The moments passed. Belknap-Jackson went to the telephone. "What? But they're not here! Very strange! They should have been here half an hour ago. Send some one--yes, at once." In the ensuing silence he repaired to the buffet and drank a glass of vodka. Quite distraught he was.

The moments passed. Again several guests exchanged seats with other guests. It seemed to be a device for relieving the strain. Once more there were scattering efforts at normal talk. "Myrtle is a strange girl--a creature of moods, I call her. She wanted to act in the moving pictures until papa bought the car. And she knows every one of the new tango steps, but I tell her a few lessons in cooking wouldn't--Beryl Mae is just the same puzzling child; one thing one day, and another thing the next; a mere bundle of nerves, and so sensitive if you say the least little thing to her ... If we could only get Ling Wong back--this Jap boy is always threatening to leave if the men don't get up to breakfast on time, or if Gertie makes fudge in his kitchen of an afternoon ... Our boy sends all his wages to his uncle in China, but I simply can't get him to say, 'Dinner is served.' He just slides in and says, 'All right, you come!' It's very annoying, but I always tell the family, 'Remember what a time we had with the Swede----'"

I mean to say, things were becoming rapidly impossible. The moments passed. Belknap-Jackson again telephoned: "You did send a man after them? Send some one after him, then. Yes, at once!" He poured himself another peg of the vodka. Silence fell again. The waiting was terrific. We had endured an hour of it, and but little more was possible to any sensitive human organism. All at once, as if the very last possible moment of silence had passed, the conversation broke loudly and generally: "And did you notice that slimpsy thing she wore last night? Indecent, if you ask me, with not a petticoat under it, I'll be bound!... Always wears shoes twice too small for her ... What men can see in her ... How they can endure that perpetual smirk!..." They were at last discussing the Klondike woman, and whatever had befallen our guest of honour I knew that those present would never regain their first awe of the occasion. It was now unrestrained gabble.

The second hour passed quickly enough, the latter half of it being enlivened by the buffet collation which elicited many compliments upon my ingenuity and good taste. Quite almost every guest partook of a glass of the vodka. They chattered of everything but music, I dare say it being thought graceful to ignore the afternoon's disaster.

Belknap-Jackson had sunk into a mood of sullen desperation. He drained the vodka bottle. Perhaps the liquor brought him something of the chill Russian fatalism. He was dignified but sodden, with a depression that seemed to blow from the bleak Siberian steppes. His wife was already receiving the adieus of their guests. She was smouldering ominously, uncertain where the blame lay, but certain there was blame. Criminal blame! I could read as much in her narrowed eyes as she tried for aplomb with her guests.

My own leave I took unobtrusively. I knew our strangely missing guest was to depart by the six-two train, and I strolled toward the station. A block away I halted, waiting. It had been a time of waiting. The moments passed. I heard the whistle of the approaching train. At the same moment I was startled by the approach of a team that I took to be running away.

I saw it was the carriage of the Pierce chap and that he was driving with the most abandoned recklessness. His passengers were the Honourable George, Cousin Egbert, and our missing guest. The great artist as they passed me seemed to feel a vast delight in his wild ride. He was cheering on the driver. He waved his arms and himself shouted to the maddened horses. The carriage drew up to the station with the train, and the three descended.

The artist hurriedly shook hands in the warmest manner with his companions, including the Pierce chap, who had driven them. He beckoned to his secretary, who was waiting with his bags. He mounted the steps of the coach, and as the train pulled out he waved frantically to the three. He kissed his hand to them, looking far out as the train gathered momentum. Again and again he kissed his hand to the hat-waving trio.

It was too much. The strain of the afternoon had told even upon my own iron nerves. I felt unequal at that moment to the simplest inquiry, and plainly the situation was not one to attack in haste. I mean to say, it was too pregnant with meaning. I withdrew rapidly from the scene, feeling the need for rest and silence.

As I walked I meditated profoundly.

CHAPTER SIXTEEN

FROM the innocent lips of Cousin Egbert the following morning there fell a tale of such cold-blooded depravity that I found myself with difficulty giving it credit. At ten o'clock, while I still mused pensively over the events of the previous day, he entered the Grill in search of breakfast, as had lately become his habit. I greeted him with perceptible restraint, not knowing what guilt might be his, but his manner to me was so unconsciously genial that I at once acquitted him of any complicity in whatever base doings had been forward.

He took his accustomed seat with a pleasant word to me. I waited.

"Feeling a mite off this morning," he began, "account of a lot of truck I eat yesterday. I guess I'll just take something kind of dainty. Tell Clarice to cook me up a nice little steak with plenty of fat on it, and some fried potatoes, and a cup of coffee and a few waffles to come. The Judge he wouldn't get up yet. He looked kind of mottled and anguished, but I guess he'll pull around all right. I had the chink take him up about a gallon of strong tea. Say, listen here, the Judge ain't so awful much of a stayer, is he?"

Burning with curiosity I was to learn what he could tell me of the day before, yet I controlled myself to the calmest of leisurely questioning in order not to alarm him. It was too plain that he had no realization of what had occurred. It was always the way with him, I had noticed. Events the most momentous might culminate furiously about his head, but he never knew that anything had happened.

"The Honourable George," I began, "was with you yesterday? Perhaps he ate something he shouldn't."

"He did, he did; he done it repeatedly. He et pretty near as much of that sauerkraut and frankfurters as the piano guy himself did, and that's some tribute, believe me, Bill! Some tribute!"

"The piano guy?" I murmured quite casually.

"And say, listen here, that guy is all right if anybody should ask you. You talk about your mixers!"

This was a bit puzzling, for of course I had never "talked about my mixers." I shouldn't a bit know how to go on. I ventured another query.

"Where was it this mixing and that sort of thing took place?"

"Why, up at Mis' Kenner's, where we was having a little party: frankfurters and sauerkraut and beer. My stars! but that steak looks good. I'm feeling better already." His food was before him, and he attacked it with no end of spirit.

"Tell me quite all about it," I amiably suggested, and after a moment's hurried devotion to the steak, he slowed up a bit to talk.

"Well, listen here, now. The Judge says to me when Eddie Pierce comes, 'Sour-dough,' he says, 'look in at Mis' Kenner's this afternoon if you got nothing else on; I fancy it will repay you.' Just like that. 'Well,' I says, 'all right, Judge, I fancy I will. I fancy I ain't got anything else on,' I says. 'And I'm always glad to go there,' I says, because no matter what they're always saying about this here Bohemian stuff, Kate Kenner is one good scout, take it from me. So in a little while I slicked up some and went on around to her house. Then hitched outside I seen Eddie Pierce's hack, and I says, 'My lands! that's a funny thing,' I says. 'I thought the Judge was going to haul this here piano guy out to the Jackson place where he could while away the tejum, like Jackson said, and now it looks as if they was here. Or mebbe it's just Eddie him-self that has fancied to look in, not having anything else on.'

"Well, so anyway I go up on the stoop and knock, and when I get in the parlour there the piano guy is and the Judge and Eddie Pierce, too, Eddie helping the Jap around with frankfurters and sauerkraut and beer and one thing and another.

"Besides them was about a dozen of Mis' Kenner's own particular friends, all of 'em good scouts, let me tell you, and everybody laughing and gassing back and forth and cutting up and having a good time all around. Well, so as soon as they seen me, everybody says, 'Oh, here comes Sour-dough--good old Sour-dough!' and all like that, and they introduced me to the piano guy, who gets up to shake hands with me and spills his beer off the chair arm on to the wife of Eddie Fosdick in the Farmers' and Merchants' National, and so I sat down and et with 'em and had a few steins of beer, and everybody had a good time all around."

The wonderful man appeared to believe that he had told me quite all of interest concerning this monstrous festivity. He surveyed the mutilated remnant of his steak and said: "I guess Clarice might as well fry me a few eggs. I'm feeling a lot better." I directed that this be done, musing upon the dreadful menu he had recited and recalling the exquisite finish of the collation I myself had prepared. Sausages, to be sure, have their place, and beer as well, but sauerkraut I have never been able to regard as an at all possible food for persons that really matter. Germans, to be sure!

Discreetly I renewed my inquiry: "I dare say the Honourable George was in good form?" I suggested.

"Well, he et a lot. Him and the piano guy was bragging which could eat the most sausages."

I was unable to restrain a shudder at the thought of this revolting contest.

"The piano guy beat him out, though. He'd been at the Palace Hotel for three meals and I guess his appetite was right craving."

"And afterward?"

"Well, it was like Jackson said: this lad wanted to while away the tejum of a Sunday afternoon, and so he whiled it, that's all. Purty soon Mis' Kenner set down to the piano and sung some coon songs that tickled him most to death, and then she got to playing ragtime--say, believe me, Bill, when she starts in on that rag stuff she can make a piano simply stutter itself to death.

"Well, at that the piano guy says it's great stuff, and so he sets down himself to try it, and he catches on pretty good, I'll say that for him, so we got to dancing while he plays for us, only he don't remember the tunes good and has to fake a lot. Then he makes Mis' Kenner play again while he dances with Mis' Fosdick that he spilled the beer on, and after that we had some more beer and this guy et another plate of kraut and a few sausages, and Mis' Kenner sings 'The Robert E. Lee' and a couple more good ones, and the guy played some more ragtime himself, trying to get the tunes right, and then he played some fancy pieces that he'd practised up on, and we danced some and had a few more beers, with everybody laughing and cutting up and having a nice home afternoon.

"Well, the piano guy enjoyed himself every minute, if anybody asks you, being lit up like a main chandelier. They made him feel like he was one of their own folks. You certainly got to hand it to him for being one little good mixer. Talk about whiling away the tejum! He done it, all right, all right. He whiled away so much tejum there he darned near missed his train. Eddie Pierce kept telling him what time it was, only he'd keep asking Mis' Kenner to play just one more rag, and at last we had to just shoot him into his fur overcoat while he was kissing all the women on their hands, and we'd have missed the train at that if Eddie hadn't poured the leather into them skates of his all the way down to the dee-po. He just did make it, and he told the Judge and Eddie and me that he ain't had such a good time since he left home. I kind of hated to see him go."

He here attacked the eggs with what seemed to be a freshening of his remarkable appetite. And as yet, be it noted, I had detected no consciousness on his part that a foul betrayal of confidence had been committed. I approached the point.

"The Belknap-Jacksons were rather expecting him, you know. My impression was that the Honourable George had been sent to escort him to the Belknap-Jackson house."

"Well, that's what I thought, too, but I guess the Judge forgot it, or mebbe he thinks the guy will mix in better with Mis' Kenner's crowd. Anyway, there they was, and it probably didn't make any difference to the guy himself. He likely thought he could while away the tejum there as well as he could while it any place, all of them being such good scouts. And the Judge has certainly got a case on Mis' Kenner, so mebby she asked him to drop in with any friend of his. She's got him bridle-wise and broke to all gaits." He visibly groped for an illumining phrase. "He--he just looks at her."

The simple words fell upon my ears with a sickening finality. "He just looks at her." I had seen him "just look" at the typing-girl and at the Brixton milliner. All too fearfully I divined their preposterous significance. Beyond question a black infamy had been laid bare, but I made no effort to convey its magnitude to my guileless informant. As I left him he was mildly bemoaning his own lack of skill on the pianoforte.

"Darned if I don't wish I'd 'a' took some lessons on the piano myself like that guy done. It certainly does help to while away the tejum when you got friends in for the afternoon. But then I was just a hill-billy. Likely I couldn't have learned the notes good."

It was a half-hour later that I was called to the telephone to listen to the anguished accents of Belknap-Jackson.

"Have you heard it?" he called. I answered that I had.

"The man is a paranoiac. He should be at once confined in an asylum for the criminal insane."

"I shall row him fiercely about it, never fear. I've not seen him yet."

"But the creature should be watched. He may do harm to himself or to some innocent person. They--they run wild, they kill, they burn--set fire to buildings--that sort of thing. I tell you, none of us is safe."

"The situation," I answered, "has even more shocking possibilities, but I've an idea I shall be equal to it. If the worst seems to be imminent I shall adopt extreme measures." I closed the interview. It was too painful. I wished to summon all my powers of deliberation.

To my amazement who should presently appear among my throng of luncheon patrons but the Honourable George. I will not say that he slunk in, but there was an unaccustomed diffidence in his bearing. He did not meet my eye, and it was not difficult to perceive that he had no wish to engage my notice. As he sought a vacant table I observed that he was spotted quite profusely, and his luncheon order was of the simplest.

Straight I went to him. He winced a bit, I thought, as he saw me approach, but then he apparently resolved to brass it out, for he glanced full at me with a terrific assumption of bravado and at once began to give me beans about my service.

"Your bally tea shop running down, what! Louts for waiters, cloddish louts! Disgraceful, my word! Slow beggars! Take a year to do you a rasher and a bit of toast, what!"

To this absurd tirade I replied not a word, but stood silently regarding him. I dare say my gaze was of the most chilling character and steady. He endured it but a moment. His eyes fell, his bravado vanished, he fumbled with the cutlery. Quite abashed he was.

"Come, your explanation!" I said curtly, divining that the moment was one in which to adopt a tone with him. He wriggled a bit, crumpling a roll with panic fingers.

"Come, come!" I commanded.

His face brightened, though with an intention most obviously false. He coughed--a cough of pure deception. Not only were his eyes averted from mine, but they were glassed to an uncanny degree. The fingers wrought piteously at the now plastic roll.

"My word, the chap was taken bad; had to be seen to, what! Revived, I mean to say. All piano Johnnies that way--nervous wrecks, what! Spells! Spells, man--spells!"

"Come, come!" I said crisply. The glassed eyes were those of one hypnotized.

"In the carriage--to the hyphen chap's place, to be sure. Fainting spell--weak heart, what! No stimulants about. Passing house! Perhaps have stimulants--heart tablets, er--beer--things of that sort. Lead him in. Revive him. Quite well presently, but not well enough to go on. Couldn't let a piano Johnny die on our hands, what! Inquest, evidence, witnesses--all that silly rot. Save his life, what! Presence of mind! Kind hearts, what! Humanity! Do as much for any chap. Not let him die like a dog in the gutter, what! Get no credit, though----" His curiously mechanical utterance trailed off to be lost in a mere husky murmur. The glassy stare was still at my wall.

I have in the course of my eventful career had occasion to mark the varying degrees of plausibility with which men speak untruths, but never, I confidently aver, have I beheld one lie with so piteous a futility. The art--and I dare say with diplomat chaps and that sort it may properly be called an art--demands as its very essence that the speaker seem to be himself convinced of the truth of that which he utters. And the Honourable George in his youth mentioned for the Foreign Office!

I turned away. The exhibition was quite too indecent. I left him to mince at his meagre fare. As I glanced his way at odd moments thereafter, he would be muttering feverishly to himself. I mean to say, he no longer *was* himself. He presently made his way to the street, looking neither to right nor left. He had, in truth, the dazed manner of one stupefied by some powerful narcotic. I wondered pityingly when I should again behold him--if it might be that his poor wits were bedevilled past mending.

My period of uncertainty was all too brief. Some two hours later, full into the tide of our afternoon shopping throng, there issued a spectacle that removed any lingering doubt of the unfortunate man's plight. In the rather smart pony-trap of the Klondike woman, driven by the person herself, rode the Honourable George. Full in the startled gaze of many of our best people he advertised his defection from all that makes for a sanely governed stability in our social organism. He had gone flagrantly over to the Bohemian set.

I could detect that his eyes were still glassy, but his head was erect. He seemed to flaunt his shame. And the guilty partner of his downfall drove with an affectation of easy carelessness, yet with a lift of the chin which, though barely perceptible, had all the effect of binding the prisoner to her chariot wheels; a prisoner, more-over, whom it was plain she meant to parade to the last ignominious degree. She drove leisurely, and in the little infrequent curt turns of her head to address her companion she contrived to instill so finished an effect of boredom that she must have goaded to frenzy any matron of the North Side set who chanced to observe her, as more than one of them did.

Thrice did she halt along our main thoroughfare for bits of shopping, a mere running into of shops or to the doors of them where she could issue verbal orders, the while she surveyed her waiting and drugged captive with a certain half-veiled but good-humoured insolence. At these moments--for I took pains to overlook the shocking scene--the Honourable George followed her with eyes no longer glassed; the eyes of helpless infatuation. "He looks at her," Cousin Egbert had said. He had told it all and told it well. The equipage graced our street upon one paltry excuse or another for the better part of an hour, the woman being minded that none of us should longer question her supremacy over the next and eleventh Earl of Brin-stead.

Not for another hour did the effects of the sensation die out among tradesmen and the street crowds. It was like waves that recede but gradually. They talked. They stopped to talk. They passed on talking. They hissed vivaciously; they rose to exclamations. I mean to say, there was no end of a gabbling row about it.

There was in my mind no longer any room for hesitation. The quite harshest of extreme measures must be at once adopted before all was too late. I made my way to the telegraph office. It was not a time for correspondence by post.

Afterward I had myself put through by telephone to Belknap-Jackson. With his sensitive nature he had stopped in all day. Although still averse to appearing publicly, he now consented to meet me at my chambers late that evening.

"The whole town is seething with indignation," he called to me. "It was dis-graceful. I shall come at ten. We rely upon you."

Again I saw that he was concerned solely with his humiliation as a would-be host. Not yet had he divined that the deluded Honourable George might go to the unspeakable length of a matrimonial alliance with the woman who had enchained him. And as to his own disaster, he was less than accurate when he said that the whole town was seething with indignation. The members of the North Side set, to be sure, were seething furiously, but a flippant element of the baser sort was quite openly rejoicing. As at the time of that most slanderous minstrel performance, it was said that the Bohemian set had again, if I have caught the phrase, "put a thing over upon" the North Side set. Many persons of low taste seemed quite to enjoy the dreadful affair, and the members of the Bohemian set, naturally, throughout the day had been quite coarsely beside themselves with glee.

Little they knew, I reflected, what power I could wield nor that I had already set in motion its deadly springs. Little did the woman dream, flaunting her triumph up and down our main business thoroughfare, that one who watched her there had but to raise his hand to wrest the victim from her toils. Little did she now dream that he would stop at no half measures. I mean to say, she would never think I could bowl her out as easy as buying cockles off a barrow.

At the hour for our conference Belknap-Jackson arrived at my chambers muffled in an ulster and with a soft hat well over his face. I gathered that he had not wished to be observed.

"I feel that this is a crisis," he began as he gloomily shook my hand. "Where is our boasted twentieth-century culture if outrages like this are permitted? For the first time I understand how these Western communities have in the past resorted to mob violence. Public feeling is already running high against the creature and her unspeakable set."

I met this outburst with the serenity of one who holds the winning cards in his hand, and begged him to be seated. Thereupon I disclosed to him the weakly, susceptible nature of the Honourable George, reciting the incidents of the typing-girl and the Brixton milliner. I added that now, as before, I should not hesitate to preserve the family honour.

"A dreadful thing, indeed," he murmured, "if that adventuress should trap him into a marriage. Imagine her one day a Countess of Brinstead! But suppose the fellow prove stubborn; suppose his infatuation dulls all his finer instincts?"

I explained that the Honourable George, while he might upon the spur of the moment commit a folly, was not to be taken too seriously; that he was, I believed, quite incapable of a grand passion. I mean to say, he always forgot them after a few days. More like a child staring into shop-windows he was, rapidly forgetting one desired object in the presence of others. I added that I had adopted the extremest measures.

Thereupon, perceiving that I had something in my sleeve, as the saying is, my caller besought me to confide in him. Without a word I handed him a copy of my cable message sent that afternoon to his lordship:

"Your immediate presence required to prevent a monstrous   folly."

He brightened as he read it.

"You actually mean to say----" he began.

"His lordship," I explained, "will at once understand the nature of what is threatened. He knows, moreover, that I would not alarm him without cause. He will come at once, and the Honourable George will be told what. His lordship has never failed. He tells him what perfectly, and that's quite all to it. The poor chap will be saved."

My caller was profoundly stirred. "Coming here--to Red Gap--his lordship the Earl of Brinstead--actually coming here! My God! This is wonderful!" He paused; he seemed to moisten his dry lips; he began once more, and now his voice trembled with emotion: "He will need a place to stay; our hotel is impossible; had you thought----" He glanced at me appealingly.

"I dare say," I replied, "that his lordship will be pleased to have you put him up; you would do him quite nicely."

"You mean it--seriously? That would be--oh, inexpressible. He would be our house guest! The Earl of Brinstead! I fancy that would silence a few of these serpent tongues that are wagging so venomously to-day!"

"But before his coming," I insisted, "there must be no word of his arrival. The Honourable George would know the meaning of it, and the woman, though I suspect now that she is only making a show of him, might go on to the bitter end. They must suspect nothing."

"I had merely thought of a brief and dignified notice in our press," he began, quite wistfully, "but if you think it might defeat our ends----"

"It must wait until he has come."

"Glorious!" he exclaimed. "It will be even more of a blow to them." He began to murmur as if reading from a journal, "'His lordship the Earl of Brinstead is visiting for a few days'--it will surely be as much as a few days, perhaps a week or more--'is visiting for a few days the C. Belknap-Jacksons of Boston and Red Gap.'" He seemed to regard the printed words. "Better still, 'The C. Belknap-Jacksons of Boston and Red Gap are for a few days entertaining as their honoured house guest his lordship the Earl of Brinstead----' Yes, that's admirable."

He arose and impulsively clasped my hand. "Ruggles, dear old chap, I shan't know at all how to repay you. The Bohemian set, such as are possible, will be bound to come over to us. There will be left of it but one unprincipled woman--and she wretched and an outcast. She has made me absurd. I shall grind her under my heel. The east room shall be prepared for his lordship; he shall breakfast there if he wishes. I fancy he'll find us rather more like himself than he suspects. He shall see that we have ideals that are not half bad."

He wrung my hand again. His eyes were misty with gratitude.

CHAPTER SEVENTEEN

Three days later came the satisfying answer to my cable message: "Damn! Sailing Wednesday.

--BRINSTEAD."

Glad I was he had used the cable. In a letter there would doubtless have been still other words improper to a peer of England. Belknap-Jackson thereafter bore himself with a dignity quite tremendous even for him. Graciously aloof, he was as one carrying an inner light. "We hold them in the hollow of our hand," said he, and both his wife and himself took pains on our own thoroughfare to cut the Honourable George dead, though I dare say the poor chap never at all noticed it. They spoke of him as "a remittance man"--the black sheep of a noble family. They mentioned sympathetically the trouble his vicious ways had been to his brother, the Earl. Indeed, so mysteriously important were they in allusions of this sort that I was obliged to caution them, lest they let out the truth. As it was, there ran through the town an undercurrent of puzzled suspicion. It was intimated that we had something in our sleeves.

Whether this tension was felt by the Honourable George, I had no means of knowing. I dare say not, as he is self-centred, being seldom aware of anything beyond his own immediate sensations. But I had reason to believe that the Klondike woman had divined some menace in our attitude of marked indifference. Her own manner, when it could be observed, grew increasingly defiant, if that were possible. The alliance of the Honourable George with the Bohemian set had become, of course, a public scandal after the day of his appearance in her trap and after his betrayal of the Belknap-Jacksons had been gossiped to rags. He no longer troubled himself to pretend any esteem whatever for the North Side set. Scarce a day passed but he appeared in public as the woman's escort. He flagrantly performed her commissions, and at their questionable Bohemian gatherings, with their beer and sausages and that sort of thing, he was the gayest of that gay, mad set.

Indeed, of his old associates, Cousin Egbert quite almost alone seemed to find him any longer desirable, and him I had no heart to caution, knowing that I should only wound without enlightening him, he being entirely impervious to even these cruder aspects of class distinction. I dare say he would have considered the marriage of the Honourable George as no more than the marriage of one of his cattle-person companions. I mean to say, he is a dear old sort and I should never fail to defend him in the most disheartening of his vagaries, but he is undeniably insensitive to what one does and does not do.

The conviction ran, let me repeat, that we had another pot of broth on the fire. I gleaned as much from the Mixer, she being one of the few others besides Cousin Egbert in whose liking the Honourable George had not terrifically descended. She made it a point to address me on the subject over a dish of tea at the Grill one afternoon, choosing a table sufficiently remote from my other feminine guests, who doubtless, at their own tables, discussed the same complication. I was indeed glad that we were remote from other occupied tables, because in the course of her remarks she quite forcefully uttered an oath, which I thought it as well not to have known that I cared to tolerate in my lady patrons.

"As to what Jackson feels about the way it was handed out to him that Sunday," she bluntly declared, "I don't care a----" The oath quite dazed me for a moment, although I had been warned that she would use language on occasion. "What I do care about," she went on briskly, "is that I won't have this girl pestered by Jackson or by you or by any man that wears hair! Why, Jackson talks so silly about her sometimes you'd think she was a bad woman--and he keeps hinting about something he's going to put over till I can hardly keep my hands off him. I just know some day he'll make me forget I'm a lady. Now, take it from me, Bill, if you're setting in with him, don't start anything you can't finish."

Really she was quite fierce about it. I mean to say, the glitter in her eyes made me recall what Cousin Egbert had said of Mrs. Effie, her being quite entirely willing to take on a rattlesnake and give it the advantage of the first two assaults. Somewhat flustered I was, yet I hastened to assure her that, whatever steps I might feel obliged to take for the protection of the Honourable George, they would involve nothing at all unfair to the lady in question.

"Well, they better hadn't!" she resumed threateningly. "That girl had a hard time all right, but listen here--she's as right as a church. She couldn't fool me a minute if she wasn't. Don't you suppose I been around and around quite some? Just because she likes to have a good time and outdresses these dames here--is that any reason they should get out their hammers? Ain't she earned some right to a good time, tell me, after being married when she was a silly kid to Two-spot Kenner, the swine--and God bless the trigger finger of the man that bumped him off! As for the poor old Judge, don't worry. I like the old boy, but Kate Kenner won't do anything more than make a monkey of him just to spite Jackson and his band of lady knockers. Marry him? Say, get me right, Bill--I'll put it as delicate as I can--the Judge is too darned far from being a mental giant for that."

I dare say she would have slanged me for another half-hour but for the constant strain of keeping her voice down. As it was, she boomed up now and again in a way that reduced to listening silence the ladies at several distant tables.

As to the various points she had raised, I was somewhat confused. About the Honourable George, for example: He was, to be sure, no mental giant. But one occupying his position is not required to be. Indeed, in the class to which he was born one well knows that a mental giant would be quite as distressingly bizarre as any other freak. I regretted not having retorted this to her, for it now occurred to me that she had gone it rather strong with her "poor old Judge." I mean to say, it was almost quite a little bit raw for a native American to adopt this patronizing tone toward one of us.

And yet I found that my esteem for the Mixer had increased rather than diminished by reason of her plucky defence of the Klondike woman. I had no reason to suppose that the designing creature was worth a defence, but I could only admire the valour that made it. Also I found food for profound meditation in the Mixer's assertion that the woman's sole aim was to "make a monkey" of the Honourable George. If she were right, a mesalliance need not be feared, at which thought I felt a great relief. That she should achieve the lesser and perhaps equally easy feat with the poor chap was a calamity that would be, I fancied, endured by his lordship with a serene fortitude.

Curiously enough, as I went over the Mixer's tirade point by point, I found in myself an inexplicable loss of animus toward the Klondike woman. I will not say I was moved to sympathy for her, but doubtless that strange ferment of equality stirred me toward her with something less than the indignation I had formerly felt. Perhaps she was an entirely worthy creature. In that case, I merely wished her to be taught that one must not look too far above one's station, even in America, in so serious an affair as matrimony. With all my heart I should wish her a worthy mate of her own class, and I was glad indeed to reflect upon the truth of my assertion to the Mixer, that no unfair advantage would be taken of her. His lordship would remove the Honourable George from her toils, a made monkey, perhaps, but no husband.

Again that day did I listen to a defence of this woman, and from a source whence I could little have expected it. Meditating upon the matter, I found myself staring at Mrs. Judson as she polished some glassware in the pantry. As always, the worthy woman made a pleasing picture in her neat print gown. From staring at her rather absently I caught myself reflecting that she was one of the few women whose hair is always perfectly coiffed. I mean to say, no matter what the press of her occupation, it never goes here and there.

From the hair, my meditative eye, still rather absently, I believe, descended her quite good figure to her boots. Thereupon, my gaze ceased to be absent. They were not boots. They were bronzed slippers with high heels and metal buckles and of a character so distinctive that I instantly knew they had once before been impressed upon my vision. Swiftly my mind identified them: they had been worn by the Klondike woman on the occasion of a dinner at the Grill, in conjunction with a gown to match and a bluish scarf--all combining to achieve an immense effect.

My assistant hummed at her task, unconscious of my scrutiny. I recall that I coughed slightly before disclosing to her that my attention had been attracted to her slippers. She took the reference lightly, affecting, as the sex will, to belittle any prized possession in the face of masculine praise.

"I have seen them before," I ventured.

"She gives me all of hers. I haven't had to buy shoes since baby was born. She gives me--lots of things--stockings and things. She likes me to have them."

"I didn't know you knew her."

"Years! I'm there once a week to give the house a good going over. That Jap of hers is the limit. Dust till you can't rest. And when I clean he just grins."

I mused upon this. The woman was already giving half her time to superintending two assistants in the preparation of the International Relish.

"Her work is too much in addition to your own," I suggested.

"Me? Work too hard? Not in a thousand years. I do all right for you, don't I?"

It was true; she was anything but a slacker. I more nearly approached my real objection.

"A woman in your position," I began, "can't be too careful as to the associations she forms----" I had meant to go on, but found it quite absurdly impossible. My assistant set down the glass she had and quite venomously brandished her towel at me.

"So that's it?" she began, and almost could get no farther for mere sputtering. I mean to say, I had long recognized that she possessed character, but never had I suspected that she would have so inadequate a control of her temper.

"So that's it?" she sputtered again, "And I thought you were too decent to join in that talk about a woman just because she's young and wears pretty clothes and likes to go out. I'm astonished at you, I really am. I thought you were more of a man!" She broke off, scowling at me most furiously.

Feeling all at once rather a fool, I sought to conciliate her. "I have joined in no talk," I said. "I merely suggested----" But she shut me off sharply.

"And let me tell you one thing: I can pick out my associates in this town without any outside help. The idea! That girl is just as nice a person as ever walked the earth, and nobody ever said she wasn't except those frumpy old cats that hate her good looks because the men all like her."

"Old cats!" I echoed, wishing to rebuke this violence of epithet, but she would have none of me.

"Nasty old spite-cats," she insisted with even more violence, and went on to an almost quite blasphemous absurdity. "A prince in his palace wouldn't be any too good for her!"

"Tut, tut!" I said, greatly shocked.

"Tut nothing!" she retorted fiercely. "A regular prince in his palace, that's what she deserves. There isn't a single man in this one-horse town that's good enough to pick up her glove. And she knows it, too. She's carrying on with your silly Englishman now, but it's just to pay those old cats back in their own coin. She'll carry on with him--yes! But marry? Good heavens and earth! Marriage is serious!" With this novel conclusion she seized another glass and began to wipe it viciously. She glared at me, seeming to believe that she had closed the interview. But I couldn't stop. In some curious way she had stirred me rather out of myself--but not about the Klondike woman nor about the Honourable George. I began most illogically, I admit, to rage inwardly about another matter.

"You have other associates," I exclaimed quite violently, "those cattle-persons--I know quite all about it. That Hank and Buck--they come here on the chance of seeing you; they bring you boxes of candy, they bring you little presents. Twice they've escorted you home at night when you quite well knew I was only too glad to do it----" I felt my temper most curiously running away with me, ranting about things I hadn't meant to at all. I looked for another outburst from her, but to my amazement she flashed me a smile with a most enigmatic look back of it. She tossed her head, but resumed her wiping of the glass with a certain demureness. She spoke almost meekly:

"They're very old friends, and I'm sure they always act right. I don't see anything wrong in it, even if Buck Edwards has shown me a good deal of attention."

But this very meekness of hers seemed to arouse all the violence in my nature.

"I won't have it!" I said. "You have no right to receive presents from men. I tell you I won't have it! You've no right!"

"Haven't I?" she suddenly said in the most curious, cool little voice, her eyes falling before mine. "Haven't I? I didn't know."

It was quite chilling, her tone and manner. I was cool in an instant. Things seemed to mean so much more than I had supposed they did. I mean to say, it was a fair crumpler. She paused in her wiping of the glass but did not regard me. I was horribly moved to go to her, but coolly remembered that that sort of thing would never do.

"I trust I have said enough," I remarked with entirely recovered dignity.

"You have," she said.

"I mean I won't have such things," I said.

"I hear you," she said, and fell again to her work. I thereupon investigated an ice-box and found enough matter for complaint against the Hobbs boy to enable me to manage a dignified withdrawal to the rear. The remarkable creature was humming again as I left.

I stood in the back door of the Grill giving upon the alley, where I mused rather excitedly. Here I was presently interrupted by the dog, Mr. Barker. For weeks now I had been relieved of his odious attentions, by the very curious circumstance that he had transferred them to the Honourable George. Not all my kicks and cuffs and beatings had sufficed one whit to repulse him. He had kept after me, fawned upon me, in spite of them. And then on a day he had suddenly, with glad cries, become enamoured of the Honourable George, waiting for him at doors, following him, hanging upon his every look. And the Honourable George had rather fancied the beast and made much of him.

And yet this animal is reputed by poets and that sort of thing to be man's best friend, faithfully sharing his good fortune and his bad, staying by his side to the bitter end, even refusing to leave his body when he has perished--starving there with a dauntless fidelity. How chagrined the weavers of these tributes would have been to observe the fickle nature of the beast in question! For weeks he had hardly deigned me a glance. It had been a relief, to be sure, but what a sickening disclosure of the cur's trifling inconstancy. Even now, though he sniffed hungrily at the open door, he paid me not the least attention--me whom he had once idolized!

I slipped back to the ice-box and procured some slices of beef that were far too good for him. He fell to them with only a perfunctory acknowledgment of my agency in procuring them.

"Why, I thought you hated him!" suddenly said the voice of his owner. She had tiptoed to my side.

"I do," I said quite savagely, "but the unspeakable beast can't be left to starve, can he?"

I felt her eyes upon me, but would not turn. Suddenly she put her hand upon my shoulder, patting it rather curiously, as she might have soothed her child. When I did turn she was back at her task. She was humming again, nor did she glance my way. Quite certainly she was no longer conscious that I stood about. She had quite forgotten me. I could tell as much from her manner. "Such," I reflected, with an unaccustomed cynicism, "is the light inconsequence of women and dogs." Yet I still experienced a curiously thrilling determination to protect her from her own good nature in the matter of her associates.

At a later and cooler moment of the day I reflected upon her defence of the Klondike woman. A "prince in his palace" not too good for her! No doubt she had meant me to take these remarkable words quite seriously. It was amazing, I thought, with what seriousness the lower classes of the country took their dogma of equality, and with what naive confidence they relied upon us to accept it. Equality in North America was indeed praiseworthy; I had already given it the full weight of my approval and meant to live by it. But at home, of course, that sort of thing would never do. The crude moral worth of the Klondike woman might be all that her two defenders had alleged, and indeed I felt again that strange little thrill of almost sympathy for her as one who had been unjustly aspersed. But I could only resolve that I would be no party to any unfair plan of opposing her. The Honourable George must be saved from her trifling as well as from her serious designs, if such she might have; but so far as I could influence the process it should cause as little chagrin as possible to the offender. This much the Mixer and my charwoman had achieved with me. Indeed, quite hopeful I was that when the creature had been set right as to what was due one of our oldest and proudest families she would find life entirely pleasant among those of her own station. She seemed to have a good heart.

As the day of his lordship's arrival drew near, Belknap-Jackson became increasingly concerned about the precise manner of his reception and the details of his entertainment, despite my best assurances that no especially profound thought need be given to either, his lordship being quite that sort, fussy enough in his own way but hardly formal or pretentious.

His prospective host, after many consultations with me, at length allowed himself to be dissuaded from meeting his lordship in correct afternoon garb of frock-coat and top-hat, consenting, at my urgent suggestion, to a mere lounge-suit of tweeds with a soft-rolled hat and a suitable rough day stick. Again in the matter of the menu for his lordship's initial dinner which we had determined might well be tendered him at my establishment. Both husband and wife were rather keen for an elaborate repast of many courses, feeling that anything less would be doing insufficient honour to their illustrious guest, but I at length convinced them that I quite knew what his lordship would prefer: a vegetable soup, an abundance of boiled mutton with potatoes, a thick pudding, a bit of scientifically correct cheese, and a jug of beer. Rather trying they were at my first mention of this--a dinner quite without finesse, to be sure, but eminently nutritive--and only their certainty that I knew his lordship's ways made them give in.

The affair was to be confined to the family, his lordship the only guest, this being thought discreet for the night of his arrival in view of the peculiar nature of his mission. Belknap-Jackson had hoped against hope that the Mixer might not be present, and even so late as the day of his lordship's arrival he was cheered by word that she might be compelled to keep her bed with a neuralgia.

To the afternoon train I accompanied him in his new motor-car, finding him not a little distressed because the chauffeur, a native of the town, had stoutly--and with some not nice words, I gathered--refused to wear the smart uniform which his employer had provided.

"I would have shopped the fellow in an instant," he confided to me, "had it been at any other time. He was most impertinent. But as usual, here I am at the mercy of circumstances. We couldn't well subject Brinstead to those loathsome public conveyances."

We waited in the usual throng of the leisured lower-classes who are so naively pleased at the passage of a train. I found myself picturing their childish wonder had they guessed the identity of him we were there to meet. Even as the train appeared Belknap-Jackson made a last moan of complaint.

"Mrs. Pettengill," he observed dejectedly, "is about the house again and I fear will be quite well enough to be with us this evening." For a moment I almost quite disapproved of the fellow. I mean to say, he was vogue and all that, and no doubt had been wretchedly mistreated, but after all the Mixer was not one to be wished ill to.

A moment later I was contrasting the quiet arrival of his lordship with the clamour and confusion that had marked the advent among us of the Honourable George. He carried but one bag and attracted no attention whatever from the station loungers. While I have never known him be entirely vogue in his appointments, his lordship carries off a lounge-suit and his gray-cloth hat with a certain manner which the Honourable George was never known to achieve even in the days when I groomed him. The grayish rather aggressive looking side-whiskers first caught my eye, and a moment later I had taken his hand. Belknap-Jackson at the same time took his bag, and with a trepidation so obvious that his lordship may perhaps have been excusable for a momentary misapprehension. I mean to say, he instantly and crisply directed Belknap-Jackson to go forward to the luggage van and recover his box.

A bit awkward it was, to be sure, but I speedily took the situation in hand by formally presenting the two men, covering the palpable embarrassment of the host by explaining to his lordship the astounding ingenuity of the American luggage system. By the time I had deprived him of his check and convinced him that his box would be admirably recovered by a person delegated to that service, Belknap-Jackson, again in form, was apologizing to him for the squalid character of the station and for the hardships he must be prepared to endure in a crude Western village. Here again the host was annoyed by having to call repeatedly to his mechanician in order to detach him from a gossiping group of loungers. He came smoking a quite fearfully bad cigar and took his place at the wheel entirely without any suitable deference to his employer.

His lordship during the ride rather pointedly surveyed me, being impressed, I dare say, by something in my appearance and manner quite new to him. Doubtless I had been feeling equal for so long that the thing was to be noticed in my manner. He made no comment upon me, however. Indeed almost the only time he spoke during our passage was to voice his astonishment at not having been able to procure the London *Times* at the press-stalls along the way. His host made clucking noises of sympathy at this. He had, he said, already warned his lordship that America was still crude.

"Crude? Of course, what, what!" exclaimed his lordship. "But naturally they'd have the *Times*! I dare say the beggars were too lazy to look it out. Laziness, what, what!"

"We've a job teaching them to know their places," ventured Belknap-Jackson, moodily regarding the back of his chauffeur which somehow contrived to be eloquent with disrespect for him.

"My word, what rot!" rejoined his lordship. I saw that he had arrived in one of his peppery moods. I fancy he could not have recited a multiplication table without becoming fanatically assertive about it. That was his way. I doubt if he had ever condescended to have an opinion. What might have been opinions came out on him like a rash in form of the most violent convictions.

"What rot not to know their places, when they must know them!" he snappishly added.

"Quite so, quite so!" his host hastened to assure him.

"A--dashed--fine big country you have," was his only other observation.

"Indeed, indeed," murmured his host mildly. I had rather dreaded the oath which his lordship is prone to use lightly.

Reaching the Belknap-Jackson house, his lordship was shown to the apartment prepared for him.

"Tea will be served in half an hour, your--er--Brinstead," announced his host cordially, although seemingly at a loss how to address him.

"Quite so, what, what! Tea, of course, of course! Why wouldn't it be? Meantime, if you don't mind, I'll have a word with Ruggles. At once."

Belknap-Jackson softly and politely withdrew at once.

Alone with his lordship, I thought it best to acquaint him instantly with the change in my circumstances, touching lightly upon the matter of my now being an equal with rather most of the North Americans. He listened with exemplary patience to my brief recital and was good enough to felicitate me.

"Assure you, glad to hear it--glad no end. Worthy fellow; always knew it. And equal, of course, of course! Take up their equality by all means if you take 'em up themselves. Curious lot of nose-talking beggars, and putting r's every place one shouldn't, but don't blame you. Do it myself if I could--England gone to pot. Quite!"

"Gone to pot, sir?" I gasped.

"Don't argue. Course it has. Women! Slasher fiends and firebrands! Pictures, churches, golf-greens, cabinet members--nothing safe. Pouring their beastly filth into pillar boxes. Women one knows. Hussies, though! Want the vote--rot! Awful rot! Don't blame you for America. Wish I might, too. Good thing, my word! No backbone in Downing Street. Let the fiends out again directly they're hungry. No system! No firmness! No dash! Starve 'em proper, I would."

He was working himself into no end of a state. I sought to divert him.

"About the Honourable George, sir----" I ventured.

"What's the silly ass up to now? Dancing girl got him--yes? How he does it, I can't think. No looks, no manner, no way with women. Can't stand him myself. How ever can they? Frightful bore, old George is. Well, well, man, I'm waiting. Tell me, tell me, tell me!"

Briefly I disclosed to him that his brother had entangled himself with a young person who had indeed been a dancing girl or a bit like that in the province of Alaska. That at the time of my cable there was strong reason to believe she would stop at nothing--even marriage, but that I had since come to suspect that she might be bent only on making a fool of her victim, she being, although an honest enough character, rather inclined to levity and without proper respect for established families.

I hinted briefly at the social warfare of which she had been a storm centre. I said again, remembering the warm words of the Mixer and of my charwoman, that to the best of my knowledge her character was without blemish. All at once I was feeling preposterously sorry for the creature.

His lordship listened, though with a cross-fire of interruptions. "Alaska dancing girl. Silly! Nothing but snow and mines in Alaska." Or, again, "Make a fool of old George? What silly piffle! Already done it himself, what, what! Waste her time!" And if she wasn't keen to marry him, had I called him across the ocean to intervene in a vulgar village squabble about social precedence? "Social precedence silly rot!"

I insisted that his brother should be seen to. One couldn't tell what the woman might do. Her audacity was tremendous, even for an American. To this he listened more patiently.

"Dare say you're right. You don't go off your head easily. I'll rag him proper, now I'm here. Always knew the ass would make a silly marriage if he could. Yes, yes, I'll break it up quick enough. I say I'll break it up proper. Dancers and that sort. Dangerous. But I know their tricks."

A summons to tea below interrupted him.

"Hungry, my word! Hardly dared eat in that dining-coach. Tinned stuff all about one. Appendicitis! American journal--some Colonel chap found it out. Hunting sort. Looked a fool beside his silly horse, but seemed to know. Took no chances. Said the tin-opener slays its thousands. Rot, no doubt. Perhaps not."

I led him below, hardly daring at the moment to confess my own responsibility for his fears. Another time, I thought, we might chat of it.

Belknap-Jackson with his wife and the Mixer awaited us. His lordship was presented, and I excused myself.

"Mrs. Pettengill, his lordship the Earl of Brinstead," had been the host's speech of presentation to the Mixer.

"How do do, Earl; I'm right glad to meet you," had been the Mixer's acknowledgment, together with a hearty grasp of the hand. I saw his lordship's face brighten.

"What ho!" he cried with the first cheerfulness he had exhibited, and the Mixer, still vigorously pumping his hand, had replied, "Same here!" with a vast smile of good nature. It occurred to me that they, at least, were quite going to "get" each other, as Americans say.

"Come right in and set down in the parlour," she was saying at the last. "I don't eat between meals like you English folks are always doing, but I'll take a shot of hooch with you."

The Belknap-Jacksons stood back not a little distressed. They seemed to publish that their guest was being torn from them.

"A shot of hooch!" observed his lordship "I dare say your shooting over here is absolutely top-hole--keener sport than our popping at driven birds. What, what!"

CHAPTER EIGHTEEN

A T a latish seven, when the Grill had become nicely filled with a representative crowd, the Belknap-Jacksons arrived with his lordship. The latter had not dressed and I was able to detect that Belknap-Jackson, doubtless noting his guest's attire at the last moment, had hastily changed back to a lounge-suit of his own. Also I noted the absence of the Mixer and wondered how the host had contrived to eliminate her. On this point he found an opportunity to enlighten me before taking his seat.

"Mark my words, that old devil is up to something," he darkly said, and I saw that he was genuinely put about, for not often does he fall into strong language.

"After pushing herself forward with his lordship all through tea-time in the most brazen manner, she announces that she has a previous dinner engagement and can't be with us. I'm as well pleased to have her absent, of course, but I'd pay handsomely to know what her little game is. Imagine her not dining with the Earl of Brinstead when she had the chance! That shows something's wrong. I don't like it. I tell you she's capable of things."

I mused upon this. The Mixer was undoubtedly capable of things. Especially things concerning her son-in-law. And yet I could imagine no opening for her at the present moment and said as much. And Mrs. Belknap-Jackson, I was glad to observe, did not share her husband's evident worry. She had entered the place plumingly, as it were, sweeping the length of the room before his lordship with quite all the manner her somewhat stubby figure could carry off. Seated, she became at once vivacious, chatting to his lordship brightly and continuously, raking the room the while with her lorgnon. Half a dozen ladies of the North Side set were with parties at other tables. I saw she was immensely stimulated by the circumstance that these friends were unaware of her guest's identity. I divined that before the evening was over she would contrive to disclose it.

His lordship responded but dully to her animated chat. He is never less urbane than when hungry, and I took pains to have his favourite soup served quite almost at once. This he fell upon. I may say that he has always a hearty manner of attacking his soup. Not infrequently he makes noises. He did so on this occasion. I mean to say, there was no finesse. I hovered near, anxious that the service should be without flaw.

His head bent slightly over his plate, I saw a spoonful of soup ascending with precision toward his lips. But curiously it halted in mid-air, then fell back. His lordship's eyes had become fixed upon some one back of me. At once, too, I noted looks of consternation upon the faces of the Belknap-Jacksons, the hostess freezing in the very midst of some choice phrase she had smilingly begun.

I turned quickly. It was the Klondike person, radiant in the costume of black and the black hat. She moved down the hushed room with well-lifted chin, eyes straight ahead and narrowed to but a faint offended consciousness of the staring crowd. It was well done. It was superior. I am able to judge those things.

Reaching a table the second but one from the Belknap-Jacksons's, she relaxed finely from the austere note of her progress and turned to her companions with a pretty and quite perfect confusion as to which chair she might occupy. Quite awfully these companions were the Mixer, overwhelming in black velvet and diamonds, and Cousin Egbert, uncomfortable enough looking but as correctly enveloped in evening dress as he could ever manage by himself. His cravat had been tied many times and needed it once more.

They were seated by the raccoon with quite all his impressiveness of manner. They faced the Belknap-Jackson party, yet seemed unconscious of its presence. Cousin Egbert, with a bored manner which I am certain he achieved only with tremendous effort, scanned my simple menu. The Mixer settled herself with a vast air of comfort and arranged various hand-belongings about her on the table.

Between them the Klondike woman sat with a restraint that would actually not have ill-become one of our own women. She did not look about; her hands were still, her head was up. At former times with her own set she had been wont to exhibit a rather defiant vivacity. Now she did not challenge. Finely, eloquently, there pervaded her a reserve that seemed almost to exhale a fragrance. But of course that is silly rot. I mean to say, she drew the attention without visible effort. She only waited.

The Earl of Brinstead, as we all saw, had continued to stare. Thrice slowly arose the spoon of soup, for mere animal habit was strong upon him, yet at a certain elevation it each time fell slowly back. He was acting like a mechanical toy. Then the Mixer caught his eye and nodded crisply. He bobbed in response.

"What ho! The dowager!" he exclaimed, and that time the soup was successfully resumed.

"Poor old mater!" sighed his hostess. "She's constantly taking up people. One does, you know, in these queer Western towns."

"Jolly old thing, awfully good sort!" said his lordship, but his eyes were not on the Mixer.

Terribly then I recalled the Honourable George's behaviour at that same table the night he had first viewed this Klondike person. His lordship was staring in much the same fashion. Yet I was relieved to observe that the woman this time was quite unconscious of the interest she had aroused. In the case of the Honourable George, who had frankly ogled her--for the poor chap has ever lacked the finer shades in these matters--she had not only been aware of it but had deliberately played upon it. It is not too much to say that she had shown herself to be a creature of blandishments. More than once she had permitted her eyes to rest upon him with that peculiarly womanish gaze which, although superficially of a blank innocence, is yet all-seeing and even shoots little fine arrows of questions from its ambuscade. But now she was ignoring his lordship as utterly as she did the Belknap-Jacksons.

To be sure she may later have been in some way informed that his eyes were seeking her, but never once, I am sure, did she descend to even a veiled challenge of his glance or betray the faintest discreet consciousness of it. And this I was indeed glad to note in her. Clearly she must know where to draw the line, permitting herself a malicious laxity with a younger brother which she would not have the presumption to essay with the holder of the title. Pleased I was, I say, to detect in her this proper respect for his lordship's position. It showed her to be not all unworthy.

The dinner proceeded, his lordship being good enough to compliment me on the fare which I knew was done to his liking. Yet, even in the very presence of the boiled mutton, his eyes were too often upon his neighbour. When he behaved thus in the presence of a dish of mutton I had not to be told that he was strongly moved. I uneasily recalled now that he had once been a bit of a dog himself. I mean to say, there was talk in the countryside, though of course it had died out a score of years ago. I thought it as well, however, that he be told almost immediately that the person he honoured with his glance was no other than the one he had come to subtract his unfortunate brother from.

The dinner progressed--somewhat jerkily because of his lordship's inattention--through the pudding and cheese to coffee. Never had I known his lordship behave so languidly in the presence of food he cared for. His hosts ate even less. They were worried. Mrs. Belknap-Jackson, however, could simply no longer contain within herself the secret of their guest's identity. With excuses to the deaf ears of his lordship she left to address a friend at a distant table. She addressed others at other tables, leaving a flutter of sensation in her wake.

Belknap-Jackson, having lighted one of his non-throat cigarettes, endeavoured to engross his lordship with an account of their last election of officers to the country club. His lordship was not properly attentive to this. Indeed, with his hostess gone he no longer made any pretence of concealing his interest in the other table. I saw him catch the eye of the Mixer and astonishingly intercepted from her a swift but most egregious wink.

"One moment," said his lordship to the host. "Must pay my respects to the dowager, what, what! Jolly old muggins, yes!" And he was gone.

I heard the Mixer's amazing presentation speech.

"Mrs. Kenner, Mr. Floud, his lordship--say, listen here, is your right name Brinstead, or Basingwell, like your brother's?"

The Klondike person acknowledged the thing with a faintly gracious nod. It carried an air, despite the slightness of it. Cousin Egbert was more cordial.

"Pleased to meet you, Lord!" said he, and grasped the newcomer's hand. "Come on, set in with us and have some coffee and a cigar. Here, Jeff, bring the lord a good cigar. We was just talking about you that minute. How do you like our town? Say, this here Kulanche Valley----" I lost the rest. His lordship had seated himself. At his own table Belknap-Jackson writhed acutely. He was lighting a second cigarette--the first not yet a quarter consumed!

At once the four began to be thick as thieves, though it was apparent his lordship had eyes only for the woman. Coffee was brought. His lordship lighted his cigar. And now the word had so run from Mrs. Belknap-Jackson that all eyes were drawn to this table. She had created her sensation and it had become all at once more of one than she had thought. From Mrs. Judge Ballard's table I caught her glare at her unconscious mother. It was not the way one's daughter should regard one in public.

Presently contriving to pass the table again, I noted that Cousin Egbert had changed his form of address.

"Have some brandy with your coffee, Earl. Here, Jeff, bring Earl and all of us some lee-cures." I divined the monstrous truth that he supposed himself to be calling his lordship by his first name, and he in turn must have understood my shocked glance of rebuke, for a bit later, with glad relief in his tones, he was addressing his lordship as "Cap!" And myself he had given the rank of colonel!

The Klondike person in the beginning finely maintained her reserve. Only at the last did she descend to vivacity or the use of her eyes. This later laxness made me wonder if, after all, she would feel bound to pay his lordship the respect he was wont to command from her class.

"You and poor George are rather alike," I overheard, "except that he uses the single 'what' and you use the double. Hasn't he any right to use the double 'what' yet, and what does it mean, anyway? Tell us."

"What, what!" demanded his lordship, a bit puzzled.

"But that's it! What do you say 'What, what' for? It can't do you any good."

"What, what! But I mean to say, you're having me on. My word you are-- spoofing, I mean to say. What, what! To be sure. Chaffing lot, you are!" He laughed. He was behaving almost with levity.

"But poor old George is so much younger than you--you must make allowances," I again caught her saying; and his lordship replied:

"Not at all; not at all! Matter of a half-score years. Barely a half-score; nine and a few months. Younger? What rot! Chaffing again."

Really it was a bit thick, the creature saying "poor old George" quite as if he were something in an institution, having to be wheeled about in a bath-chair with rugs and water-bottles!

Glad I was when the trio gave signs of departure. It was woman's craft dictating it, I dare say. She had made her effect and knew when to go.

"Of course we shall have to talk over my dreadful designs on your poor old George," said the amazing woman, intently regarding his lordship at parting.

"Leave it to me," said he, with a scarcely veiled significance.

"Well, see you again, Cap," said Cousin Egbert warmly. "I'll take you around to meet some of the boys. We'll see you have a good time."

"What ho!" his lordship replied cordially. The Klondike person flashed him one enigmatic look, then turned to precede her companions. Again down the thronged room she swept, with that chin-lifted, drooping-eyed, faintly offended half consciousness of some staring rabble at hand that concerned her not at all. Her alert feminine foes, I am certain, read no slightest trace of amusement in her unwavering lowered glance. So easily she could have been crude here!

Belknap-Jackson, enduring his ignominious solitude to the limit of his powers, had joined his wife at the lower end of the room. They had taken the unfortunate development with what grace they could. His lordship had dropped in upon them quite informally--charming man that he was. Of course he would quickly break up the disgraceful affair. Beginning at once. They would doubtless entertain for him in a quiet way----

At the deserted table his lordship now relieved a certain sickening apprehension that had beset me.

"What, what! Quite right to call me out here. Shan't forget it. Dangerous creature, that. Badly needed, I was. Can't think why you waited so long! Anything might have happened to old George. Break it up proper, though. Never do at all. Impossible person for him. Quite!"

I saw they had indeed taken no pains to hide the woman's identity from him nor their knowledge of his reason for coming out to the States, though with wretchedly low taste they had done this chaffingly. Yet it was only too plain that his lordship now realized what had been the profound gravity of the situation, and I was glad to see that he meant to end it without any nonsense.

"Silly ass, old George, though," he added as the Belknap-Jacksons approached. "How a creature like that could ever have fancied him! What, what!"

His hosts were profuse in their apologies for having so thoughtlessly run away from his lordship--they carried it off rather well. They were keen for sitting at the table once more, as the other observant diners were lingering on, but his lordship would have none of this.

"Stuffy place!" said he. "Best be getting on." And so, reluctantly, they led him down the gauntlet of widened eyes. Even so, the tenth Earl of Brinstead had dined publicly with them. More than repaid they were for the slight the Honourable George had put upon them in the affair of the pianoforte artist.

An hour later Belknap-Jackson had me on by telephone. His voice was not a little worried.

"I say, is his lordship, the Earl, subject to spells of any sort? We were in the library where I was showing him some photographic views of dear old Boston, and right over a superb print of our public library he seemed to lose consciousness. Might it be a stroke? Or do you think it's just a healthy sleep? And shall I venture to shake him? How would he take that? Or should I merely cover him with a travelling rug? It would be so dreadful if anything happened when he's been with us such a little time."

I knew his lordship. He has the gift of sleeping quite informally when his attention is not too closely engaged. I suggested that the host set his musical phonograph in motion on some one of the more audible selections. As I heard no more from him that night I dare say my plan worked.

Our town, as may be imagined, buzzed with transcendent gossip on the morrow. The *Recorder* disclosed at last that the Belknap-Jacksons of Boston and Red Gap were quietly entertaining his lordship, the Earl of Brinstead, though since the evening before this had been news to hardly any one. Nor need it be said that a viciously fermenting element in the gossip concerned the apparently cordial meeting of his lordship with the Klondike person, an encounter that had been watched with jealous eyes by more than one matron of the North Side set. It was even intimated that if his lordship had come to put the creature in her place he had chosen a curious way to set about it.

Also there were hard words uttered of the Belknap-Jacksons by Mrs. Effie, and severe blame put upon myself because his lordship had not come out to the Flouds'.

"But the Brinsteads have always stopped with us before," she went about saying, as if there had been a quite long succession of them. I mean to say, only the

Honourable George had stopped on with them, unless, indeed, the woman actually counted me as one. Between herself and Mrs. Belknap-Jackson, I understood, there ensued early that morning by telephone a passage of virulent acidity, Mrs. Effie being heard by Cousin Egbert to say bluntly that she would get even.

Undoubtedly she did not share the annoyance of the Belknap-Jacksons at certain eccentricities now developed by his lordship which made him at times a trying house guest. That first morning he arose at five sharp, a custom of his which I deeply regretted not having warned his host about. Discovering quite no one about, he had ventured abroad in search of breakfast, finding it at length in the eating establishment known as "Bert's Place," in company with engine-drivers, plate-layers, milk persons, and others of a common sort.

Thereafter he had tramped furiously about the town and its environs for some hours, at last encountering Cousin Egbert who escorted him to the Floud home for his first interview with the Honourable George. The latter received his lordship in bed, so Cousin Egbert later informed me. He had left the two together, whereupon for an hour there were heard quite all over the house words of the most explosive character. Cousin Egbert, much alarmed at the passionate beginning of the interview, suspected they might do each other a mischief, and for some moments hovered about with the aim, if need be, of preserving human life. But as the uproar continued evenly, he at length concluded they would do no more than talk, the outcome proving the accuracy of his surmise.

Mrs. Effie, meantime, saw her opportunity and seized it with a cool readiness which I have often remarked in her. Belknap-Jackson, distressed beyond measure at the strange absence of his guest, had communicated with me by telephone several times without result. Not until near noon was I able to give him any light. Mrs. Effie had then called me to know what his lordship preferred for luncheon. Replying that cold beef, pickles, and beer were his usual mid-day fancy, I hastened to allay the fears of the Belknap-Jacksons, only to find that Mrs. Effie had been before me.

"She says," came the annoyed voice of the host, "that the dear Earl dropped in for a chat with his brother and has most delightfully begged her to give him luncheon. She says he will doubtless wish to drive with them this afternoon, but I had already planned to drive him myself--to the country club and about. The woman is high-handed, I must say. For God's sake, can't you do something?"

I was obliged to tell him straight that the thing was beyond me, though I promised to recover his guest promptly, should any opportunity occur. The latter did not, however, drive with the Flouds that afternoon. He was observed walking abroad with Cousin Egbert, and it was later reported by persons of unimpeachable veracity that they had been seen to enter the Klondike person's establishment.

Evening drew on without further news. But then certain elated members of the Bohemian set made it loosely known that they were that evening to dine informally at their leader's house to meet his lordship. It seemed a bit extraordinary to me, yet I could not but rejoice that he should thus adopt the peaceful methods of diplomacy for the extrication of his brother.

Belknap-Jackson now telephoning to know if I had heard this report--"canard" he styled it--I confirmed it and remarked that his lordship was undoubtedly by way of bringing strong pressure to bear on the woman.

"But I had expected him to meet a few people here this evening," cried the host pathetically. I was then obliged to tell him that the Brinsteads for centuries had been bluntly averse to meeting a few people. It seemed to run in the blood.

The Bohemian dinner, although quite informal, was said to have been highly enjoyed by all, including the Honourable George, who was among those present, as well as Cousin Egbert. The latter gossiped briefly of the affair the following day.

"Sure, the Cap had a good time all right," he said. "Of course he ain't the mixer the Judge is, but he livens up quite some, now and then. Talks like a bunch of firecrackers going off all to once, don't he? Funny guy. I walked with him to the Jacksons' about twelve or one. He's going back to Mis' Kenner's house today. He says it'll take a lot of talking back and forth to get this thing settled right, and it's got to be right, he says. He seen that right off." He paused as if to meditate profoundly.

"If you was to ask me, though, I'd say she had him--just like that!"

He held an open hand toward me, then tightly clenched it.

Suspecting he might spread absurd gossip of this sort, I explained carefully to him that his lordship had indeed at once perceived her to be a dangerous woman; and that he was now taking his own cunning way to break off the distressing affair between her and his brother. He listened patiently, but seemed wedded to some monstrous view of his own.

"Them dames of that there North Side set better watch out," he remarked ominously. "First thing they know, what that Kate Kenner'll hand them--they can make a lemonade out of!"

I could make but little of this, save its general import, which was of course quite shockingly preposterous. I found myself wishing, to be sure, that his lordship had been able to accomplish his mission to North America without appearing to meet the person as a social equal, as I feared indeed that a wrong impression of his attitude would be gained by the undiscerning public. It might have been better, I was almost quite certain, had he adopted a stern and even brutal method at the outset, instead of the circuitous and diplomatic. Belknap-Jackson shared this view with me.

"I should hate dreadfully to have his lordship's reputation suffer for this," he confided to me.

The first week dragged to its close in this regrettable fashion. Oftener than not his hosts caught no glimpse of his lordship throughout the day. The smart trap and the tandem team were constantly ready, but he had not yet been driven abroad by his host. Each day he alleged the necessity of conferring with the woman.

"Dangerous creature, my word! But dangerous!" he would announce. "Takes no end of managing. Do it, though; do it proper. Take a high hand with her. Can't have silly old George in a mess. Own brother, what, what! Time needed, though. Not with you at dinner, if you don't mind. Creature has a way of picking up things not half nasty."

But each day Belknap-Jackson met him with pressing offers of such entertainment as the town afforded. Three several times he had been obliged to postpone the informal evening affair for a few smart people. Yet, though patient, he was determined. Reluctantly at last he abandoned the design of driving his guest about in the trap, but he insistently put forward the motor-car. He would drive it himself. They would spend pleasant hours going about the country. His lordship continued elusive. To myself he confided that his host was a nagger.

"Awfully nagging sort, yes. Doesn't know the strain I'm under getting this silly affair straight. Country interesting no doubt, what, what! But, my word! saw nothing but country coming out. Country quite all about, miles and miles both sides of the metals. Seen enough country. Seen motor-cars, too, my word. Enough of both, what, what!"

Yet it seemed that on the Saturday after his arrival he could no longer decently put off his insistent host. He consented to accompany him in the motor-car. Rotten judging it was on the part of Belknap-Jackson. He should have listened to me. They departed after luncheon, the host at the wheel. I had his account of such following events as I did not myself observe.

"Our country club," he observed early in the drive. "No one there, of course. You'd never believe the trouble I've had----"

"Jolly good club," replied his lordship. "Drive back that way."

"Back that way," it appeared, would take them by the detached villa of the Klondike person.

"Stop here," directed his lordship. "Shan't detain you a moment."

This was at two-thirty of a fair afternoon. I am able to give but the bare facts, yet I must assume that the emotions of Belknap-Jackson as he waited there during the ensuing two hours were of a quite distressing nature. As much was intimated by several observant townspeople who passed him. He was said to be distrait; to be smoking his cigarettes furiously.

At four-thirty his lordship reappeared. With apparent solicitude he escorted the Klondike person, fetchingly gowned in a street costume of the latest mode. They chatted gayly to the car.

"Hope I've not kept you waiting, old chap," said his lordship genially. "Time slips by one so. You two met, of course, course!" He bestowed his companion in the tonneau and ensconced himself beside her.

"Drive," said he, "to your goods shops, draper's, chemist's--where was it?"

"To the Central Market," responded the lady in bell-like tones, "then to the Red Front store, and to that dear little Japanese shop, if he doesn't mind."

"Mind! Mind! Course not, course not! Are you warm? Let me fasten the robe."

I confess to have felt a horrid fascination for this moment as I was able to reconstruct it from Belknap-Jackson's impassioned words. It was by way of being one of those scenes we properly loathe yet morbidly cannot resist overlooking if opportunity offers.

Into the flood tide of our Saturday shopping throng swept the car and its re-markably assembled occupants. The street fair gasped. The woman's former parade of the Honourable George had been as nothing to this exposure.

"Poor Jackson's face was a study," declared the Mixer to me later.

I dare say. It was still a study when my own turn came to observe it. The car halted before the shops that had been designated. The Klondike person dispatched her commissions in a superbly leisured manner, attentively accompanied by the Earl of Brinstead bearing packages for her.

Belknap-Jackson, at the wheel, stared straight ahead. I am told he bore himself with dignity even when some of our more ingenuous citizens paused to converse with him concerning his new motor-car. He is even said to have managed a smile when his passengers returned.

"I have it," exclaimed his lordship now. "Deuced good plan--go to that Ruggles place for a jolly fat tea. No end of a spree, what, what!"

It is said that on three occasions in turning his car and traversing the short block to the Grill the owner escaped disastrous collision with other vehicles only by the narrowest possible margin. He may have courted something of the sort. I dare say he was desperate.

"Join us, of course!" said his lordship, as he assisted his companion to alight. Again I am told the host managed to illumine his refusal with a smile. He would take no tea--the doctor's orders.

The surprising pair entered at the height of my tea-hour and were served to an accompaniment of stares from the ladies present. To this they appeared oblivious, being intent upon their conference. His lordship was amiable to a degree. It now occurred to me that he had found the woman even more dangerous than he had at first supposed. He was being forced to play a deep game with her and was meeting guile with guile. He had, I suspected, found his poor brother far deeper in than any of us had thought. Doubtless he had written compromising letters that must be secured--letters she would hold at a price.

And yet I had never before had excuse to believe his lordship possessed the diplomatic temperament. I reflected that I must always have misread him. He was deep, after all. Not until the two left did I learn that Belknap-Jackson awaited them with his car. He loitered about in adjacent doorways, quite like a hired fellow. He was passionately smoking more cigarettes than were good for him.

I escorted my guests to the car. Belknap-Jackson took his seat with but one glance at me, yet it was eloquent of all the ignominy that had been heaped upon him.

"Home, I think," said the lady when they were well seated. She said it charmingly.

"Home," repeated his lordship. "Are you quite protected by the robe?"

An incautious pedestrian at the next crossing narrowly escaped being run down. He shook a fist at the vanishing car and uttered a stream of oaths so vile that he would instantly have been taken up in any well-policed city.

Half an hour later Belknap-Jackson called me.

"He got out with that fiend! He's staying on there. But, my God! can nothing be done?"

"His lordship is playing a most desperate game," I hastened to assure him. "He's meeting difficulties. She must have her dupe's letters in her possession. Blackmail, I dare say. Best leave his lordship free. He's a deep character."

"He presumed far this afternoon--only the man's position saved him with me!" His voice seemed choked with anger. Then, remotely, faint as distant cannonading, a rumble reached me. It was hoarse laughter of the Mixer, perhaps in another room. The electric telephone has been perfected in the States to a marvellous delicacy of response.

I now found myself observing Mrs. Effie, who had been among the absorbed onlookers while the pair were at their tea, she having occupied a table with Mrs. Judge Ballard and Mrs. Dr. Martingale. Deeply immersed in thought she had been, scarce replying to her companions. Her eyes had narrowed in a way I well knew when she reviewed the social field.

Still absorbed she was when Cousin Egbert entered, accompanied by the Honourable George. The latter had seen but little of his brother since their first stormy interview, but he had also seen little of the Klondike woman. His spirits, however, had seemed quite undashed. He rarely missed his tea. Now as they seated themselves they were joined quickly by Mrs. Effie, who engaged her relative in earnest converse. It was easy to see that she begged a favour. She kept a hand on his arm. She urged. Presently, seeming to have achieved her purpose, she left them, and I paused to greet the pair.

"I guess that there Mrs. Effie is awful silly," remarked Cousin Egbert enigmatically. "No, sir; she can't ever tell how the cat is going to jump." Nor would he say more, though he most elatedly held a secret.

With this circumstance I connected the announcement in Monday's *Recorder* that Mrs. Senator Floud would on that evening entertain at dinner the members of Red Gap's Bohemian set, including Mrs. Kate Kenner, the guest of honour being his lordship the Earl of Brinstead, "at present visiting in this city. Covers," it added, "would be laid for fourteen." I saw that Cousin Egbert would have been made the ambassador to conduct what must have been a business of some delicacy.

Among the members of the North Side set the report occasioned the wildest alarm. And yet so staunch were known to be the principles of Mrs. Effie that but few accused her of downright treachery. It seemed to be felt that she was but lending herself to the furtherance of some deep design of his lordship's. Blackmail, the recovery of compromising letters, the avoidance of legal proceedings--these were hinted at. For myself I suspected that she had merely misconstrued the seeming cordiality of his lordship toward the woman and, at the expense of the Belknap-Jacksons, had sought the honour of entertaining him. If, to do that, she must entertain the woman, well and good. She was not one to funk her fences with the game in sight.

Consulting me as to the menu for her dinner, she allowed herself to be persuaded to the vegetable soup, boiled mutton, thick pudding, and cheese which I recommended, though she pleaded at length for a chance to use the new fish set and for a complicated salad portrayed in her latest woman's magazine. Covered with grated nuts it was in the illustration. I was able, however, to convince her that his lordship would regard grated nuts as silly.

From Belknap-Jackson I learned by telephone (during these days, being sensitive, he stopped in almost quite continuously) that Mrs. Effie had profusely explained to his wife about the dinner. "Of course, my dear, I couldn't have the presumption to ask you and your husband to sit at table with the creature, even if he did think it all right to drive her about town on a shopping trip. But I thought we ought to do something to make the dear Earl's visit one to be remembered--he's *so* appreciative! I'm sure you understand just how things are----"

In reciting this speech to me Belknap-Jackson essayed to simulate the tone and excessive manner of a woman gushing falsely. The fellow was quite bitter about it.

"I sometimes think I'll give up," he concluded. "God only knows what things are coming to!"

It began to seem even to me that they were coming a bit thick. But I knew that his lordship was a determined man. He was of the bulldog breed that has made old England what it is. I mean to say, I knew he would put the woman in her place.

CHAPTER NINETEEN

ECHOES of the Monday night dinner reached me the following day. The affair had passed off pleasantly enough, the members of the Bohemian set conducting themselves quite as persons who mattered, with the exception of the Klondike woman herself, who, I gathered, had descended to a mood of most indecorous liveliness considering who the guest of honour was. She had not only played and sung those noisy native folksongs of hers, but she had, it seemed, conducted herself with a certain facetious familiarity toward his lordship.

"Every now and then," said Cousin Egbert, my principal informant, "she'd whirl in and josh the Cap all over the place about them funny whiskers he wears. She told him out and out he'd just got to lose them."

"Shocking rudeness!" I exclaimed.

"Oh, sure, sure!" he agreed, yet without indignation. "And the Cap just hated her for it--you could tell that by the way he looked at her. Oh, he hates her something terrible. He just can't bear the sight of her."

"Naturally enough," I observed, though there had been an undercurrent to his speech that I thought almost quite a little odd. His accents were queerly placed. Had I not known him too well I should have thought him trying to be deep. I recalled his other phrases, that Mrs. Effie was seeing which way a cat would leap, and that the Klondike person would hand the ladies of the North Side set a lemon squash. I put them all down as childish prattle and said as much to the Mixer later in the day as she had a dish of tea at the Grill.

"Yes, Sour-dough's right," she observed. "That Earl just hates the sight of her--can't bear to look at her a minute." But she, too, intoned the thing queerly.

"He's putting pressure to bear on her," I said.

"Pressure!" said the Mixer; and then, "Hum!" very dryly.

With this news, however, it was plain as a pillar-box that things were going badly with his lordship's effort to release the Honourable George from his entanglement. The woman, doubtless with his compromising letters, would be holding out for a stiffish price; she would think them worth no end. And plainly again, his lordship had thrown off his mask; was unable longer to conceal his aversion for her. This, to be sure, was more in accordance with his character as I had long observed it. If he hated her it was like him to show it when he looked at her. I mean he was quite like that with almost any one. I hoped, however, that diplomacy might still save us all sorts of a nasty row.

To my relief when the pair appeared for tea that afternoon--a sight no longer causing the least sensation--I saw that his lordship must have returned to his first or diplomatic manner. Doubtless he still hated her, but one would little have suspected it from his manner of looking at her. I mean to say, he looked at her another way. The opposite way, in fact. He was being subtle in the extreme. I fancied it must have been her wretched levity regarding his beard that had goaded him into the exhibitions of hatred noted by Cousin Egbert and the Mixer. Unquestionably his lordship may be goaded in no time if one deliberately sets about it. At the time, doubtless, he had sliced a drive or two, as one might say, but now he was back in form.

Again I confess I was not a little sorry for the creature, seeing her there so smartly taken in by his effusive manner. He was having her on in the most obvious way and she, poor dupe, taking it all quite seriously. Prime it was, though, considering the creature's designs; and I again marvelled that in all the years of my association with his lordship I had never suspected what a topping sort he could be at this game. His mask was now perfect. It recalled, indeed, Cousin Egbert's simple but telling phrase about the Honourable George--"He looks at her!" It could now have been said of his lordship with the utmost significance to any but those in the know.

And so began, quite as had the first, the second week of his lordship's stay among us. Knowing he had booked a return from Cooks, I fancied that results of some sort must soon ensue. The pressure he was putting on the woman must begin to tell. And this was the extreme of the encouragement I was able to offer the Belknap-Jacksons. Both he and his wife were of course in a bit of a state. Nor could I blame them. With an Earl for house guest they must be content with but a glimpse of him at odd moments. Rather a barren honour they were finding it.

His lordship's conferences with the woman were unabated. When not secluded with her at her own establishment he would be abroad with her in her trap or in the car of Belknap-Jackson. The owner, however, no longer drove his car. He had never taken another chance. And well I knew these activities of his lordship's were being basely misconstrued by the gossips.

"The Cap is certainly some queener," remarked Cousin Egbert, which perhaps reflected the view of the deceived public at this time, the curious term implying that his lordship was by way of being a bit of a dog. But calm I remained under these aspersions, counting upon a clean-cut vindication of his lordship's methods when he should have got the woman where he wished her.

I remained, I repeat, serenely confident that a signal triumph would presently crown his lordship's subtly planned attack. And then, at midweek, I was rudely shocked to the suspicion that all might not be going well with his plan. I had not seen the pair for a day, and when they did appear for their tea I instantly detected a profound change in their mutual bearing. His lordship still looked at the woman, but the raillery of their past meetings had gone. Too plainly something momentous had occurred. Even the woman was serious. Had they fought to the last stand? Would she have been too much for him? I mean to say, was the Honourable George cooked?

I now recalled that I had observed an almost similar change in the latter's manner. His face wore a look of wildest gloom that might have been mitigated perhaps by a proper trimming of his beard, but even then it would have been remarked by those who knew him well. I divined, I repeat, that something momentous had now occurred and that the Honourable George was one not least affected by it.

Rather a sleepless night I passed, wondering fearfully if, after all, his lordship would have been unable to extricate the poor chap from this sordid entanglement. Had the creature held out for too much? Had she refused to compromise? Would there be one of those appalling legal things which our best families so often suffer? What if the victim were to cut off home?

Nor was my trepidation allayed by the cryptic remark of Mrs. Judson as I passed her at her tasks in the pantry that morning:

"A prince in his palace not too good--that's what I said!"

She shot the thing at me with a manner suspiciously near to flippancy. I sternly demanded her meaning.

"I mean what I mean," she retorted, shutting her lips upon it in a definite way she has. Well enough I knew the import of her uncivil speech, but I resolved not to bandy words with her, because in my position it would be undignified; because, further, of an unfortunate effect she has upon my temper at such times.

"She's being terrible careful about *her* associates," she presently went on, with a most irritating effect of addressing only herself; "nothing at all but just dukes and earls and lords day in and day out!" Too often when the woman seems to wish it she contrives to get me in motion, as the American saying is.

"And it is deeply to be regretted," I replied with dignity, "that other persons must say less of themselves if put to it."

Well she knew what I meant. Despite my previous clear warning, she had more than once accepted small gifts from the cattle-persons, Hank and Buck, and had even been seen brazenly in public with them at a cinema palace. One of a more suspicious nature than I might have guessed that she conducted herself thus for the specific purpose of enraging me, but I am glad to say that no nature could be more free than mine from vulgar jealousy, and I spoke now from the mere wish that she should more carefully guard her reputation. As before, she exhibited a surprising meekness under this rebuke, though I uneasily wondered if there might not be guile beneath it.

"Can I help it," she asked, "if they like to show me attentions? I guess I'm a free woman." She lifted her head to observe a glass she had polished. Her eyes were curiously lighted. She had this way of embarrassing me. And invariably, moreover, she aroused all that is evil in my nature against the two cattle-persons, especially the Buck one, actually on another occasion professing admiration for "his wavy chestnut hair!" I saw now that I could not trust myself to speak of the fellow. I took up another matter.

"That baby of yours is too horribly fat," I said suddenly. I had long meant to put this to her. "It's too fat. It eats too much!"

To my amazement the creature was transformed into a vixen.

"It--it! Too fat! You call my boy 'it' and say he's too fat! Don't you dare! What does a creature like you know of babies? Why, you wouldn't even know----"

But the thing was too painful. Let her angry words be forgotten. Suffice to say, she permitted herself to cry out things that might have given grave offence to one less certain of himself than I. Rather chilled I admit I was by her frenzied outburst. I was shrewd enough to see instantly that anything in the nature of a criticism of her offspring must be led up to, rather; perhaps couched in less direct phrases than I had chosen. Fearful I was that she would burst into another torrent of rage, but to my amazement she all at once smiled.

"What a fool I am!" she exclaimed. "Kidding me, were you? Trying to make me mad about the baby. Well, I'll give you good. You did it. Yes, sir, I never would have thought you had a kidding streak in you--old glum-face!"

"Little you know me," I retorted, and quickly withdrew, for I was then more embarrassed than ever, and, besides, there were other and graver matters forward to depress and occupy me.

In my fitful sleep of the night before I had dreamed vividly that I saw the Honourable George being dragged shackled to the altar. I trust I am not superstitious, but the vision had remained with me in all its tormenting detail. A veiled woman had grimly awaited him as he struggled with his uniformed captors. I mean to say, he was being hustled along by two constables.

That day, let me now put down, was to be a day of the most fearful shocks that a man of rather sensitive nervous organism has ever been called upon to endure. There are now lines in my face that I make no doubt showed then for the first time.

And it was a day that dragged interminably, so that I became fair off my head with the suspense of it, feeling that at any moment the worst might happen. For hours I saw no one with whom I could consult. Once I was almost moved to call up Belknap-Jackson, so intolerable was the menacing uncertainty; but this I knew bordered on hysteria, and I restrained the impulse with an iron will.

But I wretchedly longed for a sight of Cousin Egbert or the Mixer, or even of the Honourable George; some one to assure me that my horrid dream of the night before had been a baseless fabric, as the saying is. The very absence of these people and of his lordship was in itself ominous.

Nervously I kept to a post at one of my windows where I could survey the street. And here at mid-day I sustained my first shock. Terrific it was. His lordship had emerged from the chemist's across the street. He paused a moment, as if to recall his next mission, then walked briskly off. And this is what I had been stupefied to note: he was clean shaven! The Brinstead side-whiskers were gone! Whiskers that had been worn in precisely that fashion by a tremendous line of the Earls of Brinstead! And the tenth of his line had abandoned them. As well, I thought, could he have defaced the Brinstead arms.

It was plain as a pillar-box, indeed. The woman had our family at her mercy, and she would show no mercy. My heart sank as I pictured the Honourable George in her toils. My dream had been prophetic. Then I reflected that this very circumstance of his lordship's having pandered to her lawless whim about his beard would go to show he had not yet given up the fight. If the thing were hopeless I knew he would have seen her--dashed--before he would have relinquished it. There plainly was still hope for poor George. Indeed his lordship might well have planned some splendid coup; this defacement would be a part of his strategy, suffered in anguish for his ultimate triumph. Quite cheered I became at the thought. I still scanned the street crowd for some one who could acquaint me with developments I must have missed.

But then a moment later came the call by telephone of Belknap-Jackson. I answered it, though with little hope than to hear more of his unending complaints about his lordship's negligence. Startled instantly I was, however, for his voice was stranger than I had known it even in moments of his acutest distress. Hoarse it was, and his words alarming but hardly intelligible.

"Heard?--My God!--Heard?--My God!--Marriage! Marriage! God!" But here he broke off into the most appalling laughter--the blood-curdling laughter of a chained patient in a mad-house. Hardly could I endure it and grateful I was when I heard the line close. Even when he attempted vocables he had sounded quite like an inferior record on a phonographic machine. But I had heard enough to leave me aghast. Beyond doubt now the very worst had come upon our family. His lordship's tremendous sacrifice would have been all in vain. Marriage! The Honourable George was done for. Better had it been the typing-girl, I bitterly reflected. Her father had at least been a curate!

Thankful enough I now was for the luncheon-hour rush: I could distract myself from the appalling disaster. That day I took rather more than my accustomed charge of the serving. I chatted with our business chaps, recommending the joint in the highest terms; drawing corks; seeing that the relish was abundantly stocked at every table. I was striving to forget.

Mrs. Judson alone persisted in reminding me of the impending scandal. "A prince in his palace," she would maliciously murmur as I encountered her. I think she must have observed that I was bitter, for she at last spoke quite amiably of our morning's dust-up.

"You certainly got my goat," she said in the quaint American fashion, "telling me little No-no was too fat. You had me going there for a minute, thinking you meant it!"

The creature's name was Albert, yet she persisted in calling it "No-no," because the child itself would thus falsely declare its name upon being questioned, having in some strange manner gained this impression. It was another matter I meant to bring to her attention, but at this crisis I had no heart for it.

My crowd left. I was again alone to muse bitterly upon our plight. Still I scanned the street, hoping for a sight of Cousin Egbert, who, I fancied, would be informed as to the wretched details. Instead, now, I saw the Honourable George. He walked on the opposite side of the thoroughfare, his manner of dejection precisely what I should have expected. Followed closely as usual he was by the Judson cur. A spirit of desperate mockery seized me. I called to Mrs. Judson, who was gathering glasses from a table. I indicated the pair.

"Mr. Barker," I said, "is dogging his footsteps." I mean to say, I uttered the words in the most solemn manner. Little the woman knew that one may often be moved in the most distressing moments to a jest of this sort. She laughed heartily, being of quick discernment. And thus jauntily did I carry my knowledge of the lowering cloud. But I permitted myself no further sallies of that sort. I stayed expectantly by the window, and I dare say my bearing would have deceived the most alert. I was steadily calm. The situation called precisely for that.

The hours sped darkly and my fears mounted. In sheer desperation, at length, I had myself put through to Belknap-Jackson. To my astonishment he seemed quite revived, though in a state of feverish gayety. He fair bubbled.

"Just leaving this moment with his lordship to gather up some friends. We meet at your place. Yes, yes--all the uncertainty is past. Better set up that largest table--rather a celebration."

Almost more confusing it was than his former message, which had been confined to calls upon his Maker and to maniac laughter. Was he, I wondered, merely making the best of it? Had he resolved to be a dead sportsman? A few moments later he discharged his lordship at my door and drove rapidly on. (Only a question of time it is when he will be had heavily for damages due to his reckless driving.)

His lordship bustled in with a cheerfulness that staggered me. He, too, was gay; almost debonair. A gardenia was in his lapel. He was vogue to the last detail in a form-fitting gray morning-suit that had all the style essentials. Almost it seemed as if three valets had been needed to groom him. He briskly rubbed his hands.

"Biggest table--people. Tea, that sort of thing. Have a go of champagne, too, what, what! Beard off, much younger appearing? Of course, course! Trust women, those matters. Tea cake, toast, crumpets, marmalade--things like that. Plenty champagne! Not happen every day! Ha! ha!"

To my acute distress he here thumbed me in the ribs and laughed again. Was he, too, I wondered, madly resolved to be a dead sportsman in the face of the unavoidable? I sought to edge in a discreet word of condolence, for I knew that between us there need be no pretence.

"I know you did your best, sir," I observed. "And I was never quite free of a fear that the woman would prove too many for us. I trust the Honourable George----"

But I had said as much as he would let me. He interrupted me with his thumb again, and on his face was what in a lesser person I should unhesitatingly have called a leer.

"You dog, you! Woman prove too many for us, what, what! Dare say you knew what to expect. Silly old George! Though how she could ever have fancied the juggins----"

I was about to remark that the creature had of course played her game from entirely sordid motives and I should doubtless have ventured to applaud the game spirit in which he was taking the blow. But before I could shape my phrases on this delicate ground Mrs. Effie, the Senator, and Cousin Egbert arrived. They somewhat formally had the air of being expected. All of them rushed upon his lordship with an excessive manner. Apparently they were all to be dead sportsmen together. And then Mrs. Effie called me aside.

"You can do me a favour," she began. "About the wedding breakfast and reception. Dear Kate's place is so small. It wouldn't do. There will be a crush, of course. I've had the loveliest idea for it--our own house. You know how delighted we'd be. The Earl has been so charming and everything has turned out so splendidly. Oh, I'd love to do them this little parting kindness. Use your influence like a good fellow, won't you, when the thing is suggested?"

"Only too gladly," I responded, sick at heart, and she returned to the group. Well I knew her motive. She was by way of getting even with the Belknap-Jacksons. As Cousin Egbert in his American fashion would put it, she was trying to pass them a bison. But I was willing enough she should house the dreadful affair. The more private the better, thought I.

A moment later Belknap-Jackson's car appeared at my door, now discharging the Klondike woman, effusively escorted by the Mixer and by Mrs. Belknap-Jackson. The latter at least, I had thought, would show more principle. But she had buckled atrociously, quite as had her husband, who had quickly, almost merrily, followed them. There was increased gayety as they seated themselves about the large table, a silly noise of pretended felicitation over a calamity that not even the tenth Earl of Brinstead had been able to avert. And then Belknap-Jackson beckoned me aside.

"I want your help, old chap, in case it's needed," he began.

"The wedding breakfast and reception?" I said quite cynically.

"You've thought of it? Good! Her own place is far too small. Crowd, of course. And it's rather proper at our place, too, his lordship having been our house guest. You see? Use what influence you have. The affair will be rather widely commented on--even the New York papers, I dare say."

"Count upon me," I answered blandly, even as I had promised Mrs. Effie. Disgusted I was. Let them maul each other about over the wretched "honour." They could all be dead sports if they chose, but I was now firmly resolved that for myself I should make not a bit of pretence. The creature might trick poor George into a marriage, but I for one would not affect to regard it as other than a blight upon our house. I was just on the point of hoping that the victim himself might have cut off to unknown parts when I saw him enter. By the other members of the party he was hailed with cries of delight, though his own air was finely honest, being dejected in the extreme. He was dressed as regrettably as usual, this time in parts of two lounge-suits.

As he joined those at the table I constrained myself to serve the champagne. Senator Floud arose with a brimming glass.

"My friends," he began in his public-speaking manner, "let us remember that Red Gap's loss is England's gain--to the future Countess of Brinstead!"

To my astonishment this appalling breach of good taste was received with the loudest applause, nor was his lordship the least clamorous of them. I mean to say, the chap had as good as wished that his lordship would directly pop off. It was beyond me. I walked to the farthest window and stood a long time gazing pensively out; I wished to be away from that false show. But they noticed my absence at length and called to me. Monstrously I was desired to drink to the happiness of the groom. I thought they were pressing me too far, but as they quite gabbled now with their tea and things, I hoped to pass it off. The Senator, however, seemed to fasten me with his eye as he proposed the toast--"To the happy man!"

I drank perforce.

"A body would think Bill was drinking to the Judge," remarked Cousin Egbert in a high voice.

"Eh?" I said, startled to this outburst by his strange words.

"Good old George!" exclaimed his lordship. "Owe it all to the old juggins, what, what!"

The Klondike person spoke. I heard her voice as a bell pealing through breakers at sea. I mean to say, I was now fair dazed.

"Not to old George," said she. "To old Ruggles!"

"To old Ruggles!" promptly cried the Senator, and they drank.

Muddled indeed I was. Again in my eventful career I felt myself tremble; I knew not what I should say, any *savoir faire* being quite gone. I had received a crumpler of some sort--but what sort?

My sleeve was touched. I turned blindly, as in a nightmare. The Hobbs cub who was my vestiare was handing me our evening paper. I took it from him, staring--staring until my knees grew weak. Across the page in clarion type rang the unbelievable words:

BRITISH PEER WINS AMERICAN BRIDE

His Lordship Tenth Earl of Brinstead to Wed One of Red Gap's
Fairest Daughters

My hands so shook that in quick subterfuge I dropped the sheet, then stooped for it, trusting to control myself before I again raised my face. Mercifully the others were diverted by the journal. It was seized from me, passed from hand to hand, the incredible words read aloud by each in turn. They jested of it!

"Amazing chaps, your pressmen!" Thus the tenth Earl of Brinstead, while I pinched myself viciously to bring back my lost aplomb. "Speedy beggars, what, what! Never knew it myself till last night. She would and she wouldn't."

"I think you knew," said the lady. Stricken as I was I noted that she eyed him rather strangely, quite as if she felt some decent respect for him.

"Marriage is serious," boomed the Mixer.

"Don't blame her, don't blame her--swear I don't!" returned his lordship. "Few days to think it over--quite right, quite right. Got to know their own minds, my word!"

While their attention was thus mercifully diverted from me, my own world by painful degrees resumed its stability. I mean to say, I am not the fainting sort, but if I were, then I should have keeled over at my first sight of that journal. But now I merely recovered my glass of champagne and drained it. Rather pigged it a bit, I fancy. Badly needing a stimulant I was, to be sure.

They now discussed details: the ceremony--that sort of thing.

"Before a registrar, quickest way," said his lordship.

"Nonsense! Church, of course!" rumbled the Mixer very arbitrarily.

"Quite so, then," assented his lordship. "Get me the rector of the parish--a vicar, a curate, something of that sort."

"Then the breakfast and reception," suggested Mrs. Effie with a meaning glance at me before she turned to the lady. "Of course, dearest, your own tiny nest would never hold your host of friends----"

"I've never noticed," said the other quickly. "It's always seemed big enough," she added in pensive tones and with downcast eyes.

"Oh, not large enough by half," put in Belknap-Jackson, "Most charming little home-nook but worlds too small for all your well-wishers." With a glance at me he narrowed his eyes in friendly calculation. "I'm somewhat puzzled myself--Suppose we see what the capable Ruggles has to suggest."

"Let Ruggles suggest something by all means!" cried Mrs. Effie.

I mean to say, they both quite thought they knew what I would suggest, but it was nothing of the sort. The situation had entirely changed. Quite another sort of thing it was. Quickly I resolved to fling them both aside. I, too, would be a dead sportsman.

"I was about to suggest," I remarked, "that my place here is the only one at all suitable for the breakfast and reception. I can promise that the affair will go off smartly."

The two had looked up with such radiant expectation at my opening words and were so plainly in a state at my conclusion that I dare say the future Countess of Brinstead at once knew what. She flashed them a look, then eyed me with quick understanding.

"Great!" she exclaimed in a hearty American manner. "Then that's settled," she continued briskly, as both Belknap-Jackson and Mrs. Effie would have interposed "Ruggles shall do everything: take it off our shoulders--ices, flowers, invitations."

"The invitation list will need great care, of course," remarked Belknap-Jackson with a quite savage glance at me.

"But you just called him 'the capable Ruggles,'" insisted the fiancee. "We shall leave it all to him. How many will you ask, Ruggles?" Her eyes flicked from mine to Belknap-Jackson.

"Quite almost every one," I answered firmly.

"Fine!" she said.

"Ripping!" said his lordship.

"His lordship will of course wish a best man," suggested Belknap-Jackson. "I should be only too glad----"

"You're going to suggest Ruggles again!" cried the lady. "Just the man for it! You're quite right. Why, we owe it all to Ruggles, don't we?"

She here beamed upon his lordship. Belknap-Jackson wore an expression of the keenest disrelish.

"Of course, course!" replied his lordship. "Dashed good man, Ruggles! Owe it all to him, what, what!"

I fancy in the cordial excitement of the moment he was quite sincere. As to her ladyship, I am to this day unable to still a faint suspicion that she was having me on. True, she owed it all to me. But I hadn't a bit meant it and well she knew it. Subtle she was, I dare say, but bore me no malice, though she was not above setting Belknap-Jackson back a pace or two each time he moved up.

A final toast was drunk and my guests drifted out. Belknap-Jackson again glared savagely at me as he went, but Mrs. Effie rather outglared him. Even I should hardly have cared to face her at that moment.

And I was still in a high state of muddle. It was all beyond me. Had his lordship, I wondered, too seriously taken my careless words about American equality? Of course I had meant them to apply only to those stopping on in the States.

Cousin Egbert lingered to the last, rather with a troubled air of wishing to consult me. When I at length came up with him he held the journal before me, indicating lines in the article--"relict of an Alaskan capitalist, now for some years one of Red Gap's social favourites."

"Read that there," he commanded grimly. Then with a terrific earnestness I had never before remarked in him: "Say, listen here! I better go round right off and mix it up with that fresh guy. What's he hinting around at by that there word 'relict'? Why, say, she was married to him----"

I hastily corrected his preposterous interpretation of the word, much to his relief.

I was still in my precious state of muddle. Mrs. Judson took occasion to flounce by me in her work of clearing the table.

"A prince in his palace," she taunted. I laughed in a lofty manner.

"Why, you poor thing, I've known it all for some days," I said.

"Well, I must say you're the deep one if you did--never letting on!"

She was unable to repress a glance of admiration at me as she moved off.

I stood where she had left me, meditating profoundly.

CHAPTER TWENTY

TWO days later at high noon was solemnized the marriage of his lordship to the woman who, without a bit meaning it, I had so curiously caused to enter his life. The day was for myself so crowded with emotions that it returns in rather a jumble: patches of incidents, little floating clouds of memory; some meaningless and one at least to be significant to my last day.

The ceremony was had in our most nearly smart church. It was only a Methodist church, but I took pains to assure myself that a ceremony performed by its curate would be legal. I still seem to hear the organ, strains of "The Voice That Breathed Through Eden," as we neared the altar; also the Mixer's rumbling whisper about a lost handkerchief which she apparently found herself needing at that moment.

The responses of bride and groom were unhesitating, even firm. Her ladyship, I thought, had never appeared to better advantage than in the pearl-tinted lustreless going-away gown she had chosen. As always, she had finely known what to put on her head.

Senator Floud, despite Belknap-Jackson's suggestion of himself for the office, had been selected to give away the bride, as the saying is. He performed his function with dignity, though I recall being seized with horror when the moment came; almost certain I am he restrained himself with difficulty from making a sort of a speech.

The church was thronged. I had seen to that. I had told her ladyship that I should ask quite almost every one, and this I had done, squarely in the face of Belknap-Jackson's pleading that discretion be used. For a great white light, as one might say, had now suffused me. I had seen that the moment was come when the warring factions of Red Gap should be reunited. A Bismarck I felt myself, indeed. That I acted ably was later to be seen.

Even for the wedding breakfast, which occurred directly after the ceremony,

I had shown myself a dictator in the matter of guests. Covers were laid in my room for seventy and among these were included not only the members of the North Side set and the entire Bohemian set, but many worthy persons not hitherto socially existent yet who had been friends or well-wishers of the bride.

I am persuaded to confess that in a few of these instances I was not above a snarky little wish to correct the social horizon of Belknap-Jackson; to make it more broadly accord, as I may say, with the spirit of American equality for which their forefathers bled and died on the battlefields of Boston, New York, and Vicksburg.

Not the least of my reward, then, was to see his eyebrows more than once eloquently raise, as when the cattle-persons, Hank and Buck, appeared in suits of decent black, or when the driver chap Pierce entered with his quite obscure mother on his arm, or a few other cattle and horse persons with whom the Honourable George had palled up during his process of going in for America.

This laxity I felt that the Earl of Brinstead and his bride could amply afford, while for myself I had soundly determined that Red Gap should henceforth be without "sets." I mean to say, having frankly taken up America, I was at last re-solved to do it whole-heartedly. If I could not take up the whole of it, I would not take up a part. Quite instinctively I had chosen the slogan of our Chamber of Com-merce: "Don't Knock--Boost; and Boost Altogether." Rudely worded though it is, I had seen it to be sound in spirit.

These thoughts ran in my mind during the smart repast that now followed. Insidiously I wrought among the guests to amalgamate into one friendly whole certain elements that had hitherto been hostile. The Bohemian set was not segre-gated. Almost my first inspiration had been to scatter its members widely among the conservative pillars of the North Side set. Left in one group, I had known they would plume themselves quite intolerably over the signal triumph of their leader; perhaps, in the American speech, "start something." Widely scattered, they became mere parts of the whole I was seeking to achieve.

The banquet progressed gayly to its finish. Toasts were drunk no end, all of them proposed by Senator Floud who, toward the last, kept almost constantly on his feet. From the bride and groom he expanded geographically through Red Gap, the Kulanche Valley, the State of Washington, and the United States to the British Empire, not omitting the Honourable George--who, I noticed, called for the relish and consumed quite almost an entire bottle during the meal. Also I was proposed--"through whose lifelong friendship for the illustrious groom this meeting of hearts and hands has been so happily brought about."

Her ladyship's eyes rested briefly upon mine as her lips touched the glass to this. They conveyed the unspeakable. Rather a fool I felt, and unable to look away until she released me. She had been wondrously quiet through it all. Not dazed in the least, as might have been looked for in one of her lowly station thus prodigiously elevated; and not feverishly gay, as might also have been anticipated. Simple and quiet she was, showing a complete but perfectly controlled awareness of her position.

For the first time then, I think, I did envision her as the Countess of Brinstead. She was going to carry it off. Perhaps quite as well as even I could have wished his lordship's chosen mate to do. I observed her look at his lordship with those strange lights in her eyes, as if only half realizing yet wholly believing all that he believed. And once at the height of the gayety I saw her reach out to touch his sleeve, furtively, swiftly, and so gently he never knew.

It occurred to me there were things about the woman we had taken too little trouble to know. I wondered what old memories might be coming to her now; what staring faces might obtrude, what old, far-off, perhaps hated, voices might be sounding to her; what of remembered hurts and heartaches might newly echo back to make her flinch and wonder if she dreamed. She touched the sleeve again, as it might have been in protection from them, her eyes narrowed, her gaze fixed. It queerly occurred to me that his lordship might find her as difficult to know as we had--and yet would keep always trying more than we had, to be sure. I mean to say, she was no gabbler.

The responses to the Senator's toasts increased in volume. His final flight, I recall, involved terms like "our blood-cousins of the British Isles," and introduced a figure of speech about "hands across the sea," which I thought striking, indeed. The applause aroused by this was noisy in the extreme, a number of the cattle and horse persons, including the redskin Tuttle, emitting a shrill, concerted "yipping" which, though it would never have done with us, seemed somehow not out of place in North America, although I observed Belknap-Jackson to make gestures of extreme repugnance while it lasted.

There ensued a rather flurried wishing of happiness to the pair. A novel sight it was, the most austere matrons of the North Side set vying for places in the line that led past them. I found myself trying to analyze the inner emotions of some of them I best knew as they fondly greeted the now radiant Countess of Brinstead. But that way madness lay, as Shakespeare has so aptly said of another matter. I recalled, though, the low-toned comment of Cousin Egbert, who stood near me.

"Don't them dames stand the gaff noble!" It was quite true. They were heroic. I recalled then his other quaint prophecy that her ladyship would hand them a bottle of lemonade. As is curiously usual with this simple soul, he had gone to the heart of the matter.

The throng dwindled to the more intimate friends. Among those who lingered were the Belknap-Jacksons and Mrs. Effie. Quite solicitous they were for the "dear Countess," as they rather defiantly called her to one another. Belknap-Jackson casually mentioned in my hearing that he had been asked to Chaynes-Wotten for the shooting. Mrs. Effie, who also heard, swiftly remarked that she would doubtless run over in the spring--the dear Earl was so insistent. They rather glared at each other. But in truth his lordship had insisted that quite almost every one should come and stop on with him.

"Of course, course, what, what! Jolly party, no end of fun. Week-end, that sort of thing. Know she'll like her old friends best. Wouldn't be keen for the creature if she'd not. Have 'em all, have 'em all. Capital, by Jove!"

To be sure it was a manner of speaking, born of the expansive good feeling of the moment. Yet I believe Cousin Egbert was the only invited one to decline. He did so with evident distress at having to refuse.

"I like your little woman a whole lot," he observed to his lordship, "but Europe is too kind of uncomfortable for me; keeps me upset all the time, what with all the foreigners and one thing and another. But, listen here, Cap! You pack the little woman back once in a while. Just to give us a flash at her. We'll give you both a good time."

"What ho!" returned his lordship. "Of course, course! Fancy we'd like it vastly, what, what!"

"Yes, sir, I fancy you would, too," and rather startlingly Cousin Egbert seized her ladyship and kissed her heartily. Whereupon her ladyship kissed the fellow in return.

"Yes, sir, I dare say I fancy you would," he called back a bit nervously as he left.

Belknap-Jackson drove the party to the station, feeling, I am sure, that he scored over Mrs. Effie, though he was obliged to include the Mixer, from whom her ladyship bluntly refused to be separated. I inferred that she must have found the time and seclusion in which to weep a bit on the Mixer's shoulder. The waist of the latter's purple satin gown was quite spotty at the height of her ladyship's eyes.

Belknap-Jackson on this occasion drove his car with the greatest solicitude, proceeding more slowly than I had ever known him do. As I attended to certain luggage details at the station he was regretting to his lordship that they had not had a longer time at the country club the day it was exhibited.

"Look a bit after silly old George," said his lordship to me at parting. "Chap's dotty, I dare say. Talking about a plantation of apple trees now. For his old age--that sort of thing. Be something new in a fortnight, though. Like him, of course, course!"

Her ladyship closed upon my hand with a remarkable vigour of grip.

"We owe it all to you," she said, again with dancing eyes. Then her eyes steadied queerly. "Maybe you won't be sorry."

"Know I shan't." I fancy I rather growled it, stupidly feeling I was not rising to the occasion. "Knew his lordship wouldn't rest till he had you where he wanted you. Glad he's got you." And curiously I felt a bit of a glad little squeeze in my throat for her. I groped for something light--something American.

"You are some Countess," I at last added in a silly way.

"What, what!" said his lordship, but I had caught her eyes. They brimmed with understanding.

With the going of that train all life seemed to go. I mean to say, things all at once became flat. I turned to the dull station.

"Give you a lift, old chap," said Belknap-Jackson. Again he was cordial. So firmly had I kept the reins of the whole affair in my grasp, such prestige he knew it would give me, he dared not broach his grievance.

Some half-remembered American phrase of Cousin Egbert's ran in my mind. I had put a buffalo on him!

"Thank you," I said, "I'm needing a bit of a stretch and a breeze-out."

I wished to walk that I might the better meditate. With Belknap-Jackson one does not sufficiently meditate.

A block up from the station I was struck by the sight of the Honourable George. Plodding solitary down that low street he was, heeled as usual by the Judson cur. He came to the Spilmer public house and for a moment stared up, quite still, at the "Last Chance" on its chaffing signboard. Then he wheeled abruptly and entered. I was moved to follow him, but I knew it would never do. He would row me about the service of the Grill--something of that sort. I dare say he had fancied her lady-ship as keenly as one of his volatile nature might. But I knew him!

Back on our street the festival atmosphere still lingered. Groups of recent guests paused to discuss the astounding event. The afternoon paper was being scanned by many of them. An account of the wedding was its "feature," as they say. I had no heart for that, but on the second page my eye caught a minor item:

> "A special meeting of the Ladies Onwards and Upwards Club is   called for to-morrow afternoon at two sharp at the residence   of Mrs. Dr. Percy Hailey Martingale, for the transaction of   important business."

One could fancy, I thought, what the meeting would discuss. Nor was I wrong, for I may here state that the evening paper of the following day disclosed that her ladyship the Countess of Brinstead had unanimously been elected to a life honorary membership in the club.

Back in the Grill I found the work of clearing the tables well advanced, and very soon its before-dinner aspect of calm waiting was restored. Surveying it I reflected that one might well wonder if aught momentous had indeed so lately occurred here. A motley day it had been.

I passed into the linen and glass pantry.

Mrs. Judson, polishing my glassware, burst into tears at my approach, frankly stanching them with her towel. I saw it to be a mere overflow of the meaningless emotion that women stock so abundantly on the occasion of a wedding. She is an almost intensely feminine person, as can be seen at once by any one who understands women. In a goods box in the passage beyond I noted her nipper fast asleep, a mammoth beef-rib clasped to its fat chest. I debated putting this abuse to her once more but feared the moment was not propitious. She dried her eyes and smiled again.

"A prince in his palace," she murmured inanely. "She thought first he was going to be as funny as the other one; then she found he wasn't. I liked him, too. I didn't blame her a bit. He's one of that kind--his bark's worse than his bite. And to think you knew all the time what was coming off. My, but you're the Mr. Deep-one!"

I saw no reason to stultify myself by denying this. I mean to say, if she thought it, let her!

"The last thing yesterday she gave me this dress."

I had already noted the very becoming dull blue house gown she wore. Quite with an air she carried it. To be sure, it was not suitable to her duties. The excitements of the day, I suppose, had rendered me a bit sterner than is my wont. Perhaps a little authoritative.

"A handsome gown," I replied icily, "but one would hardly choose it for the work you are performing."

"Rubbish!" she retorted plainly. "I wanted to look nice--I had to go in there lots of times. And I wanted to be dressed for to-night."

"Why to-night, may I ask?" I was all at once uncomfortably curious.

"Why, the boys are coming for me. They're going to take No-no home, then we're all going to the movies. They've got a new bill at the Bijou, and Buck Edwards especially wants me to see it. One of the cowboys in it that does some star riding looks just like Buck--wavy chestnut hair. Buck himself is one of the best riders in the whole Kulanche."

The woman seemed to have some fiendish power to enrage me. As she prattled thus, her eyes demurely on the glass she dried, I felt a deep flush mantle my brow. She could never have dreamed that she had this malign power, but she was now at least to suspect it.

"Your Mr. Edwards," I began calmly enough, "may be like the cinema actor: the two may be as like each other as makes no difference--but you are not going." I was aware that the latter phrase was heated where I had merely meant it to be impressive. Dignified firmness had been the line I intended, but my rage was mounting. She stared at me. Astonished beyond words she was, if I can read human expressions.

"I am!" she snapped at last.

"You are not!" I repeated, stepping a bit toward her. I was conscious of a bit of the rowdy in my manner, but I seemed powerless to prevent it. All my culture was again but the flimsiest veneer.

"I am, too!" she again said, though plainly dismayed.

"No!" I quite thundered it, I dare say. "No, no! No, no!"

The nipper cried out from his box. Not until later did it occur to me that he had considered himself to be addressed in angry tones.

"No, no!" I thundered again. I couldn't help myself, though silly rot I call it now. And then to my horror the mother herself began to weep.

"I will!" she sobbed. "I will! I will! I will!"

"No, no!" I insisted, and I found myself seizing her shoulders, not knowing if I mightn't shake her smartly, so drawn-out had the woman got me; and still I kept shouting my senseless "No, no!" at which the nipper was now yelling.

She struggled her best as I clutched her, but I seemed to have the strength of a dozen men; the woman was nothing in my grasp, and my arms were taking their blind rage out on her.

Secure I held her, and presently she no longer struggled, and I was curiously no longer angry, but found myself soothing her in many strange ways. I mean to say, the passage between us had fallen to be of the very shockingly most sentimental character.

"You are so masterful!" she panted.

"I'll have my own way," I threatened; "I've told you often enough."

"Oh, you're so domineering!" she murmured. I dare say I am a bit that way.

"I'll show you who's to be master!"

"But I never dreamed you meant this," she answered. True, I had most brutally taken her by surprise. I could easily see how, expecting nothing of the faintest sort, she had been rudely shocked.

"I meant it all along," I said firmly, "from the very first moment." And now again she spoke in almost awed tones of my "deepness." I have never believed in that excessive intuition which is so widely boasted for woman.

"I never dreamed of it," she said again, and added: "Mrs. Kenner and I were talking about this dress only last night and I said--I never, never dreamed of such a thing!" She broke off with sudden inconsequence, as women will.

We had now to quiet the nipper in his box. I saw even then that, domineering though I may be, I should probably never care to bring the child's condition to her notice again. There was something about her--something volcanic in her femininity. I knew it would never do. Better let the thing continue to be a monstrosity! I might, unnoticed, of course, snatch a bun from its grasp now and then.

Our evening rush came and went quite as if nothing had happened. I may have been rather absent, reflecting pensively. I mean to say, I had at times considered this alliance as a dawning possibility, but never had I meant to be sudden. Only for the woman's remarkably stubborn obtuseness I dare say the understanding might have been deferred to a more suitable moment and arranged in a calm and orderly manner. But the die was cast. Like his lordship, I had chosen an American bride-- taken her by storm and carried her off her feet before she knew it. We English are often that way.

At ten o'clock we closed the Grill upon a day that had been historic in the truest sense of the word. I shouldered the sleeping nipper. He still passionately clutched the beef-rib and for some reason I felt averse to depriving him of it, even though it would mean a spotty top-coat.

Strangely enough, we talked but little in our walk. It seemed rather too tremendous to talk of.

When I gave the child into her arms at the door it had become half awake.

"Ruggums!" it muttered sleepily.

"Ruggums!" echoed the mother, and again, very softly in the still night: "Ruggums--Ruggums!"

*   *   *   *   *

That in the few months since that rather agreeable night I have acquired the title of Red Gap's social dictator cannot be denied. More than one person of discernment may now be heard to speak of my "reign," though this, of course, is coming it a bit thick.

The removal by his lordship of one who, despite her sterling qualities, had been a source of discord, left the social elements of the town in a state of the wildest disorganization. And having for myself acquired a remarkable prestige from my intimate association with the affair, I promptly seized the reins and drew the scattered forces together.

First, at an early day I sought an interview with Belknap-Jackson and Mrs. Effie and told them straight precisely why I had played them both false in the matter of the wedding breakfast. With the honour granted to either of them, I explained, I had foreseen another era of cliques, divisions, and acrimony. Therefore I had done the thing myself, as a measure of peace.

Flatly then I declared my intention of reconciling all those formerly opposed elements and of creating a society in Red Gap that would be a social union in the finest sense of the word. I said that contact with their curious American life had taught me that their equality should be more than a name, and that, especially in the younger settlements, a certain relaxation from the rigid requirements of an older order is not only unavoidable but vastly to be desired. I meant to say, if we were going to be Americans it was silly rot trying to be English at the same time.

I pointed out that their former social leaders had ever been inspired by the idea of exclusion; the soul of their leadership had been to cast others out; and that the campaign I planned was to be one of inclusion--even to the extent of Bohemians and well-behaved cattle-persons---which I believed to be in the finest harmony with their North American theory of human association. It might be thought a naive theory, I said, but so long as they had chosen it I should staunchly abide by it.

I added what I dare say they did not believe: that the position of leader was not one I should cherish for any other reason than the public good. That when one better fitted might appear they would find me the first to rejoice.

I need not say that I was interrupted frequently and acridly during this harangue, but I had given them both a buffalo and well they knew it. And I worked swiftly from that moment. I gave the following week the first of a series of subscription balls in the dancing hall above the Grill, and both Mrs. Belknap-Jackson and Mrs. Effie early enrolled themselves as patronesses, even after I had made it plain that I alone should name the guests.

The success of the affair was all I could have wished. Red Gap had become a social unit. Nor was appreciation for my leadership wanting. There will be malcontents, I foresee, and from the informed inner circles I learn that I have already been slightingly spoken of as a foreigner wielding a sceptre over native-born Americans, but I have the support of quite all who really matter, and I am confident these rebellions may be put down by tact alone. It is too well understood by those who know me that I have Equality for my watchword.

I mean to say, at the next ball of the series I may even see that the fellow Hobbs has a card if I can become assured that he has quite freed himself from certain debasing class-ideals of his native country. This to be sure is an extreme case, because the fellow is that type of our serving class to whom equality is unthinkable. They must, from their centuries of servility, look either up or down; and I scarce know in which attitude they are more offensive to our American point of view. Still I mean to be broad. Even Hobbs shall have his chance with us!

*   *   *   *   *

It is late June. Mrs. Ruggles and I are comfortably installed in her enlarged and repaired house. We have a fowl-run on a stretch of her free-hold, and the kitchen-garden thrives under the care of the Japanese agricultural labourer I have employed.

Already I have discharged more than half my debt to Cousin Egbert, who exclaims, "Oh, shucks!" each time I make him a payment. He and the Honourable George remain pally no end and spend much of their abundant leisure at Cousin Egbert's modest country house. At times when they are in town they rather consort with street persons, but such is the breadth of our social scheme that I shall never exclude them from our gayeties, though it is true that more often than not they decline to be present.

Mrs. Ruggles, I may say, is a lady of quite amazing capacities combined strangely with the commonest feminine weaknesses. She has acute business judgment at most times, yet would fly at me in a rage if I were to say what I think of the nipper's appalling grossness. Quite naturally I do not push my unquestioned mastery to this extreme. There are other matters in which I amusedly let her have her way, though she fondly reminds me almost daily of my brutal self-will.

On one point I have just been obliged to assert this. She came running to me with a suggestion for economizing in the manufacture of the relish. She had devised a cheaper formula. But I was firm.

"So long as the inventor's face is on that flask," I said, "its contents shall not be debased a tuppence. My name and face will guarantee its purity."

She gave in nicely, merely declaring that I needn't growl like one of their bears with a painful foot.

At my carefully mild suggestion she has just brought the nipper in from where he was cattying the young fowls, much to their detriment. But she is now heaping compote upon a slice of thickly buttered bread for him, glancing meanwhile at our evening newspaper.

"Ruggums always has his awful own way, doesn't ums?" she remarks to the nipper.

Deeply ignoring this, I resume my elocutionary studies of the Declaration of Independence. For I should say that a signal honour of a municipal character has just been done me. A committee of the Chamber of Commerce has invited me to participate in their exercises on an early day in July--the fourth, I fancy--when they celebrate the issuance of this famous document. I have been asked to read it, preceding a patriotic address to be made by Senator Floud.

I accepted with the utmost pleasure, and now on my vine-sheltered porch have begun trying it out for the proper voice effects. Its substance, I need not say, is already familiar to me.

The nipper is horribly gulping at its food, jam smears quite all about its countenance. Mrs. Ruggles glances over her journal.

"How would you like it," she suddenly demands, "if I went around town like these English women--burning churches and houses of Parliament and cutting up fine oil paintings. How would that suit your grouchy highness?"

"This is not England," I answer shortly. "That sort of thing would never do with us."

"My, but isn't he the fierce old Ruggums!" she cries in affected alarm to the now half-suffocated nipper.

Once more I take up the Declaration of Independence. It lends itself rather well to reciting. I feel that my voice is going to carry.

THE END

www.bookjungle.com *email: sales@bookjungle.com fax: 630-214-0564 mail: Book Jungle PO Box 2226 Champaign, IL 61825*

The Codes Of Hammurabi And Moses
W. W. Davies

QTY

The discovery of the Hammurabi Code is one of the greatest achievements of archaeology, and is of paramount interest, not only to the student of the Bible, but also to all those interested in ancient history...

Religion   **ISBN:** *1-59462-338-4*   **Pages:**132
MSRP $12.95

The Theory of Moral Sentiments
Adam Smith

QTY

This work from 1749. contains original theories of conscience amd moral judgment and it is the foundation for systemof morals.

Philosophy **ISBN:** *1-59462-777-0*   **Pages:**536
MSRP $19.95

Jessica's First Prayer
Hesba Stretton

QTY

In a screened and secluded corner of one of the many railway-bridges which span the streets of London there could be seen a few years ago, from five o'clock every morning until half past eight, a tidily set-out coffee-stall, consisting of a trestle and board, upon which stood two large tin cans, with a small fire of charcoal burning under each so as to keep the coffee boiling during the early hours of the morning when the work-people were thronging into the city on their way to their daily toil...

Pages:84

Childrens   **ISBN:** *1-59462-373-2*   *MSRP $9.95*

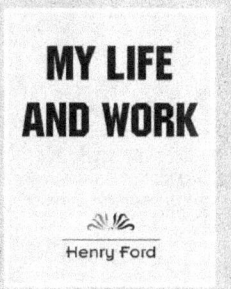

My Life and Work
Henry Ford

QTY

Henry Ford revolutionized the world with his implementation of mass production for the Model T automobile. Gain valuable business insight into his life and work with his own auto-biography... "We have only started on our development of our country we have not as yet, with all our talk of wonderful progress, done more than scratch the surface. The progress has been wonderful enough but..."

Pages:300

Biographies/   **ISBN:** *1-59462-198-5*   *MSRP $21.95*

The Art of Cross-Examination
Francis Wellman

QTY

I presume it is the experience of every author, after his first book is published upon an important subject, to be almost overwhelmed with a wealth of ideas and illustrations which could readily have been included in his book, and which to his own mind, at least, seem to make a second edition inevitable. Such certainly was the case with me; and when the first edition had reached its sixth impression in five months, I rejoiced to learn that it seemed to my publishers that the book had met with a sufficiently favorable reception to justify a second and considerably enlarged edition. ...

Pages:412

Reference   **ISBN: *1-59462-647-2***   *MSRP $19.95*

On the Duty of Civil Disobedience
Henry David Thoreau

QTY

Thoreau wrote his famous essay, On the Duty of Civil Disobedience, as a protest against an unjust but popular war and the immoral but popular institution of slave-owning. He did more than write—he declined to pay his taxes, and was hauled off to gaol in consequence. Who can say how much this refusal of his hastened the end of the war and of slavery ?

Law   **ISBN: *1-59462-747-9***   **Pages:48**

MSRP $7.45

Dream Psychology Psychoanalysis for Beginners
Sigmund Freud

QTY

Sigmund Freud, born Sigismund Schlomo Freud (May 6, 1856 - September 23, 1939), was a Jewish-Austrian neurologist and psychiatrist who co-founded the psychoanalytic school of psychology. Freud is best known for his theories of the unconscious mind, especially involving the mechanism of repression; his redefinition of sexual desire as mobile and directed towards a wide variety of objects; and his therapeutic techniques, especially his understanding of transference in the therapeutic relationship and the presumed value of dreams as sources of insight into unconscious desires.

Pages:196

Psychology   **ISBN: *1-59462-905-6***   *MSRP $15.45*

The Miracle of Right Thought
Orison Swett Marden

QTY

Believe with all of your heart that you will do what you were made to do. When the mind has once formed the habit of holding cheerful, happy, prosperous pictures, it will not be easy to form the opposite habit. It does not matter how improbable or how far away this realization may see, or how dark the prospects may be, if we visualize them as best we can, as vividly as possible, hold tenaciously to them and vigorously struggle to attain them, they will gradually become actualized, realized in the life. But a desire, a longing without endeavor, a yearning abandoned or held indifferently will vanish without realization.

Pages:360

Self Help   **ISBN: *1-59462-644-8***   *MSRP $25.45*

☐ **The Rosicrucian Cosmo-Conception Mystic Christianity** *by Max Heindel* ISBN: *1-59462-188-8* **$38.95**
The Rosicrucian Cosmo-conception is not dogmatic, neither does it appeal to any other authority than the reason of the student. It is: not controversial, but is: sent forth in the, hope that it may help to clear... New Age/Religion Pages 646

☐ **Abandonment To Divine Providence** *by Jean-Pierre de Caussade* ISBN: *1-59462-228-0* **$25.95**
"The Rev. Jean Pierre de Caussade was one of the most remarkable spiritual writers of the Society of Jesus in France in the 18th Century. His death took place at Toulouse in 1751. His works have gone through many editions and have been republished... Inspirational/Religion Pages 400

☐ **Mental Chemistry** *by Charles Haanel* ISBN: *1-59462-192-6* **$23.95**
Mental Chemistry allows the change of material conditions by combining and appropriately utilizing the power of the mind. Much like applied chemistry creates something new and unique out of careful combinations of chemicals the mastery of mental chemistry... New Age Pages 354

☐ **The Letters of Robert Browning and Elizabeth Barret Barrett 1845-1846 vol II** ISBN: *1-59462-193-4* **$35.95**
by Robert Browning and Elizabeth Barrett Biographies Pages 596

☐ **Gleanings In Genesis (volume I)** *by Arthur W. Pink* ISBN: *1-59462-130-6* **$27.45**
Appropriately has Genesis been termed "the seed plot of the Bible" for in it we have, in germ form, almost all of the great doctrines which are afterwards fully developed in the books of Scripture which follow... Religion/Inspirational Pages 420

☐ **The Master Key** *by L. W. de Laurence* ISBN: *1-59462-001-6* **$30.95**
In no branch of human knowledge has there been a more lively increase of the spirit of research during the past few years than in the study of Psychology, Concentration and Mental Discipline. The requests for authentic lessons in Thought Control, Mental Discipline and... New Age/Business Pages 422

☐ **The Lesser Key Of Solomon Goetia** *by L. W. de Laurence* ISBN: *1-59462-092-X* **$9.95**
This translation of the first book of the "Lernegton" which is now for the first time made accessible to students of Talismanic Magic is done, after careful collation and edition, from numerous Ancient Manuscripts in Hebrew, Latin, and French... New Age/Occult Pages 92

☐ **Rubaiyat Of Omar Khayyam** *by Edward Fitzgerald* ISBN:*1-59462-332-5* **$13.95**
Edward Fitzgerald, whom the world has already learned, in spite of his own efforts to remain within the shadow of anonymity, to look upon as one of the rarest poets of the century, was born at Bredfield, in Suffolk, on the 31st of March, 1809. He was the third son of John Purcell... Music Pages 172

☐ **Ancient Law** *by Henry Maine* ISBN: *1-59462-128-4* **$29.95**
The chief object of the following pages is to indicate some of the earliest ideas of mankind, as they are reflected in Ancient Law, and to point out the relation of those ideas to modern thought. Religiom/History Pages 452

☐ **Far-Away Stories** *by William J. Locke* ISBN: *1-59462-129-2* **$19.45**
"Good wine needs no bush, but a collection of mixed vintages does. And this book is just such a collection. Some of the stories I do not want to remain buried for ever in the museum files of dead magazine-numbers an author's not unpardonable vanity..." Fiction Pages 272

☐ **Life of David Crockett** *by David Crockett* ISBN: *1-59462-250-7* **$27.45**
"Colonel David Crockett was one of the most remarkable men of the times in which he lived. Born in humble life, but gifted with a strong will, an indomitable courage, and unremitting perseverance... Biographies/New Age Pages 424

☐ **Lip-Reading** *by Edward Nitchie* ISBN: *1-59462-206-X* **$25.95**
Edward B. Nitchie, founder of the New York School for the Hard of Hearing, now the Nitchie School of Lip-Reading, Inc, wrote "LIP-READING Principles and Practice". The development and perfecting of this meritorious work on lip-reading was an undertaking... How-to Pages 400

☐ **A Handbook of Suggestive Therapeutics, Applied Hypnotism, Psychic Science** ISBN: *1-59462-214-0* **$24.95**
by Henry Munro Health/New Age/Health/Self-help Pages 376

☐ **A Doll's House: and Two Other Plays** *by Henrik Ibsen* ISBN: *1-59462-112-8* **$19.95**
Henrik Ibsen created this classic when in revolutionary 1848 Rome. Introducing some striking concepts in playwriting for the realist genre, this play has been studied the world over. Fiction/Classics/Plays 308

☐ **The Light of Asia** *by sir Edwin Arnold* ISBN: *1-59462-204-3* **$13.95**
In this poetic masterpiece, Edwin Arnold describes the life and teachings of Buddha. The man who was to become known as Buddha to the world was born as Prince Gautama of India but he rejected the worldly riches and abandoned the reigns of power when... Religion/History/Biographies Pages 170

☐ **The Complete Works of Guy de Maupassant** *by Guy de Maupassant* ISBN: *1-59462-157-8* **$16.95**
"For days and days, nights and nights, I had dreamed of that first kiss which was to consecrate our engagement, and I knew not on what spot I should put my lips..." Fiction/Classics Pages 240

☐ **The Art of Cross-Examination** *by Francis L. Wellman* ISBN: *1-59462-309-0* **$26.95**
Written by a renowned trial lawyer, Wellman imparts his experience and uses case studies to explain how to use psychology to extract desired information through questioning. How-to/Science/Reference Pages 408

☐ **Answered or Unanswered?** *by Louisa Vaughan* ISBN: *1-59462-248-5* **$10.95**
Miracles of Faith in China Religion Pages 112

☐ **The Edinburgh Lectures on Mental Science (1909)** *by Thomas* ISBN: *1-59462-008-3* **$11.95**
This book contains the substance of a course of lectures recently given by the writer in the Queen Street Hail, Edinburgh. Its purpose is to indicate the Natural Principles governing the relation between Mental Action and Material Conditions... New Age/Psychology Pages 148

☐ **Ayesha** *by H. Rider Haggard* ISBN: *1-59462-301-5* **$24.95**
Verily and indeed it is the unexpected that happens! Probably if there was one person upon the earth from whom the Editor of this, and of a certain previous history, did not expect to hear again... Classics Pages 380

☐ **Ayala's Angel** *by Anthony Trollope* ISBN: *1-59462-352-X* **$29.95**
The two girls were both pretty, but Lucy who was twenty-one who supposed to be simple and comparatively unattractive, whereas Ayala was credited, as her Bombwhat romantic name might show, with poetic charm and a taste for romance. Ayala when her father died was nineteen... Fiction Pages 484

☐ **The American Commonwealth** *by James Bryce* ISBN: *1-59462-286-8* **$34.45**
An interpretation of American democratic political theory. It examines political mechanics and society from the perspective of Scotsman James Bryce Politics Pages 572

☐ **Stories of the Pilgrims** *by Margaret P. Pumphrey* ISBN: *1-59462-116-0* **$17.95**
This book explores pilgrims religious oppression in England as well as their escape to Holland and eventual crossing to America on the Mayflower, and their early days in New England... History Pages 268

QTY

The Fasting Cure *by Sinclair Upton*   ISBN: *1-59462-222-1* **$13.95**
In the Cosmopolitan Magazine for May, 1910, and in the Contemporary Review (London) for April, 1910, I published an article dealing with my experiences in fasting. I have written a great many magazine articles, but never one which attracted so much attention... New Age/Self Help/Health Pages 164

Hebrew Astrology *by Sepharial*   ISBN: *1-59462-308-2* **$13.45**
In these days of advanced thinking it is a matter of common observation that we have left many of the old landmarks behind and that we are now pressing forward to greater heights and to a wider horizon than that which represented the mind-content of our progenitors... Astrology Pages 144

Thought Vibration or The Law of Attraction in the Thought World   ISBN: *1-59462-127-6* **$12.95**

by William Walker Atkinson   Psychology/Religion Pages 144

Optimism *by Helen Keller*   ISBN: *1-59462-108-X* **$15.95**
Helen Keller was blind, deaf, and mute since 19 months old, yet famously learned how to overcome these handicaps, communicate with the world, and spread her lectures promoting optimism. An inspiring read for everyone... Biographies/Inspirational Pages 84

Sara Crewe *by Frances Burnett*   ISBN: *1-59462-360-0* **$9.45**
In the first place, Miss Minchin lived in London. Her home was a large, dull, tall one, in a large, dull square, where all the houses were alike, and all the sparrows were alike, and where all the door-knockers made the same heavy sound... Childrens/Classic Pages 88

The Autobiography of Benjamin Franklin *by Benjamin Franklin*   ISBN: *1-59462-135-7* **$24.95**
The Autobiography of Benjamin Franklin has probably been more extensively read than any other American historical work, and no other book of its kind has had such ups and downs of fortune. Franklin lived for many years in England, where he was agent... Biographies/History Pages 332

Name	
Email	
Telephone	
Address	
City, State ZIP	

☐ **Credit Card**   ☐ **Check / Money Order**

Credit Card Number	
Expiration Date	
Signature	

Please Mail to: Book Jungle
PO Box 2226
Champaign, IL 61825
or Fax to: *630-214-0564*

ORDERING INFORMATION

web*: www.bookjungle.com*
email*: sales@bookjungle.com*
fax*: 630-214-0564*
mail*: Book Jungle PO Box 2226 Champaign, IL 61825*
or PayPal *to sales@bookjungle.com*

Please contact us for bulk discounts

DIRECT-ORDER TERMS

**20% Discount if You Order
Two or More Books**
Free Domestic Shipping!
Accepted: Master Card, Visa,
Discover, American Express

www.ingramcontent.com/pod-product-compliance
Lightning Source LLC
Chambersburg PA
CBHW080726020726
47503CB00010B/2800